A DREAM OF DESIRE

"Let's try it. Right now. Here . . ." Kneeling before her, he took her hands in his own, urging her to kneel down and join him. When they were staring into each other's eyes, he directed softly, "Summon me, Molly."

"But you're so close," she murmured, aroused by the nearness of him. "It doesn't make sense."

His lips brushed hers, then he repeated, in a voice filled with both awe and authority, "Summon me. Use your magic to reach out to me. I want to feel it again. I *need* to feel it."

Almost mesmerized now, she moistened her lips, closed her eyes, and pictured him, as the sorcerer had taught her. But the picture was not of a twentieth century man in jeans and a white polo shirt. Rather, she pictured the warrior that lived in his soul, complete with a shoulder-length mane of lustrous black hair and high, windburnt cheekbones. The image of the Son of Lost Eagle—the Valmain champion—so sharp and hot that it made her almost dizzy with desire.

* * *

A DREAM APART
by Kate Donovan

Matthew Redtree is clearly a fanatic—a modern-day warrior obsessed with legends, weapons and vengeance against an ancient sorcerer. Still, Molly can't resist him and, when he becomes obsessed with *her,* the resulting torrent of passion washes away all hope of ever living without him.

But is it love? Or is she simply a pawn in his game of revenge? And if she helps Matthew defeat the wily sorcerer Aaric, who visits her nightly in her own dreams, will she shatter all hope for a rebirth of her ancestors' magical civilization?

She has finally met the man of her dreams, but is that man Matthew? Or Aaric?

Available from Pinnacle Books

KATE DONOVAN

A DREAM EMBRACED

PINNACLE BOOKS
KENSINGTON PUBLISHING CORP.

PINNACLE BOOKS are published by

Kensington Publishing Corp.
850 Third Avenue
New York, NY 10022

Pinnacle and the P logo Reg. U.S. Pat. & TM Off.

First Pinnacle Books Printing: February, 1996

Printed in the United States of America
10 9 8 7 6 5 4 3 2 1

This book is dedicated to
Jim and Ann Donovan
with gratitude and love

Prologue

In the distant past, magicians moved among the inhabitants of North America. Some chose to respect and intermarry with the various tribes of moundbuilders and hunters, while others chose to use their powers to terrorize and dominate. For a time, the most powerful of all North American magicians were twin sorcerers, who wandered into a village of proud and peaceful natives, adopting them as their own. They proceeded to build a series of burial mounds that were also "channels" to the magical powers deep within the earth. With such power, their descendants might have been able to rule benevolently and without fear of destruction. Unfortunately, the twins were murdered by malevolent lake wizards from the North before the fourth and final mound could be completed. The descendants of the twins could thereafter draw only imperfect power from the existing mounds and eventually were all but annihilated by the lake community.

Two of the mounds magicians escaped the wrath of the lakes. The first was the sorceress Kerreya, who had married Valmain, a king from across the "untraveled sea," beyond the reach of the lakes and their greedy slaughter. The second was a sorcerer named Aaric, who had been sent far into the future, by Kerreya's jealous sister Maya, to destroy the Valmain kingdom. A battle between Aaric and the Valmain champion was thus inevitable, with the victor emerging as heir to the legacy of the twins, and as avenger of the atrocities of the lake wizards.

*History became legend, yet the legend was never com-
pletely forgotten. To some it became a soothing bedtime
story, while to others it carried a message, or a warning, or
a promise of a magical world lying dormant . . . waiting. . . .*

One who heard the story centuries later and took comfort
in it was a quiet, sheltered child named Molly Sheridan. She
imagined what it would be like to be both princess and sorceress, never guessing that she was, in fact, the descendant
of Kerreya and King Valmain. She grew into graceful young
womanhood in Boston, dedicated to a career in science, unprepared for the tumult that destiny was about to thrust upon
her.

On the other side of the country, a young warrior named
Matthew Redtree was also hearing the legends of magic and
betrayal, but through a recurring dream he knew, without a
doubt, that he had been appointed to battle Aaric and to
defend a mysterious, curly-haired girl who stood always in
the shadows of his dreams, wearing white and giving him
strength through a powerful amulet. And so Matthew practiced the arts of war while traveling the world, searching for
his dream girl and his opponent. When he met Molly Sheridan he knew, and so he pursued her, and seduced her, and
convinced her that their destinies were intertwined.

With the wonder of love came the horror of battle—a vicious, dream-bound battle between the experienced, brawny
sorcerer Aaric and a noble but all-too-human young Matthew. But Matthew had Molly—the dream girl—and he had
the amulet, and in a glorious burst of love, training, and
magic, managed to vanquish his ancient foe.

With the bloodshed behind them, Molly craved only a normal life, but she was the princess of Valmain—the last hope
for the rebirth of the mounds civilization—and fate would
not loosen its grip on her heart or her soul. With Matthew
Redtree as her spouse, she was destined to bear young sorcerers and sorceresses. She was destined also to learn the
ancient magical arts of her ancestors, and for this she had

the most splendid of teachers, for Aaric the Moonshaker had remained in her dreams after the battle as mentor, friend, and ardent admirer.

Mentor, friend, admirer—and prisoner. These were not roles to which the infamous Moonshaker was accustomed. He was restless for life and deeply in love with the Valmain Princess. He longed to protect her and to be her champion but could escape from her dream and take his rightful place at her side only if and when he managed to defeat a dream opponent from the outside world and commandeer the vanquished body. He had tried twice to defeat Matthew Redtree, and twice he had failed, and so for the moment he contented himself with nightly visits from the beautiful sorceress who had given her heart to another.

Molly dared not share this treacherous secret with Matthew, who believed the Moonshaker to be dead. She dared only to love her new husband with a passion as torrid and true as any the centuries had known, hoping that one day she would find the wisdom and strength to deal with the challenges that fate had so blithely bestown upon her.

"Aaric! Stop pacing and settle down, please? You'd think *you* were the father of this baby instead of Matthew."

"If there were any logic to the universe, I would be," the agitated sorcerer declared. "This is more unbearable than any torture I have imagined possible! Never have I felt so powerless. So useless."

"Useless?" Molly Sheridan Redtree reached up to brush an unruly golden lock from his brow and insisted, "You're keeping me amused and distracting me from my labor. That's hardly useless . . . Oh, dear . . ."

"Another one?" Aaric's blue eyes flashed with alarm. "I have never known a sorceress to be so long in her travail! If the child does not come soon, you will be dead from the strain, and myself along with you."

"If the child comes *too* soon, she'll be born in the back of a station wagon," Molly gasped, holding her swollen midsection in amazement. These contractions, while intense, involved no pain at all, and so she was free to marvel, rather than wail—reason enough, she reminded herself, to be eternally grateful she had been born a sorceress. Aloud, she added, "We should be arriving at the mounds in about an hour. Matthew's determined to have our first baby born there, and you know how he always gets his way."

"His instincts are correct," Aaric grumbled. "You are at your most powerful when you are near the mounds. What he fails to realize is that, because of this dream power of yours"—he paused to sweep a mighty arm across the dreamscape, indicating the presence of three grassy burial mounds—"you do not need to physically go to the mounds. They are always with you, because they are here, in your dream."

"Since his amulet only works when he's within fifty miles of the real mounds, and since he doesn't know I can tap into my magic any other way, he thinks I need to be there, with the amulet on my wrist, if we want to guarantee a flawless birth. Oh!" Again she grasped her nonexistent waist, then grinned. "Just a little catch. Stop scowling."

"You must rest, Princess," the brawny sorcerer pleaded, slipping his arms around her shoulders and pulling her against his massive chest. "At any moment, the birthing will begin in earnest, and while it will not hurt you, it will drain you greatly. The birthing of a new magician is always thus." Stroking her long, sun-streaked curls, he added thoughtfully, "If you are carrying twins, as I have long suspected, the birth will be even more taxing. We must be prepared for that."

"First of all," Molly assured him, "it's not twins. It's one child, and she's a girl. Don't ask me how I know—I just do. And," she raised her face to his and chided, "you keep telling me to rest. Isn't that silly? I'm sound asleep. This is a dream. Remember?"

"How can I forget?" he glared. "I am trapped here, am I not?" Then his gaze softened. "There was a time when it seemed the worst of fates, to be trapped forever in a female's dream while the world outside was denied to me. But these months as your teacher, and your friend, and your admirer, have been the most rewarding of my strange life. Have I thanked you for that, Princess?"

"Only a million times," she blushed. "What would I do without you?" Pulling free, she fluffed the folds of her silver-and-white cape. "I'd better go. My nephews are stuck in the backseat with me, since Rita needed to ride up front with Matthew and nag him all the way from Los Angeles to the mounds. I'd better wake up and make sure they're all surviving."

"Your husband and his sister are arguing? Because he insists you deliver the child at the mounds?"

"Basically, yes. It's round umpteen of the same old argument. Rita thinks Matthew's crazy, because he believes the amulet is magical, and because he keeps insisting he was destined to meet me, and protect me, and etcetera, etcetera."

"She does not believe him," Aaric mused, "because magic has been lost to your world. The mounds magicians have all vanished, except for yourself, and the lake magicians have hidden themselves well. How strange and barren your world must seem."

"I wouldn't call it barren," Molly shrugged, "but you're right, no one really believes in magic anymore. I didn't believe in it myself until last year."

"When I arrived here, in your dream, to battle your champion? If only I had won that battle." Aaric's strong, square jaw was tense with frustration. "I would have been allowed to leave this dream, in the body of your lover, and the child you carry now would have been mine. And you," he added with a reluctant grin, "would be the luckiest woman, sorceress or not, on earth."

Molly laughed lightly. "I *am* the luckiest woman on earth.

I have you, here in the dream, and I have Matthew, as my husband, on the outside. I'm spoiled rotten, and I love it— Oh!" Leaning heavily into him, she added breathlessly, "I think the baby's almost ready, Aaric." Wrapping her arms tightly around his neck, she kissed his cheek and whispered, "Wish me luck."

"Princess," he groaned. "If only I could be there, to strengthen you . . ." Cupping her chin, he kissed her mouth gently. "Take care, my sweet love. Listen to your husband. In spite of his many flaws, his instincts are sound, and he worships you greatly."

"Aaric . . ." Tears were threatening at the thought of leaving him alone, with his concerns and his lovelorn heart. "I'll come back as soon as I can, and we'll celebrate." With one last, tremulous smile, she was gone from the dream, leaving Aaric the Moonshaker to his anguished pacing while she herself slowly awakened.

Her handsome husband—the father of her unborn child— was studying her in the rearview mirror of his sister's battered old station wagon and when their gazes locked, she felt a rush of love so strong it almost caused her to gasp. Matthew Redtree's eyes—those gold-flecked beacons of excitement and devotion—had always affected her that way. He knew it, of course, and, being a student of ancient cultures and legends, had diagnosed this magnetism between them as destiny's handiwork. But Molly was a student, too—of biometrics and toxicology—and so she credited chemistry, rather than destiny, for the dizzying passion that had erupted between them just one short year earlier.

She remembered how he had wooed her, with seductive stories of love and rivalry, culled from the world of legend and myth. *His* world. He had charmed her with his warm, husky voice, caressed her with his glittering gaze, and driven her mad with his scintillating style of lovemaking. Now, as their stares locked in the mirror, she remembered, and warmed, and might have melted with adoration had not a well-timed contraction—the calling card of Matthew's first-born child—drawn her back into her own more practical world.

Destiny or chemistry. Did it really matter which of these had set this love affair into motion? *No,* the wistful sorceress acknowledged silently. *All that matters now is whether it can last.*

One

"How can you do this to poor Molly? You're the worst husband in the world, Matthew Redtree. I'm ashamed to be your sister." Rita Camacho's dark eyes were narrow with disgust. "She should be in a hospital, being pampered and monitored, not lying out here in the middle of nowhere, with her contractions only eight minutes apart." Her voice lowered to an ominous hiss. "If anything happens to this baby, I'll have you committed to an insane asylum."

"Nothing's going to happen to the baby," her brother soothed. "Molly feels great, she's in perfect health, and you're a nurse. She needs to have the baby here, in our homeland."

"Our homeland? The middle of nowhere?"

Matthew Redtree's lean, bronzed arm swept to encompass two small burial mounds in the distance. "Our ancestors are here with us, Rita. If you'd just stop resisting the idea, I know you'd be able to feel it. Maybe," he added thoughtfully, "if we put the amulet on *your* wrist for a minute . . ."

"Forget it! Molly may be crazy enough to believe in all of this magic nonsense, but not me. And keep your voice down. I've told you a million times, I don't want my sons hearing all of this son-of-an-amulet mumbo jumbo."

"They need to hear it, Rita. This is their heritage."

From her resting place atop the highest of the mounds, Molly Sheridan Redtree watched and listened in fond amusement as her husband and his sister continued their long-running feud. Fortunately, Rita's two sons, who were playing nearby, had taken their Aunt Molly's cue, ignoring the debate as to heritage, confining their speculation instead to whether their new cousin would be a boy or a girl. AJ, the elder of the two boys at eleven years of age, was hoping for another male child, preferably one who would share his passion for martial arts. Robert, two years the younger, didn't care if it was a girl or a boy, as long as it was an intelligent, hopefully pacifistic, child who wouldn't be constantly trying out new judo moves on him. And Molly . . .

If it was a boy, and if that boy were half as sweet and adorable as either of these two nephews, she would be content, but in her heart she knew this infant in her womb was a little girl. Now, as her contractions intensified, and the amulet on her wrist responded by fueling her with steady power from deep within the mounds, she whispered aloud the name she and Matthew had selected—the name she had heard so often in her childhood bedtime stories. "Kerreya, . . . I can't wait to meet you. Kerreya Elizabeth Redtree."

"Molly?" Her dark-haired champion was at her side in an instant. "Did you say something?"

"I said your daughter's coming, so stop arguing with Rita and give me a kiss for luck."

"It can't be time yet, honey," Rita interrupted quickly. "Your contractions are only eight minutes apart. You've got a long way to go."

"The baby's coming," Molly corrected with a smile. "And you were right, Matthew. It doesn't hurt at all. The amulet . . ."

"Oh, for heaven's sake!" Rita dropped to her knees to examine her patient, then gasped, "It's true! I see the head. Oh, Molly, don't push yet."

"Push whenever you like," Matthew countered mischievously, kneeling also and taking his wife's hand in his own.

"Just take a deep breath, Valmain, then use the power of the amulet to deliver our first kid."

"I love you, Matthew," she sighed, then her body tensed, once and then again, and a current of hot, focused power coursed through her, gently but firmly expelling the infant into Rita's waiting hands.

"Oh, dear. . . . It's a baby girl, Molly, just like you said. A beautiful little girl." With tears in her eyes, Rita turned to her brother. "Look, Matt, I'm an aunt."

"You mean, *I'm* a father," he marveled, slipping a soft white towel around the baby, then accepting the precious bundle gingerly. "Kerreya Elizabeth Redtree, you're as perfect as your mother." Rising to his feet as soon as the cord had been severed, he held the newborn above his head and proclaimed loudly, "This is Kerreya Redtree, descendant of Lost Eagle and heiress to the Valmain kingdom!"

"Are you insane!" Rita shrieked. "Put that baby down!" When her brother complied, pulling the child snugly against his chest, she added softly, "Who would have thought you could have pulled this off, Matt? As crazy as you are, you managed to find a wife like Molly and now a little baby daughter." Running her fingers through her brother's thick, blue-black hair, she added wistfully, "Thanks for making me an aunt."

Still slightly dazed, Molly was content for the moment to see the child from a distance, in the arms of the man she loved so desperately. He looked uncharacteristically serene and happy—so content with his lot in life. Would this be the turning point for him? For them? Would he find peace of mind and stop his wandering, both physical and spiritual? Could one little baby do that for him, when all of Molly's love had been inadequate to the task?

She had hoped for such a miracle, but now it seemed irrelevant. Matthew loved this child as truly as he loved his wife, but if it still weren't enough to keep him from torturing himself over the past, so be it. For better or for worse, they all belonged together now, and Molly, for one, could scarcely believe the feelings—of love, and trust, and gratitude—that were welling inside her at the very existence of this magical child.

She needed to hold the baby close once more, as she had for the last miraculous nine months, and so she stretched out her hands toward her husband. "Matthew? Let me have her, please?"

"Sure, Valmain. Meet your daughter." He placed her gently into Molly's arms. "She's beautiful, just like Rita said."

"She looks like you," Molly cooed, cuddling the dark-haired infant. "Hi, Kerreya. I'm your mommy. I love you so much . . ."

The baby's eyes widened for just one moment, and in that moment Molly could see the sparkling flecks of gold dust that had made Matthew's gaze so irresistible and amazing from the start. Matthew Redtree and AJ Camacho, and now Kerreya—they all had that touch of magic. But would Kerreya have more than a touch?

What did you inherit from me? Molly wanted to ask the tranquil child. *Are you a sorceress like your mommy? Will you have the dream power? And if you do, will you manage it with more grace and effectiveness than I have?*

As her lips grazed the infant's forehead, she thought of her dream—and, of Aaric. He would be overjoyed to hear that the baby had arrived, healthy and beautiful. He would see this event as momentous in terms of the rebirth of the dormant mounds civilization, which had flourished more than twenty centuries earlier. He would remind Molly of her birthright—the power to draw magic from the earth through the ancient burial mounds on which she and her newborn daughter now rested.

"Molly?" Matthew's voice was soft. "Is everything okay?"

"You were right, Matthew," she admitted breathlessly.

"With the amulet on my wrist, this was a breeze. The power was so incredible. Such a tangible, manageable rush . . ."

"That's why I love it here," he nodded. "When we're within range of these mounds, and I have that thing strapped to my right wrist, I'm invincible."

"Take it back whenever you like," Molly urged. "I don't need it anymore. I've never felt better in my life." Her eyes misted slightly as she watched her newborn daughter slip into quiet slumber. "Look, Matthew. She's sleeping. I thought she'd be hungry, or crying, or cold."

"She feels safe, here at the mounds, in your arms, with me standing beside you to guard you both. This is the way it was meant to be, Valmain." He tilted his bride's chin upward and kissed her lips reverently. "Don't ever forget this moment."

"How could I?"

"Things will be different from now on, Valmain. I know I've been restless, and hard to live with, but—"

"Not now, Matthew." Her eyes had felt a sting of familiar tears. "Today, the world is perfect. Today I honestly believe there's no problem we can't solve, together."

"Right. I think we became a real family today, Molly. Not just a husband and wife, respecting each other's goals, but a family, with a common purpose. Speaking of which . . ." He glanced toward his sister. "If you're done with all that afterbirth stuff, let's get AJ and Robert over here. They should be a part of this, too."

"We're right here, Uncle Matt." Nine-year-old Robert's brown eyes were wide with questions. "When you yelled, we came." Edging closer, he murmured, "Are you okay, Aunt Molly?"

"Hi, Robert. I'm fine." Her eyes shifted toward his brother, who was sheepishly staring from a distance. "Hi, AJ."

"AJ's the oldest so he goes first," Matthew interrupted. "Hold your new cousin, AJ. Introduce yourself."

"Are you sure?" The youth glanced toward Molly for official permission and, when she proffered the sleeping child, knelt and accepted her awkwardly. Then he shifted the bundle so that he was staring into Kerreya's face, into the gold-dusted eyes that marked the true descendants of Lost Eagle. "She's beautiful, Aunt Molly. She's so tiny, and helpless." Rising to his feet, he whispered, "Don't worry, Kerreya. I'll never let anything happen to you. I promise."

"AJ!" Rita scolded. "Aunt Molly said you could hold her, not have her."

"Huh?" The boy shook his head, as though he'd forgotten there was anyone in the world but the tiny child, then he dropped back down to his knees and shoved her back toward her mother. "Sorry, Aunt Molly. I just got carried away. I guess she's just littler than I expected."

"Destiny," Matthew informed him solemnly. "You feel responsible for Kerreya, and maybe someday you will be. I won't be young forever. Someday you'll take over as the Valmain champion."

"Do you have to ruin every occasion with war talk?" Rita grumbled. "AJ, don't listen to him."

Molly touched the boy's cheek. "You're Kerry's oldest cousin, AJ. That *is* a responsibility. And now"—she turned a playful smile toward Robert—"who's next?"

Although younger, Robert betrayed none of the awkwardness AJ had initially exhibited as he took his new cousin into his arms. "AJ's gonna be your champion, Kerry," he informed the baby briskly, "but *I'm* gonna be your doctor."

Rita giggled. "Thank heavens someone around here has some common sense."

"I agree," Molly yawned. "You'll make a great doctor, Robert. Now . . ."

"Now you want to sleep?" Matthew guessed. "No problem, Valmain. We can take you back to the motel, if you want."

She touched her fingers to her husband's lips. "I want to

sleep here. Just for a while." Pausing to enjoy his surprised expression, she then added, "Rita, you and the boys don't have to stay. Go have something to eat. Matthew and I can finish the sandwiches he brought while the baby nurses, and then we'll nap."

"Matt won't nap," Rita predicted. "He has to stand guard, in case a horde of warriors descends on you." Her tone was mocking, but her smile loving. "We'll be back before dark, and then I'll insist you bring my beautiful niece indoors."

When the Camacho family had departed, Matthew again took his daughter into his arms and stood, holding her so that, had her tiny eyes been opened and focused, she could have surveyed her domain. "This is all at your feet, Kerreya Redtree. Kings and sorceresses and warriors were your ancestors, and their legacy to you was power." Turning her to face him, he added, "Your mother will teach you to be strong and pure of heart. And I'll defend you with my life, and with Lost Eagle's amulet, until the day I die."

"Matthew, . . ." Molly bit back a gentle but useless rebuke. She loved this man with a dizzying passion that made her doubt her own sanity, yet she knew she would never understand him. He was unique . . . driven . . . and, ultimately, unreachable. Or maybe this child could reach him, and tame his wanderlust, and awaken his need for love, banishing his obsession with destiny once and for all.

At that moment Kerreya began to whimper, and Matthew quickly returned her to her mother, who cooed a soft apology. "Just be happy and healthy, Kerry. Forget about destiny."

"Molly, . . ." Matthew's jaw had tensed. "Don't teach her that. You've turned your back on your birthright as a mounds sorceress, but if Kerry's one, too, let her choose to learn and use her magic. We'll find some way to train her when the time is right. Don't make her deny her heritage."

"You didn't let me finish," Molly scolded softly, then turned back to the infant and repeated, "Forget about destiny, Kerry, but never forget you're special, and your father's the

Valmain champion. The handsomest, bravest, strongest warrior the world has ever known."

"That's a little better," Matthew chuckled. "We'll discuss the rest later. For now, you need to get some sleep."

"Tell Kerry a story first. After all, she's the daughter of the most wonderful storyteller the world has ever known."

"Yeah?" He grinned proudly. "Okay, Kerreya Elizabeth, listen to this. Long ago, one of your ancestors, named Lost Eagle, lived here, among these very mounds, in a time of sorcerers and magic. And even though Lost Eagle wasn't a magician himself, he was respected as the finest warrior in his tribe and was given a magic amulet to wear on his wrist. The amulet made him invincible, but Lost Eagle made a deadly mistake by giving the amulet to a woman named Maya. Maya's lover, a sorcerer who was called the Moonshaker, murdered Lost Eagle in a fit of jealousy. As he lay dying, Lost Eagle cried out for vengeance, and years later, when the mounds themselves were destroyed, they too cried out, for a worthy descendant to inherit their power. And so, centuries later, a curly-haired sorceress with a strong, pure heart was born. She visited my dreams, night after night, wearing her cape of silver and white and urging me to come into her dream world and to do destiny's bidding. And then she tied Lost Eagle's magic amulet to my wrist"—he reached for Molly's arm and held it so that the silver spool caught the afternoon sun—"and I defeated Aaric the Moonshaker and avenged Lost Eagle. And now"—the golden eyes glittered wildly—"the dream girl has given me the greatest gift of all. A daughter. A sorceress. That's you, Kerry. I couldn't be prouder, or more humbled, or more grateful . . ."

"Matthew . . ." Molly choked on a soft sob. "When you tell it that way, it frightens me. It's so relentless. So predetermined and impersonal. Beautiful, but also hopeless . . ."

"Hopeless?" He tilted her chin upward and gently kissed her quivering lips. "Because of you, and this child, there *is* hope. For the first time in centuries. Don't you see?"

"All I see is passion. It's in your eyes, and in your voice. It makes me dizzy, and weak, and frightened . . ."

"Because you're exhausted," he murmured contritely. "Don't say another word, Valmain. Just lie here in the grass and try to sleep while I practice my kicks."

"You'll need this," Molly reminded him, untying the amulet as she spoke.

"You're sure you don't need it to heal?"

She shook her head, then tied the ends of the leather thong, securing the magic amulet to his wrist, trying not to notice the reverence in his eyes as he watched the ritual. Instead, she focused on the rest of his handsome yet humble appearance.

The ornate silver spool-shaped charm, with its turquoise stones and elaborate markings, contrasted sharply to his austere wardrobe—*always* jeans and running shoes, always a white polo shirt, and occasionally a hooded blue sweatshirt or a Red Sox baseball cap. He was a Spartan in both clothing and thought but, thanks to the silver amulet, was also a superhuman warrior when near the mounds. Now, as she rearmed him, Molly could almost feel the flood of power that surged through his lean, well-muscled body, and she almost believed, for just a moment, that she should surrender completely to his view of their future, abandon her lifelong plan to become a scientist, move to this desolate region with her warrior-husband, and study magic and folklore forever.

And you should tell him Aaric's still in your dream, she chastised herself as she watched him move a distance away to begin his daily practicing. *Matthew doesn't lie to you, or keep secrets from you, and he trusts you to be honest. He's your husband, and your champion, and now he's the father of your child . . .*

Hugging the new child close in weary confusion, she began to drift, away from Matthew Redtree, and toward Aaric the Moonshaker, the keeper of her dreams, the trainer of her talents, and the best friend she had in all the world.

* * *

"Mommy?"

Constance Sheridan barely glanced up from her fashion magazine. "What is it now, Niki?"

Twisting a lock of ash-blond hair around her finger, the four-year-old inquired hesitantly, "Did Molly have her baby yet?"

The question brought an ominous frown to the mother's otherwise-flawless face. "Who cares?"

"She's my sister."

"Your *half* sister. And the *wrong* half at that, so let's drop it."

Niki winced but persisted. "Daddy told me something."

"Oh?"

"He says when he goes to San Francisco for a consolation, he'll take me and we'll go see Molly's baby."

"Consolation?" The mother was now positively glaring. "Do you mean, consultation?"

Niki nodded. "Daddy says just me and him will go. Not you."

"Well, don't get your hopes up." Constance had regained her equilibrium and now sneered, "You'll never see Molly or her boring little brat, so forget about it."

"Daddy says the baby will call me Aunt Niki."

"That's enough!" With a single flash of her pale blue eyes, she sent the child careening backward into the wall, knocking the wind from her proud little body. "Now apologize for being such a brat, then go to your room."

Stunned and still breathless, Niki edged quickly toward the hall. "Sor-Sorry, Mommy," she managed to gasp before disappearing from view.

Constance threw down the magazine and began to pace, more disgusted with herself than with the child. What if she had bruised the girl, or broken one of her bones? How would she explain that to her husband, the devoted pediatrician?

And yet, how was she expected to discipline the whiny little brat, or to discourage her from asking tiresome questions or awakening Alexander Sheridan's long-dormant interest in his absent elder daughter, Molly?

There was only one solution and while it carried an element of risk, it was also long overdue. It was time little Niki Sheridan learned the truth—about her mother, and her half sister, and herself. Perhaps then she'd begin to show Constance the respect and fear she rightfully deserved. With a sly smile, the mother hurried to the staircase and ascended to her only daughter's room.

The girl was sobbing into the soft white fur of a five-foot-long stuffed bunny rabbit, and the vulnerable sight widened Constance's smile into a grin. This was going to be fun! "Niki?"

Red-rimmed eyes pleaded for mercy. "I'm sorry, Mommy."

"Did I hurt you?"

"Yes, Mommy."

"Good. You were very bad, and you deserved it."

"Yes, Mommy."

"And when your daddy gets home, what will you tell him?"

Niki chewed her lip, then ventured, "That I fell off my bike?"

"And?"

"And you took good care of me?"

"Well"—Constance eased herself into a chintz-covered rocking chair—"you're not as stupid as you look. Now, I have some good news for you." Before the child could react, she added, "Would you like me to tell you a secret?"

Niki hugged the bunny closer. "Okay."

Constance leaned forward. "Have you ever wondered how I can hurt you from across the room, without spanking or touching you?"

"Because I'm bad?"

"That's *why* I do it. I'm asking you *how* I do it." She smiled triumphantly. "I'll tell you how. I'm a witch, Niki. A very powerful, very important witch."

The girl's bloodshot eyes had widened with alarm. "Daddy says witches are pretend."

"If I were pretend, could I do this?" Constance rose to her feet and, as she did, her appearance changed, slowly, to that of a man in a shimmering black cape. He was handsome, with a smile so devastatingly charming that the child smiled in return—an innocent, trusting smile.

And then the man's smile twisted into a cruel leer and, within seconds, his eyes were glowing, like red-hot coals, and his hands were reaching out, with claws where his nails should have been. . . .

"Mommy!" Niki shrieked, clutching desperately at her bunny. "Mommy, make him stop!"

Constance was chuckling as her willowy body and elegant features reemerged from the illusion. "Do you still think witches are pretend? Little fool." She shook her head in feigned sympathy. "You really never suspected? Would you like me to tell you the story of my life?" When the girl simply stared, the witch added curtly, "Pay attention, Niki. From this moment on, you're going to start behaving. Now sit there on the bed and be quiet while I teach you about your magnificent heritage."

"Can I get under the covers?" the child whispered. "I'm cold, Mommy. And . . . and I'm scared."

"Good. Maybe you'll stop being such a brat." She waved her jeweled hand impatiently. "Haven't you ever wondered why I'm so beautiful? I'm the most beautiful woman you've ever seen, aren't I?"

Niki snuggled under a pink satin comforter and nodded.

"This beauty of mine is a reward. I was always pretty, but this"—she traced her chiseled face and shapely bosom—"is something I earned. I was born many centuries ago, Niki, in the place we now call New York State. In those days it was the domain of my people, the most powerful magicians in all of North America. We were called the lake magicians, because we drew our power from the waters of our lands.

"Our females were born witches, and our males, like the man you just saw standing here about to claw you, were called wizards. The wizards controlled the power. The wizards," she added sharply, "controlled everyone and everything. When I broke one of their rules, they punished me in the most hideous of ways. They disfigured my pretty face and my body so that no man would ever suffer my presence in his bed. Then they sent me into the woods, where they expected me to take my own life. I was lying on the ground, crying and cursing, when an amazing thing happened."

Niki's fear had clearly disappeared. "What happened, Mommy? Did Daddy save you?"

"Daddy?" Constance sneered. "Aren't you paying attention? This was thousands of years ago. Your daddy wasn't even born yet, and even if he had been, what could he have done? He's a powerless fool. Anyway," her voice returned to a coo, "I looked up and saw a sorceress named Maya. She was a very famous magician, from another culture—a culture that drew its magic from a set of burial mounds to the southwest of our land. We had warred with them in the past, and so I was surprised to see her in our woods, alone, without any warrior to protect her. I was even more surprised when she told me she had come to offer me a chance to be beautiful—a hundred times more beautiful than I had been before." The witch's eyes were shining at the memory. "She told me she wanted me to perform a service for her—to aid in a curse she had cast upon the future. If I did all she asked, she would give me my reward. I had no choice but to trust her, even though she was a mounds sorceress, and so I agreed.

"And then Maya told me about a king named Valmain, who had betrayed her with another woman. To punish him, Maya had cursed his kingdom with a curse of betrayal, but

Maya's father had interfered by protecting Valmain's kingdom with a spell of protection. Under such a spell a champion would rise up, at every hint of betrayal, to fight for Valmain. And so the spell would balance the curse, and each was powerful, and so Maya needed to supplement her curse if she wanted it to succeed for sure. That was *my* job. She told me she would send me into the future, to the castle of the current Valmain ruler, where she expected me to use my beauty to get close to the most powerful men in the castle. Then I was to wait until a warrior arrived—a warrior whom Maya was going to send here to meet me—and then the two of us were supposed to foment betrayal. Supposedly, at that time, a champion would arise to defend Valmain—because of the spell of protection—but my warrior would defeat that champion, and I would see to it that the curse of betrayal won out and destroyed the kingdom. If I did all of this, I would be allowed to keep my new beauty permanently.

"And so Maya put me into a deep sleep and, when I awoke, I found myself in the basement of this very house. I used my illusion power to make myself invisible, then crept up the stairs. It was like no castle I had ever imagined—small, but so luxurious! Thick carpets and sumptuous wall coverings, and so many mirrors! I wandered from room to room until I found the master bedroom. A man and woman were sleeping there, and, while the man was quite handsome, it was obvious to me that he wasn't a king. And the woman"— Constance's eyes narrowed with contempt—"was obviously common. So I left that room and made my way down the hall, to this very room, and there, tucked into bed, was the most beautiful child I had ever seen."

Niki's face was glowing with enchantment. "Me?"

"You?" the witch hooted. "I said beautiful, not ugly!" When the child's expression soured, the mother grinned. "You weren't even born yet, Niki. It was your half sister, Molly. Not," she added quickly, "that she's so beautiful now. It's just that she had a certain quality about her. A regal quality, and I knew for certain that she was the Valmain princess. She was the person I needed to get close to if I wanted to help Maya and earn my beauty. But"—she shrugged slightly—"I also was confused. There were no guards, and no servants. Nothing made sense, so I left this place and traveled until I found the barracks of my former people, the lake magicians."

She smiled at the memory. "You should have seen the First Wizard's face when he laid eyes on me that day. For hours, we barely spoke. He took me, again and again and again, as though he had been starving for a woman like me, and then he called in the others, and each wizard pleasured himself with me, until I was dizzy with exhaustion, and then," she sighed, "I told them my story, and they told me theirs.

"I was aghast, eventually, at the sorry state my people were in. They were as powerful as ever, but woefully lazy. All of their modern conveniences had made them soft, but as I told them of the exploits of their forefathers, they came alive with desire to recapture that old glory. I became the First Wizard's most valued adviser, and he, in turn, advised me on my predicament."

She stood and stretched, then wandered to the window. "So many things had changed, Niki. But the strangest news of all to me was that the mounds civilization—the civilization of Maya—had been destroyed by my people centuries earlier. Despite the greatness of individual magicians like Maya and her lover, Aaric, the race as a whole had weakened over the years because the mounds that empowered them were never completely finished.

"And therein was my dilemma. What duty did I owe to Maya, if the mounds were no more? More importantly, Valmain was no more. The kingdom, which had existed on the other side of the Atlantic Ocean, had apparently long since vanished, and I woke up in this particular house only because your half sister was the current descendant of that original royal family. But the kingdom was gone, and so how could I engender betrayal?

"But the First Wizard cautioned me, saying that my exquisite beauty might be lost if I did not do all that I had promised. He told me to come back to this house, to ingratiate myself with Molly, and to wait for the arrival of the warrior, whom Maya had promised to send to aid me. It seemed simple enough. With the wizard's help I bought the house next door and tried to get close to Molly, but it was impossible."

"Why?"

"Because she wasn't a normal girl. You couldn't flatter her. She refused to go shopping with me, even when I offered to buy her clothes, or help her with her makeup. She didn't even *wear* makeup! All she did was read and study, and when she wanted someone to talk to, she turned to her mother. They were very close. *Too* close. And so the wizard advised me to do away with the mother, which I did. I arranged for her to die in an automobile accident, but I miscalculated, and Molly almost died, too. After that, I had to work quickly. I seduced your father, with the aid of a love spell, and I conceived a child. You. I hoped that would cement my relationship to Molly, but the little bitch had a tantrum. She accused her father of being unfaithful to the mother's memory, and she refused to see us, either of us, ever again.

"I panicked and ran to the First Wizard for advice, and he told me perhaps I had done the right thing. Perhaps this betrayal—this rift between daughter and father—would fulfill my responsibility toward Maya and her curse. And that's exactly what's happened since then. Your father betrayed his first wife and his first daughter by marrying me and fathering you. That's the reason I can never allow a reconciliation between Molly and your father. And that's the reason you'll never be allowed to meet her. So," her tone grew brisk, "shut up about her from now on, understand?"

"Did the warrior come?"

Constance grinned. "So, you were paying attention, I see. No, Niki, he never came. I assume he figured out there was no longer a Valmain kingdom and so he just assimilated into the world. Or, Maya's power failed her and she was unable to send both him and me to this future world. Either way I didn't need him. I engendered betrayal all by myself, and so the curse won out over the spell of protection. My beauty is proof of that."

Niki pursed her lips thoughtfully. "Daddy might go and see Molly's baby, and it might be really cute. . . ." She shrank from the glare in her mother's eyes and added quickly, "I'm sorry, Mommy. Please don't hurt me again."

"I won't hurt you. I'll bring the wizard back and *he'll* hurt you. Do you want that?"

"No!"

"Fine, then." She crossed to sit on the edge of the frilly, pink bed. "I understand more than you think, Niki. You want to meet Molly and the baby because they're your family. You need to be a part of a larger community, and from this day on, you are. From this day on, you're a part of the lake community. Do you understand what that means?" When the girl shook her head warily, Constance revealed, "It means you're a witch, too. Isn't that wonderful?"

"I'm not! I don't *want* to be a witch!"

"No?" The mother's face hardened. "You're such a stupid fool. Perhaps you'll get your wish. Your father's human, so there's the chance you're just as powerless as you are ugly. You'd better hope not, or you'll never find a man to marry you."

"I don't need a man to marry me." The girl's chin jutted forward in complete rebellion. "I have Daddy!"

"Do you?" The witch arched an eyebrow knowingly. "Because you're his precious daughter? Just like his other precious daughter, whom he hasn't seen in over five years? You'd better smarten up, Niki. Your father's weak. I'm strong.

I can make him hate you, the way I made him hate Molly. . . ."

"He doesn't hate her," Niki whispered. "He loves her, and so do I."

Constance caught her temper and replied evenly, "But Molly hates you and your Daddy, and do you know why? She hates him for marrying me and she hates you for taking her place."

"No . . ." The girl seemed frightened by the thought. "Daddy says I look like her. . . ."

"A little perhaps, although her eyes are bluer, and her hair is thick with curls. But you're a witch, and she's not, so you needn't worry. Soon I'll take you with me to the lakes, and we'll begin your training. And one day, if you're lucky, you'll marry a wizard and your troubles will be over. I wanted to marry a wizard," she added with a sigh, "but I'm stuck here instead. At least I'm beautiful, but what a price I've paid. Married to a human, with an ugly, stubborn, stupid daughter like you."

Niki studied her mother carefully. "If Molly's a princess, did she marry a prince?"

"Who said she was a princess?" Constance snapped. "Her kingdom's all gone, and she's just a boring little graduate student. And her husband's just a regular man. Nice-looking, but not remarkable. He writes books about ancient legends." Her eyes were suddenly twinkling. "I could teach him a thing or two. About legends, and about women. I can only imagine boring little Molly in bed!"

"Does Molly know you're a witch?"

"I'm sure precious little Molly doesn't believe in magic or witches, Niki. Lucky for her. If she ever figured out I used a love spell to steal her father's heart, she'd come back, and I'd have to kill her."

"Daddy wouldn't let you." The child's tone was eerily brave. "I wouldn't, neither."

"Oh, really . . . ?"

At that moment, a booming voice invaded the afternoon with a cheerful, "Niki! Constance! Where's my little family?"

"It's Daddy!" Niki clapped her hands as though a knight in shining armor had arrived.

"Quiet! I want to spend some time alone with him. Stay in this bed and pretend to be asleep."

"But, Mommy . . ."

"Shall I bring back the wizard?"

"No! I'll be good." The child snuggled almost desperately under the satin comforter.

Constance chuckled, pleased that the brief show of courage had been so easily squelched. The perfect solution. Why take a chance on damaging the child, when the simple use of illusion could keep her so tightly under control? Patting the blanket in a mock-maternal gesture, she straightened her black knit dress and scooted into the hall, intercepting Alexander Sheridan within inches of the doorway and kissing him with playful thoroughness.

"Alex! What a wonderful surprise!" she gushed. "You must have read my mind. I've been missing you so much."

The handsome doctor returned her kiss, then pulled free and motioned toward the closed door. "Is Niki playing in her room? I've got a surprise for her."

"She's sound asleep," Constance smiled. "I was just sitting in my rocking chair, staring at her, and thinking how lucky I was to have such an angel for a daughter. And"—the smile turned suggestive—"such a devil for a husband. Love in the afternoon, Alex? How delightfully naughty."

"Sounds good, darling, but first . . ." He flushed and cleared his throat. "Maybe it's a good thing Niki's napping. There's something we need to discuss. . . ." He paused to frown. "She didn't fall off her bike again, did she?"

"She's tired from our trip to the zoo," Constance explained easily. "She talked my ear off, and, of course, we had to see *every* animal and feed *every* duck. She's so bright and curi-

ous, Alex. Such a delight. She said the cutest thing." Her
pale eyes were twinkling with motherly pride. "She said you
were going to San Francisco for a 'consolation.' Isn't that
precious?"

Her husband winced. "She told you . . . ?"

"She told me everything, and . . . ," the witch's words
came out in a rush of vulnerability and innocence, "of *course*
we should go and see Molly! She's your daughter, and the
child will be our grandchild! Don't you know by now that
all I want is to see you and Niki happy? We have to go and
mend this rift, or I'll never be able to live with myself."

His stare was a confusion of gratitude and concern. "We?
Are you saying you'd like to come along?"

"You don't want me to?"

"It's not that, darling," he insisted quickly. "It's just . . ."

"You're remembering how rude she was to me?" Constance stroked his handsome face gently. "I can't say she
didn't hurt me, Alex, but . . ." Her lower lip began to quiver.
"My only fear is that she'll say something hideous to my
poor Niki and break her sweet, trusting heart. Molly sees
Niki as the product of your . . . your infidelity. . . ."

"Don't cry," he pleaded, pulling his wife against his chest.
"I won't let anyone hurt Niki, darling. I swear it."

"Alex . . ." Pulling his head down toward her own, she
kissed him desperately as she ground her exaggerated curves
against his hungry body. "Oh, Alex, if I lost you I think I'd
die."

"I don't know what I was thinking!" he gasped. "My God,
Constance, you feel so good. . . . I can't get enough of
you. . . ."

"It's love," she assured him in a thick, almost hoarse voice.
"Make love to me, Alex. Show me you belong to me."

"I do, I swear it," he proclaimed and then, heedless of the
child on the far side of the door, pulled the witch to the
carpeted floor, mindlessly allowing her love spell to devour
him as thoroughly as it destroyed his plan for reconciliation.

Two

For a moment Molly felt almost shy as she stood in the shadows of her dream world and watched the brawny, golden-haired sorcerer pace. He had chosen to wear his short, sleeveless white tunic—Molly called this his "Greek philosopher" look and infinitely preferred it to the thick, coarsely studded leather armor he wore when in his battle mode. Either way Aaric the Moonshaker, last of the ancient ones, presented a striking figure, both in size and demeanor, and a handsome one.

Sensing Molly's presence, he now strode to her side and grasped her shoulders. "All is well?" When she nodded, he exhaled in exaggerated relief. "This dream was alive with energy and anticipation, but still I was worried for you." Pulling her against his massive chest, he cradled her gently and mourned, "If only I could have been there with you, to strengthen and guide you . . ."

"I'm fine." She blushed, pulling free enough to give him her warmest smile. "You're so sweet to care so much, Aaric. Thank you." Stroking his regal face, she added, "You and Matthew were right, as usual. It all went smoothly. The amulet gave me incredible strength."

"That is dung. It was not the amulet," he corrected. "You drew your magic directly from the mounds, Princess. You and I have no need of amulets, although your husband is just a man without it tied to his wrist." Before Molly could indignantly defend her champion-husband, Aaric grinned,

"Now tell me of your child. Is she a daughter, as you have predicted?"

"Kerreya Elizabeth Redtree. You should see her, Aaric. She's gorgeous. Dark hair, golden eyes . . ."

"Bring her immediately."

"You mean, summon her?" Molly's pulse began to race. "She's a newborn, Aaric. And I haven't summoned anyone here since Angela, and you remember how hard *that* was."

"Angela was an enemy and a witch," he reminded her. "It will be much easier to bring someone you love. Do you dare deprive me, after the long nights of watching the child grow inside of you?"

She had to smile, remembering how supportive he had been during the pregnancy—pampering her more than ever, entertaining her with stories and illusions, praising her figure despite its growing dimensions, and suspending her rigorous training in sorcery for fear of taxing her strength. "I guess you deserve to meet Kerry," she agreed fondly. "I'll do my best. . . . Oh!" The baby had appeared in her arms as though the mere thought had been a magnet, and Molly took a moment to study her anew, still in awe of the tiny fingers and shimmering eyes.

In contrast to the simple white camisole and petticoat that Molly wore under her dream cape, Kerreya was dressed in an elaborate white christening gown, decorated with freshwater pearls and a myriad of sunbursts embroidered in satiny thread along the hem. "Look, Aaric. Isn't she pretty?"

He stared for a long moment before confessing, "I did not believe she could be as beautiful as her mother, but she is."

"She looks like Matthew, don't you think?"

He nodded. "The same dark hair, and her eyes . . ." A frustrated grin passed over his face. "You always say your champion's eyes have 'flecks of gold,' but I never believed such eyes existed until now. She is a treasure."

"Look at this dress. It's so delicate and intricate. Do you think she's a sorceress, Aaric? I mean, can you tell yet?"

"Only time will tell, but I have no true doubts. To look at her is to know that she will command the magic of many mounds and the hearts of many men, just as her mother does."

"You're so eloquent sometimes," Molly blushed. "When exactly will we know if she has powers? And what about this dream power? Will she have that?"

"I have explained that this dream power is rare. In any case," he reached for the child, "she will tell us herself soon enough. We will ask her about her dreams, and if she dreams of these mounds, then we will know."

"We?" She eyed him suspiciously. For the long months of the pregnancy, she had warned, over and over, that she would never ask Matthew's child to participate in any deception and thus, Aaric could never be a part of the child's life, except vicariously, through Molly. Now he acted as though Kerreya would be joining them nightly! And as though he would train her, as he had trained her mother . . .

"You worry, when you should rejoice," Aaric scolded. "She will be the most envied of witches—a mounds sorceress. As powerful as her mother, but with the early training necessary to control it. I guarantee it. Between the two of us, we will raise her well."

"Aren't you forgetting someone?"

"Him?" Aaric scoffed. "He will neglect her, as he neglects you. If there were any justice in this strange life of mine, I would be this child's father."

"You'd make such a wonderful father."

"It is not my destiny," he shrugged. "In this strange dream world, I can be only teacher and admirer. And lover. But, of course," he added mischievously, "while destiny permits that, *you* forbid it."

She laughed gently. "The most convenient thing about my pregnancy was that it kept you from hitting on me. Now, less than an hour after I gave birth, you're at it again."

"This is too soon?" His eyebrow arched in delight. "For how long will you deny your champion?"

"Never mind," she grinned. "Anyway, you know Matthew. He'd never pressure me for such mundane needs as sex."

"He will be too patient, and you will become frustrated and hurt." Aaric nodded. "As I said, he neglects you, and will neglect this pretty new witch as well. But I will not."

"She *is* pretty, isn't she?" Molly sighed. "But a part of me hopes she's not a witch. It makes life so confusing."

"And the other part of you hopes she has great magic?"

Her smile was rueful. "I wouldn't have missed the times I've had, with you and with Matthew, for anything. If I hadn't been a witch, you and I never would have met. And even though Matthew and I would have met on campus, nothing would have come of it without magic, since, as we both know, I'm not really his type."

"That again?" Aaric scoffed. "You are every man's type, Princess. If only you did not complain so incessantly, you would be perfect."

"Very funny." Her eyes twinkled playfully. "Half the time, you're Matthew's enemy, then you start defending him just as loyally."

Aaric ignored the goading, asking instead, "Do you think he will now try to get into this dream while you sleep?"

"If we were at the motel, yes, but we're out on the mounds, and so you know how Matthew is. He's guarding me—guarding *us*," she beamed toward her daughter, "and so he'd never dare sleep. But tonight, he'll try. When he's at the mounds," she added, with a sigh, "he always tries."

"And you always block him," Aaric agreed. "You have become very skillful at that."

"I had to," Molly nodded. "Remember the last time he surprised us together? I've never seen anyone so angry. I thought he'd never forgive me. . . ."

"But he did," the sorcerer reminded her. "You should have more faith in him, Princess."

"The only reason he forgave me is because he thinks I banished you from this dream forever when I banished Maya. If he ever found out I let you stay, he'd leave me." *After more than ten months of marriage,* she added sadly to herself, *I still can't trust him to understand me. And* he *can't trust me. What a mess.*

Aaric seemed to read her mind. "You believe you will keep this secret forever, but I suspect it will not be so. Either you will learn to trust your champion—to brave his rage, knowing it will be only temporary—or you will make a mistake and reveal your powers to him, and he will know you have been trained by an expert. And since I am the only surviving expert of mounds magic, he will know the dream, and Aaric the Moonshaker, are alive and well."

Molly shrugged. "It won't happen that way. There's not much call in my world for the power to summon fire and wind, Aaric. We have matches and air conditioners. If you'd teach me something a little more useful . . ." Her blue eyes began to twinkle admiringly. "If only I had your power of illusion! That would be so amazing."

"My power here, in the dream, is amazing," he agreed easily. "I suppose it is because this very dream is an illusion of sorts. Outside of the dream my power would be impressive, but much more limited. I could change my own appearance, or become invisible, but I would never be able to create tangible forms out of mere air, like this. . . ." The sorcerer waved his hand and before them stood the image of Matthew Redtree, as he had appeared in Molly's dream the previous fall, with his blue-black hair worn long to his shoulders, and his bronzed limbs bare and glistening. An intricate red-and-black beaded headband and wristband, along with the infamous silver amulet, were his only adornments. Otherwise, his deerskin tunic and moccasins were simple and unassuming, contributing to his aura of austere nobility.

Molly moistened her lips and tried to smile, but hot tears were welling in her eyes at the sight of her lover, here where

he so longed to be. Here, in the world to which she had
denied him access for fear of losing him entirely. He was
her hero, and she wanted no other, but his temper and obsessions stood between them, and only in illusions, such as
these, could they be together without any threat of quarrels
or recriminations.

"Forgive me, Princess," Aaric murmured, erasing the illusion quickly. "I intended only to impress and amuse you."
Cupping her chin in his huge hand, he insisted, "He batters
your heart with his ignorance. Tell him everything. Tell him,
before it is too late. Trust him."

"I trust *you*," she whispered unhappily, "but I don't trust
him. How can I, when he's so blinded by destiny and legends
and obsessions? He'd make me choose between you and him.
He'd never understand that I need you both."

"No man wishes to share his woman."

The tears were now streaming down her cheeks. "Not his
woman, Aaric, his 'dream girl.' If I thought he'd be roman-
tically jealous of you, I'd jump for joy! But that's not how it
is. He's obsessed with protecting me—with being the Valmain champion—and that's why he'd want you to be gone.
The truth is," she wiped frantically at her cheeks with the
edge of her lustrous white cape, "he wouldn't care if I'd slept
with you or not! His definition of infidelity has nothing to
do with sex when it comes to me! He just wouldn't want me
sharing my magic with you—"

"That is dung!" The Moonshaker's roar awakened the
baby, who didn't cry, but simply stared as though mesmerized. Without hesitation the sorcerer began to rub the small
of her back while continuing to glare at her mother. "Do you
truly believe your champion would not be jealous if you
pleasured yourself with another man?"

Despite her tears she succumbed to gentle laughter at the
incongruous sight. Aaric the Moonshaker, with his blazing
sea-blue eyes, thick golden hair, and powerful chest, comforting a delicate six-pound baby girl wrapped in silky, in-

nocent white. "I don't know if he'd be jealous of that, but I have a feeling he'd go completely berserk if he could see you holding his baby daughter in your arms that way. So lovingly. So gently."

"You believe a warrior cannot also be gentle?" he chided. "Have you forgotten how gentle I was with you during our lovemaking?"

She arched an eyebrow in warning. "You promised never to mention that." When he smiled slyly, she blushed and added, "It would never have happened if you hadn't been masquerading as Matthew, so let's drop it."

"If you believe your champion would not object to your having an affair despite your marriage vows, why not have one with me? Have I not proven myself to you as a lover?"

"Drop it," she repeated sourly, "or Kerry and I are leaving."

Aaric grinned. "You are faithful to him because you love him and because you know, in his own peculiar way, he loves you, too. His love for you is bizarre, Princess, but it is also strong. Never doubt that."

"Fine. I don't want to talk about Matthew anymore. Let's talk about my training."

The sorcerer cocked his head. "You sound almost eager to practice."

"Until now it's been so academic, but that rush I felt during the birth changed all that. I can see how it can become almost addictive. How soon can I start again?"

"Your enthusiasm pleases me." He transferred the child back to her and folded his arms across his chest. "We will begin from the beginning, of course. It has been some time, and your control is so very erratic, and so . . ."

"Let me guess," Molly drawled. "You want me to make a spark?"

"I would prefer it to a bonfire," he chuckled, waving his hand and creating an illusion of a pile of leaves. "Let us see if you can ignite these, and then summon a breeze to extinguish the flame."

"Okay." She tingled at the thought of playing with her magic again after eight long months of neglect. "Stand back, Moonshaker. Like you said, my control might be a little rusty."

"Send the little princess out of the dream first," he insisted. "This is only a dream, yet pain is very real in this place, as you should remember from your brawl with the witch Angela."

"And you remember from your losses to Matthew?" she teased. "Okay. Give her a kiss, and I'll send her back." When the Moonshaker's lips brushed the child's forehead, Molly sighed, impressed anew by his gentleness. Then she hugged her new child close, kissed her more firmly, and sent her easily away.

"I'm getting pretty good at that," she congratulated herself. "Remember how hard it was for me the first time? Now I can bring people, and send them away, with just a thought!"

"Do not overestimate yourself," her teacher scolded. "Kerreya is your daughter. You are linked, spiritually, and so your thoughts can easily touch hers. It is different with a stranger, or an enemy."

"Spoilsport. Anyway, one little fire, and then I should leave, too. She might wake up."

"If she awakens, she will cry," Aaric smiled. "That is how it is with little ones, Princess. Do not hover. She will tell you when she needs you. For now, practice."

Molly concentrated and, in less than an instant, the leaves were aglow with flames. Then she waved her arm, and a powerful whirlwind engulfed them, extinguishing the fire while causing the witch's luminous cape to billow wildly. With a sheepish smile she managed to calm the air, but not before she had heard the Moonshaker groan with displeasure.

"Sorry, Aaric. I forgot my own strength."

"It is always thus with you," he grumbled. "Your power is almost limitless, yet you can wreak only havoc, because your control is lacking. You must try to draw slowly, Princess, as we have discussed—"

"I know, I know." She made a sour face. "I'll do better next time. For now, I'd better go." Rising onto tiptoes, she kissed his square jaw. "See you tonight."

"Wait!" He caught her by the waist and insisted, "Have I thanked you today? For the visit? For the smiles? And"—his voice grew thick—"for the little one?"

"You're so sweet."

"I am proud of you, Princess. You have given the world a new sorceress. And you have given my world meaning, and love." His rough hand stroked her long, sun-streaked hair. "Never has there been a woman such as you, who can fill a man's whole world with beauty and grace, and who can make him feel strong and needed while showing no weakness yourself."

She had heard such tributes before, so many times, and yet, as always, her heart swelled with pride and confusion. There was such fire in this man's eyes when he gazed upon her. It was the kind of love every woman dreamed of finding, but for her it was all wrong. She wanted this, yes, but only if it could be from Matthew.

"Aaric," she pleaded. "Don't do this to me. If you want to make love to someone, make yourself an illusion of Maya. . . ." Before his eyes could respond, she escaped to the safety of her slumbering body and as she awakened, she cuddled her little girl close and struggled to understand why fate had dealt her so complex a hand.

"Molly?"

To hear Matthew's voice, so soon after Aaric's—so soon after the words of passion that she so longed to hear—was simply too cruel, and so she pretended for just one moment longer that she was still asleep. *What difference can one more deception make?* she asked herself sadly.

"Valmain?" He nudged her and, as he did, also extricated their new daughter from her grip. "It's getting dark. We have to get back to the motel before Rita has a fit."

She opened one eye and had to smile. Aaric the Moon-shaker had appeared disproportionately huge holding an infant, but Matthew Redtree—the lean, mean Son of Lost Eagle and the long-awaited Valmain champion—could not have seemed more at ease. More right. The resemblance was already strong: the eyes, the raven hair, the calm disposition. Molly could only hope that for Kerreya, the calm was not the proverbial one preceding a storm, as it had proven to be for Matthew Redtree.

"She looks just like you, Matthew. I'm so glad."

"Funny you should say that. I was watching you two while you slept," he informed his wife cautiously, "and you had identical expressions on your faces. Almost as though you were both," he cleared his throat, then suggested lightly, "having the same dream."

It broke her heart, but she dared not show it, and so she forced herself to glare instead. "We had a deal. If I agreed to have our baby at these mounds, instead of in Berkeley or L.A., you weren't going to dredge up the dream. It's *gone,* Matthew."

"Sorry, Valmain." He rocked back onto his heels and studied his family wistfully. "I just hope she has the same gift of magic you used to have. If she does, and we can train her while she's still young, we've got it made."

"We already have it made," Molly reminded him. "I'm almost halfway finished with graduate school; you have a contract for three more legend books; we have great health, solid finances, wonderful friends and relatives, and now, a perfect baby girl. Try to be happy, Matthew. Please?"

"Sure, Valmain. I'm the luckiest guy in the world," he agreed, assisting her to her feet. "On the other hand"—the flecks of gold in his eyes began to dance in the way that could so easily make Molly's heart skip a beat—"anything's possible. Maybe things could be even better, right?"

If only he would kiss her, right then, she might just be able to agree, but the energy that flowed through him right now—courtesy of the amulet and his indomitable link with destiny—was of another kind. It drove him to be her champion, not her lover, and while he played that latter role well when required, this complete and total passion was reserved for moments such as these, when visions of heroic ancestors and powerful descendants filled his head and his heart.

"There's the car," Molly murmured, glad for a reason to pull free of the embrace despite her longing to surrender. "Give me the baby, and I'll—Oh!"

He had swept her, baby and all, into his arms, and despite herself she reacted viscerally—to the strength in his lean, bronzed body, the warmth in his muscled chest, and the playful grin on his handsome face. He had the ability to arouse her almost instantly and used that ability to manipulate her, yet she simply could not resist. This madness engulfed her whenever he was near, shaping her life despite lessons learned, so painfully and recently. She knew he was a fanatic. She knew he would never love her for herself rather than her magic and her heritage. She even knew she could never make him happy, and yet, when he held her this way, she lost all reason. Perhaps, if she was lucky, she always would.

He had loved the sight of them sleeping on the mound— his dream girl and his firstborn—and now, as Matthew Redtree emerged from the bathroom of their motel suite, toweling off his freshly showered body, he found himself admiring them once again. His pretty bride was trying to nurse their daughter, but the infant seemed content to simply stare up into her mother's steady, deep blue eyes.

She knows instinctively that those eyes are a reflection of Molly's magic, he told himself, remembering other times,

more than a year earlier, when he, too, had been drawn instinctively to the clear blue gaze of a curly-haired, soft-spo-
ken college girl. To think that that amazing female was now
his wife! Mother to his daughter! Heiress to the Valmain
crown and a sorceress, to boot, although she continually
sought to reject those roles.

She was still so young. Only twenty-three years old. His
uncle August had wisely advised him to back off, for a while,
from pressuring her into exploring her magical powers. Perhaps now that she was a mother, her irrational desire to pursue a career in toxicology would lessen, or, better still,
disappear entirely. Perhaps, as Kerreya's mother, she would
begin to understand the importance of heritage. And if, as
Matthew suspected, their daughter was a sorceress like her
mother, Molly would no longer be able to ignore magic.
Their lives would be filled with it! And if by some miracle
the child had the long-lost dream power . . .

He could barely contain his excitement at the thought. He
missed his nightly journeys to Molly's dream world. It was
the place where they had met, and explored their love, and
discovered the amazing powers of the amulet. It was the site
of his historic battles with Aaric the Moonshaker. Most of
all, it was the place where she had agreed to be his bride
and to share his life—a reaffirmation of their love, after being so harshly tested by betrayal. She had forgiven him for
having an affair with the witch named Angela Clay, and he
had forgiven her for secretly meeting with Aaric and for in-
viting both Aaric and his mistress Maya to live in the dream
despite the peril such an arrangement could pose.

Fortunately, they had both come to their senses. Matthew
had renounced Angela, and Molly had sent Maya and Aaric
away forever. They had emerged from the experience
stronger and more committed than ever. And wiser also. Had
it not been for their mistakes, they never would have learned
the truth about Molly's heritage. It was Deborah Clay, Angela's devious grandmother, who had first explained to Mat-

thew the fact that the mounds had been a civilization of sorcerers who had been completely destroyed by their enemies,
the lake wizards. And Maya and Aaric had confirmed such
stories in their conversations with Molly. Without this information, how could Matthew have trained or protected his
sorceresses? As ironic as it seemed, it was for the best that
he had erred with Angela, and that Molly had temporarily
entertained the Moonshaker and Maya in her dream.

Unfortunately, Molly was now unable to find her way back
to the dream. Because she was afraid? Matthew couldn't bear
the thought of his dream girl being afraid—not of her power,
or of her past, or of their future. Didn't she know he would
defend her with his life, and that he would be victorious
because, as the Valmain champion, victory was his destiny?
If only she would relax and allow the dream to find her.

In the past it had helped to make love to her at such times.
Sex relaxed her almost completely and had prepared her on
several key occasions to find the dream and perform therein,
and so Matthew had cheerfully embraced such strategies.
After all, beyond her innumerable spiritual attributes, his
bride had been graced with lustrous sun-streaked curls, a
slender, well-proportioned form, and legs so long and
shapely they could make even a disciplined warrior like Matthew breathe unevenly.

Unfortunately, his sister Rita had informed him, with char-
acteristic bluntness, that he should wait a month or longer
before making any demands on "poor Molly" and he had
laughingly promised to restrain himself. Too bad. Tonight
they were here, at the mounds, where the magic was strongest, and if he made love to her tonight, he was certain she'd
find her dream.

In any case, he intended to try to find it alone. He had
been successful many times in the past, even when Molly
was awake or otherwise unavailable, but during the past ten
months his innumerable attempts had been unsuccessful.
Somehow, without even realizing it, the dream girl was

blocking her own access and that of her champion. But she couldn't hold out forever, and so Matthew would never give up. One day he would succeed, and they would be reunited as destiny had always intended.

He had meant what he'd said to her earlier that afternoon. He knew he had been moody and restless over this first year of marriage, but now all of that would change. After all, his restlessness had been born of impatience, hadn't it? It had driven him crazy to see his bride embrace biochemistry rather than sorcery, and so he had worked out his frustrations by pursuing tangible prizes such as new weapons for his collection, or intangibles such as new legends for his anthologies.

But this afternoon everything had changed. Molly Sheridan Redtree had embraced her birthright. She had felt the power of the amulet and had used it to birth their child. After so long, she had given in to the powers of the mounds and the result had been awesome! Matthew had seen her blue eyes widening with amazement at the steady rush of magic—how often had he felt that rush himself!—and he knew this memory would be a strong one for her. Perhaps now she'd be willing to pursue the dream, or to at least try a few simple tricks like fire or wind. Matthew's research had been painstakingly exhaustive and he now felt qualified to act as her instructor, at least for such elementary lessons as fire and wind.

"I almost hate to ask you what you're thinking, Matthew Redtree," she scolded him softly from her perch on the bed. "Come over here and give your little girl a kiss good-night."

He crossed to them quickly. "She's asleep again? She's so calm, Molly. When's she going to cry for the first time?"

"I'm sure she'll have her moments. For now, why don't you take her while I call Grandma. I promised I'd let her know as soon as I could."

"Good idea." He took the tiny infant into his arms. "While you're at it, why don't you give your dad a quick call?" He didn't have to look up from his daughter's face to know that his dream girl was scowling at him, but he persisted. "Give him a break, Valmain. He's Kerreya's grandfather. And your little sister is her Aunt Nicole, right?"

"Matthew, please, just drop it? I've told you a thousand times—as long as he's still married to Constance, he's never going to be a part of my life." Her blue eyes narrowed as she added, "Don't you dare call them yourself, either. You promised."

"I'd never betray your trust in me, Valmain," he assured her solemnly. "I just thought you should look at it from Kerry's point of view."

"Kerry's point of view is simple. Warmth, love, milk . . . that's all she needs."

"But someday . . ." Recognizing the signs of true anger, he deftly changed tacks. "As much as I'd like to stay here forever, Rita wants to leave tomorrow, if you're up to it. She has to get back to work, and the boys are missing school."

"I feel great," Molly assured him. "We can leave first thing in the morning."

"I thought we'd rent a car and follow her until she's safely over the mountains, then we'll head over to my uncle's ranch. He'll be anxious to see the new mounds sorceress."

"Perfect. August will love Kerry, and vice versa." Her eyes began to dance. "Let's rent a Mustang convertible!"

Matthew smiled, amused by the illogical suggestion. "You're a mother now, Valmain. Time to give up your sports-car fantasies." Settling the baby on the bed, he continued, "I did some research on the safest cars on the road and I made a list—"

"Mustangs are perfectly safe," she interrupted. "I learned to drive on one, Matthew, and I loved it! You and Kerry can just sit back and enjoy the scenery while I chauffeur you."

"You learned to drive in a Mustang?" he murmured. "Am I about to hear about some old high-school boyfriend?"

"Hardly," she laughed. "It was my mom's car. A beautiful white convertible She loved it, and so did I."

The image sent a chill down the warrior's spine. "Are you saying that's the car she was driving when she crashed?" Gathering his dream girl against his chest, he groaned, "You've got to let go of all that, Valmain. It's morbid."

"What?"

His tone grew stern. "It's natural to miss your mother, and to mourn her, but forget about the damned car!"

"It wasn't the car's fault! It wasn't anybody's fault," she insisted, pulling free and glaring. "It's not morbid! That's ridiculous."

"It wasn't anybody's fault," he agreed, "so let it go. Be glad you survived that accident. And drive a safe car, so Kerry never has to live through a nightmare like that. So *I* never have to worry about something so awful." He pulled her close once more and whispered fervently, "We couldn't make it without you, Valmain. I know you miss your mother. I want you to keep her memory alive, but not by reliving the accident. Remember the good times. Tell Kerry and me all about them. All about her. Okay?"

"You're not listening to me," she complained softly. "I don't want to 'relive' the accident. I just . . ." Her hand stroked his face gently. "The last thing I want to do is argue with you after this perfect day. Rent whichever car you want. As long as we're together, that's all that matters."

Matthew exhaled with relief. Despite the unresolved conflicts in his young bride's heart, he could always count on her to be strong. It was this quiet, magical strength—in her heart and in her eyes—that bound him to her so completely. "Good girl, Molly. We'll go see my uncle, and then"—he tried lightly—"we could head back here for a long stay."

"Matthew, no. We've been here too long already," she protested. "I keep thinking Deborah Clay might show up and hurt Kerry. . . ."

Alarmed by the slight shudder that had dared rack his

dream girl's slender form, Matthew grasped her shoulders and insisted, "Deborah Clay is hundreds of miles away from here. Her house is all boarded up, just like I told you, and no one's seen her since they found Angela's body." When a familiar spark lit Molly's blue eyes, he added sourly, "Are you going to glare at me every time Angela's name comes up for the rest of our lives?"

"Get used to it," Molly suggested tightly. "When you have a torrid affair with an evil witch, there are consequences."

"It wasn't all that torrid, Valmain. Anyway, you got your revenge. *And* you got me. Right?"

"My revenge," Molly murmured. "That's what worries me. Deborah loved Angela—she was her granddaughter, after all—and she must realize her death wasn't a heart attack, despite what the medical examiner said. She knows we were responsible for her death, and somehow, someway, she's going to get *her* revenge. Remember how Angela threatened to find the lake community and tell them I was a mounds sorceress? Maybe Deborah's out there right now, looking for wizards or warlocks to attack me."

"Warlocks?" Matthew tried to smile, hoping Molly wouldn't sense his own concern at the thought Deborah Clay was out searching for the lakes. It had occurred to him, too, and while Molly had always claimed not to be afraid, he could see now she'd just been bluffing. In some ways it was a reassuring revelation. By acknowledging the potential for danger, she was more likely to agree to learn to defend against it, by exploring her long-neglected magical powers. "I'll protect you, Valmain."

Her gaze grew predictably amorous and she twined her arms around his neck. "My hero. Kiss me."

"My pleasure." His lips brushed hers, but only lightly, although he knew from her throaty tone she wanted more. "From now on, we're going to be together every single day, Molly, and you're calling all the shots."

"Oh, really?" Her eyes were dancing mischievously. "Every single day? Or until wanderlust strikes?"

"That's all in the past, like I told you this afternoon. From now on," he promised, "I'm staying home. As soon as you're ready, you can go back to the lab, if you want. I'm starting my new book next week, so I can watch Kerry day and night, if you need me to."

"Your new book?"

The delight in her expression pleased him. "You've been saying I should start the next one, and Zack's been on the phone nagging me for months now, so I thought I'd give it a try."

"Oh, Matthew!" Covering his face with grateful kisses, she crowed, "Whenever you write, you seem happier, which makes *me* happier, which makes life so wonderful! Tell me what it's about. More dream legends, like in *Ancient Dreams?* Or more like the first one? Will you have to do much research?"

"No research. No dream legends. This is something completely different. More philosophical. It's ambitious," he added sincerely, "but I think fatherhood is inspiring me."

"I know the feeling," she sighed, cuddling happily against him. "Tell me all about it."

"I'm not ready to talk about it yet, but I should have an outline done by Christmas, and the whole thing finished by spring. Maybe then we can celebrate by bringing Kerry back here for a long visit, assuming Deborah's still gone."

"I'd like that." His dream girl's face was shining with love. "You're being so wonderful, Matthew. Are you really okay with me going back to the lab? You'll get stir-crazy. . . ."

"I'll be too busy with Kerry and the book to even think about traveling," he promised. "Like I said, my wandering days are over. You're looking at the new Matthew Redtree, husband, author, and father." Catching her hand in his and drawing it to his lips, he pledged, "This is a new start for us, Valmain. The best days of our lives begin today."

Three

"Motherhood agrees with you, Princess," Aaric declared later that evening in the dream. "You are more breathtaking than ever. How is the little one?"

"She's wonderful."

"And your champion?"

Unable to resist—he was her confidant as well as her teacher, after all—she gushed, "He's so different! Almost normal! You should have been there tonight! Everything has changed for the better."

The huge sorcerer grinned. "So? He has made love to you, after these long months of celibacy?"

"Grow up. I'm talking about Matthew's attitude, not sex." She blushed happily. "He's writing a new book, and that alone is wonderful news, since he's always more focused and less critical when he's writing. But on top of that, he's saying I can go back to my studies and *he'll* stay home with Kerry. Permanently! No more wandering the globe. Which means I can finish up so much quicker than I'd hoped. Maybe even in less than two years! Then," she added impishly, "you can start calling me 'doctor' instead of 'princess.' "

"I will always call you Princess," he corrected, "but I will be proud that you have reached your goal, strange as it is."

"You're sweet."

"That is true. Bring the little princess now, so that we may all celebrate together."

"Okay." Molly summoned her daughter easily, placing her immediately into the Moonshaker's outstretched hands.

His eyes were soft as they studied the newborn. "She is truly remarkable. Perhaps it is true, Princess. Perhaps fatherhood will tame your champion's restlessness for a while."

"For a while?" She moistened her lips nervously. "In other words, you don't think he's really changed?"

"Do you?" Aaric handed the baby back to her mother and began to gesture rapidly. "He is a warrior, Princess. We have discussed this many times, but still you resist the truth. Just as you are a sorceress, he is a warrior. It does no good to deny the facts."

"I agree, he's a warrior. But luckily, there's no war."

"There is always a war," Aaric countered briskly. "He needs adversity, Princess. He needs to be challenged, and to overcome. Passive pursuits cannot satisfy him for long."

"Passive? Taking care of a newborn is hardly passive! And writing's hard work, too. It takes total concentration."

"It may be difficult, but it is hardly enough to satisfy a man like your husband. I am simply cautioning you, so that you will not be too disappointed, and so that you will not berate him when he is unable to keep his promise to you."

"Berate?" She shook her head, amused and annoyed all at once. "Are you calling me a nag? Just because I expect Matthew to settle down and be a normal father?"

"Yes. You knew what he was when you married him. To ask this of him now is unfair."

"You're always on Matthew's side," she grumbled, uncomfortable with the ring of truth to the sorcerer's words. How could she expect Matthew Redtree to sit home—with a word processor and a baby—while a world of weapons and ruins beckoned to him? "You think I should let him off the hook?"

"Off the hook?"

"Should I tell him to run along, while I sit home and rot?"

"You have told me that men and women in your world

share the child-raising. Would that not be a less drastic solution?"

"You mean, take turns? The only trouble with that is, if I really go back to the lab, I have to be on a schedule. He'd have to be dependable, and once he takes off on a quest, he never sticks to his original itinerary. You're right, though," she added ruefully. "If I had thought this through, I'd have realized there's no way he can do this."

"Then you must allow him off your hooks," Aaric insisted. "If you do not, he will fail. A woman should not enjoy seeing her champion fail."

"Okay, okay. He's off my hooks." Sinking to the ground, she cradled the baby against her chest and complained, "I just wanted a normal life. Is that so wrong?"

"Look at yourself," Aaric teased. "In your cape, in your dream world, with the world's most powerful sorcerer as your companion. Do you call this normal?"

Molly giggled reluctantly. "Good point. This is the kind of *ab*normalcy Matthew craves."

"Then bring him here."

"Stop saying that." Sending the baby quickly away from the dream, she sprang to her feet, hands on her hips. "If he came here he'd fight you. That's what you really want, right? Well, you can forget it, Moonshaker. I'm not putting my marriage in jeopardy just so you can have a rematch with the Son of Lost Eagle, and that's final."

Aaric chuckled. "It is true, I long to fight him. But after I fought him and won, I would explain many things to him. I would make him understand, and then your marriage would be stronger than ever." With an exaggerated sigh he complained, "You are the stubbornest witch I have ever known. Have it your own way. In the meantime we will return to your training so that, when the day for your unveiling arrives, your champion will be suitably impressed by your prowess."

* * *

"So, Uncle? Last summer I amazed you by showing up here in the middle of the night with a pure-hearted mounds sorceress. Now I'm back with two."

"And I am doubly amazed," August Redtree murmured. "Never have I seen a happier, healthier baby."

Molly hugged the old man's frail shoulders. "It's after midnight, August. Did we wake you?"

"No. I was studying the stars, for signs that all was well with you."

"It went smoothly, Uncle," Matthew assured him. "With the amulet on her wrist and the mounds surrounding her, it was awesome—"

"But it was nice having a nurse close by, just in case," Molly interrupted. "Rita knows so much, August. You really ought to let her give you an informal physical."

The old man held up his hand in protest. "I do not trust her world of medicine, daughter, although I know you do. Allow me to live, and to die, in my own way."

He was serious, and Molly knew she should back off, but his debilitated appearance concerned her. "Okay, no doctors or medicine," she agreed. "But how about a phone, at least? You're out here, in the middle of the desert, with no way of reaching help. You've got Rita worried sick, and a phone would solve the problem. Let me and Matthew give it to you as a present."

"Drop it, Valmain," Matthew warned. "He doesn't want it."

"We could call you with baby bulletins," she persisted, ignoring her husband's frown. "The first time Kerry says a word, or takes a step . . . the first time she casts a little spell." Her blue eyes twinkled mischievously. "You don't want to miss *that,* do you?"

August chuckled. "You are in fine spirits." Clearing his throat, he added quietly, "I accept your generous offer."

Molly saw Matthew's jaw tighten and knew that, until that moment, he hadn't realized how weak his uncle was feeling.

For August Redtree to accept this compromise was a signal that he suspected his time was drawing to an end.

"You should rest, Uncle," the nephew now insisted. "Molly's right. We shouldn't have woken you up."

"You've made an old man happy," August countered fondly. "I have no desire to sleep. Let me watch over this little one while you and your bride rest in my guest room."

Molly had to struggle not to blush at the thought of having her handsome champion alone in that soft, narrow guest bed for a few undisturbed hours of fun. August had played right into her hands, and she suspected he had done so knowingly. "If you're sure you don't mind," she sighed, "I really *am* a little tired. . . . Come on, Matthew."

"I'm not tired," the warrior protested. "Go get some sleep, Molly. I'll sit with my uncle in case the baby wakes up."

"She won't. I just fed her and changed her. Don't be a selfish nephew. Let August have a little time alone with her." Before her lover could argue with her or notice the twinkle in his old uncle's eyes, Molly grasped his elbow and tugged him toward the hall. " 'Night, August."

"Do not worry about the little one," their host called after them, adding predictably, "Try to dream, daughter."

Molly smiled, amused as always by the old man's stubborn insistence on mentioning the dream. He had taught Matthew Redtree well, passing on an obsession with their heritage that never wavered, although the elder's was tempered with wisdom, while his nephew's fanaticism knew no bounds. *At least August knows there's more to bedtime than dreaming,* Molly teased herself, *even if your husband has to be constantly reminded.*

"Reminding" him in the guest room would be easy, she knew. Hadn't it been the scene of one of their most frustrating nights together? Pushing open the door, she was delighted to see that nothing had changed. The bed was still so narrow that her husband would have no choice but to hold her in his arms. . . .

"I'm worried about my uncle," Matthew confessed as soon as the door was closed behind them. "Maybe we should insist he come to live with us."

"He'd say no. He's not a city dweller, Matthew. We'll just get that phone installed right away and call him every day. And we'll visit more often. How's that?" Slipping her arms around his neck, she added gently, "Try not to worry. You feel so tense. Are your shoulders stiff?"

"I'm beat from all that driving," he admitted, shrugging free and stretching broadly. "Sleep sounds pretty good."

Molly's imagination raced as her champion flexed his lean, rippling arms before her admiring eyes. "Lie down and I'll give you a nice, relaxing massage," she suggested slyly.

"Aren't you tired, too?"

She nodded. "I'll do you, and then you'll do me. Okay?"

"Sounds great." Pulling off his white polo shirt, he stretched out, facedown and still wearing his jeans, on the bed.

She savored the sight of his bronzed, enticingly muscled back for a long moment. The fact that he was truly expecting no more than an innocent massage was almost as arousing as the sight itself. Matthew Redtree could be so infuriatingly judgmental, yet at heart he was naive—charmingly naive—when it came to trusting his bride. He saw her as a simple, gentle-hearted dream girl, and it was always fun to remind him that she was, in reality, a flesh-and-blood female with a healthy libido and even healthier imagination.

Slipping out of her loose-fitting white maternity dress, she straddled his waist and rested her fingertips lightly on his shoulder blades. *Slowly,* she cautioned herself gleefully. *Remember who you're dealing with.* As she began to knead gently, she murmured, "Matthew?"

"Hmm?"

"Remember the first time we slept together in this bed?"

"Huh?"

"You were trying to seduce me," she prompted, "and I pulled a knife on you."

"Yeah . . ." He chuckled into the pillow. "Those were wild days, Valmain, weren't they?"

"Wild," she agreed, leaning down to whisper softly in his ear. "Did I ever tell you how hard it was for me to resist you that night? How much I wanted to give in to you and let you make love to me?"

"Believe me, I could tell," he assured her, his voice growing sleepy and contented as her fingers worked their magic. "It's always easy to tell when you're turned on, Valmain."

"Oh?"

"Yeah," he yawned. "Your eyes get bluer than ever, and your voice gets this little purr in it. . . ."

"A little purr?"

Almost reluctantly, he twisted enough to catch a glimpse of her face, then a deep chuckle rumbled through his back, charming her fingertips and bringing a blush to her cheeks. "Yeah, a little purr." He grinned. "You're really something, Valmain. Where's your dress?"

"I lost it." The blush became a flush when his eyes focused on her milk-swollen breasts. "I won't have my old body back for a while, I guess, but—"

"You always look great to me," he reminded her firmly. "I don't judge you by your appearance, I judge you by your beautiful heart, remember?"

"You were supposed to say I look great," she scolded, annoyed that he hadn't noticed the obvious—that her figure had not only returned, but with a vengeance! Apparently, a side benefit of her illustrious heritage was a twenty-four-hour recovery period from even so daunting a condition as pregnancy. And as for the side benefit of breast-feeding, that should have been obvious to even so pure minded a monk as Matthew!

"That's what I said," he laughed, rolling onto his back and resting his warm hands on the thighs that continued to strad-

dle him. "If you're asking for a demonstration, you'd better
be patient. Rita says a month, at least."

"I'm a sorceress," Molly reminded him, stretching provocatively. "I gave birth like a sorceress, I healed like a sorceress and now, whether you like it or not, I have the appetite
of a sorceress."

The gold flecks in his eyes were beginning to ignite. "I
like it just fine, Valmain. Believe me . . ." One rough, warm
hand moved upward to caress her breast. "You feel so incredibly smooth and soft. Like the satin of your dream
cape . . ."

"You're hopeless," she groaned, closing her eyes and sur-
rendering to the stab of pleasure his touch was providing.
"Lucky for you, you're the sexiest man on earth, and so I
forgive you for neglecting me."

"Neglecting?"

Opening one blue eye, she was pleased to see that she had
somehow challenged the warrior in him. Now he would
prove his prowess to her—with every erotic weapon in his
arsenal—and her insides began to tingle. "You've neglected
my needs for months," she goaded breathlessly. "You haven't
been much of a champion—Oh!" Her back arched gratefully
as his free hand slipped between her legs. "It's been weeks
since you kissed me like a man should kiss a woman—*Oh!*
Matthew . . ."

His fingers had penetrated her expertly and her body immediately responded with spasms of awakened need and remembered satisfaction. Flipping her gently onto her back,
he covered her mouth with his own—hot, demanding, and
thorough—coaxing a greedy groan from her throat.

She didn't care that he was still in his jeans. For the moment, at least, this was all that she could ever need: his
tongue dominating her; his bare chest crushing against her;
his fingers tormenting her, teasing her, frustrating her toward
a release so intensely craved that she was almost panicked
in her need to reach it.

But Matthew knew how to make her wait. To make her ache for it. Beg for it. Of all the erotic weapons in his arsenal of seduction, the most maddeningly effective was anticipation.

"We have all night, Valmain," he cajoled. "Just relax and let me touch you."

She wanted to plead, or chastise, or demand, but was too mindless in her arousal to do anything but writhe hungrily against his warm, rough, glorious hand. Finally she managed to murmur his name, her tone soft and sweet with desperation.

"You're almost there," he promised. "You're so hot . . . so wet . . . so tight . . . Let it happen now." In a voice almost hoarse with confidence, he instructed, "Now, Valmain," and a surge of pleasure overtook her, so acute and electrifying that she feared for a long, irrational second his hand itself might burst into flames. As she clung to him, pulsing and panting, he skillfully stroked her back and buttocks, calming her—but only just enough to allow them to continue.

"I love you, Matthew," she blurted shakily. "So much."

"Yeah, I know." He shifted, giving himself room to work the zipper on his jeans, which he shed quickly and effortlessly. When her hand was drawn immediately to him, as though by a magnet, he chuckled gratefully. "That's nice, Valmain. I've missed you, too, you know."

The sentiment amazed her. Matthew Redtree? Human after all? Then she moved her mouth to reward him wickedly for the confession, working her lips and tongue slowly, admiringly along his rock-hard arousal.

"Nice, Valmain," he groaned again. "Now come here." Then, without waiting for her to respond, he grasped her by the shoulders and gently rolled her onto her back while his mouth descended toward her flame-tipped breasts.

She knew exactly what would happen now and the knowledge made her tremble with excitement. His lips would travel slowly, relentlessly enjoying and tasting on a path across her smooth, flat stomach until, at the moment when her pleasure threatened to turn once again to exquisite pain, his tongue would plunge between her legs, ravishing her into mindless contortions. Then, and only then, would he truly take her, mounting her with a confident grin and shattering her months of need with his prowess.

Only this time she couldn't wait. It had been too, too long since she'd felt him within her that way and so, without daring to think, she buried her fingers in his lush, blue-black hair and hauled his mouth back up toward her own. Then their eyes locked, in one brief second of amused disbelief, before his lips came crushing down to thank her even as he entered her.

Her body lay drenched in a salty mixture of sweat, saliva, and satisfaction, and she could easily have drifted into sleep without a movement or word, but the insistent rhythm of Matthew's breath on her neck told her the warrior was more than wide awake—he was exhilarated. *And* he was waiting, and so she opened her blue eyes wide, smiling a smile as shy as his was triumphant.

"Any more complaints?" he demanded.

Moistening her lips, she shook her head slowly. "No complaints."

"You're sure?" His teasing tone was laced with pride and challenge. "I'm at your disposal, Valmain. Want me to kiss you like a man *should* kiss a woman?"

A nervous laugh caught in her throat. "I should have known better than to taunt a fanatic. I'm lucky I survived."

"Maybe it's not over yet," he grinned. "Maybe I'm just letting you catch your breath."

"Oh?" She licked her lips again, this time with more interest. "Is that supposed to scare me?"

Matthew shook his head. "It should, but you're wild tonight, Valmain. I guess I really have been neglecting you.

I'm sorry about that." Drawing his fingertip gently across her lips, he vowed, "It won't happen again."

A wave of frustration swept over her as she watched the boastful lover recede, replaced by the more-familiar humble servant. For a brief moment it had almost seemed as though her husband actually found her arousing! But, of course, it had simply been his duty to satisfy her—the Valmain dream princess—that had fueled his ardor. As usual.

"That was the best sex we've ever had," she insisted sadly. "Can't you just relax and enjoy it, without taking it so seriously?"

"We have our best sex at the mounds, when I'm wearing the amulet," he reminded her, slipping his arms around her waist and drawing her closer. "I wish we were there right now. Then I could really make it all up to you."

"Matthew . . ." She bit back a futile reply and cuddled against his chest instead. "You'll never know how much I love you. Here and now. Just you. Forget about mounds and amulets. You're perfect without them."

"I love you, too, Valmain," he murmured. "I'd do anything for you. From now on, if you want something, don't play games or drop hints. Just come right out and say it, okay?"

"I *like* games."

Matthew chuckled ruefully. "So I noticed."

She knew her eyes were shining with love. "Remember what you said last night? About staying home with me and Kerry, and not wandering around anymore?"

"I meant every word of it."

"Well, I want you to take it back."

"Huh?"

"I married a world-traveling, weapon-collecting, legend-recording warrior. Not a househusband." When he simply stared, she added gently, "I know you need to be in Chichén Itzá for the vernal equinox, and in Germany for the estate auctions, and in South America when your buddies start a new dig. Sometimes, when we can, Kerry and I'll go with you, but either way I want you to go wherever you need to go and stay as long as you need to stay, and come home as soon as you possibly can."

The gold in his eyes was flaming out of control. "Sometimes I forget how truly amazing you are," he whispered, his voice raspy with adoration, "because you're too good to be true and I don't deserve you, but—" his hands slid down to her buttocks and pulled her flush against himself—"you're mine, and I'm going to do my best to be worthy of you. Starting with this . . ." His mouth covered hers, rocketing her, body and soul, into ecstasy.

On nights such as these she faced a particularly bizarre dilemma: Should she go to the dream, or stay with her lover, even in her sleep? Was it disloyal to Matthew to visit with Aaric so soon after lovemaking? Was Aaric lonely, after so many hours alone in the dream world?

Or did Aaric somehow sense the passion she had shared with another man, the way he often sensed her moods? If so, there was no doubt but she should stay away. The sorcerer was all too human when it came to such emotions as love and jealousy. Molly would never knowingly hurt or provoke him, and yet she also couldn't bear to neglect him, and the thought of him alone, eagerly awaiting her visit . . .

And hadn't things changed just a bit during these last few months? The pregnancy, followed by the birth and the visits to the dream by Kerry, had certainly tempered Aaric's view of his "Princess." In fact, he had even mellowed considerably in his views of Matthew, whom he now defended frequently, sometimes almost vehemently. These days, when he spoke of the Valmain champion, he sounded less like a rival and more like an affectionate older brother.

Remember how he insisted you should let Matthew "off your hooks"? she teased herself confidently. *If he was still jealous of him, he'd never defend him that way.* Thus reassured, she hurried to the dream, suddenly anxious to inform her teacher that her "hooks" had been dutifully removed from the wandering champion.

One glance into the Moonshaker's eyes told her how very, very wrong she had been to come. The sea blue might just as well have been lagoon green, so intense was the jealous blaze that greeted her. This man had not mellowed after all, and the scintillating lovemaking had definitely not gone unnoticed.

"So?" His voice was nearly dripping with disdain. "I did not expect to see you tonight, Valmain Princess."

It was all she could do to keep from fleeing wordlessly back to the safety of her bed, but she managed to murmur, "Sorry, Aaric."

"You owe me no apology. If you wish to apologize, do so to your champion, for leaving his bed to visit another man."

"Aaric!" She flushed and offered lamely, "We don't need to do this. I'll just leave, okay?"

"You will run away? Perhaps that is wise, Princess. Who knows what might happen between us if you stay."

"Pardon?"

"You are a passionate woman. You hunger for a man's touch," he taunted, his smile almost cruelly omniscient. "It is wise for you to run."

"Aaric, for heaven's sake! I'm not running *from* you. I'm just giving you some space." When his arrogant stare challenged even that, she added more forcefully, "I'm a married woman."

"You hide behind your marriage vow, but it is cowardice, not fidelity, that restrains you."

"What?" Hot blood rushed into her cheeks and she had to force herself to take a cooling breath before demanding, "What does *that* mean?"

"It means we pretend, you and I, that your commitment to your champion prevents our lovemaking, but that is far from the truth. The truth is, you fear it, because you know

I can give you what he cannot. We both know that. We both
know it would be the end of your marriage, but not because
you have been unfaithful. It would open your eyes to the fact
that I love you in a way he cannot. I love you," he repeated
slowly, stepping toward her as he spoke, "in a way he does
not, and if I made love to you, you would realize what has
been missing and you would never go back to him."

There was an asphyxiating tightness in her chest, as
though the presence of his words in the air made that very
air unusable to her. She couldn't breathe. She couldn't answer. In fact, she couldn't think. It didn't seem to matter
whether the words were true. It only mattered that he had
conceived of them. That he had dared give voice to them.
That he so obviously believed them.

"I love you," he repeated once more, "and if I kissed you
right now, I would own you. Unfortunately"—he paused to
shrug—"I have been forced to resist the temptation to seduce
you. As easy as it would be to do so, I cannot in good conscience come between you and your champion as long as I
exist only in this dream. If I were to do that, and you were
to leave him, you would be unprotected in the world outside,
and so"—a wave of pride crashed through the vibrant stare
and into Molly's soul—"we pretend."

Something was happening. Something she could not even
begin to understand. His unfamiliar anger . . . his unmasked
passion . . . his boldly unleashed magnetism. It had been so
many months since he had allowed one of his flirtations to
flame into seduction, and she had almost forgotten what her
body had learned so graphically one torrid night long ago—
that this golden-haired sorcerer, with his magnificent body
and full, hungry mouth, could make love to a woman with
such dizzying success that she would be in grave danger of
abandoning all allegiance to anyone or anything else. Since
that night Aaric had protected her from this simple truth, out
of love and out of friendship, but now needed to remind her,
out of pride, that he was a dangerous friend. A seductive

coconspirator. A worthy challenger to the Valmain champion's position.

And he was a sorcerer, so she took a full step backward before she answered. After all, a mounds magician counted "persuasion" among his or her most useful talents, and while Molly had trusted Aaric not to use such tricks on her until now, the fire in his eyes told her all too clearly that the capacity was there. "If you made love to me," she answered finally, "it would be amazing, like everything else you do. And you're right, if it ever happened, I *would* leave Matthew, but not for the reason you think. I'd leave him, but I'd also never come back to this dream again, and my heart would be broken because the two men I love would be lost to me forever. I couldn't bear it, and I don't think you could, either, and so"—her chin rose in gentle defiance—"make an illusion of Maya, and make love to her instead. I'll come back tomorrow night and we'll pretend this conversation never took place."

"Stay," he countered coolly. "If anyone should leave, it is I." Before she could protest, he bowed slightly and was gone.

"Aaric . . ." She stopped herself, confused by the catch in her voice, and forced herself to breathe deeply for a moment while she reviewed and analyzed his absurd claims. He loved her—that was hardly news. He was jealous of Matthew—again, that had always been clear. But this unprecedented bravado . . .

Or was it unprecedented? Hadn't he made this claim once before, a full year earlier? At that time he had boasted that he could win Molly from Matthew in one long, amorous night, but that claim had been based on the fact that he would have used his magic on her. Was he threatening such a tactic again?

No. He was telling her he wouldn't need his magic. He was telling her he could give her the one thing Matthew Redtree could not—his heart. She wanted to feel sorry for him—for the futility of his love for her—but had the uneasy feeling her sympathy was premature. Despite appearances to the contrary, the Moonshaker apparently didn't feel she had unilaterally turned down his advances. He believed it was *he* who had exercised restraint, out of deference to the fact that he was confined to the dream, and that Molly needed a lover who could protect her from the dangers of the outside world! Implying, arrogantly yet persuasively, that she was his for the taking.

You've told him too much about your problems with Matthew, she berated herself nervously. *He knows you think Matthew isn't quote-unquote in love with you, and so he thinks he still has a chance with you, because . . . Well, because he is in love with you.*

There was no denying that. Aaric, who had once loved a magnificent sorceress named Maya so fiercely, was now in love with a novice witch named Molly Sheridan Redtree. And if she hadn't met Matthew first, she probably would have fallen for Aaric, if only because he knew how to combine romance with lust effectively and seemingly effortlessly. *And* he knew how to listen, and praise, and tease . . .

But you met Matthew first and you fell in love with him, even if he didn't fall in love with you, she reminded herself sternly. *Aaric's your closest friend, and he's gorgeous, so it's natural for you to feel a little confused when he comes on to you, but he's wrong to think you're his for the taking. In fact*—she squared her shoulders and tried to smile—*Aaric probably doesn't really believe that, either. He's just bluffing, because you hurt his gigantic ego.*

As brightly as she could manage she called out, "Come on, Moonshaker! That's long enough. I hate it when you sulk. Let's apologize to each other and start fresh." When he didn't reappear, she coaxed, "Please? I don't want to leave this dream on bad terms with you. Give me a break."

She glanced about herself, certain that he wouldn't resist for long, but he was nowhere in sight. Instead, she spied a soft blue cape, flung over a branch on a nearby tree, and smiled slyly. Maya's cape! If anything could get the Moon-shaker's attention, it was that. Hadn't he warned his "Princess" dozens of times not to handle or fool with this memento of Maya's visit to the dream the previous year?

Reaching up, she tugged at the satiny fabric, which came cascading into her arms. For a moment her strategy faded as memories washed over her. Memories of a beautiful, dark-haired sorceress, who called Molly "my little niece" and tried, in her own willful way, to train and protect her. Maya had even killed Angela Clay in order to protect Molly and her champion!

And you thanked her by banishing her from this dream, she accused herself sadly now. *You let Aaric stay—probably because you're secretly hot for him!—but you sent poor Maya away after all she did for you.*

"Put that down!" Without waiting for compliance the Moonshaker wrenched the cloth from Molly and muttered, "You are the most stubborn and sentimental of witches. Have I not told you a score of times to stay far from this accursed cape?"

"I was beginning to think you weren't going to rescue me." Molly smiled softly. "Welcome back."

"Do not flirt with me, Princess," he glared. "I could see you were having fond thoughts of Maya. That is a dangerous mistake."

"She was good to me."

"She was a manipulative, selfish witch," he declared. "It was arrogance on her part to leave this cape behind. This dream is yours, not hers. You banished her, and she defied your authority by leaving this behind."

"Maybe she just wanted to leave me something to remember her by."

"You are naive. Maya knew of your weakness and exploited it. But"—his vehemence subsided a bit—"you are more experienced now than when you first banished her. You are strong enough now to send the cape away as well. Try

to do that, Princess. If not for your own sake, for the sake
of the little one. She will be able to crawl one day soon and
might touch this cape and be harmed by it."

"How? I've touched it a hundred times and it never hurt
me." When his scowl returned, she added quickly, "Put it
back in the tree, then. I don't want Kerry near it, either."

"You are a stubborn witch," he complained, draping the
fabric over a branch that was far beyond Molly's reach. "I
do not know why I bother trying to teach you."

She studied him curiously. "You were in love with Maya
once, now you talk about her like you hate her."

"I loved her"—he shrugged—"and I always will. She
brought me great happiness. But I also love you, and she left
her cape here as an insult to your talent and your authority.
I cannot allow my woman to be insulted, even if my woman
is too naive to take offense."

Molly blushed. "If you'll 'always' love her, isn't she your
woman, too?"

He nodded. "A man can love two women, and a woman
can love two men. Unless, of course, the woman is you."

It annoyed her, and she shot back quickly, "I can't love
two men at the same time, and I think I'm pretty normal that
way."

"Normal?" An unsympathetic grin lit his face. "Do not
judge what you have never tried, Princess. When you are
absent from this dream, I often amuse myself by loving two
women at one time, and I find it very satisfying."

"Spare me," she drawled, resisting an urge to imagine the
leering sorcerer in so lusty a situation. "If you're trying to
pay me back by making me jealous, forget it. Make yourself
twenty Mayas, if it gives you a thrill."

Aaric's eyebrow arched sharply. "One Maya is all I need.
The second woman in my illusion is usually Angela Clay."

"What?"

Clearly pleased with her reaction, he taunted, "Your Matthew has many flaws, but his taste in women is not one of

them. First he chose you, the most beautiful female ever born, and then he chose Angela, a voluptuous and experienced temptress, and one greatly to my liking."

"I'm leaving," Molly seethed. "When I come back—*if* I come back!—I'll expect an apology."

"You are magnificent when you are angry, Princess." He grinned proudly. "I will apologize now." Taking her hand, he dropped to one knee and insisted, "I have never thought of Angela Clay with any sentiment other than distaste. If I ever decided to make love to two illusions, you would be the only woman, other than Maya, that I would even consider."

Molly laughed in spite of herself, pleased that behind the gentle mocking, the warmth and understanding that had made him such a rock over these last months had returned. "You're outrageous tonight, Moonshaker. Are we friends again?"

"Of course." He rose to his feet, still holding her hand. "Forgive my outburst. The intensity of your lovemaking with your champion caught me by surprise. It rocked this dream and filled me with envy."

She nodded. "I didn't know for sure that you could tell. . . . Anyway, from now on, I won't come here on the nights Matthew and I make love."

"Do not say that," he sighed. "Now that he intends to stay home more often, those nights will be all too frequent, and I would miss your visits sorely. And"—his blue eyes twinkled impishly—"ordinarily, your champion's pitiful efforts do not manage to shake this dream. Or at least, I do not notice it. This time it caught me by surprise—perhaps because it has been so long since he touched you."

"I guess that was it." Molly blushed.

"One of you, at least, was ravenous. I can only assume—"

"That's enough. You're such a tease." Bringing his huge hand to her lips, she kissed it gently, then confessed, "You were right about one thing. I really do love you. I wouldn't hurt you for the world, Aaric."

"You did not hurt me. You have brought me nothing but beauty and pleasure." This time his bow was deep and respectful. "Kiss the little one for me, and sleep well, Valmain Princess. It is honor enough to be counted as your friend."

After he had disappeared, she stayed for just a moment, unwilling to hurt him further by appearing to rush back to Matthew. His request that she give Kerreya a kiss good-night pleased her, helping her to focus on needs beyond those that had dominated this strange, tumultuous night. Her relationship with Aaric was complicated, yet in some ways things with Matthew were even more convoluted. Motherhood was blessedly simple in contrast and so, with a weary smile, she took leave of Aaric's world, slipped out of Matthew's bed, and tiptoed into the living room to steal her daughter from under her sleeping great-great-uncle's nose.

"Did you miss me?" she cooed after she'd bundled the infant onto the porch and offered her a swollen breast filled with milk. Before them stretched the desert, lonely and bleak, with a half-moon eerily lighting all with a bluish cast. "I love being your mother, Kerry, did you know that? And you have the best daddy in the whole world, and a wonderful aunt and cousins, and August, and, of course, Aaric. I hope it all works more simply for you than it has for me, but I'm not making any guarantees, except that I'll always be around for you."

The baby sucked contentedly, as though the warmth of the milk and the sound of Molly's voice were all she needed. The thought that, one day, Kerreya would need more—would need friends, and goals, and challenges . . . and, eventually, a man . . .

"Take my advice, Kerry," Molly instructed wryly, "don't try to juggle two at a time."

"You don't have to teach her how to breast-feed, Valmain," Matthew teased from the shadows.

"What?"

" 'Don't juggle two at a time,' " he quoted, reaching over to stroke her free breast gently. "Do you have any idea how beautiful you look right now?"

"Really?" she sighed, charmed by the unexpected flirting.

"Sure. My wife nursing my daughter. I can't imagine a more perfect sight."

"Oh, right." She shot him a withering glance. *"That* kind of beautiful. I misunderstood for a minute."

"Huh?"

"Never mind." She was suddenly weary of men and their loaded compliments. "I didn't mean to wake you up, Matthew. Why don't you go back to bed?"

"I'm wide awake. I can take Kerry while you sleep, or you can take her in the bed with you while I go for a run."

"In the dark?"

"There's plenty of light," he pointed out. "From the half-moon. Remember those stories I used to tell you, Valmain? About the Half-Moon people?"

"Bare-chested women," she nodded, glancing down at her own uncovered breasts. "I should have known, when you talked about them on our first date, that you weren't a normal guy."

"Yeah." He bent to kiss her, first on the lips, then on a rosy nipple. "I knew, even then, that you were special, and that I was lucky. And I just keep getting luckier."

Biting back an offer to allow him to get even luckier—she wasn't sure Aaric could take the strain—she settled for shifting the baby to the recently kissed nipple while she wistfully admired the lean, handsome figure of her champion as he took off for his run. "Running in the dark in the middle of the night," she muttered to her daughter. "And we were foolish enough to think fatherhood was going to settle him down. I think we'll be lucky if he stays home a week before his wanderlust rears its ugly head, Kerry. So much for returning to the lab anytime soon . . ."

Kerreya's mouth relaxed its hold on Molly, and the gold-flecked eyes opened wide, as though offering sympathy, or perhaps even advice. It charmed her mother, who enthused, "Who needs the lab, right? My doctorate can wait a few more years, until you're ready for preschool. We need this time to get acquainted. I need to teach you about men, right? Not to mention, fire and wind."

Apparently satisfied with the plan, Kerreya returned to her meal while Molly scanned the dark distance for some sign of their restless champion, but he was beyond their reach—both physically and emotionally—and her heart ached at the all-too-familiar loneliness that so willingly stepped in to take his place.

Four

"So? You have nothing new to report?"

Constance Sheridan watched as the First Wizard of the Lakes, who called himself Wolfe, carefully knotted the belt on his rich black velour bathrobe. Even through the shapeless garment, the leader's tapered, muscular form was evident. At the age of forty-three, he had the body of a twenty-five-year-old warrior, and his silver hair, rather than detracting from his image, seemed to reinforce the conclusion that he was a man of iron—a man to be feared and respected by all other men.

And as he had proven over the preceding four hours, he also had the appetites of a twenty-five-year-old male, and thus should be feared and respected by women as well. He had been brutal with Constance and, after Alexander Sheridan's fawning ways, that brutality had been more than welcome. Here, in the compound of the lakes, a witch did not need to feign innocence or tenderness. Here she could give in to her passions and, if she satisfied her wizard, could depend upon him to satisfy her in return.

"I haven't felt this good in months, Wolfe," she gushed. "I didn't come here to report anything. I came because I'm sick to death of being a good little wife and mommy. I wanted to be treated like a woman, and"—her pale blue eyes smoldered—"you didn't disappoint me."

"Of all the talents you brought from the old world," Wolfe grinned, "this animal lust of yours is the most endearing.

However," his voice grew stern, "we've had our play, and now it's time to discuss more serious things. For example, what news is there of your stepdaughter?"

"She's still in graduate school in Berkeley. Her daughter's seven months old. Her husband hasn't written a new book in ages and, according to all reports, is turning into a bum. All in all, I couldn't wish for a more fitting life for that little bitch."

"From all reports?" Wolfe frowned. "Who makes these reports to you?"

"No one, really. Molly's grandmother writes regularly to Alex—at his office, unfortunately—keeping him up to date on his precious daughter. Each time a letter comes, we have a few days of unrest at our house, and I have to struggle to keep him in line, but of course, eventually, I succeed. He cannot resist me for long."

"What man could?" Wolfe moved to the bed and ran his hand over Constance's unclothed body. "When Maya gave you this gift of ultimate beauty, she did it well."

"Wolfe . . ." Constance arched toward him hopefully. "Come back to bed."

"That's enough."

His tone, ominous and low, made her shrink from him, and she quickly gathered the sheet around herself. "As I was saying, Elizabeth keeps us informed. She's never liked Matthew Redtree; she insists he's a fanatic who doesn't appreciate poor, sweet Molly. He lives off the royalties from his books, but hasn't written anything lately. I guess he figures Molly can support them once she earns her doctorate."

"I see." The wizard scooped up Constance's discarded dress and threw it onto the bed. "Get dressed now. We've been in here too long as it is."

Constance licked her lips, intrigued by the statement. Since when did the First Wizard worry about appearances, or live by the clock? "Is something wrong?"

"Of course not," he replied smoothly. "I was simply concerned for your daughter. This is her first day of training, after all, and I'm sure our ways will seem strange to her. We should go and check on her."

"She'll be fine," Constance countered. Slipping out of the bed, she stretched her nude form for the wizard's benefit before pulling her pink knit dress over her curves. "Niki's abominably lazy, Wolfe. This training is long overdue."

"She may be lazy, but she's a pretty little thing." His tone had gone from smooth to husky. "Such golden hair, and that winsome smile—like a little doll, wouldn't you say?"

"She's only five, Wolfe," Constance drawled. "Even a First Wizard has his limits, and she's *off*-limits for ten more years."

"I didn't mean to anger you." He grinned. "Was that an outburst of jealousy or overprotectiveness?"

Constance laughed lightly. "Jealous of that skinny brat? That would be ludicrous, don't you think? And as for protecting her"—the smile faded—"she's a burden to me, Wolfe. The other witches can turn their children over to the commune to be raised, but I have no such luxury. And her father insists that I spoil her, neglecting my own entertainment and pampering. I didn't come through the centuries, with this perfect face and body, to play nursemaid to a brat."

"That's true." Wolfe stepped to within inches of the witch and reminded her coolly, "You came here as the servant of Maya, the mounds sorceress. Your beauty exists only through her grace, and through mine, and you must respect that."

"I respect you," Constance insisted, "but Maya and all of her kind are dead and gone. They need nothing from me."

"You will live out your life in the house to which she sent you. You will monitor the activities of the Valmain princess as best you can. You will see that the rift between father and daughter is never healed, and you will watch for signs that Maya's warrior has arrived to destroy Valmain. If that happens, and a champion appears to defend Valmain, it will be your job to see that the champion is defeated."

"There isn't a Valmain kingdom anymore," Constance sulked. "There aren't any real warriors in the United States, except here at our compound or in the armed forces. Even if there were, Molly hangs around with intellectuals, not warriors."

"Haven't you reported in the past that her husband collects weapons and studies martial arts?"

"Hobbies," she countered, then her pale eyes narrowed. "You suspect him of being something more?"

"No, of course not. As you said, he's an intellectual, with only a voyeuristic relationship with weapons and war. Still, it's curious, isn't it? You describe her as meek, yet she marries such a man. Shall I tell you why?" When Constance had nodded, he explained, "Her lineage is one of greatness, and although that greatness has faded, she is filled with nameless yearnings and seeks a life close to the flame. It's pitiful."

"That's the perfect word for her," Constance agreed, with a sigh of relief. "For a moment I thought you felt threatened by them. Believe me," she cooed, slipping her arms around his neck, "if Molly Sheridan had any inkling of the magic that exists in the universe—and if she was truly a princess with a champion at her beck and call—she wouldn't be stuck at home, the way she is, with a crying brat. And she wouldn't have allowed her mother to die in that car accident without seeking out magic to try to save her."

"Or to save herself," Wolfe agreed. "You told me the Valmain princess suffered serious injuries and spent months in the hospital. As you said, this was proof beyond a doubt that her world lacks magicians to aid her."

"Then let me come home." She molded herself against the wizard desperately. "I despise the life I lead. Let me come here, and sleep in your bed with you, and teach you the ways of the past."

"And what would become of Niki?"

"Niki?" Constance fought a wave of vicious envy. "I'd bring her here, to amuse you. Or we could leave her with

Alex. She's half-human, Wolfe. I'm sure she'll have some *small* talent, but she'll never be an asset to us. She's weak, and dependent on her father. Let's leave her behind."

"I don't think so." He pulled free of her arms and studied her coldly. "Are you so jealous of her that you are blinded to the truth? That girl is the key to your beauty. As long as she satisfies Alexander Sheridan's paternal instinct, you are able to keep him engaged by your love spell, which enables you to maintain your beauty. You believe you are irresistible, but a man wants more than a beautiful woman. You overrate yourself, Constance, and you don't appreciate your daughter."

Blood had rushed to her cheeks, heating them with her anger. "It's you who doesn't appreciate *me!*" she snapped. "Without me, you'd . . . Augh! Wolfe, no—" She crumpled to the floor, where she cowered at his feet, afraid to raise her eyes to his—afraid to see the red-hot coals that were a wizard's cruelest and most effective weapon. Memories from centuries earlier flooded her brain. Memories of being maimed and tortured . . .

"I have never disciplined you before," Wolfe reminded her stiffly. "It displeases me to do so."

"Forgive me! Tell me what you want me to do and I'll do it."

"I want you to stay in your cozy house with your wealthy, attentive husband. I want you to be faithful to him, unless you are here, and I want you to raise the child with care. Is that so hideous a fate?"

"No, of course not. It's generous of you, and I was wrong to complain."

"That's better." He reached down and helped her to her feet. "It pains me to discipline you, Constance. You are my favorite, did you know that?"

"You honor me."

"The others don't appreciate you," he added slyly. "The

witches are jealous of you, and the wizards doubt your loyalty."

"What?"

He sighed, as though saddened by the thought. "They say you do not know your place. They sense you feel superior to them, even though you are just a witch, and they are wizards. I suspect they would destroy you if they could."

"Oh, no . . ."

"But I defend you, and do you know why?" When she shook her head, he replied, "You are my favorite. No other woman satisfies me the way you do. You're under my protection here and, as long as I am First Wizard, you're in no danger."

"I'm grateful, Wolfe. Honestly grateful. You must know how much I adore you." Her stomach still ached from his torturous infliction, but she managed a vaguely flirtatious smile and added, "Let me show you how much."

"Very well." Taking her hands in his own, he moved them to the knot in his belt while instructing coolly, "Make me glad to have wasted this afternoon on you, worthless one."

"Well, look who's here!"

Molly turned to smile at her mentor, Dr. Ken Lewis, who had guided her education since her arrival on the Berkeley campus almost five years earlier. "Hi, Ken."

"And look at our little angel." The gentle-faced professor lifted Kerreya from her infant seat, holding her high for inspection. "You're looking good, Kerry. How old are you? Two? Three?"

"She's seven months today," Molly laughed. "Give Dr. Lewis a smile, Kerry." When the child complied sweetly, her mother boasted, "She almost took her first step today, Ken. Can you believe that?"

"I'm impressed." He settled the baby back into her seat. "Pretty soon she'll refuse to stay in this contraption, Molly."

"Kerry? Refuse? Never. She does whatever we ask, plus she likes to come to the lab and she knows sitting quietly is part of the deal."

"Just the same," he chided, "a lab is no place for a little girl. I take it your husband is off gallivanting again?"

Molly winced. Somehow she didn't think her well-meaning adviser would understand Matthew's need to spend the vernal equinox in the Yucatan, so she opted for, "He had to go to Mexico for a couple of days, then on to New York to meet with his agent."

Clearing his throat, Ken insisted, "We need to talk."

She tried to take a deep breath, but her heart was sinking too fast to allow it. Not that she hadn't expected this, of course. Despite the long hours of work and study, she had been fundamentally undependable over the last several months, and deserved whatever was coming now. "I think I know what you're going to say, Ken, and if it's any help, I agree with you completely." Extending her hand, she added sadly, "I've loved working with you, and I'm really sorry I let you down."

He was on his feet in a second, taking both of her hands and insisting, "You haven't let me down yet. If anything, I'm the one who's letting *you* down."

"Pardon?"

"I've been offered, and will undoubtedly accept, a position in Southern California. It's been in the works for months, and frankly, I've wanted it for years. It's the culmination of a lifetime of work. . . ." His eyes were filled with apology. "Of course there's a downside."

Still relieved that she hadn't been kicked out of the program, Molly smiled. "Your family lives in Los Angeles, right? It's perfect, Ken. I'm so proud of you." Hugging him briskly, she insisted, "Tell me all about it. Every detail."

"I'll be chief administrator of a privately funded institute studying drug dependency, most particularly in infants. It's not just an ivory tower, though. There's a nursery, and a staff of pediatricians, and an intensive outreach program of education and rehab. And"—his gaze locked with hers—"I can choose my own staff. So? Would Matthew consider relocating?"

Molly stared, speechless.

Her reaction seemed to galvanize her mentor's position. "He can write his books anywhere, and he's obviously lost interest in teaching. He doesn't need to be in Berkeley. In fact"—his expression darkened slightly—"he's never here, anyway, so what difference would it make?"

"I'm flattered, Ken," Molly hedged. "After my haphazard performance lately, I'm surprised you'd even want me."

"Your performance has been excellent. It's your schedule that's been a mess. That would have to change."

"I don't know what to say," she admitted. "The thought of moving to Los Angeles . . . Matthew's house is unique, as you know. He has the alarms, to protect the weapons . . ."

"After a year and a half of marriage, you still call it 'Matthew's house.' The irony being, of course, that he's never there, while you're practically a prisoner." He held up a hand to ward off her protest. "Like I said, we have to talk. We've danced around this all semester, Molly. I've watched you jeopardize your career needlessly. Now you have a chance to change all that. You can get out of that gloomy mausoleum, find some reliable child care for Kerry, get yourself a car, and get back on the track."

Molly was staring again, confused by what appeared to be an ultimatum. This ordinarily cheerful man had obviously been holding a lot inside. Did he honestly disapprove of Matthew to so strong a degree? Had he been watching and judging, all of these months, without saying a word? And could her marriage withstand such scrutiny? "You don't understand," she began lamely. "It's not as simple as you make it sound."

"Fine. Enlighten me." He moved back to his stool. "Do you like that dark, strange house? I only went there one time, for the wedding reception, but it struck me as horrific. Do you honestly intend to raise this sweet little girl there?"

"My husband collects weapons," Molly countered tersely. "That's part of who he is. And since he's also Kerry's father, she's going to be exposed to all of that. I wouldn't change that, even if I could."

"But of course you can't." Before she could respond, he was accusing, "You're virtually a prisoner of his paranoia. He's obsessed with safety, so *you* sit home, alone, with the baby, behind a ten-foot electrified fence, in a house filled with crossbows and swords, while *he* travels the world. Do you have any idea how absurd that is?"

Her stomach was churning as Ken Lewis outlined the very accusations she had leveled so often against her wandering husband as she lay awake, alone, long into the nights. Kerreya's birth had temporarily smoothed the problems, but lately the doubts had returned. Now she was hearing them spoken aloud, and they sounded more threatening and confusing than ever.

The professor shook his head. "I like Matthew, you know that. I've read his books, and I admire them. And he loves you and the baby. That's not the issue. The issue is your future. Your happiness."

"I've never been happier in my life," Molly bluffed valiantly. "It may not look that way, but it's the truth."

"But you'll think about L.A.? And discuss it with Matthew?"

"Of course." She moistened her lips thoughtfully. "We're both assuming he'll resist, but who knows? Like you said, he can write his books there just as easily, so the only real issues are child care and security. . . ." *Two insurmountable issues,* she silently warned herself. Still, she had her pride and wasn't about to confirm her professor's suspicions concerning her lack of self-determination. Squaring her shoulders, she promised, "We'll think it over. I'm not that thrilled with the thought of living in Los Angeles, but I love working with you, so . . ."

"It would be the chance of a lifetime for you, careerwise," he scolded gently.

"My career's important, but not as important as my family and my marriage. I'll make the right decision, and either way"—she touched his shoulder shyly—"I'll always be grateful to you. Okay?"

"Make your decision. I'll accept it, no questions asked. How's that?" Cupping her chin in his hand, he added gently, "The last thing I want to do is add to your pressure."

The unmistakable trace of pity in his voice stunned her more than the scolding and the criticisms had. Turning away quickly, she found herself looking into Kerreya's wide, trusting eyes, and a claustrophobic sensation—of futility and of frustration—threatened to engulf her. Grabbing the car seat, she murmured, "I'll give this my undivided attention, Ken. And I'll call you in a couple of days. Give my love to Caroline." She steeled herself, with the last of her strength, before adding, "Congratulations again on the new job. It sounds . . . like a dream come true."

"I've sent for my car, Constance. My driver will see that you and Niki arrive safely back in the city."

"I wish I didn't have to leave," the witch pouted, adding quickly, "but, of course, I understand it's my duty, Wolfe. I'm not complaining."

"Good." The First Wizard slipped his arm around her supple waist and walked her out onto the vine-covered veranda that adjoined his sumptuous rooms. "We have no choice. If your husband calls the hotel, and you don't answer, he'll wonder."

"True. I'm supposedly on a shopping spree, buying dresses for his little . . ." She caught her tongue and murmured, "For our little daughter."

"You mustn't go home without purchases or he'll grow suspicious. I'll have my driver furnish some frilly little outfits for Niki. And something for you, too, of course."

Stupid fool, the witch thought to herself, but aloud she cooed, "You're so generous, Wolfe. Where would I be without you?"

"The others may consider you a liability," he smiled, "but to me you are a treasure. Speaking of which," the wizard guided her gently into the shadows and whispered, "there's something you should know."

"Oh?"

"There's unrest in the assembly. I believe perhaps a challenge is being plotted."

"A challenge?" Constance gasped. "Who would dare challenge you?"

"I suspect it may be Fox. Or perhaps his cousin Crane." Wolfe's smile was pure confidence. "I shall annihilate any challenger, of course."

"Crane is a strange, unimaginative little man," Constance mused. "And Fox is a flirt, with no substance. Surely, the assembly can see that. It's almost laughable."

"True. I have many loyal supporters and I'll be First Wizard for many years to come. Don't worry, Constance. As long as I'm the leader, you're safe."

"I'm not frightened," she declared staunchly. "Even in my ancient times long ago, there was no magician finer than you."

The tribute clearly pleased him. "I'll keep you informed. In the meantime perhaps it's best that you stay in Boston, out of harm's way. If I need your support in the assembly, I'll send for you. Otherwise, stay safely at home." With a satisfied flat smile he urged her toward the walkway that led to his car.

As they strolled, the beautiful witch could barely contain her excitement. A challenge! How exhilarating! Whether

Wolfe won or lost, it would breathe excitement into her life-less existence, at least for a while.

If the challenger was that wimp Crane, Wolfe would pre-vail. Of that she had no doubt. But Fox was another matter. Sexy, charming, young—perhaps thirty-one or thirty-two at the most. An extraordinary lover—she remembered *that* from the last orgy! There was something special about him— an enigmatic mix of determination and nonchalance, both executed with consummate class and more than a touch of humor. Cruel in his own way, of course, but never crude. All in all, an intriguing challenger.

"Rosalie!" Wolfe was calling impatiently to his thirteen-year-old, dark-haired daughter, who was playing in the dis-tance. "Bring little Niki to us immediately." His stern look evaporated at the sight of Constance's fair-haired child, and he stooped down to greet her. "How have you been getting along, darling? Has Rosalie been helping you with your les-sons?"

"She's stupid, Father," Rosalie drawled. "She doesn't know anything. I think she's human, like Damien says."

Constance bit back an angry retort—such a remark was an insult to *her*—then, with measured civility, she reminded the pale-faced girl, "This is only her first day."

"Absolutely." Wolfe reached for Niki's chubby hand. "Don't be discouraged, darling. The first day is difficult, even for the finest witch."

Niki shrank from his touch, insisting softly, "I'm not a witch. I want to go home." Her lower lip trembled as she added, "I've been a good girl all day."

"Of course you have. Give me a kiss, then you can go home."

Again the girl shied away. "No!"

"Niki!" Constance gasped. "Give the wizard a kiss *now!*"

"I can't." Raising pleading eyes to her mother, she wailed, "I promised Daddy I wouldn't!"

Constance glanced warily toward the First Wizard and was

relieved to see he hadn't taken offense. In fact, he seemed charmed by the girl's defiance. It made little sense but was preferable to his wrath, and so she murmured sweetly, "You promised Daddy you wouldn't? Wouldn't what?"

"He said don't let people kiss my lips until I was all growed up."

"Adorable." Wolfe grinned. "That's ten years away, Niki. When you're fifteen years old, you'll be all grown up and we'll initiate you into our assembly. I'll have the honor of consummating that initiation. It's like a party. Do you like parties?"

The girl eyed him thoughtfully. "Will you have pony rides?"

"By then you'll be riding horses, not ponies," the wizard answered, smiling.

"Stallions," Constance corrected, with a smirk.

The wizard chuckled, then patted Niki's shoulder. "When you're all grown up then, do you promise to kiss me?"

"Maybe," Niki hedged. " 'Cept not if you claw me."

"Claw you?" His jaw tightened noticeably as he straightened and gestured for his twelve-year-old son to approach. "Damien, take Niki to the stables for a pony ride. And keep your hands to yourself."

Damien laughed. "I'm saving myself for her mother."

The First Wizard turned to Constance and explained curtly, "He's asked that you be the witch to initiate him into the assembly."

Resisting an impulse to grin—the boy was rapidly growing into a gorgeous young man and would be a pleasure to teach—Constance murmured, "Whatever you say, Wolfe."

"Come on, kid," Damien urged. "You can ride Blackie. He's the best of the ponies."

Niki's eyes were shining at the thought and, without a word to her mother, she eagerly followed the boy into the distance.

"Your children are very obedient, Wolfe," Constance sighed. "I apologize for Niki."

"Apologize for yourself!" he snapped, his eyes coal-like with displeasure. "It's intolerable that you used me to scare her! It's you, and not Niki, who should fear my claws."

Constance trembled, with anger as well as fear. "She's impossible to discipline, Wolfe. I wasn't trained to be a mother, and my husband won't allow me to whip her. What else am I to do?"

"Bribe her," he glared. "Shower her with candy and presents. She's much too young to threaten. That will come later, and from me, not from you. Is that understood?" Without waiting for a response, he spun on his heels and started down the path toward the stables.

Going to watch little girls ride ponies, the witch noted in silent derision. *The man has no taste and less class.*

"Constance?" a smooth voice murmured seductively from behind her. "Has our leader left you alone at last? I've been hoping for a word with you."

Her heart was instantly pounding, but when she turned to him, she knew her expression was one of pure boredom. "I can't think of anything you and I have to discuss, Fox."

"No?" His eyes scanned her curves, and she knew from his expression that he, too, remembered the last orgy fondly. "Such a waste of beauty, allowing you to spend your nights with a human. You should be the wife of a wizard, Constance. He would be the envy of all men, and you would be pampered and powerful."

She was almost trembling with relief. He *was* the challenger, and such a provocative one, with his cinnamon-toned hair, flawless complexion, and eyes a truly priceless shade of emerald green. "It's my duty to stay with the father of the Valmain princess," she reminded him coyly.

"To serve a culture that was annihilated—by us, of course—centuries ago?" the handsome wizard scoffed. "I've never understood that particular policy. You do the bidding of a mounds sorceress, when the mounds were our most distasteful enemies. It's absurd."

Not daring to engage in such mutinous talk while at the compound, Constance whispered, "It's not safe here, Fox. But my husband will be traveling most of next week. You could come for a visit." Allowing him one flirtatious smile, she added, "I can be a very entertaining hostess."

Again his eyes swept over her, with lustful thoroughness. "I can only imagine. A woman with your beauty should be more than a hostess. She should be nothing less than the bride of the First Wizard."

"Sadly, he does not agree."

"Well, things can change. Often for the better." Fox smiled slyly.

It was true! Things could change—her life could in fact be salvaged—and this was clearly the man who could make it happen. He wanted to marry her! He would challenge Wolfe and take command, and then he'd kill Alexander Sheridan—or perhaps he'd allow *her* that particular honor!—and they would rule together! Scarcely daring to breathe, she nodded slightly, then edged away, fearful that Wolfe's spies would recognize their plotting and betray them.

Fox seemed to understand and, with one last, lascivious grin, strolled gracefully away, leaving her to enjoy the gust of hope that had so unexpectedly blown into her musty existence.

"You are quiet tonight, Princess."

"Am I?"

"Are you lonely, with your champion away for so many nights?"

"It's not that. I mean, I miss him, of course, but . . ." She hesitated, then admitted, "I've got something else on my mind."

"Tell me."

"In this dream you're my teacher, right? Well, out in the world I have another teacher. A professor, who's been really good to me. He's taught me so much. . . ."

Aaric nodded. "His name is Doctor Lewis. You have mentioned him frequently."

"Have I?" She pulled her cape closer. "He's brilliant and kindhearted—you'd like him a lot—but today he made me an offer I can't accept, and I feel so torn."

"He wishes to be your lover?"

"Are you nuts?" It made her smile despite herself. "He's happily married. But he's leaving for a new job in Los Angeles, and he wants me to come, too. With Matthew and Kerreya, of course."

"But your champion will not leave the lodge of many weapons?" the sorcerer guessed.

"I'm not sure, but it doesn't matter. Even if we moved, I'd need to find someone more earthbound than Matthew to watch the baby, and Matthew would never allow it."

"Neither would I."

"Don't start with me, Moonshaker," she glared. "I'm not in the mood." When his expression didn't change, she added sheepishly, "Do you think I want a stranger watching Kerry? Believe me, I'd check any applicant out thoroughly. And I'd only be gone as little as necessary."

"Even one moment in the hands of a lake witch would mean certain death for the little one. I oppose any such arrangement."

"Fine! Why don't I just give her a sedative every morning so she'll sleep all day, and you can watch her here in the dream while I work?"

"You can accomplish this?" he marveled. "It would be the perfect arrangement. I could train her while she slept, just as I've trained you."

"You're impossible!" Molly bit back a grin. "I must be crazy getting advice from you. Aaric the Nanny. How do you propose to handle the breast-feeding?"

He grinned in return. "I can make an illusion of you, with your full breasts and your sassy smile, and she can pretend to drink, in much the same way as I pretend to make love to you when you are absent from the dream."

"Me?" Her cheeks were red-hot at the thought. "Don't you mean, Angela?"

"Never." His grin softened to a fond smile. "Bring the little princess here, so that she may have her late-night snack."

"You just want to leer at my breasts." Molly sniffed in feigned distaste.

"Breast," he corrected. "You reveal them only one at a time. You are annoyingly modest."

"And you're annoyingly lascivious, so we're even. Anyway"—her pulse quickened with delight—"tonight Kerry and I have a surprise for you, so the ogling will have to wait." Taking his hand in her own, she announced, "She took her first step today. I can't wait for you to see her."

"Bring her immediately!" he boomed. "I should have been told this the moment you arrived. Bring her, and allow her to bask in my praise."

"The way I've done whenever I've learned a new trick?" Molly beamed. "We're so lucky to have you, Aaric. To admire us, and encourage us. Do you know what I realized today?"

"Tell me."

"I realized how supportive you are of me. I know you wish I'd give up toxicology and take up magic full-time, but you know how much it means to me, and so you back off, and you support my decisions, even when you think they're wrong. I love that about you." Raising onto tiptoes, she kissed his square jaw. "Thanks."

"Bring the little one." He flushed. "Do not thank me for simple friendship. It is unnecessary."

"You're always here for me," she sighed.

"I have nowhere else to go."

"So much for sentiment," she grumbled. "In other words, if you were out of the dream, you'd take off, just like Matthew?" Almost immediately she regretted the words, not because they might sting, but because they were so blatantly impossible that they could *never* sting. There was no doubt that if Aaric the Moonshaker had a choice, he would still remain at his Princess's side, protecting and supporting with no need for more.

"Bring the little one," the sorcerer repeated gently. "I wish to see her walk."

"She can't walk yet. Just one little step—a very conservative step. You know how cautious she is. But"—her heart swelled with motherly pride—"it's so cute. She worked on it all afternoon, with the most determined little expression on her face. You should have seen her." When her companion's eyes flashed with frustration, she added teasingly, "Oh, I guess you could see her right now, couldn't you? If only I could remember how to summon . . ." When he pretended to scowl, she relented and, with the ease of a powerful sorceress, brought her daughter into the dream.

For a moment she could scarcely believe her eyes. Kerreya had indeed appeared, but not in Molly's arms, as had always been the case until this night. Instead she was standing—*Standing!*—on the very top of the highest of the mounds, with a smile as proud as it was sweet. And over her embroidered gown was a cape of dusty pink satin edged in gold braid, hanging just to her bare ankles.

"Aaric," Molly whispered. "Look at her. What does it mean?"

The mighty sorcerer, while seemingly mesmerized, managed to murmur, "She is more than we dared hope. More than we dared dream. More"—his voice was choked with a rush of emotion—"much more than has ever gone before. Look closely, Princess, and behold the future."

Five

Resplendent in her new cape, the infant stretched her arms toward her mother and her teacher. When Molly tried to go to her, however, Aaric restrained her gently. "Will you allow me the honor?"

"Of course." Molly sighed, then watched in wonder as the huge sorcerer humbly approached the newest mounds magician and knelt before her, proclaiming, "This moment will live in our hearts, little one, as a memory of deliverance from the annihilation of our people. With your birth came our rebirth, and with your cape came our greatest hope for rebuilding all that was lost. Do you understand that?"

Molly drew closer, both pleased and frightened by her daughter's shining face as the prediction filled the air. For a moment she was reminded of Matthew, and the burdens and pressures he could relentlessly impose. While Aaric's words lacked the fanaticism of Matthew's, the implication was chillingly clear. He expected more of Kerreya than to lead a happy, healthy childhood, and so, as the girl's mother, it was Molly's place to intercede. Who knew better than the Valmain princess how unfair destiny's blessings could be?

"That's enough, Moonshaker."

He turned quickly, his expression wary. "Princess?"

Without another word she took the child into her arms and cuddled her close. "I love your cape, Kerry," she whispered. "You can wear it whenever you like, but it's hard to play in it, and so"—she took a deep breath and continued—

"you can take it off whenever you want." The baby's gold-
dusted eyes were filled with questions, and in answer Molly's
own blue eyes could only fill with tears.

"Princess, are you crying? Why?" Aaric slipped his arm
around her waist. "This is a wondrous moment for all of
us."

"No, it isn't." When she blinked, the tears ran down her
cheeks and she didn't bother to brush them away. "You don't
understand, Aaric. In your world, being a sorceress was a
normal part of life. In Kerry's world it will ruin everything.
I don't want her weighed down by secrets and responsibilities
that she can't possibly understand or fulfill."

"It will be different for her," he soothed. "It was thrust
upon you in adulthood, Princess, but *she* will be raised with
it. Fire and wind will be as normal for her as taking that first
step. You said it yourself a moment ago. She needs to play.
For her, magic will be a plaything long before it becomes a
responsibility. That gentle passage was denied to you, but
for the little one it will be quite different. She will revel in
her magic, and she will thank you for gifting it to her at
birth."

"You don't know anything about our world."

"Some things cannot change. Look at her, Princess. She
is proud. She is delighted. And she is waiting for you to give
her permission to enjoy her new status."

It was true. The child's eyes, still on her mother's, were
filled with hope, excitement, and curiosity. "Is this fun,
Kerry?" Molly asked carefully. "Do you want to play with
your cape?"

In answer, the baby wriggled out of her mother's arms to
the ground, where she took one tentative step, and then another, then glanced slyly toward the Moonshaker, who applauded heartily. "Very good, little one. You must practice
this walking, day and night, do you understand? I cannot
begin to train your magic until you have mastered the skills
of childhood."

Molly exhaled wearily. "Really, Aaric? You don't want to teach her fire and wind yet?"

"What a foolish thought," he teased. "Allow her her childhood, princess." When Molly's smile was weak, he pulled her close and chastised, "You allow this moment to be darkened by your troubles. Instead, you must allow your troubles to be lightened by this moment."

"That's dung."

His laughter boomed over the mounds. "Stubborn witch. Sit there and nourish the little one now, so that she will have the strength to be the daughter of so demanding a mother."

Molly shook her long curls ruefully and settled onto the ground, then motioned for Kerreya to join her, but the girl's attention had been distracted and she was staring up into the branches of the tallest tree.

"You see the other cape?" Molly smiled. "It's pretty, isn't it? But not as pretty as yours."

"And it is dangerous," Aaric added sternly. Turning Kerreya toward himself, he instructed, "You must never touch that cape, little one. Do you understand?"

The child nodded solemnly, then fluffed her own cape, as though in inquiry.

"Yes, your cape is beautiful," he chuckled. "And your mother's cape, with its silver stitching, is a marvel to behold. My two beautiful princesses . . ." His words died on his lips as thunder rolled out of the distance and over the mounds.

The sky was darkening, and as it did Kerreya's delight visibly crumbled into fear, and she began to whimper. Even when the Moonshaker's strong arms encircled her she could not seem to find comfort.

"It's okay, Kerry," Molly murmured, joining them quickly and cuddling the child against her chest. "It's just a storm. . . ." Raising her eyes to Aaric, she mouthed silently, "Matth-ew?"

The sorcerer nodded. "Again he tries to enter this dream.

But you have blocked him well." His huge hand massaged
the baby's back as he spoke. "I have never heard the little
one cry. It is a piteous sound."

"She's never been here for this. I was hoping she never
would. It's so unnerving. And," Molly grimaced, "it makes
me a feel so deceitful and disloyal."

"He has left you no choice. It was he who made you
choose between my friendship and his love, and because you
needed both, you were forced into this deception. Do not
belabor it, Princess."

The thunder had subsided and again the meadow was
bathed in sunlight, warming and soothing the child, who was
soon nursing contentedly at her mother's breast. "It doesn't
make any sense, Aaric," Molly confided quietly. "How can
the amulet be working? Matthew's in Mexico for the equinox."

"He is at the mounds."

She started to protest, then bit her lip instead. Had it come
to this? Her husband had always been scrupulously honest—
so honest, in fact, that it sometimes broke her heart. Now
he was lying to her, and his daughter was being drawn into
the deception and hurt by it in the process.

"Do not be sad, Princess. It is his nature to persevere.
Destiny demands it of him."

"He's never lied to me before."

"Forgive him," the sorcerer advised firmly. "He hears the
call of destiny, yet it is unclear to him what he is to do. He
seeks answers to unanswerable questions. He seeks a purpose
for his life."

"He has a purpose. He's my husband and my lover. He
researches and writes his books, preserving legends and
bringing them to life for thousands of readers. He promotes
ethnic pride and cultural respect. And now, he's Kerry's father. What more does he need?" Her voice had become a
plea. "Why can't he be happy? Look at you, Aaric. Your life
here is so curtailed! You only have me—another man's

wife—and Kerry, another man's daughter. But you accept your limits, and you manage to find balance and purpose."

"Because I am training the only surviving mounds sorceresses, which gives me purpose. And I am spending time with the woman I love, which gives me pleasure."

"Why can't Matthew's books be his purpose? And why can't spending time with me give him pleasure? Why can't I be the woman *he* loves?"

"In his way, he loves you."

"You called it reverence once, and you were right. And Grandma was right when she said he only loved me because I fit the part, not because of anything personal," she lamented, loosening the baby's mouth from her breast as she spoke. "I'd better wake up now. I've got a lot of thinking to do."

"You will think about the offer made by your Doctor Lewis?"

Molly nodded. "I'd love that job. And I'd love to move out of that dark, secluded armory. I'd like to get a house like the one I grew up in. Bright and sunny, with a rose garden, and a porch that looks out over something other than bars and fences." Almost to herself she added, "I'd love to see that house again."

Aaric studied her intently. "You are considering that?"

"What? A visit to my father?" Molly chewed her lip thoughtfully. "He's Kerry's grandfather. When she took her first step, I thought about how proud you and Matthew would be, then I thought about him, and how he'd smile if he could see her. He has the greatest smile, Aaric."

"There are tears in your eyes again," the sorcerer soothed. "Life demands too much of you, my sweet love. I would give anything to help you."

"It helps just to talk to you."

He nodded. "Talk to me, and talk to your champion. But do *not* turn to the man who betrayed your mother's love while she lay dying and in pain."

Molly stared, surprised by the vehemence in his tone. "Matthew thinks I should forgive him."

"He is wrong. Until the day your father renounces the woman who destroyed your life, you must remain apart from him. Otherwise, the little princess will be exposed to that woman. I cannot abide such a thought."

"You're right. I hate to think of poor Nicole being raised by a bitch like Constance, but there's nothing I can do about that. But I can and will keep Kerry away from her."

"Away from *them*," Aaric corrected. "Your father's blame in this is great. He has undoubtedly heard that he is a grandfather, but has he asked to see the child?"

"No . . ."

"He has renounced you, Princess. Undoubtedly, the new wife will not tolerate any rivals. He cannot be both her lover and your father, and he has made his choice." Aaric's eyes were cold with disgust. "He does not deserve to be your father, or the grandfather of the little one."

"You're right." She fingered an edge of Kerreya's pink cape, then smiled wistfully. "I'm sorry I ruined this all for you. Like you said, this is an important moment. Your 'little princess' became a sorceress today and we should be celebrating."

"Time spent with you is always a celebration, Princess. Now, return to the lodge of many weapons and prepare for your champion's homecoming. When he arrives"—the sorcerer's eyes twinkled—"you will kiss him with great suggestion, and the little princess will amaze him with her walking, and then you will tell him you wish to move to a lodge where the sun shines and the flowers bloom, and because he loves you, he will agree."

"Just like that?"

"Just like that." Arching an eyebrow, he added sternly, "Do not chastise him for deceiving you. It is his destiny to find his way back to this dream. As long as you prevent his success, you cannot fault his frustration."

"In other words, it's all my fault?"

"Precisely."

"Some best friend." She grinned reluctantly. "Kiss your little protégée now." When his lips had grazed both the child's forehead and her own, the sorceress touched his cheek and, with a rueful smile, returned to the lodge of many weapons to prepare for her champion's return.

A full day passed, and her resolve began to weaken. Could she handle this dilemma wisely? Could she convince Matthew to make this move, or would he use it as a springboard for another lecture on the need for safety, leading of course to another demand that they move to the mounds permanently? She could just imagine him seductively suggesting that he would build her a light and airy house with a huge porch and an acre of rose gardens in the meadow formed by the mounds. His eyes would be bright with golden enticement. She would start to weaken, then they would make love and nothing would have changed, except that this time, something *would* be different.

Ken Lewis would be gone. It could prove as devastating a loss to her career as losing Aaric would be to her training as a sorceress. Each of these men provided a guidepost. A beacon. They kept her on course. More importantly, they kept her from being swept away by Matthew's misguided enthusiasm, or by the wave of despair that resulted whenever that enthusiasm waned.

As she tucked Kerreya into bed for the night, she mourned, "If only your daddy would come home. Or at least call. I need to talk to him, and you need to walk for him, and we all need to spend some time together soon. You miss him, don't you?" She leaned down to the slumbering child's ear and whispered, "He loves you, Kerry. If he knew how much you missed him and needed him, he'd come home. I promise." Straightening, she patted the blanket one last time and

moved out of the room and down the stairs toward the entry
hall.

"Hi, Valmain."

"Matthew!" She froze for a moment, confused both by
his presence on the landing and by his disheveled appearance. His shirt was rumpled, his hair uncombed, and his expression weary, with dark circles under decidedly lusterless
eyes. "Is something wrong?"

He shrugged. "Nothing new, if that's what you mean." His
eyes gazed past her, up to the top of the staircase. "Is Kerry
asleep?"

She nodded, then moved quickly to him, brushing a dark
lock of hair from his forehead. "You look exhausted."

"I was up all last night," he admitted, then a smile touched
his face for half a moment. "You look pretty, Valmain. Like
I always said, you get prettier every time I see you."

"It's been months since you said that," she cooed, draping
her arms around his neck. "We've missed you, Matthew.
Come to bed and in the morning you can tell me all about
your trip."

"I didn't go to Mexico or New York. I went to the
mounds."

Forcing a smile, she confided, "I knew you didn't go to
New York, since Zack's been leaving desperate messages on
the answering machine nonstop since you left." When his
expression didn't lighten, she added carefully, "Why the
mounds?"

"I think you know why."

The arms that had embraced him now fell to her sides.
Her husband was frustrated, and tired, and perhaps even angry. The fact that he had a right to be all of those things
wouldn't make this confrontation any easier, she knew. "You
were trying to find my dream?"

"That's right. Have you tried at all lately? Even once, just
to humor me?"

Her eyes narrowed slightly. He was rarely arrogant, but

when he was, she found him eminently resistible and decided now to take full advantage of the opportunity. "Why did you lie to me, Matthew? Why did you tell me you were going to Mexico?"

"I changed my mind at the airport. I would have called," he insisted, "but you always worry when I go to the mounds, so I thought I'd give you a break. I didn't lie. I'd never lie to you."

Molly winced. The arrogance was gone, and her vulnerability had rushed back into place. Still, she persevered. "I worry about you because the mounds are a dangerous place. What if Deborah Clay decided to get revenge against us by killing you? She may even have found some lake wizards or witches to help her by now."

"Wizards and witches?" he growled. "Why is it you only believe in them when it suits your purpose? When I try to protect you against them, you claim they died out years ago."

"I believe they don't exist anymore, but why take foolish chances? Anyway, we know for a fact that Deborah exists, and she must hate us for killing her granddaughter. All magic aside, she could shoot you with a plain old gun and you'd be just as dead as Angela. The amulet makes you strong, but not immortal."

"The amulet doesn't just make me strong," Matthew reminded her. "It heightens every one of my senses and sharpens my awareness of danger."

"You were wearing the amulet when you first met Deborah and Angela, and you thought they were the most wonderful people on earth!" she retorted. "You had an *affair* with Angela! Where was your heightened sense of awareness *then?* On second thought," she sniffed, "I don't think I want to hear about it."

Matthew shrugged. "I trusted them, the same way you trusted Maya and Aaric. We were both wrong. Hopefully, we've learned our lessons. I'm on my guard against the Deborahs of the world, and you know better than to get mixed up with smooth talkers like Aaric." When she simply stared, he added ruefully, "Deborah's probably dead. She was over ninety years old when I met her, and after the shock of Angela's death, she probably didn't last any longer. The motel owner in Colhaven knows everything that goes on in that area and he's sure she hasn't set foot around there since the day she boarded up her house and left."

"I still want you to be careful." She stepped into him, wrapping her arms around his waist. "I don't want anything to happen to you, and neither does Kerry. You look so tired."

"I'm beat," he admitted, "and hungry."

"Come on." She tugged him toward the kitchen. "I'll make you some eggs and we'll talk about something less volatile than Deborah."

"I'm too tired to fight," he agreed with a yawn, slumping into the first chair he encountered. "You say Zack's been calling a lot?"

"Twice a day, at least. He wants to know how far along you are in the new book." Setting a frying pan onto the stovetop, she added gently, "I'm a little curious myself."

"I'm about half finished."

"That's what you said four months ago."

"Well, it's still true."

His tone, defiant rather than defensive, warned her to drop the subject, but she prodded instead, "What's the problem, Matthew?"

"The 'problem' is that I'm not a writer. I take no pleasure in it. There was a time when it made sense, when I was searching for answers to our dreams and legends, but now it's just not for me." He seemed almost belligerent. "You've got dozens of career choices available to you, Molly. You can't possibly understand how I feel."

"You've got choices, too," she countered firmly. "Writing. Teaching. Lecturing."

"Teaching?" He frowned. "I hated that. It was convenient at the time, but now it would be intolerable."

Her patience was rapidly disappearing. "You don't like anything these days. The truth is you're very successful. Look at all your mail! What started out as textbooks have become popular with thousands of fans—"

"Fans!" Matthew spit the word contemptuously. "As though I want 'fans'? Do you know who my 'fans' are? Drug glorifiers! Elitist escapists with no individual or collective conscience! Remember that guy from Texas who insisted that I call him? Do you know what he wanted?" The pause was nothing less than damning. "He wanted to know if I could supply him with peyote. Peyote! Like he didn't really understand a damn thing about my books!"

"Did you explain to him that your philosophy is anti-drug?"

"No, I told him to go to hell."

His absolute frustration softened her and she soothed, "Not everyone who reads your books is like that. What about the students in the sociology and anthropology courses?"

"Like you? Remember? The only reason you took my course was to get an easy passing grade, not out of interest."

"Well, I'm interested now. I adored your first book and I loved the second one even more. And the next one will probably be the best yet. Why not just finish it and then you can take a long break."

"This book is different. It's not just about legends and dreams. It's about our society. . . ."

Oh, no, thought Molly. Here we go . . .

"It's about a culture that worships the god of 'convenience' above all others. A society without a social conscience. Without a social contract! A culture that despises itself. And it's infecting every other culture on earth. Too bad you toxicologists can't find a cure for that!"

He was on his feet now, pacing angrily. "Do you realize, Molly, that in every successful culture until now, each individual has identified first, and most strongly, with the group? Because he sees it working for him! He sees the value in each member. But not us! We measure our self-worth not by what we contribute but instead *by what we take out!* Most people today would gladly pillage their own society—steal from its coffers, neglect its altars—for their own personal aggrandizement."

Molly stared, fighting an impulse to fill the room with wind and fire. She had seen this fanaticism once too often and knew she had to diffuse it quickly, before it destroyed them, and so she challenged, "If your latest book is about all of that, and you feel so strongly about it, then why not finish it?"

"It can't be finished." He was suddenly as deflated as he had been animated. "The first half was easy. Describing the problem. The second half is supposed to propose solutions, and that's where it falls apart." He shook his head. "There are no solutions. We can only protect ourselves from it for as long as we can. Get away. Become self-sufficient."

"To the mounds, I suppose?"

"Wherever. In the country somewhere. It'd be good for Kerreya and eventually I think you'd come to appreciate it."

"Not me. We've been all over this. I'd hate it." The tremble in her voice belied her stiff posture. "I've compromised as far as I can, Matthew. A scientist married to someone who, at heart, is a hunter-gatherer. We knew there'd be problems, but *this* is *too much.* You've talked me out of having my own car because walking is good and pollution is bad; you totally control our diet, even though I've studied nutrition and I have a degree in biochemistry; you keep me and Kerry behind iron bars while you roam the world. You even made me give birth in the middle of nowhere with no doctor around because—"

"Wait a minute!" He crossed to her and grasped her shoulders firmly. "You admitted I was right about that. You said it was a perfect delivery, that you could feel the power of the amulet—"

"Yes! Yes! You were right! About that and about everything. Congratulations."

They locked eyes for a long moment, exhausted and wary,
before Molly whispered what she believed they both were
thinking. "Maybe we're each right, Matthew. Just not right
for each other, at least not right now."

"Molly!"

"No, wait, just listen." To her amazement her voice was
no longer shaking. "I've been giving this a lot of thought
lately. I love you. I don't want anyone else but you. So, I'm
yours. Forever."

"And I'm yours. Forever," he echoed, clearly relieved.
"So, what now?"

"You travel all the time anyway. And I hate this crazy
house, with its weapons and security system and iron gates.
So let's sell this place, for starters."

"Okay. Where will we live?"

"I'll live in Los Angeles. For a while, at least. Dr. Lewis
has a new project down there I could work on while I keep
going to school. I'd be busy and happy and working toward
a goal. I *need* that, Matthew. And you could . . . come
around . . ." She winced but persisted, "Whenever you
wanted."

" 'Come around'? What the hell does that mean?"

"It means you'd be with us when you want to be, not
under some sense of obligation."

"That's crazy," he groaned. "Who'd protect you and
Kerry?"

"I'll protect Kerreya. And I won't be in any danger. I'll
live in a safe building, or neighborhood, or something."

"Los Angeles?" He cocked his head, as though hearing
her for the first time. "How about moving in with my Uncle
August? He could help with Kerry. . . ."

"August?" Molly shook her curls vigorously. "That
wouldn't work. He's too old to watch her, and he lives too

far from the city. I know I'll have to commute, but not that far."

"You'll need a car," Matthew nodded. "I'll find you something safe, with four doors and low emissions." His eyes warned her not to mention the word "Mustang." "We can work out the details, but basically, this isn't such a bad idea."

He was thinking aloud, musing and planning, and clearly intrigued by the concept. Having expected complete resistance, Molly was disconcerted, at best. Some "champion" *he* was turning out to be! Was he actually ready to say goodbye to his wife and daughter so easily?

And Matthew was almost relentless. "There are places in the hills with some land around for security. . . . Rita and the boys could move up there, too, and she could watch Kerry for you. And you could watch the boys for her if she wants to keep her job at the hospital. . . ."

"I don't want to live *with* anyone, and I don't think Rita does either," Molly objected quickly. "She still thinks her husband's coming home some day to settle down, remember?"

"That bastard?" Matthew's eyes flashed a golden warning. "If he's smart he'll stay away forever. I'd love to tear him apart for what he's put them through. . . ." He caught himself and added more philosophically, "He's history anyway. We haven't heard a word in over three years, so forget about him. We'll find a big enough house for everyone, or we can even build one if we need to. Big, like this one, but with a better security system, and more property around it."

"Matthew!"

"Yeah?"

"You're not paying attention," she grumbled. "It's not your decision anymore. I'm leaving you."

"No way," he scoffed. "You're just confused. You've never liked this house, and you're restless to get on with your career. Believe me," he added, pulling her into his arms and nibbling on her neck, "I understand restlessness. This is a brilliant plan, Valmain. I'm glad you suggested it."

His warm breath on her neck was arousing, which she decided to find annoying. "I'm leaving you. Sex therapy isn't going to work this time, Matthew Redtree."

"Huh?" He raised innocent eyes to hers. "Sex therapy?"

"You know what I mean." She pulled free of him and accused, "Every time I try to assert my own needs and interests, you do *this* to distract me."

His eyes were sparkling on cue. "I didn't realize you had a complaint about your sex life."

"I don't," she retorted. "I have a complaint about *yours.*"

"Which means one of two things," he grinned, reaching past her to turn off the flame under the now-rubberized eggs she had been preparing. "You're talking about Angela, or about that time I offered to have a celibate marriage. I'll say one thing for you, Valmain. You know how to hold a grudge."

She raised her chin in defiance. "I'm taking you up on your offer. From now on, we'll be sleeping thousands of miles apart. Permanently celibate."

"No way. If anything, we'll be seeing more of each other than ever."

"Pardon?"

"I love Los Angeles," he explained, his tone now completely sincere. "My family's there. My favorite dojo's there, and I can practice with AJ as much as he needs. We can help my uncle more, and AJ and Robert both need to have a man around more, right? It's not as perfect as moving to the mounds, but it's a great plan anyway. I would have suggested it myself months ago, but I thought you were hooked on Berkeley until you finished your doctorate."

"I guess I was," she admitted, studying him hopefully. "You'd really prefer it?"

"Sure. The house is the key, though. When I chose this place"—his arm swept to encompass the room and beyond—"there were two main considerations. The ground around it is steep, to discourage intruders. And the fence, with the electric charge, is almost impenetrable. We'd have to duplicate all this. Something on the outskirts of the city, with a view of anyone approaching . . . some real acreage . . . something completely defensible, and big enough for my entire family, including—" he arched an eyebrow hopefully—"more babies? I'd like a son, Molly, to play with Kerry."

"Matthew . . ." She had to smile as she took his face between her hands and scolded, "You're such a fanatic. Could you just listen for one minute?"

"Sure, Valmain. What's wrong? Aren't you ready for another baby?"

"Not for a few more years," she assured him firmly, then her voice grew soft with hope. "I want a pretty little house with a porch and a garden. I want artwork on the walls, not weapons. I don't want a view of possible 'intruders,' I want a view of friendly neighbors, and children playing and riding their bikes. I want a home, not a fortress."

"Whatever you say, Valmain."

She stared in delight. "Really?"

"Sure. A little house, in a neighborhood with kids. Consider it done. Can I install an alarm system at least? And one in your car?"

"Mmm . . ." She brushed her lips across his. "Whatever you say, champion." As he swept her into her arms and carried her toward the staircase, she marveled silently, *A pretty little house! And neighbors! And a car? Aaric was right! All I had to do was ask . . .*

"Oh, Matthew! I almost forgot!" She wriggled free of him. "Guess who took her first step today!"

His grin was instant and broad. "Are you kidding? Isn't she too young?"

"She's incredibly coordinated, just like her warrior-father. Tomorrow she can demonstrate for you. But tonight . . ."

He chuckled knowingly. "No problem, Valmain. I'll try to be extra-coordinated tonight in honor of Kerry's walking."

"And in honor of our move to L.A.? Oh, Matthew . . ." She leaned into him and sighed. "I was dreading this, and instead, it's all working out perfectly."

Tilting her chin up, he locked eyes with her and insisted, "All you ever have to do is ask, Molly. The only reason I'm here on earth is to protect you and make you happy. Haven't you learned that yet?"

"You're here on earth to be Matthew Redtree," she corrected lovingly. "To preserve the past by retelling its legends, and to protect the future by explaining those legends to us, so we can learn from them."

The tribute seemed to almost stun him. "You really see me that way? That's nice, Valmain. Thanks. I've been feeling so . . ." He caught himself and chuckled ruefully. "Forget all that. Tonight I want to be the Valmain champion and make love to the Valmain princess."

"That," she assured him as he hoisted her back into his arms, "can definitely be arranged. The Valmain princess is in the mood to be ravished."

"Yeah?" He took the stairs two at a time, then strode masterfully down the hall and into the bedroom, where he lowered her carefully to her feet. "Any requests?" he teased, his breath warm on her neck as he spoke.

"Use your imagination," she sighed. "Just don't leave anything out."

"I'll be methodical, I promise," he chuckled. "Starting with your toes. Sit here"—he urged her to the edge of their king-sized bed—"and relax."

"Mmm . . ." She watched in adoring anticipation as he took her slim, bare foot into his rough hands, massaging lightly as he lifted it toward his lips. "That feels so good, Matthew. Do the other one now."

He arched an eyebrow playfully. "I promised to be methodical, not predictable. I'll come back for the other one later. For now"—he moistened his lips suggestively—"I'm setting my sights a little higher."

"How high?" She giggled nervously. "My mouth?"

"Lower." He was sliding her white satin nightgown slowly up her legs, drawing his tongue up after it, along the inside of her calf, then her thigh. When she teasingly tried to clamp her legs together, he chuckled again and forced them farther apart. "Do you want to be ravished or not? Lie back, Valmain, and relax."

"Kiss me first," she insisted throatily. "And take off your clothes, or at least, your shoes."

"In a minute," he promised, then returned his mouth to its amorous journey. Molly willingly collapsed backward onto the bed, eager to allow his tongue to control her as it worked its slow, relentless way upward until he was tasting gently of her most intimate need and thereby delivering her into ecstasy.

Six

They sold everything except the weapons, which Matthew reluctantly placed into storage. The next few weeks were filled with change, and to Molly's surprise most of it was wonderful. Of course, the olive green four-speed sedan Matthew selected for her was not exactly the vehicle she had dreamed of owning, but the two-bedroom, white brick house, with its sun porch and grape vines, was cozy and charming and, given its location just two blocks from Rita and the boys, came with instant "neighbors." AJ, in particular, was a frequent visitor, helping Molly unpack or digging post-holes with Matthew for the eight-foot fence he had insisted be installed.

"It lessens the charm of the place," Molly confided to Kerreya as they unpacked books in the sunny living room, "but it makes Daddy feel better, so I guess it's okay."

"Da-da," Kerreya nodded.

Molly stared. "You said 'Daddy'! Kerry? Say it again. Say 'Daddy.' "

"Da-da."

"Oh, my gosh! Can you say Mommy? *Please?*"

"Ma-ma."

"Oh! Oh, Kerry, wait until Daddy hears you!" She hugged her proudly. "And wait until *Aaric* hears."

"Rar-rik."

"Huh?" Molly's euphoria dissipated. "Oh, no . . ."

"Rar-rik," the baby repeated proudly.

Resisting an urge to place her hand over the girl's mouth, Molly groaned. "If Daddy hears you say that . . ."

"Da-da."

"Right. Daddy. Concentrate on saying that." She jumped to her feet and began to pace to the rhythm of the time bomb she now recognized as ticking in her life. Kerry would say "Aaric" during dinner some night soon, and Matthew would know everything!

The warmth of the sunlight through the room's bay window seemed suddenly stifling and, with an unthinking wave of her hand, the anxious witch summoned a strong breeze to cool the incendiary situation. When the gust sent newspapers swirling around the room, the baby clapped her hands in delight and Molly laughed nervously.

"Mamma!" the proud baby crowed, pointing a chubby finger toward the source of the magic.

"That's right, Kerry. Mommy did it." Unable to resist the baby's gleeful smile, she summoned a second gust, which caused the drapes to billow wildly. With a rueful grin she moved to straighten them, then caught a glimpse of Matthew through the window and sighed.

His skin was dark from the hours of laboring under the hot sun and, with his shirt off and his thick hair damp and dusty, he presented a dangerously sexy sight as he leaned on a recently cemented fence post and wiped the sweat from his brow. At that moment he resembled a warrior more than a scholar, and she remembered how it had been at the beginning, in the dream, when he had fought Aaric to win his dream girl's heart. She wondered if he knew how hopelessly in love she was. If he knew, would he be tempted to fall in love in return, or would he remain satisfied with worshiping her, as he had done for years before they'd even met?

She turned away from the window and frowned at the mess her witchcraft had wrought. "We'd better get this cleaned up before Daddy sees it."

"Da-da."

Laughing lightly, she reached down and scooped up her daughter, holding her high above her head and insisting, "You're the smartest, cutest, best baby in the whole world, did you know that? Should we go and tell Daddy the news?"

"What news?" Matthew's voice demanded cheerfully from the doorway. "Don't tell me there was a tornado in here while I was outside?" Crossing to Molly, he took their daughter and pretended to scold. "Did you make this mess, Kerreya Elizabeth?"

"Mamma," the baby explained sweetly.

"Huh?" He glanced toward his wife for confirmation of this apparent brilliance, then grinned at the child. "First you walk, then you talk, all within a month. You're amazing, Kerry."

"It gets better," Molly promised. "Ask her to say 'Daddy.' "

"Are you kidding?" He stared into the little girl's gold-flecked eyes and cajoled, "Kerry? Can you call me Daddy?"

"Da-da. Da-da, Mamma," she added, as though anticipating the next request.

While Matthew showered their daughter with praise, Molly silently thanked her for not announcing the third member of the triumvirate, then suggested, "Why don't I go make lunch while you two visit. Finishing the fence can wait, can't it, Matthew?"

"It's finished. And the alarm's wired in. You just have to memorize the codes. So . . ." His glance was sheepish. "I guess we're all set, right?"

"Right. Tomorrow Rita switches over to her evening shift, and I start working nine to three. We're right on schedule."

"And the boys will come *here* at night, right? I don't want you and Kerry over at their place until I get their alarm installed, and"—he cleared his throat hopefully—"I was thinking I might not be able to get to that until I get back."

Molly laughed. "In other words, you're leaving?"

"I wasn't planning on taking off so fast, but I have some urgent business down in Mexico."

"Urgent?" Molly teased. "If you're hot to leave, why not go to New York and reassure Zack? He's convinced you're never going to finish the book, and since it's already sold, I think that puts him in an awkward position."

"He's a great agent and a terrific lawyer. He's got the situation under control. I'm putting the book officially aside, and he knows it."

"So? What's the business in Mexico?"

"This." He pulled a large, chiseled piece of marbled stone from his pocket.

She examined it carefully. "An arrowhead?"

"That would be one heck of an arrow," he teased. "This is a spear point, Molly. It's probably nine or ten thousand years old. Some diggers I know found it in a Mayan tomb, but it's clearly pre-Mayan. They sent it to me to lure me down there and"—his grin was self-mocking—"it's working. Do you mind? It'd only be for a week or so."

"It'll take longer than a week," she smiled, "and we'll miss you, but we'll be fine. AJ's over here every day, and from what I saw of that practice match this morning, he's almost as good a warrior as you are these days."

"Don't go retiring me yet," Matthew protested, "but yeah, he's getting pretty good. So? It's settled?"

She was missing him already. "Why don't we leave Kerry with Rita tonight for a few hours? We can go out to dinner, just the two of us."

"Dinner sounds good, but we can bring Kerry. She'll behave, right, honey?" He beamed proudly at his little girl. "After all, we should celebrate her talking."

"That's not the point," Molly sighed. "I want to be alone with you. Rita told me about a romantic little hideaway, with music and candlelight. And dancing."

"I don't dance," he reminded her. "And if it's romance

you want, let's go out to my uncle's ranch, where we can sleep under a million stars."

"You're a sick man," she scolded lightly, hoping he hadn't seen the flicker of genuine hurt in her eyes. After all, as Aaric and Rita kept reminding her, she had known when she married him that he wasn't "romantic," or sentimental, or hopelessly in love. He was being himself—the man she had chosen of her own free will—and, as Rita also enjoyed reminding her, most women would love to have so attractive and devoted a mate. So, "I'll make dinner here, and we'll have Rita and the boys over, so Kerry can talk for them, and we'll make it an early night. Tomorrow I start work, the boys go to school, and you'll be heading for Mexico, so we all need our sleep."

"And I'll be back in a week, I promise." He pulled her close and kissed her gently, and with predictable ease, she melted in his arms.

"I cannot remember seeing you so content, Princess."

"I know." She sighed, fluffing her cape carefully. "Things are working out even better than I'd dreamed they would. Rita takes wonderful care of the baby, I love spending time with AJ and Robert, and the project is absolutely fascinating." Her smile was wistful. "And somehow I owe it all to you."

"Is that so?"

"You told me to just ask Matthew, and he'd agree to move to a more charming house, and it was true. You told me not to be afraid to make a few demands, and voilà! I'm practically in heaven. Of course"—her blue eyes twinkled—"he uglified the house with that fence of his, but it was a small price to pay. And for some reason he seemed to really enjoy building it, even in all that heat."

"Building the fence allowed him to feel he was protecting you," Aaric explained. "And training the boy called AJ allows him to see the future of his family being protected, too. All of these things make him more satisfied." He cocked his head and asked gently, "Have you heard from him since he left?"

"He called last night and was practically delirious," Molly smiled. "Those archaeologists who contacted him want him to do a series of articles on the black market in artifacts."

"Black market?"

"Sales that are illegal, usually because of the way the artifacts were obtained. Or because they're national treasures and some government claims title to them. There's a lot of money in those old weapons and ornaments, which encourages locals to plunder ancient sites. It's a complex ethical question, and Matthew's the perfect person to write about it. As a collector, he knows all about the black market, and as a student of various cultures, he sympathizes with the locals, who need to find a way to feed their families, even if it involves grave robbing. And, of course, he values the need for the archaeologists to carefully unearth and preserve the artifacts, so they can be studied, and placed in museums, where thousands of people can experience them. He sympathizes with everyone's point of view on the issue, except, of course, the ones motivated purely by greed."

"You are proud of him?"

"Absolutely. As much as he loves his collection, he'd never knowingly acquire any weapon that was obtained unethically." She nodded her head emphatically. "I'm totally proud of him."

"That is good. Now, you must make him proud of you by studying your magic. But first," his smile warmed, "bring the little princess. It has been four nights since she has come to the dream, and I have missed her sorely."

Molly bit her lip, then confessed, "There's a reason I haven't been bringing her."

His eyes widened with alarm. "She is ill? And you have kept it from me?"

"No, no, nothing like that," she reassured him hastily. "It's more complicated than that."

"Tell me immediately."

"A few days ago she started talking. She said 'Mommy,' and 'Daddy,' of course. Then"—she took a deep breath— "she said *your* name."

"Bring her at once. I must hear this through my own ears! Why do you hesitate?"

"Because Matthew could have heard her! What then? He would have known you were still here, and that I've been letting his daughter visit you behind his back!" Her hands were on her hips. "I've been warning you about this from the start, Moonshaker. I won't ask Kerry to keep secrets from Matthew. I think it's best if I don't bring her anymore."

"Princess!"

"Just listen. I know you think you need to train her, but that's years away, right? She's just too young to be asked to lie to her father. She wouldn't understand, even if we had the gall to ask her to. So, let's compromise." Ignoring his scowl, she suggested, "I won't bring her for a few years. During that time, if Matthew keeps mellowing the way he has been lately, maybe an opportunity to explain everything to him will pop up. And even if it doesn't"—she took a deep breath—"once she's old enough to understand why I lie to him, I'll tell her the whole story, and if she wants to be trained by you, I'll allow it. How's that?"

"That is unacceptable," he began, then changed tactics and cajoled, "I know you, Princess. You are too tenderhearted to deprive me of my opportunity to say farewell to the little one. Bring her here, one last time. It would be heartless to deprive me of that."

Molly shook her curls. "I knew you'd pull this. You don't want to say goodbye to her. You just want me to see how close the two of you are, so I'll feel like a rat keeping you apart. Believe me, I feel bad enough about it as it is." She stepped closer and took his hand in her own. "But I can't have her blurting your name out anymore. Not for the next few years, at least. Please try to understand?"

"I will not try to make you feel guilty," he promised, touching her fingertips to his lips. "I give you my word. I simply wish to embrace her one last time, before we are separated."

"Okay, I've thought this through. If you want to say good-bye to her, it will have to be on my terms."

"Which are?"

"Take Matthew's form."

Aaric stared at her in amazement. "You are suggesting *that?* You have always objected—"

"Because it was a game to you. But this is serious. I want her to be thinking about Matthew, not about you. I'm sorry if that sounds harsh, but from now on"—her eyes narrowed in warning—"if she comes here, you either have to be invisible or look like Matthew."

The sorcerer shrugged, then began to slowly dissolve into a cloud of silver light so blinding that Molly was forced to close her eyes. When she reopened them, the sight of her champion's form—lean, bare, and bronzed—covered only with animal skins and weapons, was like a jolt of electricity.

"You look as though you have not seen him in years," Aaric's voice marveled from within the illusion.

She had to moisten her lips before admitting, "Sometimes I forget . . ."

"Never forget," Aaric scolded. "He is not simply a man. He is your champion. A warrior destined to protect you. Now"—his serious expression evaporated—"bring the little princess."

Molly nodded, then summoned the baby into her arms. Without a moment's hesitation, Kerreya wriggled free and crawled eagerly into the disguised warrior's arms. "Rar-rig!"

Molly stared in amazement and frustration. "How did she know it was you?"

"She is a sorceress. She can see through my illusion. If

you would just learn to concentrate, you could do likewise," Aaric explained. "Now, little princess, try it again. Concentrate and say 'Aaric.' "

"Aaric," the baby responded dutifully. While the sorcerer chuckled and returned to his old appearance, Molly shook her head in confusion. Another mistake. She felt certain that the day was coming when she would pay for all of this deception. Still, she couldn't help but smile at the look of enchantment on her child's face as Aaric produced a cloud of butterflies for their amusement.

With a victorious grin Aaric insisted, "She looks well, Princess. This move to the place called Los Angeles has been good for her."

Molly nodded. "She loves being around her cousins, and she loves being here with you. Look at that expression, Aaric. Have you ever seen a sweeter baby?"

"Of course not. There has never *been* a sweeter baby. She is well loved by us all, and it shows." His smile turned pensive. "She is fortunate to have other children to play with. I did not have that as a child. And from all you have told me, these cousins—the little warrior, AJ, and the healer, Robert—are fine boys. Now tell me more about this Rita, whom you allow to guard my little princess. Did you find out what has become of her husband?"

Sinking onto the sweet green grass of the dream meadow, Molly patted the ground beside herself and, when the sorcerer had joined her, explained, "Matthew finally told me the whole story the night before he left and, believe me, Rita's better off without Jesse Camacho around."

"Jesse Camacho." Aaric repeated the name slowly, as though evaluating it. "Where is he?"

"They're not sure. Probably San Diego. Rita hasn't seen him for almost three years."

"He does not want to see his two sons?"

"I guess not."

"What kind of man is that?"

"According to Matthew . . . well, remember, Matthew hates him, but apparently Jesse was always extremely self-centered. Good-looking, successful with women, and in terrific shape. He was a karate instructor, and that's how he and Matthew met. Jesse practiced sometimes at the dojo where Matthew trained in high school, and when Jesse would compliment him, or spar with him, he was flattered."

"And then?"

"Well, one of the things that seemed so great about Jesse was that he had dozens of girls chasing him. Matthew was so much younger and more serious, and I guess he was easily impressed. But when Rita came to one of the competitions to watch Matthew and ended up being interested in Jesse, well, suddenly it didn't all seem so great."

"Did Matthew allow his sister to see this man?"

"No. Apparently, he went straight to Jesse and threatened him. Said he'd hit him if he didn't stay away from Rita."

"And what did Jesse say?"

"He didn't *say* anything. He 'punched Matthew's lights out,' to use AJ's expression."

Aaric burst into laughter. "So, your champion was humiliated?"

"No. That's not how it went. When Matthew regained consciousness, Jesse told him he admired him for looking out for his sister. He told him not to worry because he was going to marry Rita and promised to take care of her and respect her. And Matthew was relieved."

"And they married."

Molly nodded. "And things were okay at the beginning. Jesse went into the Navy and they ended up with what should have been an ideal situation. Living in Hawaii, both with good jobs, starting a family . . . Then one day, Rita showed up at Matthew's dorm room in tears, with a baby and a toddler, and said Jesse was tired of being tied down."

"What kind of man abandons his sons?" Aaric frowned.

"His sons *and* his wife. Don't forget her."

Aaric grinned. "You said Rita has not seen her husband in three years. That means he came back once?"

"Several times, apparently. But he drinks, and doesn't work steadily, then he gets bored and leaves. Matthew keeps trying to get Rita to divorce Jesse and find someone else, but she's positive he'll come to his senses someday. And Jesse's older brother, Rob, lives nearby—he's a widower with grown children—and he helps Rita and encourages her not to divorce Jesse. After twelve years of marriage! It's a mess." She sifted her fingers through her curls thoughtfully. "I met Rob the other day and he's pretty nice. Matthew says part of Jesse's problem was having to compete with a big brother who was always better in every way—studies, martial arts, everything."

"This Rob was a good husband before his wife died?"

"I guess so. He's a policeman or deputy sheriff or something. Really solid."

"And Rita waits?"

"I guess so. But it sounds hopeless." Her eyes clouded. "It's so unfair to the boys. They need a father."

"I agree. AJ, the young fighter, needs to see discipline, not laziness. Perhaps," he mused, "if this Jesse Camacho comes back one day soon, you can practice your persuasion on him."

"Are you serious? I'm not that powerful."

"That is dung. You *have* the power. Your problem is control. You need to practice, but you always say that you do not wish to 'manipulate' others."

"I'd definitely make an exception if I thought I could help Rita," Molly countered enthusiastically. "How would I do it?"

"You would wait for an opportunity. You would have to touch his hand or shoulder, then concentrate. Start with a small thought. Perhaps accentuate his feelings for his sons. That, above all, must be a key." He adopted his mentor tone. "Remember, you can only 'persuade' a person to acknowledge his *own* thought. You can strengthen an existing idea, but there is no magician in the world with the power to plant a thought where it is repulsive, unless a spell is involved."

"I see." She hugged him gratefully. "Wouldn't it be incredible? If my magic could do that . . ."

"There is a world of wonder at your fingertips, Princess, but first . . ."

"But first I have to practice," she finished dutifully, "so let's get started. Kerry, time for you to go back to bed. Give Aaric a kiss." When both the child and the sorcerer seemed saddened by the thought, she assured them, and herself, "Tomorrow night, and every night, we'll all visit again."

"Do you hear that, little one? The mean old witch is not going to separate us after all," Aaric teased, then his grin faded. "I am grateful, Princess. I could not bear to lose her."

"Don't worry. You're stuck with both of us. I promise. Now"—her eyes sparkled through her tears—"teach me Persuasion."

The wizard looked out over the peaceful lake and nodded, pleased with its gleam of pure silver in the high-noon sun. The power of magic—the magic of power—Fox lusted for both. He intended to have them.

The assembly would confirm him as First Wizard, he knew. Hadn't he annihilated Wolfe and his supporters? Hadn't Wolfe's own son Damien sided with Fox, along with the ancient beauty Constance and a dozen other witches and wizards? Even those who had remained neutral—including his envious rival, Crane, and enigmatic, green-eyed Sara—had seemed amused by the thoroughness of Wolfe's humiliation.

The assembly had no choice but to make this coup official. Who else but Fox could lead the lakes confidently through the troubled days ahead? And there *was* trouble ahead. Fox could feel it in the air. North America was alive with the tremors and surges that signaled a powerful newcomer. It was a challenge, but of another sort—one that the lakes had met many times before, although not within the last one hundred years. Still, new enemies were always arising, as they had since the days of the Water Masters.

Those Water Masters no longer haunted the lakes of North America; they had been forced to seek a more hospitable milieu thanks to the cunning and prowess of Fox's ancestors. And after the Water Masters, the twins had arrived, and the mounds magicians had blazed with power and purpose for nearly three centuries, but their culture had withered and died, crushed under its own imperfections, while the lakes had grown even more entrenched. More recently a band of young witches from England had challenged the lakes. As with the others, their defeat had been swift and complete. Even the Seeri of New Zealand had dared attempt to infiltrate the lakes once or twice, only to be viciously and victoriously routed.

Who was daring to challenge the lakes this time? Lake legends foretold the return of an ancient enemy, but which one? Water Masters? Seeri? *The twins?* The wizard shook his head.

Ordinarily he had no patience with such fairy tales—if there was a threat, it was a new one, not the return of a vanquished foe—but the superstitions of the lesser wizards and witches were working in his favor now that the time to select a new warrior-leader was at hand. They were frightened. They craved new counsel. They sensed Fox's confidence and longed to bask in it. In return, they would freely channel their power through him, making him invincible. The imposing, auburn-haired man squared his broad shoulders and smiled over the lakes.

"It is decided, my love."

He turned, pleased by the soft surrender in the green-eyed blonde's voice. "Is it, Sara?"

"You are First Wizard," she sighed, sinking to her knees

and embracing him with unbridled admiration. "Take me first, and I will please you well."

"There was a time when you were not so eager for my touch, Sara," he reminded her softly. "Do you remember?"

The blonde nodded. "You frightened me."

"Frightened you?" He chuckled fondly. "Explain that."

"You are *too* powerful. Too incredible," the sultry witch cooed. "I thought they might kill you from jealousy and kill *me* for being your woman."

"A brilliant answer," he congratulated her proudly. "From a brilliant witch. Perhaps one day soon I will marry you, Sara. Would you like that?"

She nodded, her eyes shining with lust for power. "Today?"

"Soon, my love. When I have had my fill of the others. However"—he urged her to her feet and moved nimble fingers to the buttons of her lacy yellow halter dress—"I'll give you a taste of such bliss today."

"Fox!" A petulant rebuke interrupted the promise of passion. "The assembly is waiting. And"—the willowy, golden-haired newcomer insinuated herself between Sara and the wizard—"you promised me I would be first."

"So I did." Fox grinned. "You have stirred both my memory and my interest, Constance."

"Fox!" Sara glared. "This bitch is married! To a powerless human. She herself has no past and small future!"

"And yet this bitch does as she is told," Fox chuckled. "Do you, Sara?"

"Yes, Fox," Sara replied quickly. "Your every wish is my heartfelt desire."

He surveyed the twosome with relish. "I will have you *both* first. Does that smooth these jealous feathers?"

The witches exchanged furious glances but nodded, unwilling to test the patience of their powerful new leader. "Shouldn't you address the assembly first?" Constance reminded him hesitantly.

"Let them wait. Let them fear me, as they fear the resurgence of the mounds, and with greater reason." His cruel laughter filled the air as he moved greedily to enjoy one of the many privileges of his newly won position.

The comforting progress of Molly's life, both within the dream and without, was rudely shattered one springtime afternoon by a call from Rita. August, ninety-four years old and always sickly of late, had taken a turn for the worse and, against his strenuous objections, Rita had decided to take him to the hospital, where she and Kerreya were anxiously awaiting the doctors' verdict. The boys' Uncle Rob had agreed to watch them indefinitely, but August was asking for Matthew, who had left no emergency number and was presumably miles from civilization. From the tremble in Rita's ordinarily strident voice, Molly knew they could lose the old man at any moment.

Panicked at the thought that her champion might miss this last opportunity to honor and thank his uncle, Molly squarely confronted her only true option and, before leaving the lab for the short ride to the hospital, stretched out on the lumpy sofa in the women's rest room and dreamed herself into Aaric's presence, where she quickly outlined the crisis, adding desperately, "I have to bring Matthew here, to the dream, and tell him what's going on. I couldn't live with myself if he missed saying goodbye to August. You'll have to make yourself invisible—*please!*—and then . . ." Her eyes filled with tears. "This is the *worst* possible time for him to find out. He'll realize everything, and he'll be furious. Poor Matthew . . . If August dies, he'll have enough to deal with without this."

"Calm yourself, Princess," Aaric soothed. "You need not bring your champion to the dream in order to summon him."

"Pardon?"

"You have the power, even while awake, to contact him."

For a moment her knees weakened with sheer relief and she had to lean into the sorcerer before whispering, "Oh, Aaric, are you sure? I haven't practiced it."

"Your control has improved. You are more than ready for this. Simply wake up. Then picture your champion in the eye of your mind and order him to come to you."

"And he'll hear me?"

"He will experience a sensation. A feeling that he must go to you. He will not suspect you are the origin. Wake up now and try. And, Princess?" He stroked her cheek with his fingertips and insisted, "I hope it is not the old man's time. I have heard the love in your voice for him, and it has touched me."

"It's Matthew I'm worried about, not me," she whispered. "And poor Kerry, and AJ, and . . ." She bit back a sob and hugged her mentor gratefully. "At least Matthew will have a chance to be there, if it happens. He'd be so grateful to you if he knew."

"Yes, he would shake my hand before he challenged me to a battle," Aaric agreed with a fond smile. "Go now, and concentrate. Summon your champion to your side."

Seven

"You must return me to my home and allow me to die with dignity," August Redtree was pleading softly. "This place means nothing to me. I cannot give up my spirit to it."

"Don't talk like that," Molly begged in return. "I left messages for Matthew at home and at the airport. He'll be here as soon as he can. Until then, just relax and get stronger. We need you, August."

"Molly's right, Uncle," Rita murmured. "You have to rest and cooperate with the doctors. They aren't going to let you die."

"To *let* me die?" The old man seemed dismayed by the thought. "If it is my time, who are they to forbid it? They are strangers to me. . . ." His voice trailed away as a soft, grateful smile lit his lips and he struggled unsuccessfully to lift his arms toward the doorway. "Matthew . . . my son. At last."

"Uncle!" The warrior crossed the room in three powerful strides. "Forgive me for being absent."

"You must get me out of here at once."

Matthew nodded. "Get his things together, Molly."

Rita's eyes were dark with anger. "Stay out of this, Matt! His condition's critical. He *needs* these doctors."

Matthew dismissed the objection, with a shrug. "I know you mean well, Rita, but we can't let him die here. It's disrespectful."

"He won't die! The doctors know what to do. *You* don't."

Molly patted August's shoulder, saddened to see the old man subjected to the endless bickering at so solemn a time. "Don't fight, you two," she warned softly.

Matthew flashed her a sheepish smile, then pulled Rita into a tender hug. "We're all worried, Sis, but we have to do what our uncle wants. We have to take him to the mounds."

"Mounds! Amulets!" the irate sister spat. "I've had enough of this legend nonsense. I'm warning you, Matthew Redtree."

"Calm down," Matthew scowled. "You'll upset our uncle. Just help Molly get his things."

"What I'll *get* is the guard." With one last glare Rita stormed from the room.

"Hurry, Valmain. There may not be much time."

"Matthew! Are you crazy? He's dying," Molly whispered tersely. "I agree we should take him out of here, but he should go back to his ranch, not the mounds. That's what he's been asking."

"We'll put the amulet on him," Matthew countered rapidly. "He's descended from Lost Eagle, too, remember? It'll work—I guarantee it—but we have to hurry."

Molly grabbed Kerreya, car seat and all, while Matthew threw his sweatshirt around the old man's shoulders and hoisted him. They had almost reached the elevator when Rita and a guard stepped into Matthew's path. Without hesitation the Valmain champion assumed a stance Molly recognized from her dream. His battle stance.

"My uncle never signed a damned thing," he growled. "This is false imprisonment. Do you want to get sued"—he advanced toward the guard menacingly—"or worse?"

The guard coughed and directed his attention to the frail old man in Matthew's arms. "Do you want to leave with him?"

"Yes," August confirmed. "This place means nothing to me."

The guard shrugged. "Sorry, Miss. The old guy wants to

go. But first"—his gaze shifted reluctantly back to Matthew—"there are papers to sign."

Molly had set the car seat on the ground and now laid her hand on the guard's shoulder, persuading, as strongly as she dared, "That can all wait, can't it?"

The man shrugged again. "I suppose."

It sent a shiver of excitement through her—persuasion! If only she could tell Matthew. Or Aaric! They'd be so proud. But there was no time for pride, or celebration. Not with August looking so pale, and the mounds so many hours away.

Rita, still choking on her anger, caught up with them as they reached the parking lot. "You'll need my car if you're going to go through with this insanity. Molly's is too small."

"Kerreya and I'll ride in the backseat with August so you two can fight all the way to the mounds just like last time," Molly informed them tersely. Without waiting for a response, she began to buckle the car seat into place, then reached out to help Matthew guide his uncle into a semi-reclined position at her side. "Rest, August," she cooed, cradling him gently. "We'll be there by morning."

As Molly had predicted, brother and sister argued almost nonstop for the first two hours, after which an exhausted, teary-eyed Rita fell asleep. Matthew drove in determined silence for another hour, then untied the amulet from his wrist and handed it back. "Here, Valmain, put this on him. Maybe as we get closer, it'll start working."

"We're hours away," she murmured, dutifully tying the leather thong to the frail wrist. "Don't get your hopes up, Matthew. He's sleeping for the moment but . . ." She met her husband's gaze in the rearview mirror. "Have you taken a good look at him, Matthew? The whites of his eyes are so bloodshot and yellow, and his skin is almost gray. It's almost as though he's already—"

"Don't say it!" Matthew ordered. "We'll make it. Remember last time? You and Rita thought I was wrong then, too, but we got there and you had Kerreya."

"That's a little different, don't you think? A birth, not a death. But," she added softly, "I hope you're right. I'd miss him so much now. I've gotten to know him a lot better these last few weeks, and I've seen how he holds your family together. And AJ and Robert adore him . . ." She sighed and fingered the amulet. To her surprise she thought she noticed a change—subtle, perhaps, but perceptible—in August's color. She stroked the silver spool again and this time there was no mistake. His appearance had improved— not dramatically, but definitely—and his breathing had become deeper and more regular. Molly glanced at her husband but his eyes had been on the road. He had noticed nothing.

With her heart pounding wildly, she pressed her fingertips onto the amulet and concentrated, forcing a rush of power, similar to the one that had fueled Kerreya's birth, to pour into the old man. This time the effect was nothing short of miraculous! Almost giddy, Molly silently chided Aaric, *Why didn't you ever tell me about this, Moonshaker?*

They didn't need the mounds! She was making a difference, right here and now, in August's condition. Her power was somehow transferable, through the amulet! She wanted to tell Matthew but was afraid to make him any more hopeful. But at least now there *was* hope, and so, for the next ten hours, while Rita and Kerreya slept, and Matthew drove like a madman, stopping only for gas, Molly and August struggled to maintain the fragile balance that could keep the man alive without destroying the witch, for it was becoming dangerously evident that there was a price to be paid for the phenomenon, and the price could be life itself.

By the time they had reached the vicinity of the mounds, Molly was weak and disoriented, holding onto consciousness by a slender thread of determination. Then the mounds themselves took over, strengthening the old man and liberating the depleted sorceress, who sank immediately into a deep, engulfing sleep.

* * *

Aaric was waiting for her, his sea-blue eyes aching with concern as he swept her limp form into his arms and carried her to the edge of a dream river. "Drink this." He cradled her close as he moistened her lips with cool, clear water. "Do not try to talk."

"Aaric . . . ," she moaned, struggling to hold on to her dream consciousness.

"I have been feeling the drain on your power, Princess, and I have cursed this prison that keeps me from springing to your side and protecting you. Tell me what has happened. Were you attacked?"

"No, no. Nothing like that. It was my magic . . ."

"Your magic?" he growled. "Are you saying your attempt to summon your champion caused this? How is that possible?"

Her mind was clearing and she could finally explain, "I kept August alive, Aaric. I'm sure of it. At first it seemed impossible, but then there was no doubt! And now that he's at the mounds, I can rest, and he's okay."

"You *what?*" The sorcerer's expression was dark with disbelief. "Have you lost your senses? Do you wish to leave the little princess motherless at such a young age?"

The richness of his anger stunned Molly. Still, it was clearly the product of love, and so she touched his face and smiled. "I'm okay, Moonshaker. I promise. I'd never desert Kerreya . . . or you."

"Dung," he mumbled. "You are toying with powers you will never understand. You have no control. You could have gone too far, and for what? That old man's time has come! Did he knowingly allow you to jeopardize your life for his?"

"He didn't even realize what was happening. Neither did Matthew."

"So?" He arched an eyebrow sharply. "Your champion has returned? Your summons worked?"

"Yes." She snuggled against him and confided, "It was unbelievable. After all these months of practicing! And I used persuasion on the hospital guard and I think *that* worked, too! I finally see what my powers can do."

"They can kill you! Do you see *that?* You could have died. Even now, you are pale and weak." The mournful tone had returned. "You must rest, Princess. Even using your dream power now is foolish. Go to sleep, here, in my arms. I will protect you."

She smiled gratefully. "I *am* tired. But I feel so good, Aaric. Let me enjoy all of this just a little."

"No." He took her face in his hand and insisted, "Promise me you will never transfer your power again. It is not for one such as you. Even Maya had to practice it for years. Promise me."

"No. I can't. Don't be angry, please."

"If you persist in this course, I want no responsibility. Perhaps I will even send myself away."

"No! Please, I need you. More than ever, now. You have to teach me to use this gift."

"It cannot be done. You will never have sufficient control. Someday you will kill yourself and me with you. Do you want that?"

"I can practice. Time and practice, remember?"

"For fire and wind!" he exploded. "Children's tricks. Even persuasion and summons, yes. With practice, those can be yours to play with as you will. But *not* transfer or infliction."

"Transfer . . . ," She savored the word, ignoring his disapproving glare. The thought that she could do this—transfer her wonderful magic to those in need—was almost more than she could fathom. "Do I always need the amulet to do it?"

"Yes. And if the old uncle had not been a kinsman of either Lost Eagle or Kerreya, the transfer would not have been successful," Aaric grumbled. "I see now that you are intent upon using this, and it concerns me, Princess. You must agree, at least, never to use such powers again without first speaking to me. Come to me for my advice."

"Yes. That I *will* promise. Gladly. I really did feel like I was in over my head during it," Molly admitted. "But it felt wonderful at the same time."

"Your touching wish to cure the sick and alleviate pain," he murmured sympathetically. "You have spoken of it so often. I know that you had to see your mother in helpless distress—twisted and in pain—for so many hours." He caressed her gently. "That memory will always haunt you. But this is not the answer, my Princess. You would be wiser to continue your study of your science and to achieve your goal in that way. This way will end in ruin."

"Not if I concentrate and practice. I should have been practicing these transfers from the start! What else didn't you tell me about?"

"This is all. You have your dream power. Fire and wind. Persuasion, confusion, transfer, and infliction."

"Tell me about confusion."

"It is an age-old power, rarely used, even in my day. It is limited, but with one significant advantage. It works flawlessly on witch, sorcerer, or wizard as well as common men."

"Wow!"

"If you choose to use it, you will engender confusion—disorientation?—in everyone within perhaps thirty strides. A single warrior, attacked by many, could find it useful." His mind seemed to wander momentarily to former pursuits. "I have, in fact, escaped certain death by confusing a band of warriors. Of course," he added hastily, "for one such as yourself, it is useless. One cannot pick and choose their targets, and more often than not, within thirty strides, you will have an ally or confederate whom you need—one whom you cannot afford to confuse or abandon."

"But if I were all alone in a room with an enemy . . . ?"

"Use persuasion, Princess. It is more easily directed. With it you can control your victim's thoughts. Confusion is imprecise."

"Would it work on you?"

"Forget all of this," he insisted. "Confusion was a lost art, even in my day. Even Maya could not master it."

"Then *I'll* master it! At least I'll be the best at something."

"You are the best at dreaming, Princess. Be content with that, and concentrate upon refining fire and wind."

"And persuasion?"

"Yes."

"And infliction?"

"No! It is *much* too dangerous. As is transference. Leave them be." He cupped her chin again and explained, "Your gift is the gift of dreaming. My gift is that of illusion, as you have seen. We are at our best when we recognize our limits. Now"—he released her chin and urged her to rest her cheek against his broad chest—"go to sleep. I will reprimand you further when your strength returns."

Molly giggled and relaxed completely against him. "I'm looking forward to it, but for now . . ." She yawned and began to drift.

As the sorcerer stroked his Princess's soft curls, he tried without success to deal with this new development—a development he recognized to be no less than catastrophic. This woman, with her soft heart and tender ways, who had harbored such pain over the suffering of her mother, now believed she had a way to avoid such tragedy in the future. Aaric knew better. He had lost friends and loved ones, despite his enormous talents, and had learned his limits again and again. Now the Princess would be forced to abide such humbling lessons, and to endure the despair and guilt that accompanied them. Worse, she might unwittingly endanger her very life to achieve the unreachable goals she was now setting for herself.

And even that was not the worst of it. Despite her claims that magic had disappeared from the land outside the dream, Aaric knew better. Even if the lakes were gone, which he doubted, there would be other enemies to take their place. There always were. And they would not look kindly on a new talent, especially one of so old and honored a breed as that of the mounds. For fire and wind, and even persuasion, the drain was slight, and the chance of discovery slighter. But if this woman now chose to wield her powers for more flamboyant causes, it would only be a matter of time before she would be detected. Detected, despised, and destroyed.

For the first time Aaric truly wished the Valmain Princess had told her champion everything, regardless of the risks. For all of his faults, the warrior called Matthew Redtree was out *there*, ready to protect her bravely from any danger—assuming he could see the danger in time. While it had been a source of pleasure and pride for Aaric to be the warrior to whom she turned in her dreams for amusement and advice, and yes, even for love, he could no longer afford to indulge himself. Not unless he was willing to risk her and the little one, and he was not.

He would have given anything, his powers included, to call this woman his wife; to call her wondrous child his daughter; above all, to be her champion, and to make love to her as he had done one glorious day so long ago.

But that had been just a dream. Nothing was real, nor would it ever be for him. Aaric the Moonshaker did not exist. He was an illusion. So why did he feel things so deeply? Why did she touch him so? Why did he ache with love, and with jealousy?

"You are my nemesis, Son of Lost Eagle," he chided Matthew softly. "You are the son of my old enemy, and the lover of the woman I would have for my own. I should hate you, and in truth there is a part of me that does, but I have also admired you for your skill—for the endless hours of unselfish training—and I have admired your loyalty to our woman, and your bravery. Can it be that you do not appreciate the danger? The lakes are out there with you, warrior. If only they were here, with me in this dream, so that I could deal with them in the age-old ways. Instead, it falls to you, and for all your devotion, you are ignorant and unready."

His Princess shifted against him in her sleep, as though comforted by the sound of his voice. With a tortured smile he murmured, "I have taught you too well, my stubborn student. If only your champion could break past your defenses and invade this dream. He would be angry, and he would challenge me, and we would fight. But I would find some way to make him listen to me, and together we would find a way to protect you." Raising his eyes to stare at the largest of the three dream mounds, he intoned, softly yet insistently, "Keep trying, Son of Lost Eagle. Struggle against her power. Be vigilant despite her stubbornness. The future of the mounds rests with me and my ability to train her, but there is no future—for the mounds or for any of us—without you and your damnable protection, and so you must come, and we must fight one last time, and you must be her champion in all worlds before it is too late."

Constance Sheridan watched in haughty delight as the assembled witches and wizards filed past her one by one. Fox—magnificent, insatiable Fox—had instructed them to leave so that he and "our extraordinary Constance" could be alone to discuss a "vital matter." It could only mean one thing—he intended to keep his promise and to make her his bride! She was free of Boston and motherhood at last!

"That was quite a celebration, wasn't it?" the new First Wizard murmured seductively in her ear.

"An orgy worthy of a master, which of course you are,"

she gushed. "Thank you for honoring me with your attention."

"I cherish you," he insisted. "You are the most valuable witch in the entire assembly. It pains me greatly to see you return to Boston."

She moistened her lips, stunned and disbelieving. *Boston?*

"Your husband will grow suspicious if you are absent much longer. And with suspicion, his paternal instinct might break through your love spell. That would be a disaster for us."

Constance stared, dumbfounded at Fox's audacity. Did he *dare* betray her? After she had risked her very existence to gain him his newfound position?

"I need you in Boston for just a little while longer," he was explaining smoothly. "Your beauty depends on your obedience to Maya's instructions. You must see that the betrayal of the Valmain heiress continues. And"—his eyes dared her to protest—"you must be there when the warrior arrives."

"The warrior?" For a moment she truly did not understand, then she demanded impatiently, "Are you referring to the warrior Maya said she was sending to help me? That's absurd, Fox! He's not coming! If he were, he'd be here by now. I've waited, bored out of my mind, and he hasn't come. Maya was overly ambitious, thinking she could send us both."

"And if she had sent him? Do you think she would have armed him with magic?"

Constance studied the wizard carefully. There was more to this than he was saying. "Yes," she answered finally. "She would have armed him with magic. Why do you ask?"

"Would she have sent a sorcerer?"

"Of course not." Impatience had crept into her tone. "If she were sending a sorcerer, she wouldn't have needed me! It was my job to use my magic to engender betrayal. The warrior's only job was to defeat the Valmain champion. She would have armed him with a defensive charm, or perhaps an amulet at the most."

"Exactly!" Fox crowed. "You have given force to my theory, Constance. Now listen, and you will see that your return to Boston is not the idle whim of a tyrant." His voice grew soft with urgency. "Someone is using magic, here in North America, without our approval."

"Impossible." When his gaze didn't waver, she added quietly, "You're certain? You've accounted for everyone?"

"Not for the silly nonsense of casual witches, of course," he shrugged. "But this disturbance, while sporadic, has real power behind it. Someone's drawing magic, either through a channel or by natural talent. I suspect the former. If it were a true magician, the draws would be more steady, and certainly more frequent. Still, we must investigate."

"Of course. But what does that have to do with my going to Boston?"

"Some of the others, including Crane, believe the old prophecies. They believe that one day the twins who established the mounds will return. That would be inconvenient, wouldn't it?"

Constance smiled reluctantly. "A bit. But we would crush them again."

"True. If anyone tried to establish a new power base here, we would crush them. Assuming we had the opportunity."

"All the more reason to keep me here! I know more about the mounds than any of you! If the twins came back, or if someone began using a mounds channel . . ." Her eyes widened as the truth hit her squarely in midsentence.

Fox nodded his approval. "My thoughts exactly. Perhaps Maya's warrior has come through time, with a charm or channel, and is using it to draw power from the mounds."

Constance took a deep breath and nodded. "That makes sense, I suppose. Maya didn't know her people would be destroyed by now. She would have instructed the warrior to defeat the Valmain champion and then join his descendants in the shadow of the mounds. Without those descendants he has possibly become a renegade, using the channel with no accountability. Which means"—her eyes grew bright with reluctant respect—"Maya managed to do everything she wanted. I thought it was simply a boast. I didn't believe she had the skill to send us both."

"She must have been an astonishing woman," Fox agreed. "It's a pity she didn't come here herself, instead of sending you. I would have enjoyed subjugating her."

Constance bit back a sneer. Did this fool think it would be so easy to subdue Maya? Fox had never had the misfortune to tangle with a mounds sorceress, and he couldn't know how powerful they could be. It would be amusing to watch! He would win, of course—he had the power of the assembly behind him, after all—but first Maya would teach him a lesson! Of course, the arrival of a mounds sorceress such as Maya would complicate things in Constance's own life a bit more than she could handle, and so she would not wish for such amusement. "If the warrior is here, he may still be confused. Perhaps he didn't come to Boston. The Valmain kingdom was across the untraveled sea, Fox, and that's where I expected to awaken after my journey. If that's where the warrior was sent, he learned quite quickly that the kingdom was destroyed, and so he must have headed directly for the mounds, hoping to find his people's descendants thriving there. When he arrived, he must have been devastated."

"Still, even though the civilization is gone, his channel would draw power."

"And he'll become intoxicated by it. He'll be easy to find. Let me go to the mounds and investigate. I'd recognize him more quickly than anyone else."

"And he would recognize you."

"Not if you allowed me to use our illusion power."

Fox shrugged. "If the disturbances continue, I'll go myself. I want that channel."

"You won't be able to use it. Their technique always involved kinspells," she countered firmly.

"If we cannot bend it to our will, we will destroy it. The last vestige of mounds power, crushed under *my* fist."

"And then will you free me from my exile?"

"Perhaps." His smile grew dangerously wide. "If you obey me well in all things, I might even kill the daughter for you."

"Kill Niki?" Constance licked her lips, unsure of how to react. "You are considering that?"

Fox burst into laughter. "Why would I kill your child? She may be half-human, but there is always the chance she may have some small talent at witchcraft. As First Wizard I would never lightly reduce our numbers." His grin told Constance he was all too aware of her feelings for her daughter. Then he sobered slightly and explained, "Your mission for Maya will be successfully completed only when the betrayal between father and daughter cannot be healed. If your stepdaughter were to die mysteriously, the rift would become irreversible."

"Oh!" Constance's heart leaped at the thought. "What a brilliant idea! Let's do it right away!"

"Patience," he chuckled. "For now, we'll concentrate on solidifying my power and tracing the source of the unauthorized practice. When the time comes for the daughter's death, it must not be by your hand, do you understand?" Moving his fingers slyly to the tiny pearl buttons on her silk blouse, he promised, "I will be your knight in shining armor and deliver you from exile, all for just a kiss. Or perhaps"—his eyes began to glow with red-hot lust—"something a bit more elaborate."

Constance closed her eyes and dutifully groaned Fox's name, but it was Maya's warrior that she craved as her body began to gyrate. How daring he was! Wielding magic through use of a charm or amulet without thought to the dangers and consequences. He had discovered that Valmain no longer existed, of course, and had seen no need to seek out Constance. If only he had! She might have taken him as a lover, protected him, and allowed him to use his charm to pleasure her. After all, he was from her own time, and she longed for someone who knew the old stories and ways, and who could appreciate her. What a shame he had chosen, instead, to become a renegade. Now Fox would travel to the mounds, find him, and kill him. Then he'd destroy the magical charm, and the last link to her old world would be gone forever.

But at least she would be free of marriage and motherhood! Once the warrior was dead, Fox would seek out and kill Molly Sheridan Redtree. On that day the betrayal would be permanent, the spell of beauty would be immutable, and Alex and Niki would be out of her life for good. It was the most arousing thought she had had in months, enabling her to service her wizard with the greedy abandon he so cruelly and consistently demanded.

"Matthew?"

"Hey, Valmain, you're awake." Jumping to his feet, he left Kerreya playing on the floor and moved to Molly's bedside. "You fell asleep in the car. You looked so exhausted, I didn't have the heart to wake you."

"August . . . ?"

"He's fine. He and Rita are in the next room." He pressed his lips to her fingertips. "The amulet saved him, Molly."

"That's so wonderful." She struggled into a sitting position. "You look worried. Are you sure he's okay?"

"He's fine. It's you I'm worried about. You were so pale and listless when I carried you in. I think this new job and the baby-sitting all night are exhausting you."

"No, Matthew. I feel wonderful. I promise." She had to struggle not to reveal her elation over the experience with the amulet. "I was just worried about August."

"You're sure? Really?"

"Absolutely. I've never felt better."

"Well, then . . ." He cleared his throat. "There's something I want to discuss with you. If you're sure you're up to it."

"Let me guess. You want to move here permanently?" Her smile was flirtatious. "You're very predictable, Son of Lost Eagle. Luckily, I find that arousing. And"—she allowed the blanket to slip down, revealing her naked breasts—"you undressed me while I was sleeping. I love it when you do that."

He smiled reluctantly. "I've never done that before."

"Well, believe me, I like it. But next time wake me up so I can enjoy it." She glanced toward Kerreya, who was cheerfully rolling an ice bucket across the room. "Too bad we have an audience."

"A very talkative audience," he agreed, somewhat obliquely. "You'll never guess what new word she said while you were sleeping." When Molly's smile faded, he intoned sternly, "Your secret's out, and, believe me, it was like a knife in my heart."

"Mat-Matthew," she stammered. "Try not to overreact. Try to remember how complicated everything is . . . was . . . has been between us all from the start . . ."

"Hey, Valmain, I'm not mad or anything." His tone was amazingly apologetic. "You really are frazzled, aren't you?"

She stared for a moment, then whispered, "You're taking this so well. I thought you'd be furious."

"Furious?" He shrugged. "Disappointed, yes, but not furious. I just didn't think you'd let her eat cookies at her age."

"Cookies?" she repeated, now completely confused.

"Don't play innocent, Valmain," he chuckled. "She said it distinctly. 'Cookie.' I couldn't believe my ears. One minute she's having only breast milk and pureed fruits, the next minute she's saying cookie."

"Cookie?"

"That's right. Junk food at nine months. What's the story? And"—he shifted closer—"it'd better be good."

She smiled in pure relief. "Cookie isn't cookie, Matthew. It's graham cracker. AJ and Robert have them after school every day with milk or pudding, or yogurt. And Rita asked permission to let Kerry have a little taste, and she adores them. And, believe me, no one overdoes it. Between Robert, the future doctor, and AJ, the fanatic-in-training, Rita and I don't get away with much of anything."

"Graham crackers?"

"You've got to let go," Molly teased, now completely recovered from the pseudo-disaster. "She's going to be a year old in a couple of months. Someday soon she'll be going to school, then dating boys with strange haircuts, then—"

"Stop." He cringed in feigned horror. "I can't take it." When Molly laughed, he joined her ruefully. "Graham crackers, huh? That sounds pretty harmless. In fact"—his smile was wistful—"it sounds familiar. I think my mom used to serve those to me and Rita after school, before we went to live with Uncle August." He glanced toward his daughter, then back at Molly. "She adores them, you say?"

"Absolutely. Second only to breast milk, and that's saying a lot."

"Do you think I could find them in that little store down the street?"

"Without a prescription?"

"Cute, Valmain." He jumped to his feet. "Hey, Kerry, want to go to the store and get some cookies?"

"Matthew?"

"Yeah?"

"Just one each."

He grinned, scooped his daughter into his arms, and was gone. Resisting an urge to return to the dream and tell Aaric of the close call, Molly rolled out of bed, dressed in a cozy white warm-up suit, and hurried next door to check on the patient.

Eight

August was sitting up in bed and, when he caught sight of Molly, his smile radiated such strength and delight that she almost burst into tears of relief as she hugged him. "You look so good!"

"I thought my time had come," he admitted quietly.

"Not for years," she protested. "We need you too much."

"Just the same, you must prepare yourself, dream girl. You haven't known death since the loss of your mother. You must learn to accept it, if only because it will continue to take loved ones from you, until the day when it takes you yourself. You must see it as a natural event, and a peaceful one. Perhaps even a fortuitous one."

"Never." She regretted her defiance immediately and added, "I agree it's natural, but let's not rush it, okay? Come and live with me, so I can take care of you."

"I wish to spend my remaining days at the ranch."

"Forget it, Molly," Rita advised dryly. "I've been trying all morning, but he's as stubborn as Matt." Her gaze fell on the amulet on her uncle's wrist. "Do you think that thing really saved his life?" Before Molly could answer, she shook her long, dark hair and laughed. "Listen to me! I almost joined the cult!" With a wave of her hand, she moved toward the door. "I'm going for some ice. Will you stay here with him 'til I get back?"

"My pleasure."

When his niece had left, August took Molly's hand and

insisted, "I've told Rita I don't wish to be kept alive, by doctors *or* by amulets. I've had every experience a man should hope to have, and I'm content. You must help Matthew to understand this. When my time comes, next time, I'll ask to remain at my ranch, and I'll expect you all to cooperate. It will be my last request, and you must honor it."

"There's plenty of time to talk about that," Molly protested. "For now, just enjoy your grandnephews and grandniece."

"Where is the little angel?"

"With Matthew, eating cookies! Can you believe it? Matthew Redtree, being decadent?"

"The demands of destiny have deprived him of many simple pleasures," August admitted pensively.

The comment intrigued her. "Simple pleasures? Like romance? Were *you* ever in love, August?"

"Yes. More than once."

"Does Matthew know?"

He smiled weakly. "He has little patience with love stories. He prefers tales of battle."

She bit her lip, then demanded, "Don't you think that's a shame? Matthew loved me before he even met me. Don't you think he's missing out on one of those experiences you talked about a minute ago? The ones every man should hope to have before he dies? He never got to fall in love."

"Instead, he has had an experience few men are privileged to have."

"A dream girl?" She grimaced.

"That is correct. The dream, and you, and the chance to meet an ancient warrior, and to avenge an age-old wrong. These experiences are unique. He has missed nothing." His eyes sought hers. "Can you say the same? Or, do you have regrets?"

"Regrets?" she sighed. "If I had to choose—between meeting Matthew, or falling in love the traditional way—I'd choose Matthew, of course. And the dream, and meeting Aaric, and Maya . . ."

"Then be content. There are many kinds of love, after all, and you have known most of them in your short life."

"Many kinds of love," she mused. "Aaric said that to me once."

"He was correct." August's eyes narrowed. "Do you sometimes miss the company of the Moonshaker?"

"Pardon?"

He chuckled and patted her hand. "A foolish question. Forgive me. And now"—his eyes closed—"I need a moment's rest. Will you sit with me, dream girl, and keep me company?"

"Of course," she whispered. "We love you so much, August. Thanks for sticking around for a while."

He smiled without opening his eyes. "I see now why I had to stay. We had to have this conversation. And now"—one eye peeked out at her—"perhaps you will rest more easily. You may even have your dream again."

"Who needs the dream?" she scoffed. "All I need is my family, and I have that. Just sleep and get better, okay? When Kerry gets back, she's going to want to visit you."

"That will be a delight," he murmured, then his breathing steadied and sleep overtook him.

Molly watched in wonder, remembering the tense, exhilarating tug-of-war, between his life force and her own, that had taken place so recently. So miraculously. As she sat and stared down at the gentle man, she vowed to find more ways to use her wondrous powers.

"Valmain? Is he okay?"

"Oh!" She jumped to her feet. "I didn't hear you. Where's Kerry?"

"She's right behind me, with Rita. She wants to nurse."

"And when she's done," Rita's voice announced mischievously from the doorway, "I'm giving you two a whole hour alone together as a reward for saving my uncle."

Molly shot her sister-in-law a grateful smile. "The perfect gift."

"Right," Matthew enthused. "We'll go to the mounds. I've been wanting a chance to talk, undisturbed."

"Talk?" Rita scoffed. "You haven't seen your wife in weeks, Matt. I think she'd rather have a kiss."

"No problem." He moved to Molly's side and touched his lips to her cheek, then hoisted Kerreya into her arms. "I'm going to run ahead, Valmain, for a little exercise, while you feed the baby. When you're done, drive out to meet me."

"Matthew, wait!" She caught his wrist and insisted, "Don't go running around without the amulet. Deborah could come back, or someone else. Please put it on."

"I can't, Valmain. What if my uncle gets worse?"

"He's stable, Matt," Rita assured her brother dourly. "Go ahead and take your toy."

Matthew hesitated, then slipped the thong off August's thin wrist, securing it to his own. He took a deep breath, as though momentarily engulfed by the rush of power, then patted Kerreya's head and headed for the door.

"He's one of a kind," Rita drawled when he'd disappeared.

"That's true." Molly cuddled her nursing daughter close.

"Amulets and mounds." The dark-haired nurse expertly took her sleeping uncle's pulse, then collapsed onto the empty second bed and teased, "You and Matt were made for each other. We heard about you for years, Molly. The dream girl with the curly hair. It's romantic, in a bizarre sort of way."

"I suppose. It would have been nice the other way, too, though. August and I were just talking about that," Molly sighed. "Falling in love. Matthew never got to do that. He came into this relationship with his feelings already in place and"—her voice caught in her throat—"those feelings have never changed."

"That's good, right?" Rita pursed her lips and added thoughtfully, "I guess I see what you're saying. I remember how Jesse was, in the early days, when *he* was falling for me. He used to sing to me, and bring me roses, and panic whenever he saw me within five feet of any other guy . . ." As though suddenly inspired, she sat up and announced, "You're right! You and Matt *should* have that. You know what you need?"

"What?"

"A second honeymoon." With a frown she demanded, "Did you ever even have a *first* one?"

"We were supposed to go to Paris, but we ended up on Easter Island, remember?"

Her sister-in-law winced. "That's pitiful. You have to insist on a better one, right away. Leave Kerry with me, and go to some hideaway, drink wine, make love on deserted beaches . . ."

Molly shook her head. "Matthew hates trips like that. He wants to explore."

"Fine. Let him explore you," Rita teased. "Buy a sexy new wardrobe—anything but white!—and drive him wild. You've got the body for it, Molly. Use it." Her dark eyes were twinkling with inspiration. "Go shopping with my neighbor Tori. You've seen *her* clothes, right?"

Molly smiled at the reference. Tori, a skinny would-be actress with a wild mane of red hair, had an almost daily habit of washing her car in front of her house while clad only in a bikini, a habit which alternately fascinated and embarrassed Robert and AJ.

If only it were that easy to catch Matthew's eye. Shaking her head, Molly reminded herself that she had tried all such tactics, only to be told, quite gently by Matthew, that he preferred her in white; that she didn't need sexy dresses, because it was her purity that made her beautiful; and, above all, they didn't need "props," because the love they shared was so deep and so complete. True romance to Matthew was sleeping under the stars with his dream girl, preferably at the mounds, with the amulet charged and the promise of magic in the air. . . .

"Molly?"

"Oh, sorry." She shook her head and shifted a dozing Kerreya to her second breast. "I was thinking about your neighbor. She's the same age as me, did you know that? But she seems like a kid, and I seem like a dud."

"She's a flake at twenty-four and she'll be a flake at fifty," Rita grinned. "I'm not telling you to act like her, just *dress* like her occasionally. She may be a flake, but she knows men." A rueful laugh bubbled in her throat and she added, "Maybe we *both* should take lessons from her. I'm in worse shape than you. At least Matt comes home regularly. With Jesse . . ."

Molly smiled sympathetically but said nothing. What *could* she say? Three years was too long to wait, yet from the wistful glow in Rita's eyes when she had discussed their courtship, she simply was not yet ready to let go.

And Rita was right about one thing. Matthew was here, and she intended to take advantage of that, and so she carefully laid her daughter onto the bed, kissed her cheek, and headed for the mounds.

The sight never failed to seduce her—her champion, so lean and handsome, standing proudly in the shadow of the mounds he loved with all his heart. With the amulet on his wrist, he was indefatigable, both physically and emotionally, and his confidence radiated like warmth, beguiling and inspiring her despite her best intentions. Now she moved eagerly into his arms, willing to be overwhelmed by the energy and determination of this wondrous fanatic.

His kiss was fiery, as it always was when the amulet fueled him, and Molly surrendered to it, allowing the heat to spread from her hungry mouth throughout her trembling body. As his hands caressed her breasts, skillful fingertips took inventory of every impressionable nerve ending, totally focused on pleasing her, and she was too weak with anticipation to wish he might be more selfish, if only to prove he was as needy as she.

"We belong here, Valmain," he groaned, pulling her to the ground. "How can you deny it?"

"Deny?" she gasped. "Who's denying? Make love to me, Matthew. Don't ever stop."

"In broad daylight? Someone could come . . ."

"No one will come!" she insisted, pawing at the muscled chest under his damp shirt as she spoke. "No one ever comes here but us. Us, and of course"—she roused herself slightly from the erotic euphoria—"Deborah, armed and dangerous. I guess we *should* stop."

"We'll camp here tonight," he promised, "and it'll be better than anything you've ever imagined."

"Really?" She rested her cheek against his shoulder and waited for her breathing to return to normal. "Promise?"

"Yeah. And for now, we need to talk anyway. There's something important we have to discuss."

"Oh? Did Kerry say another bad word?"

"Hardly," Matthew chuckled. "She just kept asking for AJ and Robert. I guess they're getting to be close cousins. I like that." He cleared his throat and added, "Something happened when I was in Mexico, Molly. Something incredible. We need to talk about it, and I need for you to listen with an open mind. You'll say it was just my imagination, but I know it wasn't."

Curious, she lifted her face to his and was instantly enchanted by the glittery display of gold in his eyes. She had seen this look before. In fact, she had been seduced by it, more than once, and even now could scarcely resist it. "Tell me," she whispered. "I'll believe you if I can."

He smiled gratefully. "I was examining those spearheads I told you about, and I was concentrating completely, and then suddenly, it was like you had reached out and beckoned to me. I didn't hear your voice, exactly, and there weren't any words, but the feeling was so real . . ."

The trust in his eyes, more beautiful even than the gold dust, captivated her, and she knew she had to give him this, at the very least. She owed him this, after all his dedication. He was the Valmain champion, and his love affair with magic had been mandated, centuries earlier, by destiny itself. "I believe you, Matthew."

"Huh?"

She enjoyed his sincere disbelief for a few seconds before repeating, gently, "I believe you, because that's exactly what happened." Touching his lips with her fingertips, she explained, "We had no way of reaching you, and I couldn't bear the thought you might not get to say goodbye to August, so I . . . I just made you come home. Don't ask me how I did it. I just did."

He nodded, as though slightly dazed. "I know. I just didn't know *you* knew! You're saying you did it consciously? Summoned me?" When she nodded, he exclaimed, "Just like you summoned Angela to the dream! Do you understand that, Molly? You used your magic to send for me, and I heard you, thousands of miles away!" Jumping to his feet, he pulled her to her own and then hugged her joyously. "Do you have any idea what this means? You affirmatively used your magic! You can reach me, wherever I am, day or night! It's incredible!"

She laughed lightly when he began to pace, talking as much to himself as to her, outlining all of the marvelous ramifications of this miraculous development. He was in heaven, pure and simple, and she didn't care if this eventually led to her downfall. If he began to suspect, belatedly, that she had greater access to her magic than she had let on, she would have to live with that. It was worth the risk. Seeing him this way—animated and deliriously happy for the first time since Kerreya's birth—was worth any price.

"We'll practice, of course," he was insisting eagerly.

"Over short distances, and with different messages, although I'm pretty sure we can't refine it into anything more than a sensation, but believe me, Valmain, that sensation was *so* strong, it was like you reached into my brain and squeezed it with your hand! And once we've practiced, I'll go back to Mexico, to wrap things up, and we'll set a specific time, right? For you to contact me. We'll synchronize our watches, and if it happens again, over all that distance . . ." His pacing stopped abruptly and again he pulled her into his arms. "Let's try it. Right now. Here . . ." Kneeling before her, he took her hands in his own, urging her to kneel down and join him. When they were staring into each others eyes, he directed softly, "Summon me."

"But you're so close," she murmured, aroused by the nearness of him. "It doesn't make sense."

His lips brushed hers, then he repeated, in a voice filled with both awe and authority, "Summon me, Molly. Use your birthright to reach out to me. I want to feel it again. I *need* to feel it."

Almost mesmerized now, she moistened her lips, closed her eyes, and pictured him, as Aaric had taught her. But the picture was not of a twentieth century man in jeans and a white polo shirt. Rather, she pictured the warrior that lived in his soul, complete with a shoulder-length mane of lustrous black hair and high, windburned cheekbones. The image of the Son of Lost Eagle—the Valmain champion—so sharp and hot that it made her almost dizzy with desire.

Her eyes remained closed, even when he softly spoke her name. Even when his rough fingertips brushed a teardrop from her cheek. Then his hands rested on her waist, pulling her close. "I could see you, Valmain. You were wearing your cape . . ."

"I know." She tried to smile as she finally met his gaze. "It's the magic, I guess."

"It's the magic," he repeated, clearly as subdued as she. "You touched me. You made me ache to be with you . . ."

"I felt it, too," she confessed in breathless wonder. "Like I was touching your soul, Matthew. Last time . . ."

"I know." One hand moved up, slowly, until it was cupping her chin. "Last time there was such urgency. But this time . . ." Seemingly at a loss for words, he chose to kiss her lips carefully, as though afraid he could damage her, or the moment, or both.

Now utterly seduced, Molly draped her arms around his neck while her tongue encouraged his mouth to savor her more thoroughly. He hesitated for only a moment, then pulled her to the soft green grass of the mounds and began to caress her, first through the soft white lace of her sundress and then under it, his hands seeking and finding the soft, damp folds that had grown so warm with need of him. Sliding her lace panties quickly down her legs, he stripped off his jeans and entered her without the usual, complex rituals, as though the simple act of joining had become his only purpose.

As he filled her with his love, Molly's long legs wrapped around him and her arms stretched outward, pleading for his mouth to return to her own. When he kissed her, it was a kiss filled with such adoration and passion that their loins began to throb in unison, a gentle, hypnotic throbbing unlike any they could remember. Movement seemed unnecessary—almost perilous—to the subtle balance of sensation and need that their gentle spasms were maintaining. Then Matthew groaned—a low, confused groan of manly need—and a dam of raw, unnamed yearning broke, flooding them both as they began to move together. Madly. Desperately. Joyously, until they climaxed together in one last rush of sensation and appreciation and, when finally each was satiated and still, they lay in one another's arms, their lips barely touching, their eyes wide with gratitude, their hearts beating in steady unison while each silently relived the summons, and the images, and the magic that had been gifted to them as a reward for their enslavement to destiny.

It was Matthew who managed to speak first, and while his voice was shaky, it was filled with determination. "I'll wrap things up in Mexico as quickly as I can. When I get back we'll practice night and day. We can't let this pass us by again."

"Night and day," Molly repeated, stretching slowly and sensuously. "I'm for that."

It brought a proud grin to his face. "I meant, practice your magic, not sex. Magic is the goal here, Valmain."

"As long as making love is the reward, I'm sold," she laughed. "I love seeing you this way, Son of Lost Eagle. Your eyes are so gold they're almost other-worldly."

"*Your* eyes," he countered firmly, "are filled with magic. Incredible magic. It's always been there, but we couldn't access it. Now, at last, we've found a way. Don't try to fight it, and don't be afraid of it, okay?"

"I'm not afraid of anything when you hold me," she assured him, molding herself hungrily to his lean, hard form. "Just kiss me, Matthew, and tell me you're hopelessly in love with me, and I'll never ask for anything else."

"Ask for the world," he countered, his voice resounding with confidence. "It's all at your feet now, Valmain. This world"—his arm swept to encompass the mounds—"and the other one, in your dreams. It's destiny's gift to you through me."

But I didn't ask for the world, she reprimanded him in wistful silence. *I asked you to tell me you're in love with me. Without that, the world is empty for me, and so are destiny's gifts.*

"Did you trick me, Moonshaker?"

The sorcerer shrugged. "We had no choice. Matthew had to be informed of the old uncle's condition. You had to use your summons power."

"That's true." She eyed him with amusement. "But you told me he'd never suspect I was the source."

"I was wrong."

"Except, you're never wrong," she reminded him playfully. "And now it's just a matter of time before he figures out the rest, right? I think you planned it this way. You want us to have a big argument. And you want him to come storming into this dream so you can have your chance for a rematch with him."

"It is long overdue." He shrugged. "And this time I would easily defeat him. Speaking of which"—his blue eyes began to twinkle—"did your summons cause him intense pain?"

"Pain?" She flushed, remembering the pleasure that the second summons had precipitated. But the first . . . What was it Matthew had said? "He said he could almost hear my voice. And something about me reaching into his brain and squeezing . . ." She grimaced slightly. "Are you saying I hurt him? Why didn't you warn me? I used every ounce of power I could summon . . ."

The sorcerer was laughing heartily. "I'm surprised he survived. There were times when a summons from Maya could actually cause me to double over with distress."

"And other times . . . ?" When he didn't seem to understand, she prodded, "Weren't there other times when she'd summon you gently, and it would feel . . . nice?"

"A summons can be weak or strong, but never pleasant," Aaric shrugged. "The suffering is unavoidable, Princess, which is the reason a magician never summons a loved one without good reason."

"I see." She moistened her lips pensively. If that was true, how would Aaric explain the gently erotic experience she and Matthew had shared on the mounds? Had she tapped into some power other than summoning? One Aaric had not yet explained to her? Or perhaps one Aaric didn't even know existed!

"Do not concern yourself, Princess. The pain of a summons is only momentary and never causes permanent injury. You did what you had to do, to bring Matthew to his mentor's deathbed. It was unavoidable, just as bringing him here one day will be unavoidable."

"Seeing him these last two days, in seventh heaven over my witchcraft, has made me almost eager to tell him the whole thing and be done with it."

"You have learned to trust his love?"

"Trust? Love?" She shook her head. "I've just decided he's too obsessed to stay away from me forever. I'm the dream girl, right? And he's the champion. That's his whole life. He won't turn his back on it."

"On it? Do you not mean, on you?"

"Me? I'm irrelevant," she quipped.

The sorcerer frowned. "When you speak this way, it alarms me, Princess. If you are unhappy—"

"Me? What do I have to be unhappy about? I have a big strong husband who worships the ground I walk on, and a bigger stronger teacher who adores me"—she paused to kiss his cheek—"and a beautiful daughter, a great boss, and"— the flippant tone softened into true appreciation—"August is doing better every day. Really, Aaric, I'd be crazy to be dissatisfied, so I've decided to be deliriously happy, just like Matthew."

"That is dung."

She grinned mischievously. "Watch your language. All I need is for Kerry to say that to Matthew when he gets home."

Aaric chuckled reluctantly. "When will that be?"

"In a couple of weeks. And then, of course, he plans on training me night and day. Which means I've got to get as much done at work as possible while I can. I've got meetings with Dr. Lewis scheduled for every single evening this week."

"You are working too hard. Perhaps your mood is the result of such weariness."

Molly nodded. Despite a few lingering misgivings over

the lack of hearts-and-flowers-style romance in her life, she was basically content, and regretted having burdened Aaric so frivolously. "I'll see you tomorrow night, Moonshaker," she promised, kissing his cheek lightly and returning to her bed just in time to hear the alarm that signaled the beginning of another hectic day.

Twelve hours later she was flying up the steps to Rita's house, worried that her late return from her evening meeting would inconvenience AJ. Of course, the eleven-year-old would be sweet about it and she would then feel doubly guilty for taking advantage of his generosity as a baby-sitter. He was so gentle and responsible for his years that Molly had come to rely on him as much as she had Rita.

She bounded into the living room and stopped short, confronted by a stranger—a stranger who was strangely familiar. Tall, dark, and powerfully built, he was dressed in black jeans and a maroon muscle shirt worn tight across a rippling chest. His five-o'clock shadow and the tattoo of a crossbow on his bulging upper arm served as warnings to her, although she wasn't sure of just what they warned.

She was staring and she knew it, but somehow was unable to stop. He was physically imposing in a way the men in her life, with the exception of Aaric, had never been, and he had, without a doubt, the most devastatingly handsome smile she had ever seen—wide, playful, and completely decadent. His chocolate-brown eyes were traveling lazily over her body and, to her mortification, she wanted him to like what he saw! Then she brought herself sharply back into line and managed a neutral smile. "Hello."

"Let me guess," he drawled. "You're Matt's little dream girl, right?"

"And you're Jesse?" she managed to counter.

"Guilty." His eyes played over her again, this time with open admiration. "Look at you. All legs and eyes. Just my type." With a conspiratorial wink he confided, "Know what turns me on quicker than just about anything, Auntie Molly?"

"Looking in the mirror?"

To her chagrin he roared with good-natured laughter. "I didn't know Matt liked his women so bratty!" Stepping to within inches of her, he took her arm and urged her toward the sofa. "Come on in and make yourself comfortable. But"—his tone dropped seductively—"you'd better stop staring at me with those big blue eyes, or I just might have to fall in love with you."

Nine

"Make yourself comfortable," Jesse Camacho repeated cheerfully. "Want a beer?"

"No, thank you," Molly sniffed, pulling her elbow free.

"A cigarette?" He grinned when she frowned. "Sit down. Let's get acquainted. I bet Matt's told you all kinds of interesting stories about me."

Molly's eyes narrowed. "Where are the boys? They were watching my daughter."

"Yeah. What's her name? Karen? Cries a lot, doesn't she?"

"Not usually." Molly took a deep breath. "Where are they?"

"Relax," he advised, slouching onto the couch. "My kids took her for a walk. All that crying was getting on my nerves. It was a hell of a homecoming," he added with a rueful chuckle. "For a minute I thought she might be *Rita's* kid."

Molly stiffened. So, Matthew had been right all along. Jesse Camacho didn't deserve to be a part of Rita's life, but here he was and she had a sinking feeling Rita was going to be ecstatic. It was, therefore, imperative to fix things, just as Aaric had suggested. Remembering the sense of wonder and exhilaration that had accompanied her use of magic on August, she surveyed her next victim with cautious determination.

He was handsome, just as Rita frequently claimed—brawny, with dark skin and darker hair. Rugged and independent at best, lazy and undependable at worst. As the witch

studied him, he lit a cigarette, then offered her one mischievously.

"So, Jesse," she began smoothly. "Does Rita know you're
back?"

"No. The kids said she'll be home around midnight."

"Right. And she'll be so excited." Molly settled onto the
couch beside him, then reached for his hand, squeezing it
gently. "It must be wonderful to see the boys again."

"Yeah," he grinned. "Wonderful."

"She's told me so much about you. I'm glad we have some
time alone together like this. To get to know one another. I
can see you're a fine man." She edged closer, tightening her
grip. "You want this homecoming to be special, don't you?"

"I think we both want the same thing," he assured her,
pulling her toward himself with a proud chuckle. "Matt sure
got himself a handful when he married you!"

Shocked, she tried to wriggle free and, when Jesse's playful embrace held, she abandoned persuasion completely and
turned, almost instinctively, to infliction, flooding his arms
with pain.

"Hey!" He jumped to his feet, shaking the affected limbs
frantically. "What the hell was that?"

"You keep your hands off me! How dare you!"

"Hey, Auntie, *you* came on to *me,* remember? What's your
problem?"

Trembling with anger, she hurried from the room and onto
the porch. *So much for persuasion,* she acknowledged
grimly. She'd better *stop* following Aaric's advice and *start*
following Matthew's. He had told her bluntly to stay away
from Jesse Camacho, should "the bum" resurface. The only
possible silver lining to this cloud was that she had finally
had an opportunity to try out her power of infliction which,
in contrast to persuasion, had been amazingly effective.

"I'm going to find the kids and take Kerreya home!" she
called back through the window. "Can I trust you to stay
here with the boys until Rita gets home?"

"Sure." Jesse appeared in the doorway and chuckled weakly. "Calm down, will you? I'm going to take a nap. Tell the kids not to bug me."

"Sure. Whatever you say." *What a creep,* she added in silent disdain. *You haven't seen your sons in three years and you're going to take a nap? Jerk!*

She was storming toward her own house when she heard someone calling her name and turned to see Tori, Rita's red-haired neighbor, dressed in jean shorts and a bikini top and waving cheerfully. "Molly!"

Taking a deep breath, Molly managed a tight smile. "What's up, Tori?"

"Did you *see* him? What a hunk! I think he's the famous Jesse," the sparkling-eyed female gushed. "Rita didn't exaggerate after all. He's gorgeous."

"He's also married."

"I know." Tori tossed her wild mane and pretended to pout. "All the best hunks are. I'm just saying, he's gorgeous. Rita's *so* lucky."

Molly grimaced. "I have to go find the kids."

"They went toward your house."

"Thanks." She turned to leave, then frowned when Tori began to saunter up Rita's walkway. "Tori? Where are you going?"

"I thought I'd welcome him to the neighborhood."

"I thought so. Listen to me." She grabbed her by the elbow, persuading sternly, "Rita's your friend, and Jesse's her husband. There are plenty of other guys, and you *don't* want to come between them."

"I guess you're right." The girl seemed completely bewildered by her change of heart and was still shaking her head as she walked back toward her own porch.

Weary and disheartened, Molly turned again toward home and was relieved to see her nephews turning the corner, pushing Kerreya's stroller as they went.

"Aunt Molly!" AJ called out, his golden eyes dancing. "I

knew he'd be back! Robert thought he was gone for good but I knew he'd miss us. What did you think of him, Aunt Molly? He's *really* strong! I bet he's even stronger than Uncle Matt."

"He looked very strong," she agreed quietly, reaching out to stroke the boy's warm cheek. "But he seemed tired. You and Robert let him rest until your mom gets home, okay? And if you need anything, you call me. I can be here in three minutes."

"We won't need anything now that Dad's home."

Molly bit her lip and sighed. AJ's resemblance to Matthew at that moment was strong, with his confidence and sincerity making him seem all the more vulnerable to Jesse's eventual misbehavior. Then there was Robert. Poor little thing. Pretending to be unmoved by his father's return. In some ways it was more pathetic than AJ's enthusiasm. When she hugged the young scholar, as she always did, and he didn't pull away, as he usually did after a second or two, she knew his pain was acute. "I love you guys . . ."

"Come on, Robert, let's *go!*" AJ insisted and the two sped toward home.

"You're a lucky little girl," Molly cooed sadly to Kerreya on the short walk to their own little house. "You've got a great daddy. We miss him, don't we?" Then she winced and added, "Let's hope Daddy comes home in a mellow mood, though. I can see how he'd *love* to take that creep Jesse apart."

Rita Camacho poured herself a cup of tea and settled down at the kitchen table, glancing with disinterest at Molly's paperwork. "It was a real shock. I got home from work and there he was, asleep on the couch."

Molly nodded but couldn't quite meet her gaze. "I'm happy for you, Rita."

"Are you?"

Rita's tone had been pointed, and Molly looked up in surprise. "Yes, if he's what you want, then I'm happy for you. I mean, Matthew's told me a little about how things have been but . . . You're an intelligent woman. You know the score, so to speak."

"I'll tell you the score, Molly." She leaned closer, her voice cold and accusatory. "Every good woman friend I've ever had has ended up falling into bed with Jesse. Not that I blame them. He's gorgeous and oversexed and I know it. But I kind of expected more of you. You're not just a friend. You're my brother's wife." Settling back against the chair, she folded her arms across her chest as though waiting for an apology.

Molly shrugged. "I don't know what happened between Jesse and your other friends, but I'm in love with Matthew, remember?"

"That's why you send him traveling thousands of miles away while you pursue a career he disapproves of? No, wait!" Her dark eyes flashed with disgust. "Let me finish. I think things can work between Jesse and me this time. He's seems more focused. Rob noticed it, too. And you should see how really proud he is of how the boys are turning out. I think he's finally ready to be a father to them."

"I hope so. I'll do anything I can to help."

"Like last night? He told me all about it."

"All about what? Rita, come on. You know me. If Jesse said anything . . ."

"Jesse has his faults, Molly, but he never lies to me. Never. He says you came on to him, but when he responded you backed off. And I believe him."

"What!"

"If you're this hung up on falling in love, fine. Leave my brother and find a guy who'll sweep you off your feet. Anyone but my Jesse. Understand?"

"Falling in love?"

"You said you and Matt never had the chance because of all the dream-girl nonsense. Remember?"

"And so you think I'd make up for it by having an affair with my own brother-in-law? It's ridiculous."

"I know. I assume that's why you backed off when he started to take you up on your offer."

"My offer?" Molly glared. "You think I 'offered' to have sex with him, there on the couch, knowing the kids could walk in at any minute?"

Rita seemed suddenly weary. "He has that effect on women."

"He's *your* husband. And frankly"—she paused for emphasis—"he's *hardly* my type. Maybe he never lies to you but I swear he misunderstood my intentions yesterday." Grasping her sister-in-law's wrist, she persuaded anxiously, "I was just trying to make friends, believe me."

Rita was nodding slowly as the persuasion worked its magic. "You were just being friendly and he took it the wrong way?" She seemed at once embarrassed and relieved. "It's just so important for it to work this time."

"I know." Molly loosened her hold, silently thanked Aaric, then assured Rita, "We all want it to work. Speaking of which"—she drew a deep breath—"with Jesse back, maybe we should make new arrangements about the kids. He can watch the boys for you now, so you don't need me, and you two should spend time together alone, so—"

"No! What would you do with Kerry? You can't leave her with strangers. And I'd *miss* her." Rita's eyes were bright with auntly indignation. "Jesse and I aren't newlyweds, Molly. Kerry won't be in the way. And it's time she started to get to know her Uncle Jesse."

Molly squirmed. "Talk to him. I don't want to cause any strain."

"Give him a chance, Molly. I know he looks like a tough guy, and he is, but he can be really gentle, too. But"—she smiled an enchanted smile—"you're right about the boys.

They'll want to spend all their time with their dad." With impulsive, almost schoolgirl delight, she confided, "He really missed me, Molly. He's been very attentive. Like in the old days, when I first met him."

"That's nice."

"Promise me you'll give him a chance. Don't go by what Matt says. I love my brother but the truth is he's always been a little jealous of Jesse."

Oh, right, thought Molly sarcastically.

"Did he ever tell you about the time he and Jesse had a fight?" When Molly nodded, the sister-in-law added devilishly, "Did he tell you who won?" When she nodded again, Rita beamed, "It was *so* romantic. Jesse swept me off my feet, Molly, and I guess you saw why yesterday. He's big and strong and sexy and funny. And tenderhearted, despite what Matt says. You'll think he's great when you get to know him."

"Robert has his eyes," Molly admitted quietly. "And AJ's built like him. The fact that he's their father means a lot to me, Rita. I think he's great just for giving me such great nephews."

"Then it's settled? I'll still watch Kerry?" Before Molly could answer, she was being hugged again. "She's so smart. She'll be calling him Uncle Jesse by the end of the week!"

For the next two weeks, Molly saw little of the Camacho family. Jesse was usually asleep when she dropped Kerreya with Rita in the morning, and when she returned to pick her up, the boys almost always had their little cousin out on the front lawn, bag and baggage, ready to go home. Missing her visits with the family, Molly was delighted to find AJ on her doorstep one hazy springtime Saturday.

"Hey, stranger! Come on in," she gushed. "Is Robert coming over, too?"

"No. He's reading. As usual. I was just walking by and . . . well . . ."

"You don't need a reason to visit me," Molly assured him quickly, ushering him into the kitchen where she served up two tall glasses of lemonade. "I've missed you. What's new? Are you hungry?"

"No, I just ate. Mom's working an extra day today."

"Oh?" Molly tried to appear casual. "So your Dad's in charge? Does he cook for you?"

"Dad? No, we cook for him. But he's not home today. He had an appointment. Probably a job interview."

"Really? Great."

"Yeah. He's had lots of offers," the boy insisted, "but he's waiting for just the right one."

"That's wise."

"Yeah." AJ was pacing now, in an almost uncanny impression of Matthew Redtree. "Yeah. Dad's great."

"Okay, AJ." Molly planted herself in front of him playfully. "Something's bugging you. What is it?"

"Nothing." He was uncharacteristically defensive, almost hostile. "I thought you said I didn't need a reason to visit here."

"You don't. You just reminded me of Uncle Matthew for a second. He paces like that when something's bothering him."

"That's him. Not me."

"Okay." She slipped into a chair and sipped her lemonade in cautious silence.

"Where's Kerry?"

"She's asleep. She had a little fever last night." The boy's instant alarm touched her and she assured him hastily, "It's just a mild cold. She's doing fine now."

"Can I see her?"

"Sure."

He tiptoed into the nursery, then emerged moments later, looking enormously relieved. "She's sleeping," he announced. "She looks bigger."

Molly nodded. "Do you miss her? I mean, now that we

don't get together with you at night anymore? You still see her every afternoon, don't you?"

AJ's face was flushed, and he was pacing again. "Yeah. I've been thinking about that."

"What about it?"

"Well, I'm older now. I'm almost twelve. I think I'm old enough to watch her over here for you in the afternoon, instead of at our house. So that," he fumbled slightly, "well, so that she can have her toys around and all."

Something was clearly bothering the boy and so his aunt measured her words carefully, not wanting to discourage his confidence. "That's too much responsibility, AJ. I know you'd do a great job, but you've got homework and judo practice. And what about your friends? You need to spend time with them."

"I watch her almost every day now, anyway." He, too, seemed to be choosing his words with great deliberation. "When we get home from school, Mom leaves Kerry with me and Robert, so she can run errands. She gets stuff for dinner and all, you know. Dad likes Mom to get all that out of the way as soon as we get home."

"So your mom goes out? And you and Robert watch Kerreya?" Taking a deep breath, she blurted, "And what does your dad do?"

AJ stared at her. "This isn't about *him,* Aunt Molly."

She stood up and stared back evenly. "I think it is. Should I talk to you or to him?"

"He sleeps. That's all! And . . . it really bugs him when Kerry starts crying, or whatever. It gets on his nerves. He's not used to having a baby around. So why can't I watch her over here?"

"Is that all of it? Come on, AJ. I need you to be straight with me. What else goes on?"

"That's it. I promise. The crying gets on his nerves and when Dad's around she cries more."

"Because . . . ?"

"Because she's scared of him." The words were now tumbling out. "I swear, Aunt Molly, he's never done anything to hurt her. I mean, he yells sometimes and she's not used to that, so I guess she's scared of him. He doesn't mean to be mean. He's just got a loud voice. It even freaks *me* out sometimes."

"And he's never touched her? Or hit her?" Molly demanded.

AJ seemed aghast at the thought. "No! I swear, Aunt Molly, he just wants her to be quiet. He'd never hurt her, honest."

"I believe you." She touched his burning cheek and smiled in relief. "I understand completely. Not everyone likes to be around babies. You did the right thing, telling me like this." She pulled him into a brisk hug. "Thanks."

"So, I can watch her over here? And you aren't mad?"

"I'd be proud to have you watch her over here. But not every day. You need time to be a kid."

"No, I don't. Really, Aunt Molly, I don't care about kid stuff. Neither does Robert. He'll help me. And I can go to practice in the mornings, and we'll do our homework at night."

"Mrs. Jacobs down the street has been begging me to let her watch Kerreya," Molly countered firmly. "And now that the project's going so smoothly, I've been considering cutting down my hours anyway. So how about a compromise? Say, twice a week, you come over after school and get her from Mrs. Jacobs and take her here and wait for me? I'd really appreciate that."

AJ winced. "Mom can still watch her during the day before we get home. It's just after school that needs changing."

"No. Your mom and dad need time alone, AJ. I've been insensitive about that." She laughed at his skeptical frown and gave him another, more effusive hug. "I love you, AJ. There's no one in this whole world I'd trust more with my little girl."

He blushed proudly. "Thanks, Aunt Molly. And thanks for not, you know, getting mad at Dad."

"No problem, honey. Don't give it another thought."

"What are you going to tell Mom?"

"Don't worry. I'll just explain that Mrs. Jacobs is more convenient. Which is absolutely true. Okay?"

"Yeah. So?" He glanced around hesitantly. "I guess I'll go. You're sure it's just a cold?"

"Stop worrying! She's almost as safe with me as she is with you, remember?"

AJ laughed. "Yeah, I remember." Again he hesitated. "Can I ask you something else?"

"Sure. What is it?"

"Have you heard from Uncle Matt? Is he coming back soon?"

"I haven't heard from him in almost a week but I have a feeling he'll be home soon. Why?"

"I don't know. It just seems like he should be here. You know what I mean?"

"Definitely. He'll be back soon, AJ." She studied him wistfully. "Would you like to take a trip with me today? Out to August's place? We haven't seen much of him lately."

"I'd like it a lot," AJ nodded. "Is it okay for Kerry?"

"We'll bundle her up. She'll love it."

"She likes all the goats and the chickens. She's a real animal nut, isn't she?" It was as though a staggering weight had been lifted from his young shoulders. "I'll go get Robert."

Molly watched through the window as he raced down the street, wondering what she could do for her vulnerable nephews. Probably nothing. For Rita? Probably even less. But she could, and would, keep Kerreya away from Jesse Camacho from now on. And she'd talk to August. If nothing else, she hoped the old man's advice would give her some much-needed insight into Matthew's eventual reaction to this hopeless situation.

* * *

"Stay away from him! And keep the little princess away from him! Summon your champion. I do not like the sound of this."

Molly smiled at her mentor's predictable overreaction. "I'm handling everything just fine, Moonshaker."

"That is dung! You did not handle the persuasion at all. And using infliction could have angered him and placed you in jeopardy."

"My persuasion worked just fine on Rita and Tori. And on the hospital guard."

"You need protection from Jesse Camacho, not from Rita and those others. Stay away from him and summon Matthew."

"I don't want Matthew to fight Jesse and I really think that's what would happen. The guy's so obnoxious I'm tempted to take a swing at him myself."

"Do you think he would defeat your champion?"

"Are you kidding? He may have been in great shape once, and even now he seems impressive, I guess, at first glance, but he's almost always hungover and tired, lying around the house and smoking and drinking. He's out all night, every night, I'm sure."

"Then you must encourage Matthew to fight him," Aaric insisted. "To teach him to behave like a man."

"Rita would be furious. She'd never speak to us again. She's convinced Jesse's reformed."

"Then leave her to her fate, but keep yourself and my little princess far away."

"Don't worry. If it weren't for the boys, I'd probably move to the other side of the city, but I'm worried about them."

"You think he'd harm *them?*" Aaric marveled.

"Not physically. But he's already hurting them with his indifference and his cruel jokes. And someday it's all going to be too much for AJ. Robert hides his head in a book and escapes, but AJ sees everything. He won't be a kid forever, Aaric. In a few years *he's* the one who's going to take a swing at Jesse."

"That is how he sounds," Aaric agreed, as though proud of this boy warrior despite never having seen him. "I am grateful to him for his devotion to my little princess. He will be a champion, like Matthew and Lost Eagle. Take him to the old uncle as often as possible, to be counseled and encouraged. To think"—he shook his head ruefully—"this Jesse has something I could never have, and he does not appreciate it."

"Sons?"

"Yes. It angers you, I know, when I say you should give Matthew a son, but for men such as us, it is important."

"Because you're chauvinists. Matthew has a perfect daughter. But," she added softly, "I agree it's a shame you never had children. You would have been a remarkable father."

"Would I?" The sorcerer shrugged. "You see me as I am now. As you have made me become. The old Aaric was not like this. Still, I would have been better than this Jesse." With impatience he added, "For once you should obey me and summon the Valmain champion."

"We'll see. I might, if things get any worse. For now, Rita seems happy and that's worth something, right?"

"Do not ask my opinion. You will only ignore it."

"So let's change the subject. Help me figure out what I did wrong with Jesse. If we fine-tune my persuasion, maybe I can try it on him again soon."

When Molly did finally decide to take the Moonshaker's advice and to summon the Valmain champion, it had little to do with Jesse Camacho, except perhaps that his presence at Rita's contributed indirectly to Molly's loneliness. It was, however, much more than loneliness that prompted her decision. She ached for Matthew Redtree, both for his touch and for his strength, and so she arranged for an afternoon off from work, left Kerreya in Mrs. Jacobs's capable hands, and turned her attention to their little home, intent upon preparing it for his return. If all went well she would summon him that very evening and hopefully he would arrive within twenty-four hours.

She was putting the finishing touches on the newly waxed hardwood floors when, to her amazement, he appeared in the doorway of his own accord. Running to him eagerly, she exclaimed, "Matthew!" then drew back, alarmed by his lukewarm response. "Matthew? Is something wrong?"

He eyed her carefully. "Could be."

She had seen that look before. He was just about to lose his temper and was aimed right in her direction. What could it be? Had he talked to Rita and found out about Jesse? Surely, he couldn't blame *her* for any of that!

Her curiosity outweighed her feelings of foreboding and so she prodded gently, "You're upset? Tell me what's wrong."

"You tell me, dream girl." His monotone was ominous. *"Have you had your dream lately?"*

From the look in his eye, it was almost as though he knew for certain, but that was impossible and so she bluffed, "Why? Has something happened? Have *you* started dreaming again, Matthew?"

"No. I've tried. Over and over. *With* the amulet, *at* the mounds. I should be able to get in, but I can't because *you're* blocking me."

"Pardon?"

He took a deep breath and shook his head. "This may take a while. Shouldn't we go over to Rita's and get Kerreya first?"

Fine, thought Molly. *Just what this situation needs. More bad news.* "I'll go get her. She's next door with a neighbor."

"What?"

"Give me a little credit, Matthew," she retorted, as indignant as possible under the circumstances. "I had my reasons. Jesse's back with Rita and I didn't feel comfortable leaving Kerry there anymore."

The warrior's jaw tensed. "I can't believe that asshole had the nerve to come back again! You did the right thing, Valmain. I don't want him near Kerreya *or* you." To Molly's relief the news seemed to be bringing out Matthew's feelings of protectiveness toward her. Perhaps that would give her the time she needed to work this through once and for all.

The Valmain champion was pacing madly. "I *knew* something was wrong."

"Nothing's wrong, Matthew. Jesse's just a fact of life for the time being. He'll leave again soon. I'm almost sure of it." She reached for his hand and sighed. "The worst thing you could do would be to make a scene and alienate Rita and the boys. They're going to need us when he goes."

"I hate this. But," he grimaced, "you're probably right. Let's just hope he goes soon. For now, let's go get Kerreya."

"She'll be so excited. She's been asking for you." Leaning into him hopefully, she murmured, "She missed you. So did I."

For a moment he responded to her shy, sweet kiss, then he pulled back abruptly. "We'll get the baby. Then we'll have our talk."

"I don't want to fight in front of Kerry." Squaring her shoulders, she reminded herself she had prepared for this battle, and the accompanying revelation, for months. And Aaric was so sure Matthew would understand. "You mentioned my dreaming?"

Matthew got right to the point, or, at least, what he apparently believed to be the point. "Remember Deborah?"

"Of course. I mean, I never met her, but . . ."

"But you remember how knowledgeable she was about magic and the mounds?"

"What I 'remember' is that she was Angela's grandmother. What else do I have to know? I don't even like hearing her

name," Molly frowned. "You aren't going to tell me she
dared to contact you, are you?"

"Actually, I contacted her."

"What?"

"I heard she was back, visiting her nephew near the
mounds. I figured we should discuss the incident with Angela—"

"The *'incident'* with Angela? The *'incident'!"* Molly
heard herself shrieking and didn't care. Matthew had clearly
lost his mind! While *she* had been agonizing over her failure
to tell him about Aaric, he had dared to seek out relatives of
the witch who had seduced him! The witch who had tried
to kill them all!

"Calm down, Valmain. There's nothing sinister about it. I
just wanted to see if—"

"To see if she had any more beautiful, dark-haired witch
granddaughters for you to have *incidents* with?" Molly
hissed. "You're crazy, Matthew Redtree! How *dare* you!
You're supposed to *protect* us from her, not expose us!"

Matthew the inquisitor had been rapidly replaced by Matthew the peacemaker. "Hey, come on. Calm down and listen."

"Don't tell me what to do!"

He grabbed her hands in his own. "Listen to me! Deborah
knows things, that's all. I have questions. Things that have
been bothering me. I had to find out—"

"What? What could be so urgent that you'd talk to someone like that? Don't you remember what Angela tried to do?
Do you doubt that Deborah was involved in all of that?"

"I was careful, believe me. I just wanted to know . . ."
His eyes were suddenly desperate. "I had to see if she knew
anything about the dream power."

"My dream power?" Molly gasped. "You told her . . . ?"

"No. It turns out, she had already figured it out."

"Oh, no. Oh, Matthew . . ."

"It's not a problem, Molly, believe me. She's harmless now."

Anger flooded through her and she spat, "This is too much! Get out of here! Go back to your mistress's grandmother and talk about my dreaming behind my back!" Hefting his knapsack from the floor beside him, she pushed it against his chest. "Get out!"

A book fell from the sack and, with panic in his gold-flecked eyes, the Valmain champion fumbled to retrieve it, insisting frantically, "Look, Molly. I brought you a collection of herbal remedies."

"*Herbal* remedies?" Her wrath flared into red-hot fury at the insult and, as it did, the offending book burst into flames.

Ten

The blazing book dropped to the freshly waxed hardwood floor and the Valmain couple stared at it in silence until the fire had slowly died away. Even then, try as she would, the mounds sorceress could not bring herself to meet her champion's gaze.

"Incredible," he whispered finally. "Do you realize . . . ? Do you know . . . ?"

"Matthew, please . . ."

"No. Molly, let me say this." Pulling her against his chest with one strong arm, he cupped her chin in his free hand. "I am so monumentally sorry."

Her heart seemed to miss a beat. "You're sorry?"

"Can you ever forgive me?" His voice was choked with remorse. "Can't you see? You were right. That book! I had it with me when I visited Deborah! She must have done something to it, put some kind of spell . . ." His embrace tightened fiercely. "I endangered you with my damned curiosity and suspicions, just like you said! I was so sure she was harmless now, but *you* were *right!* She wants revenge against us—against *you*—for killing Angela. Can you forgive me?"

Molly closed her eyes and suppressed a groan. In some ways it would have been preferable for him to simply guess the truth, go berserk, and storm away. At least the worst of it would be over. Finished. Perhaps forever.

Forever—without hearing his husky, resonant voice,

charming her with legends, promising her a future filled with discovery and magic. And his touch—could she live without that? Could she be expected to bear such a loss? Had her deception been as heinous as that? *No!* She couldn't bear it, and so, for the moment she would accept this bizarre reprieve.

"I've missed you so much," she murmured desperately. "I didn't want your homecoming to be like this."

"Neither did I," he whispered. "I missed you, too. It's just that I . . ." When she began to draw away, he amended quickly, "I just want to hold you. To make love to you and forget all this. I want you to forgive me for being such a beast."

She nodded with relief. *Yes, make love to me, my champion. Make all of this go away. Don't ask any questions, or mention Angela, or rant about Jesse. Just hold me. Just for tonight. One last night of innocence before I bring you back to my dream.*

"So. It will finally be said. Good!"

Molly grinned darkly at her delighted coconspirator. "In a way I agree. I should have told him from the start. Now, on top of everything else, I have to tell him I've been deceiving him for over a year, just as he suspects."

"He will be furious." Aaric seemed annoyingly pleased at the thought. "But you will make him understand. Try to remember, Princess. If it were not for his quick temper, you would have told him long ago. He bears some responsibility."

"That's true. Thanks, Aaric."

"I have more advice."

"Anything!"

"Do not set any more books on fire."

"Very funny. Although"—she smiled in spite of her predicament—"we'll probably be lucky if I don't accidentally set some poor *goat* on fire! If I get up the nerve to tell him at August's ranch tomorrow, like I plan."

"It is a good idea. The old uncle will help you."

"That's what I think. We're going to try to bring AJ and Robert with us, and that'll make it easier, too. They'll keep Kerry occupied while we talk. Matthew's been pushing the same plan. I think he's intending to have it out about my dream. Little does he know . . ."

"He will be amazed."

"I hope so. It depends on what old Deborah told him. I wish I knew. Any ideas?"

The sorcerer pursed his lips thoughtfully. "She knows you are blocking him, either consciously or unconsciously. If it were unconscious, she knows it would not be totally effective, and that you must be returning, at least occasionally, to this dream. And so she suspects you are consciously blocking all access—using your magic, and then deceiving Matthew when he asks about your power. Yes," he reasoned finally, "she knows for certain you are deceiving him in some way."

"So, I suppose he's prepared for the truth about the dream. Of course, the truth about *you* is another matter."

"Perhaps his joy over your training will outweigh his anger over my return. He will burst with pride when he sees how much you have learned."

"Maybe so," she agreed hopefully. "Anyway, I'd better go. It'll be morning soon. I want to get everything ready so we can leave as soon as we call the boys. I want them to come to our place." Grimacing slightly, she explained, "The last thing I need is for Matthew to have a run-in with Jesse over at Rita's. That wouldn't put him in a very receptive mood."

"You will all travel in the 'gutless box'?"

Molly laughed in rueful delight. "I forgot to tell you the *latest* humiliation. After Matthew shamed me into buying that four-cylinder mess, *he* shows up yesterday in a brand-new eight-cylinder four-wheel-drive mega-vehicle that *he* just bought for himself! It has leather seats, a sun roof, and oodles of chrome and power, and he has the nerve to tell me it was a practical decision. What a hypocrite."

"It is a superior vehicle?"

"Top of the line."

"That is understandable," Aaric insisted. "He is accustomed to the airplane that flies like a bird through the skies. Of all the wonders you have described, it is the airplane that I would most want to experience."

"Really?" She paused to consider this, then nodded. "It's pretty amazing, I guess."

"Across the seas! Over the mountains! In one day!"

"I wonder where you'd go," she mused.

"To the pyramid, at the time of the vernal equinox, to see the serpent that slithers along the great steps."

"You're kidding!" It was almost as depressing as it was amazing. "You're so much like Matthew. Impressed by the same strange things."

"You were also impressed by it," the sorcerer reminded her. "I remember when you came to the dream that night after your champion took you to see it. You were carrying the little one in your womb . . ."

"Right. So I lucked out and didn't have to climb all the steps on that pyramid with Matthew," she quipped.

"You were awed by the sight you had seen. You told me of how the afternoon sun cast a shadow along the steps, and suddenly the shadow became a long, majestic serpent, and a hush fell over the crowd, and you felt privileged to witness it."

"I said all that?" she mused. "In those words?"

"You have chosen to forget, because you do not wish to be impressed by mysticism or unseen power. You wish only to be impressed by your science."

"That snake shadow appears on those steps because scientists—ancient astronomers and architects—made it happen," she argued. "That's what impressed me, Aaric. Not mysticism or cosmic forces."

The sorcerer shrugged. "Nevertheless, it is a miracle. And it is no wonder your champion cannot remain in one place, with so many such miracles all over the world, entirely within his grasp, thanks to the amazing airplane that carries him where he wishes to go."

"Well, he'll probably be on one of those amazing planes by this time tomorrow, running away from me."

"And you will merely summon him here—to this dream. And *I* will make him understand." Aaric's eyes sparkled at the thought.

"Forget it, Moonshaker. You had your chance to get out of this dream by defeating Matthew in battle and you blew it."

"You are a harsh witch."

"That's right," Molly grinned. "Anyway, I won't allow any more fighting here, understand?"

"We shall see."

"Aaric . . ." Her amusement faded. "I want your word. If I bring him here tomorrow, you'll make yourself invisible, at least for the first few visits. Please? Let him get used to one lie at a time."

"You have my word." Taking her hand, he kissed her fingertips and murmured, "I have enjoyed being the only man in your dreams, my Princess."

The remark caught her off guard and, as the meaning behind his words registered, her eyes filled with unexpected tears. It was true! Their precious friendship would change now, perhaps radically. At the very least, the intimacy would be gone. Forever. "I've loved this too, Aaric," she insisted. "It'll never be the same, but"—her lips brushed his—"there's nothing else I can do."

His sea-blue eyes had clouded. "This may be the last time we are alone together. The last time I can tell you how much I love you. The last time . . ." He hesitated, as though waiting for permission, and when she nodded shyly he pulled her into a tender embrace.

When his mouth covered hers, the need behind the kiss almost caused her to reel, yet she did not try to pull free. Not this time. This one last time. Right or wrong seemed irrelevant to this fervent goodbye.

It was Aaric who ended it, pushing her gently to arm's length and reminding her, "He will ask if we are lovers and you must say I am as a brother to you."

She nodded, dazed and unhappy, searching for the words that would ease their grief. Before she could find them, the sorcerer chose to save her the trouble and gallantly disappeared.

The Valmain sorceress squirmed uneasily as her champion pulled his shiny new vehicle up to the front of Rita's house. They had tried in vain to reach the boys by phone, with only a relentless busy signal to greet their efforts. She imagined that Rita was probably working a day shift, Jesse was out cold on the couch, and the boys were taking advantage of their mother's absence to listen in rapt confusion to the endless telephone chattering of AJ's new, not to mention first, girlfriend.

"Those boys definitely need a trip to the country," she whispered to the sleeping Kerreya, trying to ignore the fact that Matthew had just bolted up the steps and disappeared through the front door. *Jesse's* front door. After he had solemnly promised to go no farther than the porch!

She decided to use this time to rehearse her speech one last time. It was short and hopefully sweet. "Matthew," she insisted aloud, "I know it was magic and destiny and my dream that brought us together, but I've lived in fear, every day since then, that those same things would drive us apart one day." She paused to allow time for Matthew's standard response—that *nothing* could drive them apart—and then continued, "I feel like I'm at a crossroads now, with my magic. I need your advice, but your temper scares me. You have to give me your word, as the Son of Lost Eagle, that you won't get angry with me if I confide in you. You have to promise to give *my* instincts the same respect that you give your own. . . . Ooh, that's good," she congratulated herself, digging quickly in her purse for pen and paper to record the Matthewesque phrasing.

A shrill female voice interrupted her notemaking, awakening Kerreya in the process, and the Valmain princesses stared out the window toward Tori, who was waving wildly from Rita's porch and shrieking, "Molly! Hurry! They'll *kill* each other!"

"Oh, no . . ." The situation was clear from a glance at the girl's clothing, or lack of it—she had apparently pulled a man's T-shirt over her naked body in quite a rush. The panic was contagious and Molly's fingers began to tremble as she tried to unbuckle Kerreya from the car seat. "I'll do that," Tori gasped when she'd reached the vehicle. "You go stop them. Please!"

Kerreya seemed willing, and so Molly instructed tersely, "Bring the baby into the living room and keep her distracted," then rushed up the walkway and into the house.

The sounds of flying fists and furniture led her up the stairs to the master bedroom, where Matthew had apparently discovered an "incident" and was now in the process of ensuring that Jesse would think twice before ever again humiliating Rita. Molly considered intervening but could see that Jesse was in no real danger and felt unashamedly proud to see justice meted out so decisively by her powerful, cross-trained champion.

Finally she touched Matthew's shoulder. "He's had enough."

The warrior hesitated, then stood up slowly and contemptuously. "Listen, asshole. I want you out of here before my sister gets home."

"And before the boys see all of this," Molly added firmly.

She turned to the wide-eyed Tori. "Where are Robert and AJ?"

She shuffled nervously. "At his brother's house. The cop."

"Rob? Good. I'll call him and see that they stay there. Where's Kerry?"

"In the crib in the kids' room."

"Okay. You'd better get dressed and get out of here."

Tori nodded, gathered up her clothes, and edged for the bathroom.

Jesse had dragged himself across the room and onto the bed. For a moment Molly thought he was going to speak but he merely shook his head, completely defeated. Matthew stood guard over him in contemptuous silence while Molly called Rob Camacho and gave him the highlights of the encounter.

"Come on, Matthew," she urged after she'd finished speaking with Jesse's brother. "Let's go home and wait for Rita. She's going to need us. Rob's on his way. He can take over here."

Matthew nodded and slipped his arm around her waist, ushering her toward the doorway. They had almost reached it when they heard Jesse snarl, "This isn't over yet, Matt. *Turn around slowly.*"

Molly had assumed that, given her exposure to weapons over the last two years, the sight of a firearm or sword would no longer be shocking to her. But she had never had a cold revolver pointed directly at her head—had never seen a face so twisted with contempt and humiliation as Jesse's now was—and she literally froze with dread and disbelief. All she could think about was Kerry, in the next room, trusting and innocent, not ready to be motherless. *Don't do this to her,* she pleaded with destiny. *Don't take me from her. Not yet. Not Kerry . . .*

Then Matthew stepped protectively in front of her and she grabbed instinctively for the amulet on his wrist, transferring every pulse of power she could muster to the father of her baby. As life itself abandoned her body, the room—distorted and spinning—seemed to swallow her whole.

"Please wake up. *Please,* Molly. I don't know who else to turn to." It was Rita, sobbing over her, as Molly pulled herself back into the world she had almost relinquished forever.

"Rita?" the sorceress murmured, groggy and disoriented.

"Take it slow. You're at the hospital," Rita whispered. "Oh, Molly, thank heavens you're all right! Everything's so awful."

Molly's memory cleared with a jolt. "Jesse had a gun! Did he shoot Matthew? Is Matthew okay?"

"Matt's fine." There was an unmistakable edge to Rita's voice. *"He's* just fine. It's poor *Jesse* who's hurt."

"Jesse?" Molly considered trying to get out of the bed but knew that her legs had no strength. "Where's Kerry?"

"She's fine, too. She's downstairs with August. And the boys are with Rob's housekeeper."

"And where's Matthew? Rita, please tell me what happened."

Rita nodded. "Tori gave me all the details. Matt and Jesse had a horrible fight. You passed out during it, and I don't blame you. It must have been so . . . so gruesome." She began to sob again and Molly grew impatient.

"Jesse had a gun, Rita! Tell me what happened."

"That gun wasn't loaded. It never is. Jesse knew it. He was just trying to scare Matt. That was wrong, I'll admit, but Matt had no business coming into my home and starting a fight with my husband! Poor Jesse!"

"If Jesse got hurt—"

"Hurt? He's dying!"

"Dying?" Molly struggled for an even tone. "That's awful, Rita, but you can't blame Matthew for defending me. That gun was pointed right at my head. If Matthew hit Jesse—"

"Hit him? He went berserk! Tori says he tore the gun from Jesse's hand and then he tore . . . and then he tore . . ."

Stunned by her sister-in-law's shuddering sobs, Molly took her into her arms and cooed, "Shhh . . . Everything'll be okay."

"It'll never be okay. My husband murdered by my own brother! It's hideous. What can I say to my boys?"

"Murder's a pretty harsh word, isn't it?" Molly chided.

"That's what the police are calling it."

"The police?" Molly frowned. "Didn't Matthew explain it was self-defense? And defense of me?"

"Rob says once Matt took the gun away from Jesse, it wasn't self-defense anymore. The danger was all gone. But that didn't stop Matt. Tori says he was like an animal! And if you could see what's left of poor Jesse, you'd believe it. He tore Jesse to bits! He was. . . . he was . . ."

"Rita! Are you telling me they *arrested* Matthew?"

"Of course. What do you expect? At least he's alive, Molly. They won't even let me see Jesse now. I may not even get to say goodbye! You're the lucky ones."

"Don't be like that! Talk to me. Does Matthew have a lawyer? Get me out of here. I have to see him." She tried to rise but fell back, exhausted.

"Don't! You're still weak. They still don't know what's wrong with you, Molly. You have to stay put." Rita's voice had gone soft with concern. "There's nothing you or a lawyer can do for Matt. He confessed already."

"Confessed," the impaired witch murmured. "Confessed to what? Assault?"

"Attempted murder, I guess. That's the charge, according to Rob. And if Jesse dies . . ."

"Are you crazy? Do you hear what you're saying? He's your brother! Why would he confess, anyway? It doesn't make sense."

"He threw Jesse, or rather what was left of him, through a second-story window, for heaven's sake. Do you call *that* self-defense? Matt himself says he should be locked up. He says he's ashamed, and he doesn't want to get near you or Kerreya! I love him, Molly, don't get me wrong, but there's a dark side to him—there always has been!—and we have to acknowledge it now."

"Shut up! I won't listen to this! Get me my clothes and then get out. Find August and tell him I need him." Molly tried again to stand and, although pale and weak, succeeded. Rita was crying, begging her to get back into bed, apologizing for her bluntness while furiously summoning the nurses. They arrived en force but could not deter the determined patient.

Only the timely appearance of August and Kerreya brought a moment of fleeting comfort and stability. While she dressed, Molly learned that Matthew's agent, Zack, was on his way. That was something, at least, although she had a feeling that a New York literary attorney, even one as dedicated to Matthew as Zack Payton, would be no match for a California confession.

In a bizarre way it was all beginning to make sense. Molly remembered the transfer of her power. That was clearly the key. Matthew was accustomed to a steady stream from the mounds to the amulet, not a burst from a frightened witch. She had overridden his instincts, giving him raw power with no controls. She had turned him into an animal and now he was facing possible murder charges!

Even worse, thought Molly in desperation, *he's sitting in a cell somewhere thinking that he's actually capable of this. Responsible for it!* She couldn't allow him to torture himself. She had to get to him right away.

As the speeding cab transported the Valmain princess to the jail, she forced herself to concentrate, fearful that she would again pass out. She hadn't felt this weak since the transfer to August! If Aaric could see her . . . She leaned back wistfully. The luxury of sleep, and Aaric, felt so close, she was tempted to give in to it, but there was no time. They had arrived.

A grim-faced Rob Camacho hurried to assist her as she stumbled toward the front desk.

"I need to see him, Rob."

"No way, Molly. I'm sorry. You're a victim here, too— don't think I'm not sensitive to that—but Matt sees no one. Except a lawyer, which he refuses."

"Refuses? Oh, Rob, please, don't you see? I *have* to talk to him. Please get me in there?"

"No way. You'd better get to a doctor. You don't look too good." He tightened his grip on her arm and, as he did, she looked deep into his eyes and persuaded gingerly, "Rob, you know I have to see him. You can't be this cruel. Please? Just five minutes?"

Rob licked his lips, as though wrestling with the idea. "Maybe just five minutes," he agreed finally. "But that's it."

"Right. Thanks." Molly leaned into him for a few seconds, weakened almost into a faint by the persuasion's drain on her power, then took a deep breath. She had to remain conscious long enough to make use of the opportunity. "Let's go."

She couldn't have prepared herself for the chilling stare that greeted her when her champion was ushered into the private visiting room. "I told them not to let you see me," he insisted. "You shouldn't be around me. Just the sight of my . . . my atrocity . . . made you pass out earlier today, remember?"

"I passed out. That's true. But not because of what you did, Matthew." She ached to touch him but didn't dare. Not yet. Stepping closer, she pleaded, "I have to talk to you."

He backed away quickly. "Get out of here, Molly. I need to be alone. I . . . hey!" He caught her just as her legs began to buckle. "Are you still sick? Here, sit down, I'll call the guard."

"Just listen. Please. I'm so weak." Her voice trembled with despair. "I'm too weak to argue."

He sat down next to her, distracted for the moment from his own anguish. "I won't argue, Valmain. Go on. Say what you came to say."

"I'm a sorceress. *No!* Listen to me. I'm *really* a sorceress. I have powers. Not just dream power or summoning. I can do things but I'm not very good. I don't control the flow of magic. Oh, Matthew, I'm so sorry." She wrapped her arms around his neck and wailed, "I did it! Don't you see? I sent you my power through the amulet. Think! You must remember."

He deliberated carefully. "Your power? Through the amulet? You can *do* that?"

"I did it with August. On the way to the mounds. It makes me very weak. And I guess it made you very, very strong."

Matthew's eyes widened. "It made me go insane. I always hate Jesse, but . . ." He gathered her closer and marveled, "The amulet? That's just how it felt. But like you said! The power just burst through! There was no way to control it."

"Right." She sighed with relief. "So please stop confessing! Zack's on his way, but we need a criminal lawyer."

"Who called Zack? He's going to really be on the spot," Matthew predicted. "He knows better than anyone how much I hated Jesse. He may even believe I wanted to kill him."

"No way. No one would believe it. Except of course all the people you've confessed to," she amended wryly. "So cut it out. And hold me."

"My pleasure." His lips brushed her curls. "Is Jesse going to make it?"

"Rita says the doctors don't think so. I'm scared, Matthew."

"We'll work something out. And even if we don't, it's such a relief knowing there isn't something malignant inside me that made it happen. If I end up in prison, I'll survive."

"Don't even say that! I'm a witch, remember? I'll help."

"Any more help from you and I'll be in the electric chair," he drawled. When she winced, he tilted her chin upward and instructed sternly, "Promise me you'll let me deal with this by myself."

Molly grimaced but nodded.

"Good." His lips brushed her dampened cheek. "We'll make it through this, Valmain, just like we made it through the battles with Aaric and that mess with Angela. Trust me to handle it, okay? Go get Kerry, take her home, and then both of you try to sleep."

She was about to plead, one last time, to be allowed to help, then Rob Camacho appeared in the doorway, scratching his chin as though still bewildered by his having allowed Molly's visit. "I guess I did the right thing letting her in here. You don't look so wasted, Matt. Are you ready to see a lawyer?"

Matthew crossed the room and extended his hand. "That's pretty decent of you, Rob."

Rob's eyes were cold as they noted, then ignored, the outstretched hand. "Don't misunderstand, Matt. If my brother dies, I want you to get what you deserve. I just don't ever want to wonder if I was unprofessional."

"Fair enough. That's still pretty decent." Turning back to Molly, he kissed her again and whispered, "Remember what I said. You stay out of this. Understand?"

"Yes, Matthew," she assured him quietly. "As soon as I leave here, I'm going to go straight to sleep."

Aaric stared in abject horror as the day's events tumbled from his weakened Princess's lips. "You could have died, Princess. You do these things—I know it is your beautiful heart that prompts them—but I have told you . . ." When she began to sob, he abandoned the rebuke and soothed, "We will not allow the Son of Lost Eagle to be locked in a dungeon. It is unthinkable. But *you* must obey his command and do nothing but rest. Let me give it my thought. There must be a way. . . ."

"I don't understand why I didn't come here when I passed out or while I was unconscious in the hospital."

"You had no power. Not even enough with which to dream. To be so fully drained . . ." He shuddered. "You must promise not to use your power again."

"But Matthew needs me!"

"You can do nothing for him. If only I were out there . . ." His voice trailed away and he stood, as though possessed, and began to gesture—talking aloud, but to himself, in a language Molly had never heard. Finally he turned, a triumphant grin replacing the worried scowl. "Bring him here. Now."

"Why? He'll be furious."

"Do not argue. There is no time. Did you not say he could die at any moment?"

"Die? No, he's in jail but—"

"In jail! With such injuries! Barbaric!"

"You're talking about Jesse?" Molly whispered. "You want me to bring *Jesse* here?"

"Who else? And quickly! If he dies we are lost."

"You think you can cure him? Oh, Aaric, that would be perfect! Except"—her burst of elation faded—"Rita says he's too far gone. He's got massive injuries. Are your healing powers that strong?"

"Yes and no." He smiled enigmatically. "I cannot cure him unless I kill him."

"Kill?" He was making no sense. Or was he? He would kill Jesse, and then he would cure him—by becoming him! Molly shook her sun-streaked curls frantically. "We can't! We can't!"

"Not this again!" Aaric growled. "Surely this is different! This man will die at any moment, with or without my actions! But if he dies out there, Matthew is a prisoner. If he dies in here, Matthew goes free. And so do I."

"Free. Alive." She struggled to her feet and touched his cheek. "I want that for you, Aaric. You must know that. But I have to think."

"There is no time. Bring him before it is too late. Before he dies. *Now,* Princess."

She nodded and, with a mixture of dread and hope, closed her eyes and summoned Jesse Camacho. The sight of his mangled, lifeless body shocked them both and the Moonshaker hesitated, as though for a moment he could not accept such a fate. Then he knelt alongside the unconscious man and felt for his pulse. "He is almost gone. Leave us, Princess. There is no need for you to watch. I will be with you soon."

Molly reached for the sorcerer's hand, removing it from Jesse's wrist. "This has to be said first, Aaric. If you take over Jesse's body, you become him in every way. Rita will be your wife. AJ and Robert—"

"Yes, yes. If that is how you wish it."

"Swear to me, Aaric! *You can never be with me.* You can never hurt *them.* And you can never, never tell Matthew. Swear it."

He nodded impatiently. "Yes, yes. Anything. Now hurry. He will be dead in a moment. Go!" When Molly flinched, he grabbed her and amended contritely, "Wait, Princess. Yes, sweet darling. I swear I will never tell. And I will never hurt the ones you care for. And I will not force my attention on you, although I will be sorely tempted. But," he added lovingly, "I will always be near. I will always protect you. Will you allow me that?"

"It would kill me to lose you," she admitted, her voice trembling with confusion and hope. "I love you, too." Moving away quickly, she averted her eyes, unable to leave, unable to watch, unable to fully comprehend what she had done.

And then it was over. Somehow she knew. Turning slowly, her heart filled with trepidation, not certain what to expect, she saw only that she was alone.

Eleven

There was no time for subtlety at the hospital. The staff was buzzing with the news of Jesse's remarkable turnaround and Molly simply would not be stopped. Grabbing the doctor's hand, she instructed, "Mr. Camacho and I are very close. I need five minutes with him."

"Five minutes," the doctor agreed cheerfully. "But don't tire him out."

"Should I ask Rita to step outside so you can give her an update?" Molly persisted carefully.

The doctor shrugged. "Sounds like a good idea."

Before he could change his mind, Molly tiptoed into Jesse's room, where Rita's face immediately lit up with delight. "Molly! Look! It's a miracle."

Not yet daring to glance at the patient, Molly hugged her sister-in-law and murmured, "The doctor wants to see you in the hall, Rita. I'll sit here with Jesse while you're gone."

After one long, longing glance toward the motionless figure of her husband, Rita hurried away.

Slipping into the vacant bedside chair, Molly took his hand and stroked his dark, curly hair, whispering, "Aaric?"

"Call me Jesse." He seemed to be trying to smile but couldn't, and even his eyes communicated only agony.

"You're in pain?" Molly gasped. "I didn't know! I thought . . ."

"Don't worry, Princess. It's not so bad. Just sit here with me and hold my hand for a while."

"Oh, Aaric . . ." She covered his forehead and cheeks with gentle kisses, taking care not to contact the swollen, purple bruises around both eye sockets. "I didn't expect this. You should have told me!"

"Why? It does not matter. What matters is, we did it. We were just in time." Pulling himself up on one elbow, he insisted, "I didn't have to kill him, Princess. I swear it. He died as I touched, as I . . ." Too weak to finish, he fell back, shaken and dangerously short of breath.

"Oh, Aaric, don't!" she sobbed, throwing herself onto Jesse's broad chest. "You don't have to justify anything. I would have killed him myself with my bare hands to accomplish what you've done. I'm so grateful."

"Call me Jesse," he repeated weakly. "It will take some time for me to heal—the internal injuries are extensive—but I'll be fine. Promise not to worry. You should be with Matt now."

"No! I want to stay with you," she pleaded. "Let me help."

"My wife will stay with me," he corrected, managing a faint smile as he added, "You didn't tell me she was so lovely."

"You're really something, Moonshaker." Molly brushed a tear from her cheek. "You're going to keep your promise, aren't you?"

"Of course." He closed his eyes just as Rita peeked through the door.

Turning tearful eyes to her sister-in-law, Molly lamented, "I guess I should go home now. Take good care of him, Rita."

"Don't worry. I almost lost him . . ." She caught Molly by the arm. "I'm sorry about the things I said earlier. About Matt. Forgive me?"

"Let's just concentrate on getting things back to normal," Molly suggested softly.

"You should rest, Molly. You've been through a lot."

"I got a little sleep during the cab ride." Smiling toward

Jesse's bed, she confided, "I had the most wonderful dream of my entire life, Rita. I think things are going to be perfect now."

"Well, you *are* the dream girl," Rita quipped, adding wistfully, "Let's hope you're right. Let's hope this is a second chance for all of us."

When only four days of healing had passed, the doctors agreed that their miracle patient was well enough to go home. In fact, as it turned out, he was well enough to orchestrate and preside over a huge "welcome home" barbecue in his own honor, where he shamelessly bragged about his sons, flirted with his wife, and entertained family and friends with an unceasing display of boisterous good humor.

Rita Camacho, while charmed and attentive, was also clearly bewildered, as was August Redtree, who observed quietly from a lawn chair, shaking his head in occasional disbelief. Even Jesse's older brother, Rob, seemed wary, as though waiting for his sibling to revert to his usual, irresponsible style. Instead, Jesse seemed to grow more entrenched in his new personality with every passing hour.

The attraction Molly felt toward this amazing man was nothing less than magnetic, and while she told herself it wasn't sexual, she found herself blushing whenever he flashed his devilish grin her way. While she hadn't made the connection in the dream, Jesse Camacho's build was eerily similar to Aaric's, from his huge forearms and hands to his broad shoulders and muscle-bound chest. And while their coloring was technically opposite—with dark hair where the fair had been, and warm brown eyes in place of sea blue— each had a thick unruly mane of hair and well-weathered skin, with thick eyebrows that arched playfully at the slightest provocation—and he was clearly "provoked" whenever the Valmain princess ventured too close.

There had been so many times when Aaric had been the

most real and solid thing in her tumultuous existence, but he had never truly been real or solid until now, and Molly could hardly control her stare as he ate, and drank, and tapped his foot to the music of his "son's" boom box, generally adapting to life in modern-day Los Angeles as though he had been born for it.

Throughout the festivities, Matthew had kept his distance, ostensibly conferring with Zack Payton, who had decided to stay in town for a few days' visit. But when Robert approached them seeking a partner for a badminton game against AJ and their Uncle Rob, the Valmain champion took the opportunity to pair his agent with the boy and to thereafter pull Molly aside to demand, "Haven't you paid enough attention to Jesse for one day?"

"Matthew! He's an invalid." With a teasing smile she prodded, "Don't tell me you're jealous!"

"Hardly," he drawled. "I just don't like seeing you waiting on him hand and foot. The guy's not worth it, Molly."

"That was the old Jesse," she insisted. "You once considered him a friend, Matthew. Give him another chance. He's trying so hard."

"Why shouldn't he try? He's got everyone, including *my* wife, fussing over him."

"It's in our best interest that he make a full recovery," she reminded him coolly. "Anyway, it was pretty classy of him to refuse to press any charges or testify against you. Rob says he told the police he drove you into a frenzy by threatening to shoot me. He told them he deserved everything he got."

Matthew's jaw tightened in frustration. "I know, I know. I'm grateful, I guess, but I'm also suspicious. He's still Jesse."

"Look at Kerreya," Molly whispered in sudden delight. "She used to be so afraid of him! Look at her there on his lap."

"Just like old friends," Matthew acknowledged grudgingly. "Okay, maybe I'll lighten up. But one false move . . ."

"Of course, Matthew. But in the meantime, let's try to enjoy the fact that *you're* out of jail, *he's* out of the hospital, and we're all relatively safe and healthy."

"I'm just glad the whole thing got resolved without any crazy interference by you," Matthew grumbled. "We've still got a lot to talk about, Valmain."

"But I'm still weak . . ."

"Don't give me that routine." He was laughing in spite of his frustration. "I still want the whole story. Soon."

"Are you going to be angry?"

"Angry?" He shook his head. "I'm confused about your keeping so much to yourself, but not angry."

"I kept it from you because I didn't know whether you'd be proud, or angry, or jealous . . ."

"Jealous? Of you?" Matthew chuckled. "That's hilarious. You're like the little kid whose big dog takes *him* for a walk."

"Meaning what?"

"Meaning you don't control your powers. They just happen. I've got more useful power, through the amulet at the mounds, than you have being a full-fledged sorceress."

Molly frowned. "Watch it, Matthew. I may be a little klutzy, but I could set this whole place on fire if I wanted to."

"On fire? *Fire?* Are you telling me that recipe book . . . ?"

She nodded smugly. "That was me, so try not to make me mad anymore." When he simply stared, she added gently, "I didn't do it on purpose. You made me mad and then *voilà!*"

Matthew's eyes were twinkling with pride. "Starting next week, no more 'voilà'! We're going to practice, two hours every day, until your control is flawless."

"Whatever you say, teacher."

"Zack and I were thinking we'd take our annual fishing trip to Oregon now, while you're resting and Rita still needs help with Jesse. But when I get home, your lessons will start. We'll begin with wind, not fire."

"Why?"

He grinned slyly. "If you accidentally start a bonfire, I want you to be able to put it out. Or"—the gold dust was beginning to shimmer—"we could try persuasion. Uncle August says Aaric was supposed to have that power, so maybe you do, too."

His enthusiasm—like a child confronted with a pile of gifts, trying to decide which to open first—charmed her. She'd have to remember to tell Aaric about it. Except, of course, Aaric wasn't Aaric anymore. He was Jesse now. And playing it to the hilt.

As though echoing her thoughts, if not her sentiments, Zack approached at that moment, complaining, "I say, give that man an Academy Award."

"What does that mean?" Molly frowned.

"It means, he's too good to be true. No one can change that much, not even with a near-death experience. Not even if a dozen angels danced on his pillow, showing him the light. He's conning you all—and doing a pretty good job."

"Don't be such a cynic," Molly chided.

"I know all about brothers-in-law," Zack shrugged. "My sister's husband can be great, too, when he wants something—usually money—but it never lasts."

"Well, you're entitled to your opinion," Molly sniffed, "but we're genuinely impressed."

Zack turned directly toward Matthew. "He's putting one over on you, man. Making a fuss over the sons he used to call 'brats,' and calling Molly 'princess.' It's a con."

"Princess?" Matthew scowled.

Molly laughed nervously. "I told him the Valmain story, and I guess he took it seriously." To Zack she explained, "Kerry and I are descended from royalty—a king named Valmain—so technically, we *are* princesses."

"Whatever," Zack growled. "I still say, once a bum, al-

ways a bum." He hesitated, acknowledging a warning signal
from Matthew, then chuckled. "Okay, okay. I'll back off.
Who knows? Maybe I'm wrong. There's a first time for everything. And"—his grin widened—"if you're right, maybe
I should beat *my* brother-in-law to a pulp. Maybe then *he'd*
be a new man."

"Very funny," Molly glared. "Maybe you two shouldn't
wait until morning to leave on your little fishing trip. Maybe
you should go right away. In the meantime, I'm putting Kerry
down for a nap. Excuse me."

When his wife had stormed away, Matthew applauded ruefully. "Smooth, Zack."

"What's with her, anyway?" the agent retorted. "She's
changed. Why does she care what I think about that creep?"

Matthew shook his head. "I've been asking myself that
for days. I guess she's just so grateful to him for not dying—
and for not prosecuting me—that she's lost her perspective."

"I'm grateful, too," Zack admitted. "During the plane ride
here, I kept imagining having to associate with some California criminal attorney and trying my first murder case.
Believe me, it's not something I was looking forward to.
But"—his grin faded—"it still doesn't add up. One minute
he's a loser. A drifter. Now he's suddenly Mr. Wonderful?
Buying a ranch even? Aren't you curious where all the
money's coming from?"

"He won the lottery, remember?" Matthew grinned wryly.
"His luck has completely changed, I guess. And Molly's
right, in a way. He seems to be genuinely trying, so I'm
going to give him the benefit of the doubt for now. But one
false move . . ."

His scowl seemed to reassure Zack. "Now that's the Matt
Redtree I know! I was beginning to think you'd gone soft
down here in Tinseltown." He glanced around the small yard.
"Speaking of Jesse's ranch . . ."

"Yeah?"

"I always thought *you'd* be the one to end up on a place like that."

"If he gets the spread he's been talking about," Matthew agreed, "it sure will be strange. I'd give anything . . ." He caught himself grimly. "At least AJ and Robert are finally getting a break. And maybe, if they do move way out there, Molly won't be so caught up in their lives all the time."

"Relax, Princess," Jesse was advising Molly later that week when she drove out to meet him on the five-hundred-acre parcel he had so magically acquired. "I'm not going to let you down."

"I'm not worried. You're doing great. You talk like him, you move like him . . . Sometimes I almost believe you *are* Jesse."

"Sometimes I almost believe it myself," he chuckled, adding more soberly, "It's strange. I thought I'd be the warrior I once was. And of course I am. But I'm also Jesse Camacho. With his memories. And his weaknesses."

"That explains the cigarettes," she complained lightly.

"I can stop whenever I want, but I don't want to make Rita suspicious."

"Oh, sure," Molly laughed. "What other weaknesses are you going to blame on Jesse?"

"Maybe weakness was the wrong word," he admitted. "I should have said 'frustrations.' *That's* what he was filled with. I think I can understand Matt's frustrations better now, too. Being a warrior in a world such as this!" He shook his head as though bemused. "Of course, Matt was lucky. He had his dream and his legends to give his life direction. Jesse had nothing to work toward. And the only things he did well, his brother did even better. He was a misfit."

"And now? What about you? You're a warrior, too."

"Yes, but I appreciate every moment, every breath. It's a magnificent feeling. And of course, I have certain advantages over the old Jesse. Remember?" He winked and placed his hand over her eyes. When he removed it she saw August standing before her.

"Aaric! What if someone sees? Change back! Hurry!"

"Obey your champion, dream girl." He was mimicking the old uncle's voice perfectly. "Try to find the dream."

Molly giggled. "Cut it out! Change back, *please.*"

Jesse was back, laughing. "That was your chance to tell the old guy off once and for all."

"I'm telling *you* off! Don't play around with your powers, at least not when the boys or Matthew might see you. Promise?"

"No. I promise to be discreet, but I have to have my fun. And you could use some fun, too. Lighten up, Princess!"

The casual, more colloquial style of speech, in contrast to Aaric's formal English, amused Molly, who put her hands on her hips and pretended to scold. "You need a new hobby, Moonshaker. That's why I'm here. I brought you a present. Watch Kerreya while I grab it." Turning away, she began to rummage in the trunk of her brand-new, shiny white Mustang convertible.

"Nice car," he observed smugly.

"How many times do I have to thank you?"

"Me? You won it in that contest."

"You mean the contest I never entered?"

He shrugged offhandedly. "I guess someone must have entered for you."

"Entered for me and then fixed it for me, just like that lottery of yours? But anyway"—she smiled wistfully—"I do love it. It's just what I always wanted. But"—the smile faded—"you've got to stop all this. Matthew's not stupid. He'll think I'm using *my* powers to get these things."

"And you say he's not stupid?"

"Watch it, Aaric. Anyway," she glance around furtively and then thrust a heavy copper axe into his hands. "Here."

"An axe! And a fine one. It's very old."

"Right. It's a collector's object. That's your new hobby."

"I would guess it was once owned by a wizard," he murmured, stroking the rough blade admiringly.

"Really? That's how I reacted to it, too. Like it was magical. Do you know how to use it?"

"Sure. Watch." He hurled the axe toward a nearby sapling, splitting its trunk into perfect halves, then repeated, "It's a fine axe."

"Aaric! I meant can you use its *magic*. You aren't supposed to throw it around! Have a little respect. It's a keepsake."

"It's just an axe, Princess. I'm not Matt. I won't hang it on a wall and study it. I'll make good use of it. As for the magic"—he shrugged—"I have no sense of how to access it. I don't think it's a source." He ambled across the lawn and retrieved the weapon. "Maybe it's a channel, like the amulet. It's not of the mounds. The lakes, maybe." He examined it carefully. "Of course, this handle is recent and not very authentic. And it's lashed incorrectly. But the head's solid and well balanced." He threw it again. "Thanks, Princess."

"If I'd known you were going to abuse it, I might not have given it to you," she pouted.

"Why didn't you give it to your husband?"

"The truth is, I originally bought it for him. Almost two years ago. But then I found out about his policy—*no* weapons are added to his collection unless he knows the origin." She grimaced, then explained, "He doesn't like to encourage unscrupulous dealers, so I never bothered to give it to him. He wouldn't have appreciated it."

"Where did you find it?"

"I bought it from a dealer. I think he was reputable, but who knows?" She shrugged her shoulders. "Anyway, now it's yours. Try not to wreck it."

"I'll teach AJ to use it. His aim's phenomenal. He'll master it in no time."

"He's a little young, isn't he?"

"Young? His training has been neglected for too long already. I arrived just in time." His brown eyes warmed with pride. "That boy will make us all proud one day."

"He reminds you a little of Matthew, doesn't he? Or I guess Lost Eagle, right?" When Jesse started to protest, she hugged him quickly. "I guess all that seems pretty far away these days."

"It wouldn't if you'd just allow me back to the dream occasionally."

"I've explained that, Aaric," she countered defensively. "I'd feel unfaithful to Matthew. It was one thing when you were living there, but for me to call you there, when he would *love* for me to bring him there . . ." Her voice trailed into a sigh.

"He's still fishing in Oregon with his agent?"

Molly nodded. "They make this trip once a year. When he gets back, my training begins." Blushing, she added truthfully, "I miss training with you, Moonshaker."

"What do you do in the dream all alone? Do you practice?"

"Practice, practice," Molly smiled. "Your solution to everything. I hardly go there anymore, anyway."

"Because you're lonely? You would have me back?"

Her cheeks reddened and she admitted shyly, "Yes, but not if it meant you couldn't be Jesse anymore."

"You should have a warrior in your dream. If not me, then summon Matt."

"I'll think about it." She fumbled for her keys. "Just don't tell AJ, or anyone else, who gave this axe to you. And be careful. Now I'd better go."

She buckled Kerreya into the car seat, then turned to find herself in Jesse's arms, being kissed with exaggerated intimacy. Releasing her just as abruptly, he instructed, "Drive carefully, Princess."

Molly blushed again, nodded, and left in speechless confusion. Aaric was so like Jesse Camacho in manner and speech, and of course appearance, but he was still her Aaric in strength and sentiment—in every way that counted. And he was still the only person in her life who loved her by choice, rather than familial duty or destiny's design. She could keep him out of her dreams, but never out of her thoughts.

Five-year-old Niki Sheridan was sitting on the front steps of her Boston home, her eyes scanning anxiously—first to the left, then to the right—for any sign of her daddy's silver Mercedes. Overhead, a robin was singing to her while a pale yellow butterfly enjoyed a newly planted bed of purple pansies, not five feet away. Niki, however, did not dare be distracted by these harbingers of summer. She had to be a "good little lookout," like the bad man Fox had instructed.

She hated it when the bad men came, especially this one named Fox. He even *looked* like a fox, although not nearly as cuddly, of course. And the one named Wolfe had looked like a wolf, but he had been nicer to Niki, and she was almost sorry he had had to die. Anyway, he had liked her because he thought she was a witch like her mommy, and when he found out she wasn't, he could have been mean to her, too, she was sure.

But she didn't want to be a witch and she was sure she wasn't. Witches were bad, and Niki wanted to be good. And Daddy had told her a lot of times that there weren't any such things as witches, and Daddy was the smartest man in the world. And Mommy said even Molly didn't believe in magic, and Molly was *sooo* smart! Daddy had said that a lot of times, too. He said Molly was always reading books and studying smart things when she was little. So if Molly *and* Daddy didn't believe in witches, maybe Mommy was wrong. Maybe there were no witches at all! Just mean ladies, like Mommy, and mean men, like Fox and Wolfe.

This visit, Fox hadn't just been mean. He had been scared, too. He was worried about some secret—a secret he said only he and Mommy knew—and if he knew Niki had heard them talking about it through an open window, he'd probably claw her! She didn't even want to hear their stupid secrets and had been glad when they had moved from the living room and up to Mommy's room, like they always did when they started being sexy. Mommy always brought the bad men up to the room to be sexy, and always made Niki watch for Daddy, and Niki always did her best because she didn't want him to get clawed.

Twin sorcerers. That was part of the secret. They were dead, but Fox was still afraid of them, so Niki knew they must be ghosts. Except, of course, Daddy said there were no ghosts, either, so Niki wasn't really afraid of them. But Fox was really, *really* afraid of them, because he kept telling Mommy that if they came back he wanted to kill them again! And Mommy had told him he was crazy, but after he hurt her with his red eyes, she didn't say that anymore.

Maybe Mommy was right. Maybe Fox and Wolfe were crazy men, and that's why they clawed little girls and killed twins who were already dead. If only Niki could talk to Daddy about it! Or Molly. That would be the best. If she could talk to Molly, maybe Molly and Daddy would make up, and they could all live together—with Mommy, too, *if* she promised not to be mean anymore. That would be the very, *very* best.

The warm glow that comforted her at the thought was gone in a flash when a silver Mercedes turned the corner and headed for the Sheridan home. For a second Niki thought her little legs were going to fail her, but she *had* to warn Mommy in time, or else Daddy would get dead like the twins, and so she lurched into the house and up the stairs, trying to call out, but too frightened to make a sound, until she reached the half-closed bedroom door, which she pounded with all her might.

* * *

He made his way through the shadows, an intruder rather than a visitor, until he reached the sensor-laden fence that protected the Valmain princesses while they slept. Matthew Redtree was still in Oregon, as he had been for the past three nights. And, for the past three nights, the intruder had moved through these shadows, disarmed the security system, and entered the house, moving quietly to the bedside of the dreamer.

His heart began to pound in his chest as he thought of her—of being with her, again. He missed her so fiercely, it was as though she were life itself to him. She had barred him from her dream, and he had sworn to keep his distance from her, but he was weak with need for her, and so again he used the codes she had so innocently shared with him and, within minutes, he was in her little home.

When he caught sight of his reflection in a hall mirror, he grinned sheepishly and chided himself, "You are woefully out of practice, Moonshaker. For a moment you were almost fooled by your own illusion!" Then he scowled slightly, displeased at the image of Matthew Redtree—the son of that accursed enemy Lost Eagle!—staring back at him from the looking glass. "To think I have been reduced to this! To playing games and deceiving her, when I respect her above all women."

But he knew his respect was due, at least partially, to her unwavering fidelity to her champion, and so, paradoxically, respect and deceit were destined to coexist, perhaps forever. And so he would take her champion's form, at every opportunity, and would indulge both love and lust, knowing that in her heart she both suspected and forgave.

He had reached her bedside and now gazed for a long moment, drinking in the sight of this veritable sleeping beauty. As always, she sensed his presence and roused herself, murmuring groggily, "Matthew? I thought . . ."

"You thought I was in Oregon," he whispered, slipping into the bed and molding her nude body to his own, "but I couldn't stay away from you."

She was quickly melting under his lustful touch. "Matthew Redtree! What's gotten into you! Ooh, that feels good." Each kiss was deeper and more arousing than the one before, and his Princess responded with breathless appreciation, urging him to take her to himself as his woman.

Later, as she lay sleeping, he kissed her again, this time with bittersweet gentleness. "Forgive me, Princess. I broke my word. Again. Each time I intend for it to be the last, but the nights are unbearable without you. And so, again"—he touched her brow lightly—"forget that you have seen Matthew this night. He is in Oregon with Zack after all. When you awaken, you will not remember. But I will remember." The sorcerer's husky voice almost broke. "I will never, never forget."

Twelve

It soon became clear that Jesse's ranch had captured the Valmain champion's imagination. He spoke of it often and was clearly intrigued. Skeptical, but intrigued. *He's tempted to move out there, too,* thought Molly in amazement. To her further amazement she realized that she, too, would love it. The location was perfect—close enough to the city so that she could continue to work part-time on the project and perhaps even someday receive her doctorate. Kerreya and the boys would have fresh air, and she could visit Aaric whenever she wished, although, technically, she could see how that might be a drawback as well as an advantage.

When Matthew wasn't thinking about the ranch, he was badgering Molly about her powers and, just as Aaric had done for so many months, insisting that she practice. He coached, applauded, and prodded for details. Always focused and always proud. No longer did he rage against modern civilization. He was sensing that he could again find a purpose in life.

It was the most contented she had ever seen her champion. Even when August Redtree died in his sleep at the end of May, both Matthew and Rita seemed calm and accepting. It was Molly who wept bitter tears, berating herself for leaving the old man alone. Both Matthew and Jesse did their best to reassure her that August had chosen his time, prepared himself, and passed away peacefully. They tried to help the sor-

ceress understand that August would not have wanted or
looked kindly upon any further interference with his time.

Through it all, Matthew was a rock. Past worlds and un-
solved mysteries seemed to have lost some of their urgency.
He spoke of settling down . . . raising horses . . . writing
again. Still, like Rita, Molly was wary of drastic changes in
husbands. It was not a question of if, but rather *when,* the
old Matthew would erupt. It came precariously close one
early summer afternoon during "practice."

"I've got a question for you."

"Okay."

"This is a yes-or-no question, Valmain. Are you ready?"

"Shoot."

He visibly braced himself. "When Jesse was lying in that
bed, in the hospital, dying. Beyond hope. And I was in jail."

It was Molly's turn to brace herself. "Yes?"

"Did you go to his hospital room and give him one of
your power transfusions and save his life?"

"Matthew Redtree!" Molly gasped. "How long have you
been—"

"Yes or no," he interrupted sternly.

"No." She returned his stare defiantly. "No, no, no. I
swear I didn't."

He looked disappointed—almost defeated—and so she
prodded gently, "What made you think such a thing? Remember how weak I was that day? I couldn't have healed a
paper cut."

"I remember. I guess I was just looking for an easy answer," he admitted. "You and Jesse seem so connected. Like
old friends, almost."

"I *like* Jesse. I wasn't around for all the bad years. I've
seen mostly the good side."

"I guess that makes sense."

"There's something else," she added cautiously. "He
saved you from prison, Matthew."

"I know, I know. But you're forgetting we wouldn't have

been in such a mess in the first place if he hadn't been cheating on my sister! Not to mention threatening us with a gun."

"That's true, but . . ." She stopped herself in rueful recognition of the fact that Matthew Redtree was not yet ready for the whole truth.

He confirmed that thought immediately by insisting, "He's a jerk, Molly. Like you said, you weren't around for all the bad years, but Rita was. I watched her spend the best years of her life waiting for that bum to grow up and accept responsibility. She had to raise those boys on her own—she even had a miscarriage once, after one of Jesse's famous stopovers, and did he even know about it? No, he was gone as soon as the fun was over, like usual. Now that he's faced death, he's trying to change—I'll give him that—but don't ask me to admire him."

"Okay, okay." Molly winced. "Sorry I mentioned it. Let's just get back to work. Stand back and I'll bring in a little breeze." With a wave of her hand, she summoned a powerful gust of wind, blasting Matthew directly in the face.

"Cute, Valmain." He grinned. "I get the hint. No more Jesse-bashing."

Someday soon, he'll be ready to hear the whole story, she consoled herself. It was her second favorite fantasy, imagining that Matthew would one day be delighted to discover a powerful sorcerer, right in the midst of his family, who could unlock incredible secrets. The temptation to tell him was equaled, however, by the potential for disaster, and so she willingly postponed the revelation. Perhaps, when Matthew showed some genuine appreciation for the new Jesse, she could dare to bring it all into the open.

Nothing was ever simple where Matthew Redtree was concerned. Without any prior signs of an appreciable shift in his opinion of his brother-in-law, he suddenly proposed to include him on one of his camping-hunting trips, and the thought of the two warriors, out in the wilderness, armed, panicked the Valmain princess.

"You can't be serious! If you need company that bad, *I'll* go with you."

"School vacation started yesterday and I've been promising to take AJ to the mounds," Matthew explained. "It's time he saw them again. Someday he'll hear the *whole* Lost Eagle story and this will give him some background. When he asked if his dad could come, I was trapped. I hoped Jesse would say no but, frankly, now I'm glad he's coming. It's good for AJ." He glanced at the clock, then smiled apologetically. "I'm supposed to pick them up in an hour, so I'd better start packing. We want to get over the mountains before dark."

"I'll come, too," Molly insisted. "My powers might come in handy."

"Don't make me laugh. All we need is you using too much power and then collapsing on the ground," he chuckled. "We'll be fine, Valmain. Just stay home and practice."

"Will you call me every night, at least? I won't be able to sleep unless you do."

He grinned mischievously. "Because you're worried? Or, because you'll miss making love? Ever since I got back from Oregon, you've been all over me."

"I don't know what you're talking about." She blushed, silently acknowledging that, in fact, for reasons she couldn't fathom, she had been literally starved for his touch after that celibate week apart. Not that he didn't always have that effect on her, of course. Moving into his arms, she slipped her hand under his shirt, enjoying the feel of his densely muscled chest. "Take me with you," she cajoled sweetly. "We could make love under the stars. Doesn't that sound wonderful?"

"With AJ three feet away? Nice try, Valmain, but you're staying home and practicing. This is an all-male camp out." He studied her quizzically. "You don't really think I'd hurt Jesse again, do you?"

"I'm not worried about Jesse. I'm worried about you! You

know how obnoxious he can be, Matthew. He might goad you into fighting with him, just so he can make up for the times you've gotten the best of him."

"He'd be nuts to do that," Matthew laughed. "He's not stupid, Molly. He knows he's past his prime. All the drinking and wild living, and neglecting his training—he may have been a fighter once, but that was years ago. He talks big, but that's about it, believe me."

"You don't know him as well as I do, Matthew. He's very competitive *and* he's a show-off. And he can be a bully, too."

"I like this," Matthew grinned, pulling her into his arms. "For once you're not defending the bum. I was beginning to wonder whose side you were on."

"Matthew!"

He nuzzled her neck seductively. "I'll be back in a week, safe and sound, and then you can show me how much you missed me. *And* how much you've practiced. Okay?"

She cuddled protectively against him. "Promise you won't let him make you mad? He can be such a pain."

"I promise." He tilted her chin upward and murmured, "After this trip I'll stay home for the rest of the summer. We have a lot of practicing to do. And I need to spend time with Kerry. In fact"—he cleared his throat cautiously—"I've been thinking about moving to a bigger place. With more land. Would that be okay with you? You'd still be able to commute into the city, and I'd build you a house with a porch, just like you wanted."

"It sounds wonderful," she sighed. "You know, Jesse keeps offering to let us build out with them."

"No! I want our own place." His smile turned sheepish as he admitted, "I want to have you to myself, with no competition from the Camacho males."

"The Camacho males are no competition for you, believe me" she drawled, adding sharply, "Just make sure you give Jesse Camacho the message—that I said *no fighting* on this camping trip—or he'll have to answer to me."

* * *

She tried again. For the tenth time. Such a simple thing. *Just gently blow the leaf off the table.* Despite her best attempt at concentrating, her effort yielded a gust of wind so powerful that it blew not only the leaf, but also the Sunday paper and Kerreya's bib, across the room. It was almost a relief when an unexpected visit from Rita and Robert interrupted the witch's practice. Soon, Robert was pushing Kerreya on her rope swing while the women sat on the porch, enjoying a frosty pitcher of iced tea.

"I'll bet Robert misses AJ." Molly sighed as she watched the children play.

"We both do, but neither of us likes camping, so . . ."

Molly nodded. "Just the same, I wish I'd gone with them." She stretched wistfully. "Have they only been gone two days? It feels like two weeks."

"Actually, I've kind of needed a break. Does that sound terrible?"

"No, but I'm a little surprised," Molly hedged. "I thought you and Jesse were doing okay."

"We are. And then again we're not. You know? He pretends to be happy but . . ." She bit her lip, then blurted, "Molly, if he left again, now, it would be so hard on the boys."

Not nearly as hard as it would be on Aaric, the indignant witch observed silently. *For his sake, Rita had better be wrong.* "What makes you think he's only pretending?"

"He's just so out of character. I mean, this whole ranch thing, for one. Jesse on a ranch? Up at dawn and all that? It's ridiculous," she declared. "And this camping trip with AJ and Matt! Bizarre. *And* he keeps talking about having *another baby!* Can you top that?"

"I think it's kind of sweet."

"Sweet? Jesse? Puh-lease." She dropped the mocking tone and confided, "I don't know what's gotten into him, and I don't think it'll last, but it doesn't matter. I can't have another baby. Physically, I mean."

"I didn't know."

"It's true. I had a couple of miscarriages. Matt remembers. I had such bad scarring in my tubes that I just gave up and had them tied. And even if I hadn't, I could never have carried a baby to term. So that's that."

Molly's heart sank at the realization that Aaric had once again been thwarted in his quest for fatherhood. "I'm sorry, Rita. Sorry for both of you."

"Don't be. He had his chance. I admit, there's a part of me that would love another baby—I've gotten such a kick out of Kerreya—especially if Jesse really was going to stick around this time, but I've put it out of my mind. And I wish Jesse would, too. He has two wonderful sons, after all."

"He loves them," Molly nodded. "He'll adjust. And AJ's already twelve years old. Jesse'll have to wait for his grandchildren."

Rita brightened. "Now, that sounds really fun. All the pleasure and none of the work, right? I knew you could make me feel better, Molly. Thanks."

Molly, however, could not make *herself* feel better. Poor Aaric. He had wanted a baby with Maya and had been denied. Now it was happening again. Could she still demand that he stay married to Rita? Shouldn't she let him find someone new?

She recoiled from the thought, knowing how many people it would hurt, but her heart ached for her friend and mentor, and she vowed to do for him what he had done for her so many, many times—she would argue, cajole, and bully but, ultimately, would support his decision in this matter. It was the very least she could do after all he'd done for her *and* for Matthew, and she wouldn't allow misplaced sentiment to dissuade her from that decision.

* * *

A seemingly interminable week passed, and then Matthew was home, dropping a load of fish onto the counter and hugging each of his sorceresses in turn. "Did you two miss me?"

"You never called, you know."

"I forgot. And there were no phones where we were."

"Forgot? Does that mean you had a good time? What about AJ?"

"AJ had a great time. 'The best time of his life,' to use his exact words. And so did I." He flashed her a rueful smile. "It turns out you were right about Jesse. The guy knows a little something about . . . well, everything, basically. He taught me to spearfish—"

"Yuck."

"No. It was amazing. The guy can stand perfectly still. For hours, I'll bet, if he needed to. Totally calm."

"Did you talk to them about things? Like the amulet?"

"I told them about Lost Eagle, of course, but not the amulet. Actually"—his eyes twinkled—"my stories were pretty tame compared to Jesse's. He can be hilarious! Listen to *this!*"

Molly's head was spinning as Matthew rattled on. Was this *her* Matthew? Raving about Jesse Camacho? It was unbelievable, not to mention unnerving. "So, you two are friends now?"

"Friends? That's kind of strong. Let's just say I don't think he's a total asshole anymore." He grinned. "Now I want to see if you two have been practicing. Let's see some block building and breeze summoning, pronto."

"Gladly. You smell like fish." Molly laughed, ventilating the kitchen effortlessly. "But I still can't resist you. Welcome home, champion." After a reverent yet promising kiss, she admitted, "I was afraid you and Jesse would fight or compete in front of poor AJ . . ."

"AJ loves to watch us compete. He eats it up. He's a real warrior, Molly. When Jesse and I were sparring—"

"What?"

"Relax. I took off the amulet first," he assured her nobly.

"You took off the amulet? Matthew Redtree, you're hopeless."

Missing her point, he insisted, "Jesse wasn't in any danger. In fact, I think he could have beaten me if we hadn't been interrupted."

Molly almost laughed, imagining how Aaric, with his trickery and extra dream hours of practice, could probably have repaid Matthew for both the two dream losses *and* the thrashing Jesse's body had taken only two months earlier. "I'm glad you were interrupted," she smiled. "I wouldn't want *either* of you getting hurt."

"The interruption," he announced mischievously, "was AJ. Guess what he did?" Before she could answer, he blurted, "He put on the amulet."

"Oh!"

"Right. He's descended from Lost Eagle, so it gave him an incredible jolt. You should have seen his face."

"How did you explain it?"

"Luckily, Jesse jumped in and said all the right things. About certain places and experiences being so moving, they seem almost magical." His grin widened. "I was dying to tell them the truth, but I just kept my mouth shut."

Molly shook her curls, amused at the convoluted deception. "Maybe someday the whole truth will come out and we'll all be closer because of it."

"Maybe so," Matthew mused. "Now"—he scooped his little daughter into his arms—"let's go find those blocks."

"So? You dared to fight Matthew at the mounds?" she accused indignantly as soon as she had cornered the Moonshaker alone on his new ranch. "After I warned you not to? And when he wasn't even wearing the amulet?"

The warrior was unrepentant. "I would have beat him, but AJ interrupted us. Did Matt tell you?"

She nodded. "I wish I could have seen his face. A little champion, right there among the mounds."

Jesse grinned. "Did Matt tell you the rest? About how charming and entertaining I was?"

"A little too entertaining," she agreed. "What are you up to?"

"I want him to build on my land," he shrugged. "I'm willing to give him half-ownership. Outright. It's as simple as that. So I'm gaining his trust."

"Are you using persuasion on him?"

"Princess! You underestimate me. I'm charming enough without my powers. Of course, with them I'm totally irresistible."

"Stop teasing. I'm serious," she warned. "Don't manipulate my husband. And back off on this land-sharing thing. I'm not sure it's wise."

"I don't want wise. I want *you.* I miss you. I want to see you every day, like before."

"It's not like before. It never will be."

"No. It can be better." His eyes twinkled. "You and Matt need me. I can make life go smoothly for you. And he enjoys the idea of a ranch. And more children. All of the things *I* want. So, it makes sense." He held out a piece of his lunch. "Want some duck, Princess?"

"You're the only person I know who barbecues duck!" she chastised. "You didn't kill this poor little bird yourself, did you?"

"No, Princess." He waited until she was enjoying her second mouthful before adding, "AJ shot him with an arrow, dead center."

"*AJ?* Jesse Camacho! That's disgusting. Does Rita know?"

Once again, the sorcerer was unrepentant. "AJ needs to learn. His aim's phenomenal, Princess. When Matt's too old, AJ will take over as Valmain champion, to protect you and Kerreya."

"Matthew will never be too old. Anyway," Molly sniffed, "by then, Kerry will have her own husband to protect her."

"Husband?" He seemed to find the thought appalling. "Don't marry her off so easily, Princess!"

"Are you going to be an overprotective uncle?"

"Absolutely. Just as you are an overprotective aunt to my sons."

"Oh, that reminds me." She reached for his hand and squeezed it. "I know how much you want to be a father—"

"I *am* a father."

Molly paused to beam with pride, then continued, "I'm talking about a baby. You and Rita. She told me all about it."

"I knew you'd be worried," he smiled. "You're afraid I'll prefer the new child to my sons? Don't worry, Princess. AJ's my firstborn. My right arm. And Robert may never be a warrior, but he's just as important in my eyes. Just as valuable. He'll be the thinker. The healer!"

"Jesse, listen," Molly pleaded. "There *won't be* a third child. At least not with Rita."

"She told you of her infirmity? She's very brave about it. I'm proud of her."

"And you're not upset?"

"I was momentarily frustrated. But I won't let it stop me from having another son."

Molly's tender mood vanished. "Oh, really? Listen to me, Jesse Camacho, if you're even considering finding another woman, just forget it."

"You've got that book-burning look in your eye," he chuckled. "Calm down. My solution is simple and will hurt no one."

"Oh, really?"

"Do you remember what I told you about Maya? How I tried to persuade her to have my child?"

"Yes. It's so unfair, Aaric. Twice in one—or should I say, two?—lifetimes."

"Remember the details? There was a spell. A lake spell."

"Sure. You called it a carrying spell, and said it would allow another woman to bear Maya's child." She caught her breath. "Oh, no! What are you thinking? What other woman do you have in mind?"

"Rita herself, of course. Think, Princess. Rita cannot conceive. Because of some unfortunate blockage that keeps her egg from traveling to her womb. She drew me a picture, and I think I understand the problem well enough to propose a solution. We'll bypass the blockage."

"Listen to yourself!" Molly grinned reluctantly. " 'Bypass the blockage'? Suddenly you're a doctor? And who is this 'we'?"

"I need your cooperation. This spell is for two. And it *will* work." His tone grew impatient. "Would you deprive me of this child?"

"Me? I can't do spells, remember?" she retorted. "I have no control."

"I will supply the control." Staring deep into her eyes, he cajoled, "Do this for me, Princess. I need you."

"Don't try that persuasion stuff with me, Moonshaker. If I'm going to consider this crazy idea, you'd better convince me there's absolutely no danger to Rita. Or the baby. And"— she was struggling to resist a wave of enthusiasm at the thought of so magnificent a venture—"you have to promise not to get your hopes up. We don't know that we can bypass anything."

"Yes, yes, yes. I promise. It's perfectly safe," he assured her. "You and I will be there to help her. You remember Kerreya's birth? Painless. Simple. Because of your powers and Matt's amulet. Which are impressive but nothing compared to *my* powers. It'll be a breeze. And in nine months you'll be an aunt again."

"Next you'll tell me you'll name it after me if it's a girl," she teased.

"It will be a boy. But you may choose his name."

His grin was contagious, and Molly relented. "Okay. What do you want me to do?"

"We'll work the spell tonight. At midnight. While our families are asleep."

"No! Aaric, I can't get away on such short notice."

"Your champion will sleep soundly tonight, and so will the little princess."

"I won't ask how you know that," she muttered. "So? Should I meet you at your house?"

"You will meet me in the dream."

"Oh, of course! But, Aaric, what about—"

"Midnight," he repeated, then the form of Jesse Camacho disappeared from her sight.

"Oh, Aaric!" She glared in disgust at the empty spot. "You and your stupid illusions." Reminding herself that as a sorceress she should be able to easily see through the illusion, she concentrated—but without success—and so, with a frustrated pout, she returned home to prepare for yet another miracle, courtesy of Aaric the Moonshaker.

It was one of the most incredible nights of Molly's life. There was Aaric, *as Aaric,* standing over Rita, who was serene, angelic, and in the deepest of sleeps in the dream meadow, completely unaware of having been summoned. The sorcerer was in full warrior garb, from his thick leather chest plate to his iron-studded wrist guards—fierce, and yet there was a nobility to him born of his regal bearing, luxurious blond locks, and deeply bronzed, almost leathery skin. His fingertips, charged with fever and ice, worked their magic while his thunderous voice exhorted the mounds themselves to fuel his design. And the Valmain sorceress— the dreamer—trembling yet undeniably powerful—followed his unspoken instructions, binding the spouses together at the wrists with strands of Rita's hair intertwined with her own. She dared not speak, for fear of breaking Aaric's concentration, yet she was silently filled with praise for him. His control was nothing less than phenomenal, causing the magic of the mounds to almost dance through her hands.

Only once before in her life—during the revitalization of August Redtree months earlier—had she stood in such awe of her heritage and her destiny. Life seemed eerie and impossibly mystical, and she longed, illogically, for the moment to last forever.

Then it was done, and Aaric was touching her shoulder gently. "Send Rita back to my bed, Princess."

"Oh . . ." Tears flooded her eyes. "Oh, Aaric, it was so beautiful."

"Send her," he repeated, adding, almost sadly, "I must go, too. Immediately. There is one last duty I must perform."

"Oh, of course." Heat had rushed to her cheeks at the thought and she quickly sent Rita away. "Go ahead. And, good luck. And, Aaric?"

"Yes, Princess?"

"Thank you. I'll never forget this."

"Nor will I." His lips brushed hers and he frowned slightly. "You're trembling."

She flushed again and managed a shaky smile. "Go on, Moonshaker. I'll be okay."

He was so clearly torn, it almost broke her heart and, when he made his reluctant choice and disappeared from her dream, the resulting loneliness was unbearable. Sinking onto the cool grass of her meadow, she began to sob with uncontrollable anguish until her chest and ribs ached from the strain.

"You're hysterical," she taunted herself unhappily. "What's *wrong* with you? It's like you're jealous!"

But of whom? Rita? Because she was making love at that very moment with Aaric? No! That couldn't be true! The truth, as insane as it seemed, was something quite different. Molly was indeed jealous—in fact she was *seething* with jealousy—but not over a simple night's lust. It wasn't Rita's husband she wanted after all. *It was Rita's baby!*

Thirteen

"Wake up, Valmain!" Matthew Redtree switched on the bedside lamp and shook his dream girl anxiously. "Molly! You're having a nightmare!"

"Matthew . . . ?"

"Damn, you scared me," he whispered, pulling her trembling body close. "I couldn't wake you up." As he stroked her perspiration-drenched curls, he forced his own heartbeat to return to a less frantic pace, displeased with himself for having panicked so easily. *You're supposed to be a balanced warrior, not an alarmist,* he chided himself sternly.

But she *had* alarmed him. His precious bride, trembling in terror so palpable that even in his deep sleep he had responded to it. It had been all the more frightening given her usual calm. Even now, as he held her close and caressed her, he could feel the aftershocks of her nightmare racking her slender frame. "Talk to me, Valmain," he pleaded. "Let me help."

"Matthew?" Her eyes opened at last—those stupendous blue eyes—and Matthew's heart sank. Where was the legendary strength? He *needed* that strength almost as much as he needed air or water. This wondrous female had inspired him during childhood, years before they ever met, and had fueled him for his battles with Aaric the Moonshaker. She was everything to him, and he was her champion, sworn to protect her, but felt useless against so unseen and intangible a foe as this unnamed fear that had dared invade her trusting heart.

"Matthew, help me," she was imploring. "Please . . ."

"I'm here, Valmain. Just talk to me. Tell me what scared you and I'll make it better." His arms tightened protectively around her. "Nothing can hurt you when you're with me, Molly. I swear it."

"I need you."

"I'm here."

"I want a baby." She began to sob against his chest. "Please, Matthew?"

"A baby?" He took another deep breath and tried to fathom the nature of this request. A baby? What could it mean? "Did you have a dream about Kerreya?" he probed carefully. "Did you dream something bad happened to her? Is that what scared you?"

The huge blue eyes were literally begging him to understand. "Make love to me, Matthew. I *need* to have a baby. I'm so lonely. So empty . . . so empty . . ."

"Listen to me, Valmain," he insisted in his most reassuring tone. "You had a nightmare. You're still shaking. Let me get you some brandy."

"No! I *don't want* brandy, I want a baby. I'm begging you, Matthew." She sandwiched his face between her feverish hands. "Do this for me. You're my champion. I *need* you."

"Whatever you say," he soothed. "One baby, coming up." To himself he added grimly, *Okay, Son of Lost Eagle, let's see just how well you perform under pressure.*

For the days and weeks that followed, Matthew found himself standing by in helpless silence as his dream girl proceeded to neglect both her work at the lab and her practice with him, spending her time instead playing with Kerreya and sewing tiny quilts and gowns. She seemed unable to fully recover from the nightmare—or procreation impulse—

or whatever had prompted her manic behavior. She didn't want to sleep. She didn't want to eat. She wanted a baby and seemed certain one was on the way.

Matthew certainly hoped she was right. He had wanted a second child himself for months. Aside even from that, however, he wanted his strong, centered bride back. She was so distant from him that, for the first time since the "incident" with Angela, he felt their legendary, fated bond being strained.

Given her moodiness, he hadn't pressed her to practice. Her concentration was off—that much was glaringly clear—and if in fact she was pregnant, the drain on her power might somehow affect the child. He tried to remember the pregnancy with Kerry. Had Molly been this aimless and tense during those months? No. She had been tired but jubilant, humming while she sewed, and flirting, in that cute way she had, with her warrior-husband. This was hardly the same.

Because it's the second kid, he assured himself firmly. *And Molly's older and wiser and knows how much work is involved. Or maybe she knows this is a boy—last time she knew from the start it was a girl—and it's affecting her differently.* It made a certain amount of sense and so Matthew gratefully adopted it as his theory. He also resolved to arrange a get-together with the Camacho family soon. That was a surefire way to bring a smile to her pretty face.

Robert and AJ had been regular visitors, as usual, but Jesse and Rita had been keeping to themselves lately, undoubtedly preoccupied with fixing up their new ranch. Matthew imagined they could probably use a break as much as Molly did! In fact, the more he considered it, the more anxious he was to implement this idea. Abandoning his work on a rusty iron spear he had recently acquired for his collection, he went looking for his dream girl.

He found her in the kitchen, crying, and hurriedly gathered her into his arms. "What's wrong, Valmain?" His gaze was drawn to an empty cardboard box on the table, and then to a tiny plastic test tube. "What's this? A home pregnancy test? Oh, no . . ." Cupping her chin, he turned her tearstained face up toward his. "Sorry, Valmain. Don't cry. We'll just have to try again, right?" Nuzzling her neck, he added lightly, "Kerry's still napping. We could make love right now."

She pulled free and scowled, "I'm not in the mood. Plus, I'm not ovulating, so what's the point?"

He refused to take offense. "Let's do something else, then. It's a beautiful day. We could practice . . ." He winced at her haughty reaction. "Or we could go out and see what Rita and Jesse have done with their new place. Would you like that?"

"Just go by yourself," she suggested wearily. "I don't feel like socializing. Just go, and I'll stay here and catch up on some studying."

"I don't want to leave you alone."

"I've spent most of our marriage alone. I think I can survive one more afternoon."

Matthew shook his head. "I've never seen you like this. Is something else bothering you besides this pregnancy thing?"

She shook her curls and sighed. "I'm just disappointed, Matthew. I'm sorry I've been so bitchy."

"Don't apologize. Even dream girls are entitled to fall apart occasionally," he teased gently.

To his surprise the comment seemed to offend her. "I'm not in the mood to be anyone's dream girl today," she sniffed. "This whole childhood-sweethearts thing leaves me cold."

"What does that mean?"

"It means, I'm a woman, not a girl. I'm flesh and blood, not a dream. And"—her amazing blue eyes flashed—"I don't appreciate the fact that you loved me before you even met me. In fact, I think it stinks." Without warning, her lower lip began to quiver, and she added plaintively, "I miss August! And I miss my mother! And I miss . . ." A sob caught in her throat. "Oh, Matthew, I'm sorry. You're right! I *am* falling apart."

He reached confidently for her, relieved that her illogical anger had vanished so quickly. Now he could begin to help her, and so he soothed, "I know what you were going to say, Valmain. You miss your dad, right?" Before she could respond, he assured her, "He misses you, too. I know it. August and your mother are gone, and I know it's rough, but your father's still alive, in Boston, waiting for you to forgive him. And little Nicole is waiting—"

"And sweet, wonderful Constance?" The dream girl had pulled free of him once again. "Never mind, Matthew. You'll never understand. You'll never see why I can't forgive my father, and you'll never see why I don't want to be the dream girl. You just don't know me at all. *That's* the problem."

"There's no one in this world who knows you better than I do," he corrected firmly. "We're soul mates, and lovers, and partners." He reached tentative fingers toward her crimson cheek and stroked it gently. "I love you, Molly. Let me help."

She stared for a moment, then nodded, allowing him to embrace her. "Sorry, Matthew. I'm just not myself these days. Maybe I'll go and take a nap."

"I'll join you." He moved his hand to her breast and murmured, "Let me make love to you. That always relaxes you."

"I'm not ovulating," she reminded him sadly. "And I think I hear Kerry. Why don't you get her up and feed her while I rest, then you and I can have dinner a little later."

"Sure, Valmain." He watched with concern as she drifted out of sight. Never before had she successfully resisted one of his seductions. If anything, she had always been a little *too* preoccupied with making love, given the many other, nobler tasks destiny had assigned to them. He had hoped she would one day embrace those other responsibilities, including her lessons in magic and her study of the lore of the mounds. Still, the rejection was amazingly frustrating . . .

Because you're thinking like a guy, not like a champion, he chastised himself quickly. *Remember who you are. Remember who she is! Even if she never let you make love to her again, you'd still be the luckiest man on earth, so get a grip.*

Thus reoriented, he hurried down the hall, anxious to quiet Kerreya's cheerful calls for "Mommy" and "Daddy" before they disturbed the dream girl's much-needed rest. For the next few hours, father and daughter ate freshly mashed squash and graham crackers, built block towers, and otherwise entertained one another. Then, after watching an almost mystically vibrant sunset, Matthew bundled the little girl back to bed for the night. He had just turned toward the master bedroom, with intentions of seducing Molly, when a frantic knocking at the front door detoured him and he sprinted to open it.

"Rita!" He pulled his sister into the living room, alarmed by her expression. "What's wrong? What are you doing out alone at this hour?"

"I'm sorry to bother you so late, Matt, but . . ." Rita scanned the room desperately. "Where's Molly?"

"I'm right here," Molly assured her, rubbing sleepy eyes as she emerged from the hallway. "Are you okay? Are the boys—"

"Everyone's fine. I'm just glad you're both here. I needed someone to talk to, and I didn't know who else to turn to."

"Take a deep breath and tell us what's wrong," Matthew instructed briskly. "Are you sick? You look so pale—"

"I feel lousy but I'm not sick," she confided obliquely. Then she grimaced and explained, "I'm pregnant."

"Oh, Rita!" Molly gasped. "Are you sure?"

When his sister started to cry, Matthew hugged her shoulders and soothed, "What's wrong, Sis? Are you afraid you'll lose this one, too? What do the doctors say?"

"I haven't seen a doctor yet. Until today I thought I was

just imagining things. I had my *tubes* tied, remember? But the test results were positive."

Molly's eyes were dancing with delayed delight. "This is so wonderful! Don't be scared, Rita. Just relax and enjoy it. It's the best possible news!"

"I feel awful." Rita's words came tumbling out. "I feel trapped. I don't even *want* a baby! They're too much work! I see you with Kerry, and I'm just not up to it. And even if I was"—her tone grew shrill with despair—"I'll miscarry! I *know* it. I can't go through that again, Matt. To fall in love with it only to lose it. I can't!"

"We understand," Matthew assured her. "Have you told Jesse?"

"That's the problem," Rita explained tearfully. "He's *so* excited. He'd die if he knew I was even thinking about . . . you know . . ." She raised plaintive eyes to her brother. "You know I love Jesse. I want to please him but, damn it, he may have missed the boys' childhoods but *I was right there*. Stuck, twenty-four hours a day. I paid my dues."

"Of course you did." Matthew settled her into a chair and began to pace. "So, let's talk about it. I know I've always been against abortion—that's what we're talking about, right?—but it's *your* body, Rita, and we know you'll miscarry anyway, and so—"

"Matthew Redtree!" Molly gasped. "Don't talk like that! Rita, please, listen to me. The last time you had babies, you were alone. It wasn't fair. But now you have Jesse. You have us! Especially me! I'll help. I'll do whatever you want."

"Molly!" He sent her as stern a warning glance as he dared. "You're not listening to her. She doesn't *want* to have a baby."

"She's just scared. It's intimidating." Molly knelt before her sister-in-law and cooed, "Poor Rita. It's going to be okay. I promise."

Rita shook her head sadly. "You don't understand, Molly. You're ten years younger than me. Your delivery of Kerreya was a breeze. I was there. I remember. My deliveries have always been torture, and that was years ago. Even if I could carry this baby, even if I could stand the pain and discomfort, there's all the years of being tied down . . ."

"That's what I'm saying," Molly insisted brightly. "I'll help with all that! I promise. Anytime you need me. And you won't miscarry—I guarantee it!"

"Excuse us, Rita." Matthew grabbed his wife by her elbow, dragged her into the kitchen and, after backing her carefully but firmly against the wall, exploded, *"What the hell do you think you're doing?"*

Molly was momentarily startled by the vehemence of her champion's reprimand, yet the news was so incredible—at long last, Aaric the Moonshaker was going to be a daddy!— that she simply could not remain cowed for long, and so she wriggled free, flung her arms around his neck, and crowed, "They're going to have a baby!"

"Are you crazy?" Matthew growled. "Didn't you hear a word she said? She came here for *support*. What's with you?"

"I'm just excited. It's so wonderful."

"Stop saying that. And butt out. Now."

"But I can help them."

"Why? Suddenly you're available? You've been anxious to get on with your career and your life, just like Rita. It's all I heard for years. Now suddenly *you* want another baby, and you want *them* to have another one? What's going on?"

Rita hurried into the kitchen, putting her hands on both their shoulders. "Don't argue, please. I shouldn't have come."

"Don't be silly," Molly countered eagerly. "Listen to this, Rita. Matthew and I have been trying to have another baby, too! He's always wanted a son, and our babies could play together!"

"Molly!" Matthew barked. "Cut it out!"

She ignored him frantically. "Wouldn't it be great? We could give each other moral support for the pregnancies, and the kids would grow up together, with Kerry—"

"Valmain, would you please *shut up!*"

The two women stared at him in dismay, then Rita edged away, murmuring helplessly, "I'd better go . . ."

Molly hurried after her, catching up with her on the porch. "I'm sorry, Rita. Matthew's just confused. He wants to tell you that whatever you want is the right thing, and of course that's true, and in my heart, I know you'll make the right decision. But I also know this baby is special. I just feel it."

Rita nodded. "It feels special to me, too. But I'm scared. And now I'm scared for you and Matt. I can't believe the way he yelled at you." Her eyes were filling with tears. "You're his dream girl."

"I haven't been very dreamy lately. I guess he finally ran out of patience."

"Please go in and make up with him. I won't be able to sleep knowing I've caused all this trouble."

"Don't worry. If there's trouble, it's old news," Molly assured her. "Go home and get some sleep. And forgive me for getting so excited. And"—she couldn't resist one last attempt,—"listen to Jesse. Let him be strong for you. Okay?"

"Okay. And thanks, Molly. Tell Matt I'm sorry."

Molly waved with forced cheerfulness until Rita's car was far out of sight. Even then she stayed outside for what seemed like hours, hoping Matthew would give up and go to bed. When she found him, still up and clearly still agitated, she approached, with a cautious smile. "Matthew? Have you been pacing all this time? I'm surprised there's any carpet left."

"Is there an explanation for what happened here tonight?" he demanded coolly. "If there is, I wish you'd tell me. I feel like I don't know you at all and, frankly, I'm not sure I ever did."

"Did you ever want to?" she countered wearily.

"What the hell does *that* mean? You've been taking shots like that all week. All month! Why don't you just say whatever it is you want to say, instead of taking it out on me, and now Rita."

"I'm sorry about that. I admit I got a little overzealous. I already apologized to Rita." She sank onto the couch, pulling her legs up under her. "This whole baby thing just has me on edge, I guess."

"You've been acting like a bitch for weeks. Now this!"

"If I've been such a bitch, why have you stayed?"

"Why does any man stay? You're my wife."

"Just don't say you're 'destined' to stay!" she snapped.

"Why not? It's the truth." He raked his fingers through his unruly black hair. "You've never understood, have you?"

"Open your eyes and grow up, Matthew. You're not a little boy anymore and I'm not a dream girl. I'm just a woman. I just want a man. A man to fall madly, passionately in love with me. And that's never going to happen as long as . . ." She caught herself, aghast at what she'd almost said.

But Matthew had heard the unspoken words and growled, "It won't happen as long as *I'm* around? Fine. Consider me gone." Without a backward glance he stalked into the bedroom, emerging in less than a minute with his fully packed knapsack flung over his shoulder. She thought he might say something then, but he proceeded directly to the front door and then into the night.

She wanted to run after him—to explain that yes, she wanted a man to fall in love with her, but that man *had* to be Matthew Redtree! She never wanted another. Not ever. She would love him until the day she died, with a hungry, precious love that transcended all else. Had she dared imply otherwise?

But she couldn't go after him because she knew he had

read the truth in her eyes. She was miserable without the kind of love she craved from him, and while he was the man she wanted, he was simply incapable of giving her what she needed. He had been programmed by the dream, since childhood, to eschew romance in favor of a more legendary type of drama—the drama of nobility, and honor, and loyalty to a cause. He demanded so much from himself, there was nothing left for her, and yet, in a tragic, hopeless way, it was *all* for her!

She would never find another man to love her with such mindless devotion and utter dedication. Unless of course she turned to Aaric. The thought almost made her cry out in confusion, but instead she whispered, "I've made such a mess of it all. I have to try to sort it out before Matthew comes home. . . ." And she knew he would come home— that was part of the dream deal, after all. He would go to the mounds, to think and to regroup, and then he would come back to his two sorceresses. She had to prepare herself for that moment. She owed that much to everyone concerned.

The master bedroom seemed too far away and much too empty, so she stretched out on the couch. Should she go to the dream? she wondered. What was there for her? More memories, but no champion, and no mentor.

Should she go to Boston? Could it ever be home again? Or would it always represent the place where her mother, after hours of excruciating pain, had died in the automobile accident that had almost claimed Molly and that had, in fact, led to the severance of her ties with her father. No, she wouldn't go back to Boston. At least, not yet.

Ireland? Her grandmother's house was there. Maybe that would be the right choice. But it held too many memories of Matthew, and the love that had been so confused with devotion from the very start. She had no place. No one . . .

"Valmain, wake up."

She responded hungrily to his voice, opening her eyes and marveling, "Matthew! You came back!"

"Did I startle you? You were sleeping so soundly."

"I can't believe you came back. You were so angry. You had a right to be angry," she added sadly.

"I was worried about you. I didn't want it to end like that." His smile, while tender, was enigmatic. "Aren't you just a little glad to see me?"

"I'm so confused," she murmured, slipping her arms around his neck. "I want to be glad to see you, but—"

He put a finger lightly over her mouth and, when she had stopped speaking, kissed her gently. He was going to make love to her, and she wanted that so much, but what would it solve? And where was all his righteous anger? Why was he being so understanding? So much like . . .

"AARIC!" Unnerved by the sorcerer's audacity, she jumped to her feet and wailed, "This is *too* much! How could you dare do this?"

"Forgive me, Princess. I needed to see you."

"Are you crazy? What if Matthew had been here?"

"He stopped by the ranch on his way out of town. He's on his way to the mounds."

"That figures," she nodded. "But what if he decides to come back? My heart's still pounding! What if he walks in right now and sees . . . well, sees *himself* here, with me?"

"I don't think he's coming back, Princess."

Molly's anger disappeared as she absorbed his meaning, then she sat down, trying to think of something—anything— to say. "Did Rita come home after she left here?" she murmured finally.

"Yeah. She's sound asleep. Like a baby," he added, a grin sneaking through his solemnity.

Molly took his hand and pressed it to her lips. "The news was wonderful, Aaric. I just wish Rita was happier about it."

"She's better than she was. Again, I'm grateful to you." His hand stroked her cheek. "That's why I had to come. I couldn't let you be alone with this, after all you've done for me. I'm so sorry, Princess."

"Forget about Matthew and me. Let's talk about the baby. Are you sure Rita won't change her mind again?"

"I'm certain. Whatever you said worked. You are so remarkable," he added fondly. "You don't need your power of persuasion. People respond to you because you care about them."

"What about that? You didn't use persuasion on her, did you?"

"Before she came to see you, my power was useless on her. That's how much she *didn't* want my son. But when she returned, it was easy."

"Aaric! You can't abuse her like that. You have to respect her feelings. It's *her* body."

"It's *my* son. And her fears are groundless. Everything will be easy and painless. The birth will be uncomplicated. And after that, if she feels tied down, you and I will raise the child, as you offered."

"When did I offer that?" Molly demanded. "I told her I'd help her out, but that's hardly the same as *raising* the child! Especially now! With Matthew . . . by the way, do you think you could stop the illusion? It's a little awkward talking *about* him *to* him, if you know what I mean."

"Sure. Who shall I be? Jesse? Or Aaric?"

Resisting her first impulse, she advised, "You'd better be Jesse. I don't think . . . Oh!" Her heart melted as he slowly rematerialized, bronzed, golden-haired and invincible. "Aaric! You always look so magnificent!"

"Of course I do. Why are you surprised? Come here now and tell me your troubles, just as you once did in the days of the dream. I'll make you feel better."

"I love you!" she declared, hugging him passionately. "Now change back and go home to your wife. My troubles will wait until tomorrow."

"You shouldn't be alone."

"I'm not alone. Kerry's here and plus, I have a lot of thinking to do. I might even take a little trip," she added, surprising herself as well as the sorcerer with the tentative thought.

"A trip? To the mounds?"

"No. Actually, I've been thinking this may be a good time to go and make peace with my father. Maybe then I'll be able to think about Matthew, and my life, more clearly."

"No! You must stay here! I need you," Aaric protested. "You can't leave us alone right now, Princess. What about my son? Your unborn nephew?"

"If Matthew and I get a divorce, your son won't be my nephew anymore, Aaric," Molly sighed. "He won't be legally related to me at all."

The sorcerer's eyes were wide with shock. "I never thought of that! I'll make a will immediately, naming you guardian."

"You can't do that," she chided. "People will think we had an affair or something."

"If you get divorced, maybe we will." When she remained silent he cocked an eyebrow and teased, "No protest?"

She shook her head. "What a mess. And poor Kerry's caught in the middle."

"You should make a will, too," he urged. "If anything happened to you, the little one should be with me. She needs training. Developing. I don't want her to end up like . . ." He hesitated, grinning apologetically.

"Like me?" Molly finished with a reluctant smile. "I don't think she will. She's so precocious. Grandma says *I* didn't walk until I was almost a year old."

"Ah, yes," Aaric mused. "Grandma Elizabeth. I still haven't met her. But if you insist upon going to family for a visit, why not go to see her?"

"That would be nice, except"—she paused to grimace—"it might get her hopes up. She never wanted me to marry Matthew, remember? She's a little mellower on the subject now that Kerreya's in the picture but she still calls him a 'legendmonger' and all that. On the other hand," she added,

more to herself than to Aaric, "it would please Grandma to
know I'd made some effort to reconcile with Dad. He's never
even seen his only grandchild."

"He forfeited that right when he betrayed Kerreya's grandmother!" Aaric retorted. "Have you accepted *that?* His fla-
grant affair with another woman while your mother was
dying?"

"Of course not. You're right," she admitted, more confused
than ever. "I hate this. Everything's so hopeless. Except, of
course, your baby." The thought soothed her. "Rita said she's
been feeling a little sick. Is that a problem?"

"She's weary, but that's normal." His eyes narrowed. "You
seem pale yourself. Have you been ill?"

"Not at all. Just tired, I guess. Stressed out."

"Let Rita and I take Kerreya for a few days so you can
rest."

"You just want to start training her," she teased, adding
softly, "Don't worry. I'll sleep once Matthew's home and
we've dealt with all of this once and for all."

"Then at least let one of my boys stay with you. There's
no school now, Princess."

"I'm a big girl," Molly countered firmly. "I'll just concentrate on work and sewing more clothes for the new baby.
That'll distract me."

He studied her carefully, then nodded. "If you're sure, I'll
go. It's best not to leave Rita alone with her lingering doubts.
Tomorrow I'll come back and we'll have a long talk."

"I'll call you when I'm ready to talk," she hedged. "Just
stay with Rita until then."

"Agreed. And, Princess?" He hesitated, clearly concerned.
"You wouldn't ever leave town without telling us first, would
you?"

"Of course not. Anyway"—her smile grew wistful—"you
pretty much blew my travel plans away."

"I didn't mean to make you sadder."

"Sadder but wiser, right? Calling my father would probably just add to my stress. I guess the only real solution for now is a good night's sleep."

"That's true." He embraced her gently, then shrugged to his feet. "Go to the dream. If you need to talk, summon me to meet you."

"Okay. And, Aaric?" She stood and took his huge hands in her own. "Congratulations again. You'll make an outstanding father."

"Thanks, Princess." He turned toward the door, then added sternly over his shoulder, "Sleep."

"I will, I promise." She managed to maintain a half-smile until he'd gone, but his words were ringing in her ears.

I don't think he's coming back, Princess.

"He'll come back," she whispered aloud. "He'll come, or he'll call. Or, I'll take Kerry to Ireland to meet Grandma. Or"—her voice began to tremble with innocent, childlike hope—"maybe we'll go see Dad."

Fourteen

"Hello?"

"Hello." Molly took a deep breath. "May I please speak to Dr. Sheridan?"

"Dr. Sheridan is unavailable. Could I take a message?"

Resisting an impulse to break the connection, she persisted, "May I speak to Nicole, please?"

"Who is this?"

"Constance? This is Molly." She took another deep breath and blurted, "I'd like to speak to my father. Or my sister."

"Your sister?" The stepmother's voice dripped with amusement. "What's the occasion?"

"Are they home?"

"Your father and his daughter are riding their bikes."

"Oh." Molly thought of other days, and other bike rides, and tears stung her eyes. "That's so cute. And I'm sure Nicole's cute, too, Constance. I've really enjoyed the pictures of her that Dad sends every Christmas."

"The pictures *I* send," the now-cold voice corrected. "He and Niki are very close."

"I remember what that's like."

"Do you really?"

"She's lucky to have a father like him."

"No. *He's* lucky to have a *daughter* like her."

"I see. Goodbye, Constance." Placing the receiver gently back into its cradle, Molly's gaze swept sadly over the open photo album filled with snapshots of a handsome, fair-haired doctor and a perky blond angel. *They're not your family,* she told herself ruefully. *Is Matthew? Jesse? There's Kerreya, of course, but . . .*

"Aunt Molly?"

She spun gratefully toward the cheerful voice. "Hi, AJ."

"Dad just dropped me off." Hefting a duffel bag into view, the boy grinned. "You've got company for a while. Okay?"

"It's better than okay. I *needed* a friendly face." Rumpling his thick hair, she suggested gratefully, "Let's go see what Kerry's up to."

Aaric stopped by every day for a week, listening patiently as she alternately bemoaned Matthew's absence and railed against his very existence. When she confided she was considering divorce, her mentor simply shrugged and assured her he would stand by her whatever she decided. When she cried against his shirtfront and wailed that she missed her champion, he offered to go to the mounds and talk to him, warrior to warrior. When she admitted she didn't know *what* to do, he claimed she was the most intelligent woman in the universe and would undoubtedly make the correct decision.

Finally she let him "off her hooks," instructing him to stay away until she sent for him again, and reminding him that Rita needed him during these early days of the pregnancy. Thereafter, it was AJ who became her rock and, like a true son of Lost Eagle, he proved more than equal to the task. As she watched him "train" his infant cousin over the ensuing days, she was slowly able to find genuine peace at last.

"You're wonderful with Kerry, AJ."

"It's good practice for when Mom's baby comes," the boy enthused. "Except Dad says it's going to definitely be a boy. I think Mom wants a girl, though."

"You're excited about the baby?"

"Sure. So's Robert." He began his telltale pacing. "When's Uncle Matt coming home?"

"Soon, I'm sure."

"He's at the mounds?"

"Yes, AJ."

"I had the best week of my life there with him and Dad." He hesitated, then asked, "You know that spool you gave him?"

Molly nodded cautiously. "Yes, AJ?"

"Have you ever put it on your wrist?"

"Twice. Once before Uncle Matthew and I were married, and once when Kerry was born." She was touched by AJ's breathless, trusting anticipation. It would be so easy to confirm the obvious suspicions of this young descendant of Lost Eagle. "That spool's been in my family for a long time, AJ. It's very special to me and to Matthew. I'm glad it's special to you, too."

"Special?"

"On the right person's wrist," she smiled, "it's almost magical."

"Yeah." The boy's voice was hushed. "You really understand?"

"So do your uncle and your dad. They just don't want to confuse you just yet."

"Until my 'training' is done?" AJ laughed. "That's what *Dad* would say. He's always thinking of some new job for me. He has this old axe, made out of copper—real ancient!— and we use it every day! Uncle Matt would have a fit if he saw how Dad treats it."

"Maybe not." Molly smiled. "An axe is pretty unique. It's not just a weapon. It's also a tool. *Mostly* a tool."

"But this one feels mostly like a weapon! When I throw it I feel like a real warrior."

"You be careful with that," she chided nervously. "It's not a toy."

"Sure, Aunt Molly. I promise. Now"—the roles shifted abruptly—"you go and rest. Dad's orders."

"Let me watch a little longer," Molly cajoled, intrigued by Kerreya's progress. Under AJ's careful tutelage she had begun to develop a keen interest in, and aptitude for, throwing her red rubber ball into a nearby bucket.

Molly was mindful of Aaric's prediction: Kerreya Redtree would be trained to become a powerful sorceress; AJ would protect her as Matthew had protected Molly. The foundation was being laid even now, Molly decided with halfhearted enthusiasm. Kerreya and AJ—both almost fanatical in their willingness to practice a skill; their acceptance of endless repetition as a form of amusement; and, their devotion—not to mention their *deference*—to one another!

"Look, Aunt Molly!" AJ boasted. "She never misses now."

"You're a good teacher, AJ."

"Look, Mommy!" Kerreya echoed proudly, tossing the ball with ease.

"That's very good, Kerry."

"We'll practice every day—while *you* rest—until Uncle Matt gets home," AJ promised. "Do you think he'll be impressed?"

"He'll be proud of you both. I guarantee it." *And,* she decided firmly, *it's time.* With the quiet concentration of the mature witch she was being forced to become, she moved a short distance away and prepared to summon her champion.

When three distinct attempts at summoning her wandering husband proved futile, Molly's annoyance became tempered with concern for his safety. Her powers, never dependable, were becoming oddly erratic, so much so that she dared not use them, even to amuse herself in the lonely hours between sleep and work. She needed professional advice but was determined to be discreet, so she decided not to call Aaric at the ranch. AJ had innocently revealed that his father disappeared into Los Angeles every day between four and six in the afternoon, and she surmised he had either found a mistress or a hangout. Hopefully, the latter.

Digging through her purse, she found a matchbook he had left on her porch after one of his visits. It had amused her at the time. The Moonshaker's fascination with matches had not yet subsided, and his smoking habit had, if anything, worsened. Was this Chaste Scene, as the bar was apparently called, the spot to which he disappeared so often?

She waited until almost four, then slipped into a modest white shirtdress, left Kerreya in her warrior-nephew's capable hands, and headed for town.

It was a surprisingly nice club. *Very tasteful,* she thought nervously, smoothing her prim outfit apologetically and trying to ignore the curious stares of the regular patrons, most of whom were wearing jeans. *You should have just summoned him,* she reproached herself as she scanned the stools and booths. *He's obviously not here and you're wasting valuable time.*

Annoyed with herself, she was about to make a hasty retreat when a handsome figure caught her eye and she smiled in recognition. He wasn't Jesse—at least, not quite. He was more like Aaric—fair-haired, but leaner and taller. Abandoning the two young women he had been entertaining, he moved quickly toward his Princess.

"Do I know you?" he inquired smoothly. "You look familiar. Could I buy you a drink?"

"Cut it out, Aaric. I'd know you anywhere."

"Aaric? You're mistaken." He took her hand and kissed it mischievously. "I'm Nicholas."

"Nicholas? I like that. It suits you." She felt herself melting before his attentive gaze. His eyes, alive with flecks of shimmering gold, were so . . . "Aaric! *You're using Matthew's eyes!* I can't believe you! Is nothing sacred?"

"They're the best," he acknowledged, with no trace of remorse. "Women instinctively trust them. If Matt would just get some decent clothes and lighten up a little, he could have women crawling all over him."

Molly bit back a smile. "I *like* the way Matthew dresses."

"Of course you do. You know he won't attract any women in that dismal getup."

"I'll admit one thing," she mused. "When I would attend his lectures, back at school, before I'd actually met him, he used to wear an old tweed blazer, and all the female students had incredible crushes on him. Not me, of course. I was too studious in those days." She shook her head in wonder. It all seemed so long ago. What had happened to that jacket? To that studious young woman?

"If you persist in your plan to divorce him, I'll have to give him some pointers." When Molly's smile faded, Nicholas added hurriedly, "I'm kidding. Hey, Princess, what's wrong? Don't tell me you're missing him? One short week ago you were ready to serve papers on him."

"I'm worried about him, Aaric. It's been so long since he left. I finally tried to summon him. Twice yesterday, and once today. All I got for my trouble was a headache."

"A headache? What do you mean? Are you ill?"

"It just hurts. And I've been feeling a little weak and dizzy," she admitted reluctantly.

"Dizzy?" He frowned. "Is it possible you're pregnant?"

"No. Definitely not. I just haven't been sleeping well."

"And you summoned him? To the dream?"

"No. I didn't even think of it," she admitted. "Maybe I should try that."

"If you're feeling weak you should do nothing but rest. A summons can be draining. Rest your power. Matt's probably just ignoring you," he added gently. "Now that he knows about you, he'll understand the summons and resist it, especially if he's still at the mounds. With the amulet he could even resist a *dream* summons."

"That's what I thought at first," she agreed. "But it would worry him. I *know* it. He'd wonder if maybe something was wrong with Kerreya and he'd call you and Rita, at least."

"That's probably true," Nicholas conceded. "There's only one way to be sure. *I* will summon him. If he's able, he'll come. He won't be able to ignore such a jolt."

"Thanks, Aaric. I can always count on you." She gazed around wistfully. The soft glow of candlelight and the strains of light-rock love songs filled the room with sensuous comfort, reminding her of the courtship that had never been. "Go on back to your fun. Tomorrow will be soon enough. I'd better get going. I left the baby with AJ." She squeezed his arm gratefully. "Having him stay with me may have been the best of all your ideas."

"Don't rush away, Princess. Let me buy you a drink."

"What if someone sees us?"

"Us? They know me as Nicholas, not as Jesse. If you're serious about divorcing Matt, you'd better get used to seeing other men."

"*Other* men. Not you in different disguises. Anyway"—she sighed—"I have to be sure he's all right before I think about divorcing him, right?"

Nicholas threw up his hands in disgust. "You're not 'worried' about him. You just miss him. You're hopeless."

"Are you angry?"

"At you? Never. Thanks to you, I will be a father in less than a year."

She kissed his cheek. "Do you have any idea how much I love you? You're my best friend."

"Yeah, I know. Come on, let's go. I'll get him back for you in less than twenty-four hours. Guaranteed."

* * *

Constance Sheridan's gaze shifted from the ornate, spool-shaped amulet in her hand, to the inscrutable expression on the First Wizard's face, to the child standing, staring, in the doorway. "What are you waiting for, you stupid brat?" she chastised nervously. "Go and watch for your father's car!" When the girl had scurried away, she inquired sweetly, "Wherever did you find this, Fox? It's quite remarkable."

"Is it of the mounds?"

"Almost certainly. Do you see these markings? The mounds, and the twins." She pressed the amulet to her right wrist, and then to her left, then sighed. "Of course, we cannot manipulate it. Still, it's remarkable. It brings back such old memories."

"They had many such artifacts?"

His tone was smoother than ever, Constance noted. As though he had rehearsed this conversation time and again. If so, then she had better get *her* lines right. "These amulets were very rare. The mounds magicians were unable to combine their powers and so, to fashion such a charm as this, one magician would need to drain himself—or herself—to a dangerous degree. There were many stories of sentimental fools dying in a vain attempt to create such an amulet, or a similar one, designed for protection rather than offense. This amulet," she added thoughtfully, "would allow its owner to draw power directly from the mounds. Such a person would then be quite formidable." Taking a deep breath, she dared to inquire, "Where did you find this?"

"I took it from the wrist of a dark-haired warrior."

"Oh! My warrior!" she gasped. "Has he come at last? Did you kill him?"

"He's not *your* warrior, he's *hers*."

"Pardon?"

"He is the husband of your stepdaughter. He is Redtree."

For a moment the room seemed to spin as the impossible fact assaulted Constance's equilibrium. Finally, and with great effort, she managed to murmur, "I don't understand."

"Of course you don't." The wizard's eyes were glowing a dangerous shade of red. "That's because you're stupid and worthless. You had only one duty, you pitiful bitch, and you failed."

"No!" She backed away quickly but forced herself not to cower. "That isn't fair! I stayed in this boring house with Alexander. I brought about the betrayal. You can't deny that!"

"But when the warrior came, where were you? Shopping? Whoring? Whining? And so he went to the Valmain girl instead, and she won his heart."

"Maybe he was just trying to get close to her," Constance reasoned desperately. "So he could be there when the Valmain champion arose."

"He *is* the champion! Are you a complete idiot? Can't you see that the spell of protection has triumphed? Maya's curse has been foiled, thanks to you. Her servant has become her undoing."

"Then why am I still beautiful?"

It seemed to confuse Fox for a moment, and to her relief his eyes returned to their less volatile green. Finally he admitted, "I hadn't thought of that. Maybe it's not over yet."

Eager to exploit his momentary calm, she insisted, "This is wonderful news, Fox. Don't you see? You spoke of disturbances in North America, and now we know the source. Maya sent this warrior, and he's been practicing near the mounds, drawing power from them. It makes perfect sense. And"—she stepped into him, positioning herself provocatively against him—"now that you've disarmed him, he's powerless. You're a hero to us all, Fox. Allow me to honor you."

He grinned reluctantly. "In a moment, perhaps. I have a few more questions for you."

"Oh?" She pretended to pout. "What now?"

"Can this simple amulet explain tremendous power surges?"

"Absolutely," she soothed. "With this on his wrist, his strength and stamina must have been unequaled." She paused to imagine little Molly in bed with such a man and laughed enviously. "Without it he is now nothing. I guarantee it." She cocked her head to one side. "You allowed him to live?"

Fox eyed her knowingly. "I almost killed him for you, my love, but he has something else I want."

She was intrigued by the undercurrent of ambition and lust in his voice. What could a legend spinner have that a wizard could covet so fervently? Had Matthew Redtree come to this century armed with more than one amulet? Or was it something less dramatic? A woman, perhaps? Certainly not Molly, of course, but another?

"Never mind for now," the wizard chided. "If you behave, and keep all of this confidential, I'll tell you the rest soon enough."

"Confidential?" She frowned. "You haven't informed the assembly? Is that wise?"

"You doubt my wisdom?"

Constance winced. "Certainly not. I just thought they should be told, so they could praise you for disarming so deadly and challenging an enemy."

"You sound as though you admire him," Fox taunted. "How unfortunate that he chose your stepdaughter over you."

"He didn't choose her *over* me. He never met me." Her eyes flashed as she added, "I'm one thousand times more beautiful than Molly. Maya's spell guaranteed that. I could steal him from her in an instant if I wanted. Or rather," she amended quickly, "if *you* wanted me to."

"Perhaps it isn't simply beauty he was looking for," Fox smirked. "If that were all a man needed, would I have married Sara when I could have had you?" Before she could answer, he assured her, "Some women have more than beauty, my love. Perhaps your stepdaughter is like my Sara. Perhaps she has grace, or fire, or imagination. Those qualities can be quite intoxicating." He laughed when Constance scowled with jealousy, then teased, "Would you like a chance to prove me wrong?"

Constance nodded, immediately confident, and, after a quick glance through the window to ensure that her brat daughter was at her post, resolved to teach this tasteless fool a lesson—in fire *and* imagination—he would not soon forget.

Hefting the last of the suitcases into the trunk of his Cadillac, Jesse Camacho turned to his Princess and chided, "Try to smile, for the little one's sake. She knows you're upset, and it's frightening her."

"We're all frightened, even you. Don't deny it."

"I'm concerned," he corrected. "That's why we're going to the mounds. But," he slammed the trunk lid and insisted, "I am never frightened."

"You've been summoning him for two days."

"He's stubborn, and the amulet aids his resistance."

"Or he's hurt. Or worse."

"Such talk is useless. We'll know the truth soon enough." He scowled when AJ appeared in the doorway with the cordless telephone in his hand. "Great, another delay."

"Maybe it's Matthew!" She flew to her nephew's side, demanding, "Is it him?"

The boy shook his head, his eyes round with apprehension. "It's some guy, Aunt Molly. He said he's a doctor."

"A doctor?"

"He said he's calling from Peru."

"Peru?" Molly frowned. "Did he ask for Uncle Matthew?"

"No. He asked if I was Matthew Redtree's son and then he said I should get you. Right away."

Jesse had come up behind her and now urged gently, "Answer it, Princess. Don't keep him waiting."

The doctor's voice was soothing yet insistent. A man "identified" as Matthew Redtree had been "found" three days earlier, wandering and delirious. He was being "treated." He was doing "very well, actually, all things considered," but it would be best if the family could send a "representative" right away . . .

"Calm down, Princess," Jesse consoled her. "We'll go right away. We're all packed, remember? And they say he's not in any danger. This is *good* news," he added firmly. "He's alive."

"But, Aaric . . ."

"Call me Jesse." He glanced toward AJ, who was trying to distract an increasingly agitated Kerreya. "Smile now, and let's get going. We'll drop the kids at the ranch."

"I want to bring Kerry with us."

"That is unwise. Rita will take fine care of her."

He hurried her along after that, refusing to allow her to speculate. He reminded her of their powers, and of Matthew's excellent conditioning, and of the amazing progress that her science and medicine had made in the last dozen centuries. In what seemed like only minutes, they had delivered the children to Rita and were rushing into the airport.

"The gate is this way, Princess."

"We need tickets," she protested. "And we're already late."

"Tickets aren't technically necessary, as long as the flight isn't full," her wily escort insisted. "I do this at least twice a week."

"What?"

"Don't you remember? I told you flying was the thing I wished to try the most."

It brought a fleeting smile to her face—her wonderful Moonshaker! He could always make her feel better! Then she remembered Matthew. If only Aaric could do the same for *him*. Matthew Redtree, lying in a hospital! His greatest anathema.

She would get him out of there immediately. She and Aaric would transfer their power to him through the amulet, then whisk him away to the mounds. It would work for Matthew just as it had worked for August.

"You use your persuasion so effortlessly," she marveled as they boarded the twelve-hour flight for Cuzco. "What would I do without you, Moonshaker?"

"You would pay for your ticket," he grinned. "Flying is very expensive that way, Princess. Would you like a drink now?" He motioned for a flight attendant, who seemed only too eager to abandon her boarding duties and cater to the couple.

Ordinarily, Molly might have protested such abuse of their magic, but she welcomed the distraction from thoughts of Matthew's plight. "Do you often use persuasion on women, Jesse?"

"Usually I travel as Nicholas. Women do his bidding with no need for persuasion."

"He's handsome," Molly agreed shyly. "But so is Jesse."

"No flirting, Princess."

"Jesse!" She shook her head. "You're having fun, aren't you? Just like you predicted, you love flying. Tell me everything. I want to know where you fly to, and how often."

"I've taken many short flights. To the mounds. To Mexico. To the lakes or, should I say, the former location of the lakes."

Molly patted his arm. "You're disappointed, aren't you? That it's all gone?"

"Don't be deceived, Princess. The mounds are deserted, I agree. I've searched in vain for our descendants. If they were here, I believe I would sense them. Instead, all is quiet. Except, of course, when Matt's using his amulet or you're making a mess."

"Very funny."

"The lakes are another matter. When I'm there I feel electricity in the air. They're active, Princess. Unfortunately, they've relocated, although their base must still be in what you call New York, or at least in that vicinity."

"And you're afraid they pose a threat?"

"If they knew about you, they would kill you. If they suspected Kerreya's strength, they would launch an all-out assault on us."

"And if they knew about you?"

"If they knew that the Moonshaker had returned, they would quake. No, don't smile," he cautioned sharply. "That's not an idle boast. They feared me, and with good reason."

"And Maya? Did they fear her?"

"Maya never allowed her hatred for them to show. She flirted with them, in order to gain access to their secrets."

"Flirted?" Molly frowned. "Did she ever get involved with a wizard? They all sound so ugly and evil . . ."

Jesse closed his eyes and remembered. "No, Princess, Maya never gave herself to a wizard. She would never have chanced a pregnancy, knowing that any child of a wizard would owe first allegiance to the lakes, just as the child of a mounds sorcerer would be loyal to the mounds."

"That's chauvinistic," Molly complained. "You just assume in a mixed marriage, the child would be loyal to the father's culture, not the mother's."

"It's academic. We of the mounds allowed no marriage to outside magicians, lake or otherwise. We were vulnerable as it was, and such infiltration could have been disastrous. Perhaps," he added sadly, "that's what happened. Perhaps we were destroyed by just such a mistake."

"But we're *not* destroyed," Molly soothed. "You and Kerry and I—and the baby who's coming—*we're* the mounds. All of the Redtrees, through the amulet, are the mounds, and we grow stronger with each passing day."

"I've never heard you speak this way," Jesse murmured. "It's ancient music to my ears. Are you beginning to understand?"

"I guess so. I want to be strong."

"Because your champion is injured?" He patted her hand. "You must try to sleep. I have this situation under control."

"How can you? We don't know how serious his injuries are yet."

"He was found wandering in the jungle. My guess is he's suffering from exposure. It's rare in your day but in my time it was an ever-present danger to the traveler. I've used my powers to restore such victims dozens of times."

"Have you, Aaric? I know you're exaggerating," she added with a rueful smile, "but have you cured it at least once? Honestly?"

"More than once. Of course," he hesitated, then revealed, "when I help him, he'll be aware of my assistance. He'll know immediately that I'm not Jesse Camacho."

"I see." Molly squared her shoulders, accepting the implications. "It can't be helped. My powers are weak. Yours are strong. Matthew will be 'restored' by you and then we'll deal with his anger."

"I'll be temporarily weakened by the experience," he predicted quietly, "but when my strength returns I'll use my powers to persuade him to hear us out. No"—he shook his head vehemently—"don't argue. Foolish pride is an enemy we cannot afford, Princess, as your grandfather once told us. Close your eyes now." He stroked her hair and, while she knew he was using persuasion on her to force her to rest, she had no strength or will to resist and gladly slipped into a deep, replenishing sleep.

Fifteen

Cuzco presented unique problems for the young witch, who found herself clinging to Jesse's arm as a wave of dizziness swept over her almost immediately upon alighting from the plane. "Altitude sickness?" she moaned.

"The Peruvians call it *soroche.* We're thousands of feet above sea level here, Princess. Sit down." He led her to a bank of chairs. "I'll see if I can find you something to drink." He was back in less than a minute. "They tell me there's a tea called *maté de coca.* We'll find you some before we proceed to the hospital."

"But we have to hurry. And I . . ." The room spun and, as she passed out, she was dimly aware of Jesse's booming laughter as he caught her in his arms.

"So? You're finally awake?"

"Aaric?" Molly's head was swimming as she struggled to focus on his grinning face. "Where are we? Where's Matthew?"

"We're at the hospital. You've been out for twenty minutes." His chuckle was tempered with love as he chided, "You're more trouble than any woman I've ever known. Would you like to meet your husband's doctor?"

She stared past him, into a pair of sympathetic eyes, and extended her hand in a silent plea for good news.

"Mrs. Redtree? Please don't be distressed. Your symptoms will subside when you've adjusted to our altitude."

"And my husband?"

"He's recovering well, physically," the doctor assured her. "His body is in excellent condition."

Molly turned to Jesse. "What does *that* mean?"

"He's saying Matt has amnesia, Princess."

"What?"

The doctor touched her shoulder and explained, "We knew you'd want to be with him. And we're hoping the sight of you will stimulate his memory."

"His memory?"

"He was delirious for a while. Then, two days ago he became totally lucid—as though someone had shaken him or called to him—except . . ."

"Except he has no memory," Jesse finished. "Is there no medicine for this, Doctor?"

The kindly man shrugged. "He refuses to consent to any drug therapy. And even if he did, we don't really understand his condition. There was a blow to the head, and several other wounds, but nothing that would explain amnesia."

"A blow to his head? Did someone hit him?"

"We may never fully know what happened," the doctor hedged. "But he's doing well. None of the injuries are critical."

"Can we go in?"

"Yes. Hopefully, as I said, the sight of you will trigger something. If not, try not to upset him. He's not a man who enjoys being infirm."

Molly nodded and took hold of Jesse's arm. "Let's go."

She braced herself as they proceeded to the room, but even so, the sight of Matthew Redtree in a hospital gown, propped against pillows and surrounded by sterile walls, was unnerving. He eyed them quizzically, first Molly, then Jesse, and then, with an increasingly dumbfounded expression, turned back to Molly and asked nervously, "Do I know you?"

"Matthew?" She choked back her shock and moved slowly toward the bed. "Matthew, are you all right?"

He was still staring. "Who are you?"

"I'm Molly. I'm your wife." She managed a weak smile and added, "I love you. I'm here to take care of you."

He shook his head. "When they told me I was married, I pictured you so . . . completely different." He continued to study her. "Are you sure?"

"Of course." She tried to sound reassuring. "Just give it a little time. You've been through a lot."

"But I don't recognize you. You look . . ." He shook his head again.

"She isn't usually this green," Jesse offered helpfully and, to Molly's surprise, Matthew laughed easily. Jesse strode across the room then and offered his hand. "I'm Jesse Camacho. Your brother-in-law. I'm married to your sister, whose name is Rita."

"Rita?" Matthew was clearly trying to make a connection. "Jesse?" He shrugged but shook Jesse's hand firmly. "Nice to meet you. Thanks for coming."

It seemed to Molly that Matthew was now trying to avoid looking at her, and although she knew better, she felt rejected. The feeling intensified when a petite, dark-haired nurse sailed into the room and proceeded to fill his water glass and fluff his pillows, addressing him in Spanish in a proprietary, almost intimate, fashion. When the patient thanked her with a degree of warmth apparently reserved for everyone but his wife, the witch lost her temper and focused her wrath on the offensive water jug in the equally offensive woman's hands.

"Eee!" The nurse dropped the pitcher into Matthew's lap and shook her hand rapidly, as though trying to shake off a flame, then stammered a bewildered apology to Matthew, who didn't notice Jesse reprimanding Molly with a stern

glance. The unrepentant witch shrugged coolly—it was nice to see that her powers hadn't disappeared completely, she congratulated herself—and Jesse took the hint, quickly escorting the nurse into the hall before any more jealousy could erupt.

Left alone, the spouses exchanged awkward smiles, then Molly tried, "They say you're doing well. Do you want to go home?"

"I don't know." He was attempting to deal with the soaked bedsheet as they talked. "Listen, if I seem rude . . ."

"Don't worry about it. I understand. I'm just glad you're okay. There'll be plenty of time later for us to sort this out."

"Thanks. I know this must be uncomfortable for you, too. You're just so totally different than I pictured you."

"You mentioned that," she muttered under her breath.

"I've been having vivid dreams . . ."

"Dreams?" Molly brightened. Surely *that* was a good sign. "Tell me about them."

"They're strange. There's this woman. Tall, with dark hair, dark eyes. I guess I expected—when they told me I had a wife—that she . . . I mean, you . . . would look like the one in the dream. But you don't. Not at all." He leaned back wearily, remembering. "She was so beautiful."

Molly bristled. This was too much. Even with amnesia, Matthew could apparently remember to be impossible. The doctor didn't want him upset, but if this kept up . . . Well, it was time to put an end to this episode and so she approached the bed boldly, intent upon transferring some power, and hopefully some sense—if not tact—to this annoying champion. It was then that she noticed his bare wrist for the first time.

"Matthew! Where's your amulet?"

"Pardon?"

"Your amulet. It's a bracelet. You always wear it."

He shrugged. "It's probably with my clothes. Although, I thought they'd shown me everything." He seemed wary of her concern. "Was it valuable? They said I didn't have any money or identification. I was robbed, so I guess it's been stolen."

Speechless, Molly summoned Jesse sharply. He joined them in an instant, demanding, "What's wrong?"

"The amulet's missing! Matthew thinks it was stolen!"

"Don't panic," Jesse advised. "Maybe they put it away for safekeeping."

"They *showed* him everything! It's gone! What will we do now?"

"We'll be calm," he reminded her. "And we'll talk to the police. Maybe it'll turn up. And if not"—the sorcerer shrugged—"he'll just have to learn to live without it."

"Me?" demanded Matthew. "I'm not the one who's worried about a bracelet. I'm the one who's lucky just to be alive, remember?"

Molly winced at his annoyed tone. "When you get your memory back, Matthew, you'll understand why we're upset. In the meantime you're right. We should count our blessings and get you home. There's someone else who's anxious to see you." She hesitated, then pulled a picture of Kerreya from her wallet. "Here. See? Our daughter, Kerreya Elizabeth Redtree."

"This is too much," Matthew whispered, shaking his head as though profoundly saddened by the development. "I don't remember my own daughter?"

"You will, Matthew. Soon you'll remember. Right, Jesse?"

Apparently not content with "soon," Jesse pushed past her to the side of the bed, put his hands on Matthew's shoulders, and spoke commandingly. "You are Matthew Redtree. Descendant of Lost Eagle. This woman is the dream girl. The Valmain Princess. You must remember all of this immediately."

Matthew stiffened, his countenance darkening. "I appreciate your intentions, but I'd appreciate it even more if you'd *take your hands off me."*

Jesse's arms dropped to his side and, for the first time, he seemed worried. It was Molly's turn to be reassuring, and so she stroked his cheek lightly. "Time is what he needs. Don't worry. We'll figure this out."

Jesse nodded, recovering quickly. "Perhaps time *is* the answer. If not," he winked, "I have a few other tricks up my sleeve."

She smiled, then glanced sheepishly toward Matthew, who was studying their interaction with growing suspicion in his eyes. "He's kidding," she explained. "Anyway"—her smile faded in the face of her husband's judgmental stare—"just try to rest while we get you released."

"You should have seen him on the plane, Rita," she was complaining to her sister-in-law when they'd been home less than a week. "Incredibly uncomfortable with *me* but with the *flight attendants* it was a different story. And it's been that way all week. I don't even think he likes me."

"Don't be silly," Rita soothed. "He's just uncomfortable. You're a stranger to him, but you're also his wife. That has to be weird for him."

"When I walk into a room, he gives me that zombie stare, like he can't imagine talking to me, much less *marrying* me. And," she lowered her voice and glanced toward Kerreya, who was busily crumbling crackers on the tray of her high chair, "he gives his own daughter the creeps. She won't even go near him, did you notice that?"

"That's not fair, Molly. Kerry takes her cue from you. So does AJ." She shook her head in clear disgust. "My son treats poor Matt like an alien."

"He acts like an alien," Molly grumbled. "And he spends too much time at your place, and not enough time with me."

"He spends his time looking through his old books. Looking at photo albums. He even took his stupid weapons out of storage. They're all over our barn. And last night"—her eyes narrowed in defense of her brother—"he stayed up past midnight reading some paper you wrote for his class. He's trying, like I said. And you probably intimidate the hell out of him with all that amulet, dream-girl stuff."

"I've hardly mentioned any of that," Molly protested. "The doctors said take it slow, and I have. But I had to tell him how we met—how he recognized me as the girl he'd dreamed about."

"Exactly!" Rita crowed. "Can you imagine how crazy that sounds to him?"

"You could help, you know," she accused softly. "You could tell him *he* used to believe all of it, too."

"I do, but in my own way. I'm caught in the middle, you know. And frankly, it's kind of nice to have a sane brother for a change."

"You're *glad* he doesn't believe it anymore, right?" Molly snapped. "For heaven's sake, Rita, we need your help!"

Rita shrugged to her feet and headed for the door. "I've got some advice for you, Molly," she drawled over her shoulder. "If you really care about my brother, you'll try to see this from his point of view. I think you're being a little selfish."

She was gone before Molly could think of an appropriate retort. *Selfish,* she muttered to herself finally. *Matthew Redtree drags me into the world of mounds and amulets and then he forgets about it!* And *about me. And I'm selfish?*

"Sad Mommy," Kerreya soothed.

"Oh, Kerry!" Molly quickly rescued the girl from her high chair. "I've been ignoring you, haven't I?" She kissed her cheek in apology. "Time for some fun."

"Play!"

"Right. I'll fill your panda pool with water, and we'll put on our swimsuits, and float boats for the rest of the afternoon. And"—she bundled the child down the hall and into the master bedroom—"look what I sewed for us." Pulling two soft white terry cloth beach cover-ups off her sewing table, she waved them before the child's eyes. "Aren't they pretty?"

"Capes!" Kerreya exclaimed, clapping her hands in delight.

"Well, not really. But I suppose . . ." Molly draped the smaller garment over the toddler's shoulders and nodded. "Not bad. We'll wear them like that. Let's change now, okay?"

Within minutes mother and daughter—dressed in sleeveless white leotards and "capes"—were ready for an afternoon in the shade of their backyard willow tree. Molly filled Kerreya's plastic wading pool while the baby arranged a fleet of tiny boats along the grass, ready for sailing. They were just about to launch the first ship when Matthew appeared at the gate.

The sight of him standing there, so lean and powerful, made his bride's heart beat faster, and she ached for the days when that reaction had been mutual. Now he was simply staring, as though confounded anew by her very existence. Reminding herself through her hurt that the situation was only temporary, she waved and gave him the reassuring smile that never seemed to quite reassure him. "Look, Kerry. It's Daddy." When the girl hid behind her mother's bare legs, she added apologetically, "Hi, Matthew. What a nice surprise."

"I didn't mean to intrude . . ."

"Don't be silly. You live here." Nervously unwrapping Kerreya's arms from her legs and settling her next to the pool, she moved across the small yard and extended her hand toward his. "We're glad to see you, Matthew. Come and sail boats with us."

He so clearly didn't want to touch her that she quickly dropped her hand back to her side before offering him a cool drink.

"Thanks, but I'm not staying," he murmured. "I just wanted to see if you needed anything."

"If I needed anything?" It was all she could do to keep from glaring at the ridiculous thought. If he had come out of a sense of obligation . . . "We're fine. We're worried about you, of course, but we're fine."

"Good. If you need anything, don't hesitate to call me."

"Thanks. I've got Rita's number," she grimaced. "Is that all you came to say?"

"I'm sorry," he insisted sadly. "I don't know what else you want me to say. I'm trying to remember, Molly. It's just not coming back." Wincing, as though momentarily disoriented, he glanced toward a pair of lawn chairs. "Do you mind if I sit for a minute?"

Flooded with guilt over having pressured him, and with concern over his condition, she sprang to his side, then hovered helplessly as he settled into the chair. "Does your head hurt? Can I get you something?"

"Ike cube?" Kerreya added sympathetically from a safe distance.

When Matthew smiled at their daughter, Molly breathed deeply in relief and explained, "We use ice cubes around here as an all-purpose remedy."

His smile grew broader. "Ice sounds great."

"Run and get some for Daddy," Molly instructed the child, who nodded and bustled toward the kitchen door.

"She's the cutest kid," Matthew grinned. "She's so smart. And she's got your smile."

"And your eyes."

He flushed slightly but nodded. "Yeah, I noticed. Rita's son AJ has them, too." He hesitated, then added, "Is it just me, or is that kid hostile?"

"It's just you," she confirmed with a gentle smile. "I guess he can't handle seeing you injured. You've always been his idol, in a way. The ultimate, unbeatable warrior."

"I get along better with Robert."

"You and he always related as intellectuals, not warriors, so it's easier for him to adjust."

"Because I'm still an intellectual, but I'm no longer a warrior?" His tone became faintly mocking as he added, "No more Valmain champion?"

It shocked and saddened her to hear him joke about so sacred and intimate a connection between them, but she wasn't about to chastise him again—it wasn't his fault, after all. Still, it hurt and she could think of no response other than silence. Then Kerreya was back with a cupful of melting ice, which he applied to the back of his head, announcing after a second, "That's just what I needed. Thank you, Kerreya."

Molly could identify with the helplessness in her daughter's eyes—she was hearing the voice, and seeing the body, yet missing the man even as he stood there. Matthew seemed to understand, too, and his smile was apologetic as he shrugged to his feet. "I'd better be going."

"You could rest inside for a while."

"No, thanks. Rita's fixing dinner. I'm sure you and your daughter are welcome to join us," he added quickly.

She's your daughter, too! Molly wanted to remind him. Instead, she suggested, "Come back soon. There are so many things we need to talk about. Things that might help with your memory."

"Like the dream?" He seemed amused at the thought. "The whole thing sounds pretty romantic, Molly, but I have to admit, I'm still surprised we took it all so seriously."

"Romantic?"

"I dreamed of a woman in white for years, but I couldn't see her face, right? Then when I met you, I was sure you were her. I can see how that must have been romantic. And then you started dreaming about me, too." He flushed deeply but continued, "I don't see how that proves anything, other than the fact that we were involved—obviously madly involved—with each other."

"Romance had nothing to do with it, Matthew. I *am* the woman in white." When his eyes flickered over the skimpy white beach cover-up, then down over her bare legs, she glared, "You used to dream of *me,* but now I guess it's that other woman."

"Pardon?"

"You mentioned her in the hospital," Molly reminded him, amazing herself with the jealous edge to her voice. "You said she had dark hair and dark eyes, and you thought she was your wife, and she was *incredibly* beautiful."

He seemed mortified at the apparent accusation. "I haven't had those dreams since the hospital, and she wasn't any better-looking than you, believe me. If I implied that, I'm sorry."

"Well, thanks for the compliment," Molly sniffed.

Matthew chuckled nervously. "I'm sure I did better when we were dating. With compliments, I mean. I'm sure"—his eyes traveled over her once again—"I raved about your legs about a million times back then."

"Not even once!" Molly snapped. "The Matthew Redtree *I* fell in love with doesn't judge women by such superficial standards."

"Huh?"

"You used to compliment my steady eyes," she informed him proudly, "and my pure heart." A lump formed unexpectedly in her throat—how *could* he have forgotten!—and she turned away, desperate not to cry.

"Hey, I'm sorry." He grasped her arm and turned her back toward his stricken face. "I didn't mean to upset you."

"I'm the one who should apologize," she whispered mournfully. "You were just trying to be polite. Let's drop it, okay? When your memory comes back, you'll understand."

"Somehow," he muttered, half under his breath, "I doubt it."

"What?"

"Never mind." He rubbed his eyes wearily. "I'd better

head back to Rita's. Goodbye, Kerreya," he called toward the pool. "And, Molly? Maybe you should get some rest, too."

"Right. Thanks." She hesitated, then touched his cheek, knowing he'd flinch but needing the contact. "Come back soon, Matthew. Please?"

"I'll do my best," he murmured, then left without a backward glance.

The two sorceresses resumed their afternoon of play, but a cloud of confusion hung over the pool, dissipating only when Jesse arrived, a golden retriever puppy for Kerreya under his arm and a determined look in his eye for his sorceress-apprentice.

Kerreya was enchanted by her new playmate and, watching her trying to teach the pup to fetch a ball, Molly found herself genuinely relaxing for the first time in weeks. "Thanks, Jesse. We needed a lift. This whole thing has been hard on everyone's nerves, including the baby's."

"The puppy's for Kerreya. I've got something better for you."

"A present?"

"Not exactly. A recommendation."

Molly stiffened. "Forget it. I know what you're going to say. You want me to summon Matthew to my dream and I absolutely refuse. The doctor says everything should be approached in an even and tranquil manner, no matter how uneven and untranquil it makes *me* feel. One step at a time. He's not ready for the dream, believe me. He thinks it's all just a fairy tale and he thinks I'm nuts."

"He doesn't think you're crazy. He thinks you're susceptible."

"Excuse me?"

"That's the word he most often uses to describe you. It means you're easily swayed."

"I *know* what it means. Did you tell him who did the original swaying?"

"I've stayed out of it. I'm Jesse, remember?"

"Jesse, Nicholas, Matthew, Aaric. You're lucky. You can be anyone you want. I'm stuck with being the wife of a zombie."

"He's actually a very serious, intelligent man," Jesse insisted. "He remembers much of his training and schooling. He's an expert on many cultures. It's fascinating, actually. He can't remember the items in his collection specifically, but he can identify artifacts in general quite precisely. His memory may be gone, but his instincts are as sharp as ever."

"You sound like Rita. Like you think this is the improved version of Matthew Redtree."

"Hardly. But he is impressive in many ways."

"Well, somehow I've missed it. Around me he's just a zombie. He won't even shake hands with me," she added sadly.

"Because he's embarrassed, knowing he has made love to you. Knowing he has held you and caressed you . . ." Jesse took a deep breath and grinned. "You're a beautiful woman, Princess. If he's tongue-tied around you, it's because he's in awe of you."

"Somehow I don't think that's it," Molly grumbled, "but thanks for trying. He's just not comfortable with the thought that he's my husband, and it's making me uncomfortable, too. And *don't* tell me to give him more time."

"He's had enough time," Jesse agreed. "He's forming new attachments, new memories . . ."

"Attachments?" she repeated carefully. "Has he been seeing another woman? Is it that stewardess?"

"There's no other woman. In fact, thanks to you, I think he's afraid of *all* women," Jesse teased. "But these attachments *are* a threat to you. He's building new memories. Without you and the little princess. I'm convinced we'd better act now."

"In the dream?"

"Yes, but listen to my idea before you reject it."

"Okay. I'm desperate enough for almost anything."

"I want you to summon him to the dream tonight. I'll already be there. Don't waste your powers. I'll come on my own." He eyed her cautiously. "How are you feeling, by the way?"

"You mean my magic? I'm still a mess. The last time it worked right was on that nurse in Peru."

"That was beneath you, but very amusing. Anyway, assuming your dream power is unharmed, you'll bring him. When he arrives, I'll create an illusion—a reenactment—of everything. The dream, the amulet, and the battles. He'll see you, magnificent in your cape. All will be clear to him, and he'll remember."

She nodded. It was a good idea. Even if Matthew didn't remember, he'd at least have to believe them. And Aaric's illusions were always so convincing, maybe they really would jog his memory! "Okay. Let's do it."

"Provided you can handle it. Did the dream power ever fail you during your first pregnancy?"

"No, and stop thinking I'm pregnant. I told you, it's not possible. I even took another pregnancy test yesterday, you had me so confused." She flushed, remembering the disappointment she had felt, and reminding herself that having the baby of an amnesiac would probably be more than she could handle, in any case.

At that moment, Kerreya bounded into Jesse's arms, exclaiming, "Look, look!"

"What, little princess? Where is your puppy?"

"My *baby*," she corrected solemnly, gesturing toward the stroller.

Molly peeked at the contented pet, sleeping peacefully under Kerreya's blanket, and giggled. "See what happens when you talk about babies too much, Jesse Camacho?"

"Too much? Not enough, if you ask me. I haven't even

told you the news. Yesterday I heard my son's heartbeat for the first time!"

Molly hugged him. "How wonderful! And so soon? I remember what a great day that was for me with Kerreya. A miracle. Now"—she pulled her daughter into the embrace and sighed—"let's hope for another miracle tonight."

Almost as though she knew what was required, Kerreya went cheerfully to bed early that evening, and an excited Molly was soon nestled under her covers, anticipating that it would take hours to fall asleep, and intending to use those hours to plan exactly the right words that would reassure Matthew following the shock of a dream summons. Before she had manufactured even a simple greeting, she dozed off and found herself in the grassy meadow. "Wait for Aaric," she counseled herself, but the power and the possibilities were too enticing and so, with a shiver of anticipation, she waved her hand, summoning the Valmain champion.

In an instant he was there, pulling her into a desperate embrace and exclaiming, "Molly! You're all right! I was worried about you . . ." His hands were caressing her frantically. "It's been a nightmare! I couldn't find you. I couldn't find anyone!"

"Oh, Matthew," she murmured, almost weak with relief. "You know me? You remember?" Her head was swimming at the enormity of the apparent success, then she pulled away and demanded sharply, "Aaric? If this is your idea of a clever illusion . . ."

"Aaric?" Matthew scowled. "What the hell does he have to do with this? What's wrong with you, Valmain?" Then his amazed eyes traveled over the dream landscape and he whispered, "You found the dream again. *We* found the dream. Finally!"

She studied him with cautious hope, almost certain it was her champion. Still, the recovery seemed too good to be true, which was usually a sign of magic afoot. "I'll think of a question. Something only Matthew would know."

"Ask me about my books," he suggested impatiently.

"That's no good. Jesse's read them all."

"What the hell does *Jesse* have to do with it?" Matthew threw up his hands and began to pace. "What's going on, Molly? First Aaric and now Jesse? Did you tell Jesse about this dream?"

He had an annoyed look on his face that Aaric could never have mustered while addressing his Princess. *And* he was pacing! Throwing herself into his arms, she gushed, "Matthew! I can't believe how simple this was! I've been resisting this solution, even though Jesse was sure—"

"Molly! What are you talking about?"

Her arms tightened desperately around his neck. "I'm just so glad to have you back. I love you so much!" After covering his face with kisses, she continued, "I was so worried. And I missed you. It was so bizarre, seeing you look at me and knowing you didn't remember the dream, or the amulet, or Kerreya."

"Kerreya?" He frowned. "How could I forget her? What are you talking about?"

"You don't remember having amnesia?" When he shook his head in disbelief, she soothed, "It doesn't matter. You remember us now, and that's all that matters."

"Amnesia?" He was clearly trying to reconcile this with his own memories. "It was more like a coma, Molly. Like I was trapped somewhere. There was no sense of time or place. Almost like a sort of limbo."

"What's the last thing you remember?"

"I was hiking in the jungle. Something was going on with the amulet . . . Hey! Where is it?"

"We think it was stolen. By the thieves who hurt you. We'll probably never get it back, Matthew. I'm so sorry."

"Thieves?" His eyes had darkened at the memory. "They hit me on the head, right?"

"Probably. They robbed you and left you, and you wandered around. Finally some servant of some art collector in Cuzco identified you and they called me."

The champion surveyed his bare wrist mournfully. "It took so many years to find it the first time and now I lost it. I shouldn't have been fooling around with it, but . . ." He pulled her against himself and kissed her thoroughly. "I'll find it again, somehow. For now, it sounds like we're lucky we ever got a chance to do this again. How's Kerry? How long has it been since I passed out?"

"It's been a month since you left—since that awful, awful fight—and I think you were injured about ten days ago. And"—she smiled fondly—"the baby's fine, and she'll love seeing you. She hasn't been too crazy about not being recognized by her own father."

"Poor kid! Let's go see her right now. I guess you have to send me, right?" Again he mourned the loss of the amulet, then his eyes narrowed and he demanded, "How did you manage to find the dream after all these months?" When she winced, he added apologetically, "Never mind. I guess desperation can do strange things to anyone, even a sorceress. And"—his lips brushed hers gently—"I'm just so glad to see you and this dream again, I can hardly stand it."

"I know what you mean," she sighed, kissing him more fully, then adding briskly, "You'll wake up at Rita's house, but your Jeep's there so just come over. I'll have Kerreya awake when you get home, and we'll celebrate for the rest of our lives." Flashing one last loving smile, she sent him out of her dream, then followed quickly, intent upon telephoning Jesse with the good news and a heartfelt thank-you.

The sorcerer was clearly amazed. "Are you serious? It's all over? I haven't even gone to bed yet! I thought you were going to wait for me. . . ." He abandoned the rebuke and chuckled. "It sounds like you handled it fine by yourself. Nice work, Princess."

"He'll be out of his bedroom and on his way here any minute. Just pretend you don't know anything about it for now. But guess what? I'm going to tell him *everything* tonight."

"That's a good idea," Jesse agreed, adding half to himself, "I didn't even know he'd gone to bed. I thought he was out in the barn with Robert." His voice began to trail into uncertainty. "The light's still on out there . . . Hold on, Princess, I'm going to check something."

"Jesse? Aaric! Don't just . . ." *Darn,* she thought in complete frustration. *I can't just hold on here forever! I've got to get the baby up soon.* She considered hanging up but decided instead to give him a minute. After all, it would take Matthew at least forty minutes to get home, even at breakneck speed.

Then Jesse was back on the line, his tone grim. "Princess?"

"Aaric! Why did you do that?" she demanded. "Is everything okay?"

"Listen. And don't panic."

"I *am* panicking. What's wrong?"

"I just spoke to Matt. He's in the barn. He hasn't slept at all tonight. And"—he cleared his throat nervously—"he still has amnesia."

"What?"

"Take a deep breath, Princess, and then"—the sorcerer's tone turned grim—"tell me again about your dream."

Sixteen

"There's nothing to tell! He was Matthew Redtree, good as new. He remembered everything!" Molly's voice was shrill with confusion. "He wanted to see the baby! He *kissed* me. Aaric, help me."

"Go to sleep right away," Jesse ordered quietly. "I'll meet you in the dream in a couple of minutes. Do you understand?"

"Yes, Aaric. Hurry."

They went over all of it, word by word as they stood together once more in the peaceful meadow of Aaric's former exile. "He said it was like he was trapped in limbo?"

"What does it mean?"

"I'm not sure, but it sounds uncomfortably familiar."

Her eyes scanned his anxiously. "You're saying it sounds like it used to be, for you? Here in my dream?"

"Yes. Except this dream was a pleasant place. Confining, but pleasant. It sounds as though it's different for him."

"He called it a nightmare. And he's still there, isn't he?"

"There's only one way to find out. Bring him back. I'll make myself scarce for a few minutes."

Molly didn't hesitate. She summoned Matthew again and the horrified expression on his face confirmed their worst suspicions.

"I was still in the coma," he whispered.

"I know." She drew him into a tight embrace. "I have to

tell you something, Matthew. Try not to panic. We'll solve this problem together, just like we did against Angela."

"I'm listening," he promised grimly. "I'll do whatever it takes to wake up."

"You already *are* awake."

"Huh?"

"You have amnesia, but you're wide awake. At this very moment, you're in Rita's barn, talking to Robert. Somehow you're conscious on two levels at the same time, or something."

"Okay." He was visibly trying to maintain his balance. "I've never heard of anything like this."

"We'll sort it out. We have help. We have Aaric."

"No way," Matthew growled. "I don't know what makes you think you can bring him back after all this time, but don't try it. Sending him away was right two years ago and it's still right. We'll figure this out together."

"This will take special skills. Aaric has—"

"Forget it! I forbid it. I'm still your husband, Molly."

"Forbid?" Her eyes flashed with frustration. "Who gave you the right to forbid me to do anything?"

"Okay, okay. Maybe 'forbid' was the wrong word," he soothed. "Don't get so upset, Valmain."

"Upset? I'm *furious!*"

"Why? Because I left?"

"Yes! And because you never *listen* to me! And now you have the nerve to forbid—"

"Fine! Call your damned Aaric! Call whoever you want. Just don't be so angry."

"Why? Aren't dream girls supposed to have tempers? But champions can have fierce ones? You never did tell me the rules, Matthew Redtree. But it doesn't matter because as soon as you're better, *I'm getting a divorce.*"

"Now there's a clever solution," he drawled. "Just like with your father, right? He made a mistake, so he was out of your life forever. Now *I'm* out. That's convenient."

"Hypocrite! *You* left *me,* remember?"

"I only left to think. I always come back."

"Don't bother!" she snapped.

"Fine. I'm leaving now and this time I *won't* be back."

"You can't leave. I *summoned* you, remember? You'll leave when I say and not before."

He stared as though completely fascinated. "I've never seen you so mad. Do you still love me?"

"Don't you *dare* ask me that!"

"Fine." He raked his fingers through his hair. "If you're so hot to try to get Aaric back here, go ahead."

"It won't be very hard." She straightened defiantly and announced, "He's Jesse."

It seemed, several times, as though Matthew were about to speak, then he wandered away. Thinking. Piecing it together. For her part Molly waited, knowing she was ready for him. She had rehearsed this speech a million times, but when he again stood before her, she could see that he had reasoned most of it out. Still, she carefully went over the details—the friendship, the pangs of conscience, the training, and finally, the transformation. "He saved you from a murder charge. And he kept his word. He's been good to Rita and the boys."

Matthew nodded. "And it explains why you were so irrational about their baby."

"Oh, right," she sighed. "There's something you need to know about that. I mean, there's a lot you need to know, but I'm not hiding anything anymore. There's just so much to tell . . ."

"The baby?" he prodded.

She grimaced slightly. "Jesse and I did a spell to make Rita get pregnant. Remember the spell Aaric wanted to do with Maya that made her angry and made her go off with Valmain? It's called a carrying spell."

Matthew shook his head. "How could you work a spell on my sister without her permission?"

"Don't be so negative. Rita's very excited about the baby these days. I'd do it all again if I had to."

"Fine. I don't like any of this but I guess I understand. Not that it matters, at this point," he added ruefully. "I just wish you'd told me sooner. I would have gotten upset, probably, but—"

"You would have *left* me. For good."

"You really think that?" His eyes softened with regret. "I guess I've really screwed things up with you, Molly. I swear I never would have left you."

"You left me once before," she reminded him sadly. "When I brought Maya back, you left me and went off with Angela Clay because you felt I'd betrayed you. I didn't want to go through that again. Anyway"—she squared her caped shoulders proudly—"no more secrets—not from you, *and not from Aaric*. Let's just get him here and get you cured."

"Okay."

"And *don't* fight with him."

"Don't worry. I'm not anxious to see whose side you're on."

"I'm on my own side this time," she shrugged, then summoned her mentor without further discussion. When he appeared—as Aaric rather than Jesse, and wearing battle gear and an enormous grin—she knew she had cautioned the wrong warrior to behave.

He confirmed this immediately, greeting the Valmain champion with a hearty, "Brother-in-law!"

"Aaric!" Molly warned. "No teasing."

"It's okay, Molly." Matthew grasped Aaric's outstretched hand firmly. "Molly told me how you've helped us. I'm grateful."

"That's why I'm here," Aaric boasted. "To bail you and the Princess out of your calamities."

"Aaric!"

He winked toward the angry sorceress, then turned back to Matthew. "Now tell us the whole story. You were in the jungle? What do you remember?"

"I had the amulet. It was working, sporadically . . ."

"In Peru?" Aaric frowned. "How is that possible?"

The warrior began to pace. "It was giving me spurts of energy, like it does when I'm just coming within range of the mounds. I was wandering around, fascinated, trying to determine the source, and then when I was resting for a minute, trying to get it to work again, someone must have hit me." He shook his head. "I let my guard down, like a fool, and lost the amulet."

"We have to get it back," Aaric announced briskly. "It's safe to assume your amnesia resulted from one of the surges of power, combined with the blow to the head."

"Why were you in Peru in the first place, Matthew?"

"When I left our place after the argument, I went camping at the mounds. One of my dealers contacted me there with a message from a collector in Cuzco. This particular collector owns a weapon I've wanted for over a year, and he's never been willing to even discuss selling it before, so when he sent for me, I went immediately. It was a false alarm, though."

"He didn't really have it?"

"He had it, all right. In fact, it was *this*." Pulling his obsidian dagger from its scabbard, he brandished it proudly. "Not just a replica like the one I gave you, Molly. The one Paul Aganyer has is authentic. I'm sure of it."

"That's amazing," Aaric interjected. "When all of this is over, we must purchase it at any price."

"It's not for sale," Matthew grumbled. "Aganyer wants to *trade* it for something I don't even own. That's what got me so frustrated, so I went hiking, to let off some steam. I intended to come home in a few days. Now," his voice softened, "I'm wondering if I'll ever come home."

"What do you think, Aaric?" Molly demanded anxiously.

"I think that this, standing before us, is a part of Matthew Redtree. Just as Maya sent a part of me into the future. The very fact that you can summon him while his body is awake is proof that his former consciousness has been completely severed from his physical self. We need to reunite them."

"Are you powerful enough?"

"Perhaps. It's dangerous, though. The only safe solution is to regain the amulet. Or leave him here, in your dream—"

"No!" Matthew seemed horrified by the prospect. "I'm willing to take my chances with any spell you can dream up. I can't face this timeless existence."

"I understand. I'll recover the amulet," Aaric assured him.

"No," interrupted Molly. *"I'll* get it back. You can't go to Peru again, Aaric. This time it could take weeks. You have to be with Rita." She ignored their skeptical reactions, insisting, "I'll go see that collector in Cuzco. I'll offer to pay him whatever he wants to use his connections to find the amulet."

"He *did* admire it," Matthew conceded. "Aganyer's a strange guy, Molly. I get the feeling the only reason he values the obsidian knife is that he knows how much I want it. At first, when he noticed my amulet, he was only mildly interested, but when I wouldn't take it off so he could examine it, he really got curious. He even offered to buy it."

"Do you think he might have had you followed and robbed? The doctor who treated you said a servant of some local art collector identified you . . ."

"Who knows? Maybe he did have me robbed, although that doesn't seem to be his style. He has enough money to get whatever he wants, and I think part of the allure is the negotiating. I don't think he'd enjoy simple robbery."

"Still, it's a good place to start." Molly smiled, exuding forced confidence. "I'll leave tomorrow."

"No!" Aaric objected. "You aren't strong enough. And you'll undoubtedly experience *soroche* again. Stay with Rita. I'll go."

Matthew shook his head. "Molly almost has to go. I think Paul Aganyer will see her, out of curiosity if nothing else. He won't see strangers. He wouldn't even see me until lately. The guy's basically a recluse."

"No problem. I'll just pretend to be you. I can hold the illusion for several hours." Aaric's eyes twinkled as he added, "I've done it before."

"Yeah, I'll just bet you have," Matthew growled.

"I can go alone," Molly interjected nervously. "You're forgetting, Aaric, you can't leave Rita. Your persuasion could fail, and she could change her mind about the baby."

"Take Zack then," Matthew suggested. "He'll protect you."

"I hardly know him. I'd rather go alone."

"There's one option we haven't discussed," Matthew sighed. "You could take *me* with you."

"Very funny."

"No. I'm serious. Take this alter ego of mine. He's still me, right? Aganyer will agree to see him, at least, and he's physically trained as a fighter. He can protect you."

"He is well trained," Aaric agreed, "but he's also naive. And he doesn't believe in the power of the amulet. Most importantly, he doesn't feel allegiance to our Princess."

"Aaric's right," Molly sighed. "The zombie has no feelings for me. And I don't think I can persuade him to go with me. My powers are messed up these days, Matthew."

"Huh?"

"It's not serious," she assured him hastily. "Just incredibly inconvenient."

"That's not a problem, Princess," Aaric interrupted. "I'll work *my* persuasion on your 'zombie.' "

"What about Kerry?" Molly worried. "She's never been away from me for more than a night."

"She can visit you at night in the dream. And she'll be comfortable with Rita and me during the day," Aaric assured her. "And the enchanted dog will offer extra protection."

"Her new puppy?" Molly's composure weakened. "He's hexed?"

"This is incredible," Matthew grumbled. "It's like a circus. And you're the ringleader," he accused Aaric sourly. "If you're so clever and powerful, why don't you just try to put me back into my consciousness right now?"

"Our powers do not work that way. They are strong, but limited. I could, for example, convince you to give me all your money. Or the Princess here could set you on fire."

When Molly giggled, her champion shook his head. "This guy's a riot."

"Speaking of money, I'd better take a lot, I guess."

"No problem," Aaric assured her. "I'll get it for you."

"Money isn't Aganyer's first love, though," Matthew warned. "He may want to trade. Now I really wish I had that damned copper axe."

Molly and Aaric exchanged amazed glances. "Copper axe?"

"Yeah. That's why Aganyer had me flown down to Cuzco. A dealer I used to know died recently and, according to his records, I own some ancient copper axe. But it's a mix-up. I've never even seen it."

"And Aganyer wants it?"

"Indirectly. It's really a man in Michigan who wants it. A man named Fox. He's contacted me a dozen times. I thought I'd finally convinced him the records were wrong but I guess not. It's generated a ton of controversy. Fox must have told Aganyer, who—like I said—can't resist a game. So I went all the way down there for nothing."

"We have it, Matthew." Molly quickly related the story. "We can trade for the amulet."

" 'Trade,' again?" Aaric was growing annoyed. "If he has the amulet, we should just take it!"

"His place is a fortress. I don't want Molly to take any chances. Trade the axe for the amulet, Molly. We'll sort everything else out later."

"I'll make a deal with you," Aaric suggested slyly. "I'll let you borrow my axe to deal with Aganyer—to trade for the dagger and for the amulet. When we're done, you'll help me recover my axe. You'll own the amulet. I'll own the axe *and* the dagger."

"Aaric!" Molly gasped.

But Matthew was grinning triumphantly. "That's more like it. Let him show his true colors. I'm not crazy about being in his debt, anyway, so I *prefer* a trade."

"Well, I'm ashamed," Molly sulked. "What possible justification do you have, Moonshaker?"

"My sons have no magic. They're unprotected. The axe, to be so strangely coveted, must have remarkable power. I'm sure of that now. And the dagger, if it is the one from this dream, has strong magic as well. My sons must have these weapons."

The proud witch blushed and looked toward Matthew. "See?"

Matthew nodded. "That's fair. More than fair." As though to cement the agreement, he again took the dream knife from his belt, handing it to Aaric. "Here. For AJ."

"For AJ," agreed Aaric heartily. "This is a fine weapon. When the Princess stabbed me with it, there was a sensation beyond pain. Almost venomous."

"Oh, Aaric! I'm so sorry!"

"No need to apologize," Aaric grinned. "You were defending yourself. Things were different. Now we are family. Speaking of which"—his blue eyes twinkled—"bring the little one here now to see her father, Princess."

The baby flew instantly into her father's loving arms and a joyful family reunion ensued, with Matthew being enlightened, Kerreya being entertained, Molly being reassured, and Aaric being the "ringleader," just as Matthew had claimed. As dawn approached, the sorcerer provided Kerreya with a pony and took her for a ride while Matthew and Molly traded information.

"There's something else you should know."

"Do you realize how many times you've made that statement in the last hour?" Matthew teased. "You've had a real secret life going when I wasn't around. How did you manage to find time to work?"

"It's been spread out over more than two years, remember? And I was asleep most of the time. It didn't come out of your time."

"My time. His time. Interesting concept," he drawled. "And now I suppose we've reversed roles, right?"

"Hardly. I've still got the zombie to deal with when I'm awake, remember? He can be as annoying as you ever were."

"Good." Matthew studied her wistfully. "You know, I used to sit there at night and watch you sleep. And I *knew* it! I knew that wasn't the expression of someone who's dreaming about test tubes and periodic tables."

"You used to do that? Watch me?"

"Yeah. I always wanted to figure you out. I still do." He fluffed her sun-streaked curls, then prodded, "So? What's this 'something else' I should know about?"

"Well, Kerreya is, or will be, a sorceress, too. Or did you guess that?"

"I noticed her cape right away," he chuckled. "That seems to be a dead giveaway around here."

"Aaric wants to train her, so she won't end up like me."

"I'll train her when I think the time is right."

"We'll decide when the time is right," Molly countered stubbornly. "And I agree, *we* should be the ones to guide her, but it would be foolish not to accept Aaric's help."

"He's manipulative. He gets you to do things—"

"No, Matthew. He rarely manipulates me, and I'm willing to bet he'd *never* manipulate Kerreya. He adores her."

"He adores you, too, but it hasn't stopped him. He tricked you into helping with Rita's pregnancy, didn't he? He'd better not try to use Kerry for any of his schemes. I'm still her father even if . . ." He broke off, staring silently into the distance, and Molly knew he was worrying about his daughter's future, should the amulet not be recovered. She wished she could convince him to trust Aaric, but Matthew had spent a lifetime seeing him as an opponent. It would take time. Perhaps, once the amulet was back on his wrist, and he was back in the real world, Matthew would feel more comfortable. Aaric as Jesse would surely be a little easier to take than Aaric as the Moonshaker.

At that moment the sorcerer returned, leaving Kerreya at the top of the large mound. "She wants to show you something, Princess."

Molly's eyes narrowed. "In other words, you're trying to get rid of me? No way. No secrets."

"Go ahead, Molly," Matthew urged. "I want to hear what he has to say."

"Don't keep the little one waiting, Princess."

"I don't know why you bother to call me Princess," she grumbled. "I don't seem to have any authority here."

"Your kingdom is gone, and your authority is nonexistent," Aaric chuckled, "but you are the Valmain Princess nevertheless. Now," he added abruptly, *"run along."*

"Ten minutes, and *no* fighting?" When they'd each nodded, she squared her shoulders and hurried away.

Matthew Redtree faced his old nemesis and guessed, "There's more? Some other danger Molly doesn't know about?"

"Yes. Many times in the last month, the Princess has spoken of contacting her father. Trying to reestablish that tie. And I get the impression you've encouraged this."

"Sure, I think it's great. What's the problem? Her father may have screwed up, but he's still her father."

"It's not that simple." Aaric's gaze was locked on the distant figures of his princesses. "Think about it, warrior. Did your woman get her extraordinary nature—her strength, her loyalty, or her compassion—from a man who would play games behind the back of his dying wife? A man of low character? Impossible."

"He was lonely. Stressed out. His wife was dying, and his daughter was lying in the hospital with a concussion and compound fractures . . ." Matthew's conviction was fading rapidly. "What are you trying to imply?"

"I'm saying that, at the time of the so-called accident, the Princess's life was at a crossroads with her destiny. Finishing the cape was going to trigger our conflict. But because of the accident, she ceased working on it for all those years, using her powers to repair her own battered body, and attempting unconsciously to save her dying mother—a hopeless cause. Powers that should have been building to an imminent climax were instead drained to a dangerous degree. She has never recovered her control." The Moonshaker paused, as though momentarily mourning the loss to the mounds. "This woman, this Constance. Has the Princess told you much about her?"

"Just that she's beautiful and treacherous."

"She tried to befriend the Princess. When that failed, she became friends with the mother. Did you know that the Princess wasn't supposed to be in the car the day of the accident?"

"Yeah, she mentioned that. What do you make of it?"

"I think Constance came to Boston to influence the Princess, but couldn't because of the strong tie with the mother. She decided to break the tie in order to gain control of the Valmain Princess. Her interference almost prevented the dream. It wasn't until you met, years later—until you were drawn together in Berkeley by destiny—that the Princess returned to the dream and finished the cape. *That* was the catalyst. But it should have been finished years before, when she was younger. The so-called accident—"

"You keep saying that! You think it *wasn't* an accident? You believe Constance murdered the mother?" Matthew was pacing furiously. "You can't tell Molly any of this until you're sure."

"We must *never* tell her," the sorcerer agreed briskly. "She would want revenge."

"Why would Constance have wanted to influence Molly in the first place? How did she even know Molly was a sorceress?"

"She may still not know. If my suspicions are correct, she knows only that the Princess is the descendant of King Valmain—a fine man, but no magician. Remember the reason Maya sent me through the centuries? Because she was obsessed with revenge. Who's to say whether she sent another? She wanted to ensure her own victory—meaning my victory against you—and sending someone to confuse the loyalties of the Valmain Princess would have helped accomplish that."

"You think Maya sent Constance? Was Constance a friend of hers?"

"A friend? No. More like a tool. If I am correct, this Constance is of the lakes. In exchange for power, or beauty, the witch became Maya's revenge." His frown deepened. "You would have to know Maya the way I did. She was very impetuous. And she had no maternal instinct whatsoever. And yet"—his eyes narrowed—"when Maya was here in the dream last year and the Princess told her the story of losing her mother, Maya sobbed and wailed as though her heart were broken."

"Molly told me about that," Matthew nodded. "She thought Maya was wonderful to care so deeply. But you're saying . . ."

"I'm saying Maya was consumed with guilt, not grief. She sent me here, to destroy Valmain, and she sent a lake witch to do the same, not stopping to realize, until the damage was done, that the lake witch might commit an unholy act, such as murdering an innocent woman, leaving our sweet Princess motherless."

Matthew weighed the theory cautiously. If it was true—if

a lake witch killed Molly's mother in cold blood, and even now controlled the father who had been so shamelessly seduced—then maybe Molly *should* be told. It certainly explained why the few attempts the father had made to contact his daughter had been so feeble. Then he winced and demanded, "What about Molly's half sister?"

Aaric shrugged. "The child could easily be ignorant of all this. Lake witches aren't maternal toward their daughters, especially when the daughter is half-human. They're a jealous, secretive lot. And the rivalry between lake wizards, father and son, would shock you!" He spoke rapidly, his eyes fixed on the return of his princesses. "The truth is, even Constance herself probably didn't fully understand her mission. Information is power, and Maya wouldn't have given any more than was necessary. Even if she told Constance that Valmain's descendants might be magicians, she definitely wouldn't have told her about this dream power, since not even Maya could have predicted such a gift. *Constance must never find out!*"

Matthew nodded slowly. "Can we confirm any of this? If we went to see her . . ."

"She might hear your thoughts. Or worse, she might perceive my strength. All of this could endanger the princesses. It's best to let it lie. Constance shows no interest in any of us."

"But her father! We can't just leave him in the hands of a witch."

"There are worse fates," Aaric reminded him slyly. "Think back to your nights with Angela. He is undoubtedly a happy man. Deluded perhaps, but enjoying it."

"Poor guy." Matthew grimaced. "I *do* remember. Molly would zap me if she knew how well."

"She may 'zap' you anyway. She is very displeased."

"Tell me about it. I can't say anything right," he grumbled. "Why do I feel like I won all the battles and still lost the war?"

"*You* got the prize."

"That depends on whether the prize was Molly's body or her heart."

"That heart is tender, and easily broken," Aaric chided. "It hurts her to think you didn't choose her as your mate of your own free will. She knows it was destiny's choice, not yours."

"I know. I know. She can't accept the fact that we never, quote-unquote, fell in love."

"No! She cannot accept the fact that *you* never fell in love. Do you see the difference?"

"Oh." He fought a wave of confusion and shame. "I couldn't love her more than I do."

"Nor could I. But neither of us seems to be able to offer her what she really needs. If it cannot be me—and it apparently cannot—then I would prefer that it be you. But we must both be prepared for the possibility that she will find another someday. It seems inevitable. She has a strong need to be courted and romanced."

"How can I prepare myself for something like that?"

"You're asking the wrong person."

Matthew chuckled reluctantly. "You're right. Maybe *you'd* rather see her with me than with a stranger, but I'd rather see her with *anyone* else than you!" He shook his head. "I always thought I had it made, because she was part of my destiny. But she's part of *your* destiny, too. I'll never forget that again."

"Here she comes. Will you keep this all from her, at least for now?"

"Yeah. She's got enough on her mind. I'm not sure she's equipped to handle all this."

"The Princess?" Aaric chuckled fondly. "You're forgetting my first meeting with her—when she stabbed me in the leg! Don't worry about her. She's a fighter, despite the way she behaves around you."

"What does *that* mean?"

"She's not always herself around you," he shrugged. "Don't take offense. I'm just telling you the truth. Think about the day she burned the book right in your hands! *That's* your wife. She's a fighter. Do you even know her?"

Matthew's jaw tightened. "I know her well enough to know she doesn't want to be lied to about her father. Once I get back to normal, *I'll* decide when and what to tell her."

"Fair enough," agreed Aaric. "Now I'll be going. Another time I'll give you more background on the lakes, so that you can more fully appreciate the dangers. Tell the Princess to telephone me as soon as she wakes up. I'll get to work on 'persuading' your alter ego to escort her to Cuzco."

The young witch approached cautiously. "Why did Aaric leave? What did I miss?"

"Just some strategy. Where's Kerry?"

"I sent her back to bed. It's almost morning."

He stroked her cheek longingly. "You'd better get some rest, too. If Aaric successfully persuades 'me' to go with you, you have a long trip ahead of you. I'm worried about this weakness of yours. Are you sure you're not pregnant?"

"Is that what he wanted to talk to you about?" Molly groaned. "No, no, no. I took another pregnancy test the other day and since then, *believe* me, your zombie body hasn't been beating down my bedroom door."

My 'zombie body' doesn't know what it's missing." Pulling her close, he murmured, "You're trembling. Are you still mad?"

"No." She raised her eyes to his and admitted, "I've missed you so much. No matter what else has happened, or will happen, being in your arms will always be a dream come true for me."

He cupped her chin in his hand. "I honestly love you, Molly. I know it hasn't been enough for you, but . . ."

Her eyes were sparkling with tears. "It's not a question of how much, Matthew. Anyway, all I want is to get you back in one piece. If we do that, I'll never complain about anything again. Or at least, I'll try not to."

"Do you love Aaric?"

"As a friend. As a brother. A lifeline, a teacher." She tasted his lips gently. "Not as a lover. I swear that."

He nodded, relieved. "Can I make love to you?" When she melted against him, shy but willing, he felt a rush of reverence and adoration so strong it threatened to engulf them both and, as he pulled her into the sweet green grass of the dream, he vowed to prove, once and for all, that she needed no other love. With tender thoroughness he caressed and kissed, coaxed and probed, until she was mindlessly aroused. Then and only then did he bring her into ecstasy so perfect and so complete that he was satisfied at last no doubts could possibly have survived.

Seventeen

"What do you mean he's gone?" Molly wailed the next morning when Jesse appeared at her front door with news that the "persuasion" would have to be postponed.

"He left last night," Jesse repeated. "While I was asleep. Rita says he wanted to see his old house in Berkeley."

"That's just like him! To take off without saying goodbye to me *or* to Kerry. What a jerk."

"We'll just have to be patient," the sorcerer soothed. "He'll be back soon. And he left a note asking Rita to tell you all about it."

"Well, I'm not waiting around for him. He won't be any help, anyway."

"No! Matthew was correct. You'll need him. Aganyer will agree to see him, he speaks Spanish, he's strong . . ."

"So what? Like you said, he feels nothing for me. After all," she grumbled, "I'm *only* his wife."

"But he's obviously anxious to regain his memory. That's good. We'll tell him you believe the amulet will stir some memories."

"Okay," she conceded, "but keep it scientific. He doesn't believe the amulet is anything more than a keepsake."

"I'll be careful." He hesitated, then asked gently, "What did you do with your champion last night after I left? Did you send him back to limbo?"

"He insisted," she sighed. "I felt terrible sending him away, but . . ."

"He was correct. It would be a drain on you to keep him in the dream." The sorcerer's brown eyes were filled with admiration. "His instincts in these matters are always good."

"So, now we wait? I guess I can make good use of the time. I'll go on into work and quit." She almost laughed at the concerned expression on her mentor's face, then explained, "I've taken off so much time lately, and now this trip! It doesn't matter anyway. I can't concentrate on work until we have the amulet, and Matthew, back, safe and sound."

"Do what you have to do, then," Jesse nodded. "And be patient. Play with the little princess. I'll let you know as soon as he gets back to the ranch."

When her husband did return, he chose, to Molly's surprise, to stop at her place before heading out to the ranch. "I hope I'm not disturbing you. I thought about calling first . . ."

"Don't be silly. This is your house, too, remember?" She winced in apology as she motioned for him to join her at the kitchen table. "Sorry. I *know* you don't remember."

"That's okay." His smile seemed genuine. "You've been great through all this, Molly. I'm afraid I can't say the same for myself. It's just been so strange."

"For both of us," she agreed. "But harder for you. You don't owe me any apologies."

"Maybe I do. I've been confused—by all the Valmain stuff. And"—he eyed her carefully as he took a seat directly across from her—"by your close relationship with Jesse."

She blushed but admitted, "He's my best friend these days."

"I understand that now. But at the hospital, you two seemed more like . . ." He seemed to be groping for the right word. "Like conspirators, I guess you'd say."

The heat in her cheeks was intensifying rapidly. "Conspirators?"

"It's okay," he assured her firmly. "If anything, I should be grateful to Jesse for doing what *I* should have been doing all this time. Taking care of you. And your—I mean, *our*—daughter. I don't have any reason, or right, to distrust his motives, and I don't."

"Good." She flashed an encouraging smile. "So what's next? I mean, where do we go from here?"

"Actually, I've been thinking about going back to Cuzco." Misunderstanding Molly's gasp, he insisted, "Don't be worried. I'll be perfectly safe, and it's the next logical move. That's where I lost my memory, right?"

"I think it's a *wonderful* idea," she gushed. "Let's leave today. Rita and Jesse can watch Kerry for us."

"Us?" His vacant stare had returned. "You want to come with me?"

Molly's insecurities overpowered her reason and she glared. "I suppose being with me for so long would be like some kind of jail sentence to you? Go alone, then! See if I care. I have a life, too, you know, Matthew. I have better things to do than run off with a perfect—and I use the term loosely—stranger."

"What *is* it with you?" he demanded, raking his fingers through his lush hair as though absolutely stymied. "One minute you're calm and rational, and the next you're erupting, like some volcanic avenger of imagined slights!"

"How *dare* you call me that!"

"It's obvious to me," he persisted doggedly, "you have a lot of pent-up hostility against me. Maybe when I get my memory back, I'll remember whatever it is I did to you to make you so mad, but for now . . . ," he took a quick breath and suggested, carefully, "we need to have a truce. And"—he took another, deeper breath—"you're welcome to come with me to Peru. It just hadn't occurred to me. You got so sick the last time, and you weren't there when I lost my memory anyway, but if you want to come, come."

"That's a very enticing invitation," she muttered, "but I think I'll go on my own, if you don't mind. And the truth is, I may have been more useful than you think. For one thing"—she paused dramatically—"I happen to know the name of the person you originally went to Cuzco to see."

"You mean Paul Aganyer?"

"How do *you* know *that?*"

"He called me a couple of times when I was in the hospital, to check on my condition. He sounds like a nice guy."

"You're so naive, Matthew. Paul Aganyer is probably the person who hurt you and stole your amulet."

"Why do you say that?"

She shrugged unhappily. "Never mind. I don't know. I just want you to be careful."

"So?" He hesitated, as though regretting the words as he spoke them. "Are you coming with me?"

Swallowing her pride, she forced herself to smile. "Thank you, Matthew. I'd love to."

"Fine. I'll call you with the details."

She watched numbly as he hurriedly made his escape from her—the "volcanic avenger of imagined slights." Did he honestly see her that way? For all of her heartache with the old Matthew, she had always been able to count on respect and adoration. To this new stranger, Molly's existence was more frustrating than valuable. And from the way Kerreya shied away from him, Molly knew without a doubt that none of the old devotion remained.

She realized unhappily that if they didn't find the amulet, her marriage was over. If she didn't bring up the subject of divorce, *he* eventually would. Her world was falling apart, with even her magic failing her more and more often. She had no parents or siblings to offer her support. She had lost her job and was probably in danger of forfeiting her entire career. She would be a single parent, separated from the man she loved, loved by a man she could never have, haunted by the remnants of a romance that never was. . . .

"Pull yourself together!" she commanded herself in a loud voice. "As Jesse would say, this is *good* news. The zombie's going with you to Cuzco. He *wants* to go. No persuasion necessary. And once you're there, you'll find the amulet and clamp it to his wrist and he won't be a zombie anymore. And"—she shuddered with bittersweet anticipation at the thought—"you'll be his dream girl again."

"His reaction is totally understandable," Aaric soothed her later in the dream. "He thinks you'll just be in the way."

"Thanks. I feel better."

Matthew laughed. *"We* know you'll be a help, Molly, but how can he—I mean, I—"

"Call the other one 'Matt,' " Aaric interrupted. "Otherwise we'll go in circles with all of this."

"Call him 'heartless zombie,' " Molly suggested bitterly. "Anyway, for better or worse, as they say, we're leaving in the morning. I'm dreading the flight. Twelve hours! I won't know what to say to him."

"He probably won't want to talk to you, either," Aaric teased. "Just bring a book, and sleep a lot. You'll survive."

"What about the axe?" Matthew demanded anxiously. "Do you think they should bring it with them, Aaric?"

"No. For now, let's keep this man Aganyer in the dark. If he stole the amulet, he would certainly not be above stealing the axe."

"True. And if he didn't steal the amulet, then we move on to Fox."

Molly winced. "Who?"

Aaric was nodding. "The man from Michigan? He's an intriguing suspect. After all, he's the one who really wants the axe."

"Right."

"But you *told* him you didn't have it!" Molly protested. "And if he didn't believe you, why would he go to all the trouble of stealing the amulet? Why wouldn't he just come to L.A. and try to steal the axe from our house?"

"If he's a lake wizard," Aaric explained quietly, "he stole the amulet out of curiosity, knowing mounds magic could not be accessed by him. But the axe is another matter. He wants it for lake magic, and to access it, his possession must be legitimate."

"It's protected?" Matthew's eyes were glittering gold. "If he steals it, or kills for it, it won't work for him? Incredible! I've heard about spells like that. He has to buy it, like he already tried . . ."

"Or receive it as a gift," Aaric added. "Or find it, if it has been abandoned. These are his only options."

"But if he stole the amulet and is holding it for ransom, how is *that* legitimate?" Molly grumbled. "This is too far-fetched, Aaric. I vote for Aganyer as our culprit. It makes more sense."

"Let's hope so," Matthew nodded. "But my guess is, he's not dangerous, just mischievous."

"The zombie agrees with you," Molly grimaced. "He thinks Aganyer's a nice guy."

"Hardly 'nice.' Just not a robber." Matthew turned back to Aaric. "You think the axe is a channel?"

"I used to think it was, but now I'm not sure. I've used it almost daily on the ranch, to clear and to chop. AJ uses it, too, and . . ." He seemed to be reasoning as he spoke. "I'm skilled with such tools, of course, and AJ is a talented boy, but I can see that, even so, we've had much luck with that axe. It doesn't miss. It never fails." His eyes flashed with inspiration. "Maybe we should have the Princess try to use it. If her aim is true, then we would have proof the axe is empowered."

"One insult after another. Thanks, Moonshaker." She ignored their appreciative laughter and continued, "Suppose it *is* magical? What's so valuable about an axe just because it never misses? Why not just put a spell on another axe?"

Aaric shrugged. "All I know is, if it's lake magic, it will work only for its rightful owner. To steal it would be to render it useless. It works for me, as owner, and AJ as one to whom I have given permission. Do you see?"

Matthew held up a hand in interruption. "We have to assume there's more to it than we know. Molly's right. No one would go to all this trouble just for an axe that flies straight. And she's right about something else, too. If Fox—or Aganyer—stole the amulet, isn't that a little like stealing the axe? I mean, if he forces us to trade the axe for the amulet, will he be the rightful owner?"

"That, I believe, is why he hasn't contacted you. He doesn't intend to trade. He took the amulet to learn more about you and, perhaps, because he suspects it gives you power. Now he waits for you to make a move. It would have been better if we had just known soon enough to sell the axe to Aganyer and be done with it. You would still have the amulet, and you probably would never have been injured."

"So let's offer to give it to them," Molly suggested. "Isn't that obvious? We'll offer it to them with our blessings in exchange for the amulet, Let's *make* them the rightful owners." When they didn't respond, she glared. "Am I missing something?"

"It's not that simple now, Princess. To give a man the axe is to give him power. What he then does with that power would become our responsibility."

"Aaric's right," Matthew agreed. "Suppose he killed someone with it? It would be our fault."

"This is the twentieth century. If he wanted to kill someone, wouldn't he use a gun?"

"There's an old story about an axe," Aaric insisted, his frustration clearly mounting. "Maya would remember. She always listened to the old lake tales. I rarely did. Most of them were lies and ridiculous boasts. But there was something about an axe . . ."

"I've been thinking the same thing," agreed Matthew. "It seems like Deborah once mentioned an axe."

"If she knows the tale, then we must speak to her!"

"No!" Molly protested. "That old woman's dangerous. She's Angela's grandmother, Aaric!"

"She would quake before me, Princess. Do not worry. Summon her here. Now."

"I never met her, so I can't picture her."

"Then we can't do anything for now. If you and Matt don't have success with Aganyer, I'll have to go to Deborah."

"She scares me," Molly sighed. "And she'll probably lie anyway. You said Maya would have known." Reaching toward the blue cape in the tree branches, she proposed, "Try to read the markings on her cape."

"Don't touch that!" The sorcerer turned to Matthew and explained tersely, "Maya left that cape here as one of her little tricks. I'm sure of it. And the markings are just decoration. Not like the stories on the Princess's cape."

"Don't touch the cape anymore, Molly," Matthew agreed softly.

"If only we could talk to her. For just a few minutes."

Aaric's blue eyes narrowed. "That's impossible. You're wasting time with such thoughts. We must pursue this old Deborah woman. I'll go to the mounds when you return."

"I'll come with you."

"No. She might see how weak you are. You can't let anyone know how vulnerable you are, Princess. You're strong in this dream, but outside something's wrong."

"Aaric's right again, Molly. Let him go alone. He can handle Deborah."

"I have to help, too," Molly protested. "I'll go crazy just waiting."

"You'll take care of Rita and the children. It's always possible our enemies could show up in Los Angeles. You'll need to stay—"

"Wait!" Matthew's fists had clenched at his sides. "If you really think she's in danger in Los Angeles, I don't want you leaving her or Kerry alone there ever."

"She won't be alone. She'll have you," Aaric reminded him. "And she'll have AJ and the puppy. And the axe. I give it back to her, formally, here and now. So should you. There must be no mistake as to ownership."

Matthew nodded. "It's all yours, Molly. Let's hope you never have to use it."

Molly winced at the concern in Aaric's eyes. "Are you sure you're telling us everything?"

"All that I remember. You know how it is with me, Princess. I didn't spend my childhood at the mounds. I didn't hear all the old stories. And even if I had, the tale I'm trying to recall is a lake story. Now," he smiled, "speaking of childhood, bring Kerreya here. Morning approaches and she should see her father."

"Very subtle, Aaric. Why don't you just admit you don't want to tell us?"

"There's nothing to tell. Bring the little princess."

Matthew gladly welcomed his adoring daughter but refused to allow Aaric to avoid Molly's questions. "Why didn't you spend your childhood at the mounds?"

It was Molly who answered, her tone guarded. "Aaric's mother was Maya's mother's cousin. She ran away with a man who didn't live at the mounds."

"Where did he live?"

Aaric interceded impatiently. "On the seas, with others like him. They had no permanent home. I was born on their ship. When I was AJ's age, Maya's father found out about me and summoned me to the mounds. As a child I never sat with the women, listening to old stories."

"Let me get this straight." Matthew winked toward Kerreya. "Your father was a pirate?"

"That's correct." Aaric's tone was cool. "Do you wish to pursue this subject? Notice first, of course, that your wrist is bare, and that I have your dagger."

With a disapproving shrug Molly sent both warriors away, then played in the meadow with her daughter, trying not to think of the upcoming trip to Peru, or the heartache it could bring.

This plane ride proved much less stressful than their last, with Molly staring through the window, and Matt, far from noticing the flight attendants, dozing off almost immediately. *He's still not fully recovered,* Molly realized in dismay. *We shouldn't have pushed this so soon.* Still, perhaps it was the strain of being in his dual state that was tiring him and, if so, they were wise to proceed without delay.

When he awoke, he apologized sheepishly for having been such poor company. "I was up all night sorting through these papers." He pulled a large, tattered envelope from his knapsack. "I thought it might help if I read these with you, so you could give me some background."

"It's Matthew's manuscript! The one he—I mean, you— started last year. You gave it up, did you know?"

"I guessed that. It definitely reaches an impasse. Still, it's fascinating. Have you read it?"

"No. He never lets anyone see it until it's all finished. I feel guilty even holding it like this."

"I'm giving you permission, Molly, remember?" His smile relaxed her and she eagerly perused the first chapter. She had always wondered about this unfinished work, and now she had permission. A loophole, really. Matthew would just have to understand.

As she read, her elation faded into sadness. *No wonder he couldn't finish it. He's torn our world apart—our only world. Exposed its ugly flaws. He calls out to destroy it and to replace it—-but with what? Poor Matthew.* A lesser man, she knew, would be content to couch his social blueprints in generalities and double-talk, but to Matthew Redtree that would have been unthinkable. He had tried—tried and failed.

She felt tears sting her eyes for the man who had focused so single-mindedly on his predestined conflict—who had trained so relentlessly, fought so bravely, triumphed so nobly—only to have it all end in chaos. Glancing toward her companion, she realized that he, too, was touched by the words on these pages and the frustrations of the author. The hours flew by thereafter as they read and shared, analyzing and admiring Matthew's style while wondering at the intensity of his conflict.

"Was I happy, Molly?"

"Sometimes. There were moments of pure happiness, I think."

"And other moments of pure discontent?"

"You wanted a lot. Total reorganization of society. You were really bitter about drugs, and you hated what you referred to as the worship of the 'god of convenience.' On the other hand, you were impressed by simple things and you loved stories. . . ."

"Legends and anecdotes?"

"Yes. You knew hundreds of them. From all parts of the world. You collected them as avidly as your weapons." Her eyes were damp with memories. "When we were traveling together in Ireland, you told me old stories—some gruesome, some amazing—trying to force me to appreciate my Celtic heritage as much as you did. And you loved the woods, and the ocean, and cave paintings and ruins. There was a lot about our world you loved."

"It's the legend business that fascinates me, though. I get the impression that you and I believed some of them."

"One or two, I guess," she sighed. "Most of them you saw as fables. Teachings. But there were one or two . . ."

"The ones about your dreams? I read that Valmain thing,

and your term paper, but what about the rest? Why do you suppose I never wrote about them?"

"You never wrote about yourself," she smiled. "That wasn't your style. And you were protecting me, in a way . . ."

"Yeah. I guess there would have been a lot of crank calls if people knew you were a . . . princess, right?"

"It was more serious than that. You wanted to keep my heritage a secret because of the danger from unscrupulous magicians. I know, I know, you don't believe I'm descended from a sorceress, and you don't believe I have my dreams. . . ."

"Everyone has dreams, Molly. And yours must be incredibly vivid. They're real to you and, somehow, they were real to me, too," he admitted. "That's obvious from my notes."

"Tell me what you dream about now."

"No way," he laughed. "For once we're getting along. I'm not going to blow it."

"You're afraid of me?" she sighed. "Sorry. I never knew what a jealous person I was until lately."

"That's okay." He smiled, patting her hand casually. "It's kind of flattering."

Molly turned back quickly to her reading, not certain what response he expected. She decided they had talked enough. As he'd said, for once they were getting along. Why spoil it?

"Why did we live in Los Angeles of all places, Molly?"

"*I* lived in Los Angeles. You lived all over the world."

"Did that bother you? You know, being the jealous person you are."

"I think I liked it better when you were afraid of me," she laughed, charmed by his playful grin. "Anyway, the wandering bothered me sometimes, but he—I mean you—always invited me to come along. And you invited the baby, too, for that matter. We made compromises. I had my career. I wanted to continue my education." Slowly the subject had turned to Molly, and her escort's gentle, sincere questioning over the next few hours disarmed her. Soon the pilot was announcing their approach to Cuzco.

"Eleven thousand feet," she groaned. "I'm doomed. I wish I had some sort of medicine."

"You don't need drugs," Matt objected. "You said their tea worked well last time."

"That tea *is* a drug," she muttered under her breath.

"What?"

"Sorry. For a minute you reminded me of . . . well, of yourself. The antimedicine crusader. Anyway, the tea will work just fine, I'm sure."

"You already seem a little pale," he worried, slipping his arm around her shoulder protectively. "Is there something else wrong?"

"I haven't been sleeping well," she admitted, shifting shyly away from the unexpected show of concern. "But I'll be fine once we find the amulet."

"I know you're hoping the amulet will restore my memory. I hope you won't be too disappointed if"—he gestured toward himself pointedly—"if this is all there is."

His obvious vulnerability saddened her. "I want you to get your memory back for yourself and Kerreya, not just for me. You must admit we have to try."

Matt nodded. "Sure. But at some point *you'll* have to admit we should give up and start over." Releasing his hold on her, he leaned back and closed his eyes.

Start over? The thought was intimidating. Was he asking her to pretend the last two years had never happened? To start over together, or apart? She could think of nothing else to say, and so she said nothing, staring instead at Cuzco, rushing up to envelop her.

Fox didn't care for puzzles, especially when he suspected he hadn't been given all the pieces. Studying Matthew

Redtree's silver amulet solemnly, he forced himself to cata-
logue the facts as he knew them.

The infamous mounds sorceress Maya had borne a grudge
against a pre-Celtic king—undoubtedly based on some sort
of sexual infidelity—and had ordained that his kingdom
would be destroyed by betrayal. To ensure such a downfall,
she had sent the bitch Constance and the warrior Redtree
through time to mount a surprise attack on a future genera-
tion of Valmain. But only a harmless remnant—a Boston
princess turned scientist—remained, and only a slight betrayal—that of father toward daughter—had been required
to fulfill Constance's duty.

And the warrior, armed with an amulet and expecting to
be welcomed by legions of mounds magicians, had found
himself unneeded and alone. He had also undoubtedly realized quickly that he was unique to this modern world and
so, abandoning all loyalty to his ancestors and their cautious
ways, had begun to draw magic for his own purposes. Heady
with power and ambition, he had seduced the pretty Valmain
princess, believing himself beyond the reach of Maya's wrath
over so blatant a perversion of his mission.

*This girl Molly must be utterly delectable to have captured
his heart so strangely,* Fox silently taunted himself. *Perhaps
you've missed something, despite all the females at your disposal, wizard. Before you die, you must taste of Redtree's
wife.*

But first he needed to recover the copper axe. Matthew
Redtree had been clever to purchase it. Undoubtedly, he had
recognized it immediately as the sacred weapon that had
killed the accursed mounds twins so many centuries before.
"A brilliant move, warrior," Fox murmured aloud to the absent opponent. "I cannot kill you as long as you are the
owner of the axe. It's your insurance against us, for now. If
I wish to gain possession—and I *must* gain possession, and
soon—it must be through legitimate means. If only I knew
more about you!"

Hopefully, such information would be forthcoming soon. Fox had sent three spies, including the ambitious scholar Crane, to investigate. Until their return, he would have to be patient. If the assembly sensed his panic over this bizarre development, it would panic as well, spouting old wives' tales about the "return of the twins," the "rebirth of the mounds," and other such nonsense.

The twins would never return, Fox knew. But he also knew how suspicious and gullible the assembly was. If it began to fear such an event, it could lead to a challenge by Crane for First Wizardship.

"Never!" the wily leader proclaimed with thunderous confidence. "I'll find a way to recover the axe if I have to torture every member of Redtree's little entourage to do it. Then I'll kill them all, but only after the princess and I have our rendezvous. Then"—he eyed the amulet contemptuously—"I'll crush this trinket, and with it the last hopes for any future rebirth. The lakes will prevail, as always, and the mounds will be dark and cold forever."

Eighteen

Molly's head was swimming by the time Matt had retrieved their luggage, and so he left her—collapsed in a chair and sipping her *maté de coca*—while he contacted Paul Aganyer. The curious recluse immediately sent his limousine, along with a message that he insisted they stay with him. The curves along the mountain road that led to the Aganyer estate did nothing for Molly's disorientation, and she instinctively buried her aching head against Matt's familiar chest, without the strength to worry that she might be making him uncomfortable or embarrassed. Then the car rounded the final bend, a palatial stone fortress came into view, and she momentarily forgot her misery. "Look!"

"It's like something out of a Gothic novel," Matt agreed, his gold-dusted eyes wide with admiration.

"Can you imagine what it's like inside?"

"I guess we're about to find out." He helped her from the car, steadying her gently before ushering her up the steps, into a grand marble hall and then, at the insistence of the driver, directly into Paul Aganyer's study.

In the dream Matthew had prepared Molly for the wealthy recluse's confusing appearance: the toned, well-built upper body poised in sharp contrast above the withered legs. His most striking feature—silvery, almond-shaped eyes—were alive with curiosity. "You're still suffering from amnesia? It's fascinating. And this charming female is your wife? She's nothing like I pictured her."

"That seems to be the general consensus," Molly smiled wryly. "But I *am* Molly Redtree. And I'm pleased to meet you."

He kissed her fingertips, then turned to Matt, eyeing his bare right wrist intently. "Where is your silver charm?"

Taking a deep breath, Molly monitored Aganyer's reaction as she announced, "Matthew wasn't wearing it when they admitted him to the hospital. He'd been robbed. His backpack and money, and the amulet, were gone."

"I'm not surprised," Aganyer admitted. "Wandering around the jungle may be exciting but it certainly isn't safe. You shouldn't have taken anything valuable with you."

Matt shrugged. "My wife's anxious to recover the amulet. She thinks it will jog my memory."

"You remember nothing? Your childhood? Your family? Our meeting several weeks ago?"

"Nothing, although I'd like to thank you for your servant's intervention and for your contacting me in the hospital."

Aganyer nodded. "You were lucky to be alive. When I heard they'd found an American man wandering in the jungle, delirious, I knew it was you! You remind me of myself ten years ago. Reckless. Foolhardy—"

"About the amulet," Molly interrupted. "Can you think of anyone who would have wanted it?"

"Myself, for one. Don't look so alarmed. I would never commission stolen property, at least not knowingly. And whoever has it, they haven't yet offered it to me."

"Why would you want it? It's just a trinket."

"Is it?" He studied Matt slyly. "It was intriguing. When I asked for permission to examine it during your last visit, you wouldn't allow it. It was as though it were a part of you."

"Apparently, it had great sentimental value. It's been in my wife's family for years," Matt explained easily. "Like I said, we're anxious to recover it. Can you help us?"

"I can make inquiries. If I hear something, I'll contact you, but you may have to pay an exorbitant price for its return. Of course," Aganyer added hastily, "if it were up to me, it would be returned immediately and at no cost. But . . ."

"We'll pay," Matt assured him. "I have some fairly valuable items in my collection. I can sell them, or trade with the amulet's new owner."

Aganyer nodded again. "It's too bad you don't have the axe. *That* would attract some interest, and we'd undoubtedly get faster results."

"The axe?"

"Yes. A copper axe. I keep forgetting," he chuckled, "that you don't remember our last conversation. A collector in Michigan is very anxious to get his hands on a certain copper axe. It was rumored to be in your possession."

"I haven't seen anything like that in my collection. What's it like?"

"It's a North American ceremonial axe. The collector is very eager. He'd do almost anything to get it."

"Even hit Matthew over the head and leave him for dead in the jungle?" Molly demanded.

Aganyer seemed amused. "For dead? What purpose would that serve? But I do believe that this particular man—a Mr. Fox—is capable of stealing the amulet with the intention of holding it for ransom, so to speak. Not that I'm accusing anyone," he added quickly. "A plausible theory, however."

Matt was staring at the Incan masks that decorated the room. "These pieces are incredible. What else do you collect besides weapons and masks?"

"I collect everything! The last time you were here you were very intrigued by this." He opened his desk drawer and produced the obsidian dagger.

Molly's heart beat furiously as Matt expertly handled the knife. "It's a real nice piece. I own a similar piece—a copy, but an excellent one also. And my nephew is learning to work with obsidian." He smiled proudly. "It's tricky, but I think someday he's going to produce one exactly like this."

He handed it back and returned his attention to the masks. "These are *really* something, though. Do you mind if I hold one?"

"Of course not." Aganyer shook his head. "I must confess, Matthew, I paid a fortune for this dagger on the strength of your once-strong interest." When the younger man simply shrugged, his host chuckled and offered, "Would you like to see some other masks? Older ones?"

Matt eagerly accepted but Molly, whose stomach and head were in turmoil, declined and was shown to a sumptuous guest room, where she immediately collapsed on a majestic four-postered bed, desperate for rest and a consultation with Aaric, whom she summoned immediately to the dream.

"Summon Matthew, too," the sorcerer urged.

"But he's awake."

"So was I until a moment ago," he complained good-naturedly. "Rita will begin to think less of me if I keep dozing off in the middle of my chores. But in this case it's Matt who's awake, not Matthew. Summon your champion."

When she had reported every detail, Matthew shook his head. "I wonder what Aganyer's up to. Last time I was there, he wouldn't even let me *touch* those masks. Or anything but the dagger. Why is he suddenly so accessible?"

"Do you think I shouldn't have left them alone?"

"Matt can take care of himself," Aaric assured her. "Maybe he'll find out something useful."

"I'm more sure by the minute that Fox stole my amulet," Matthew added.

"I agree," Aaric intoned. "Which means I need to visit Deborah as soon as the Princess and Matt return. In the meantime," he touched Molly's shoulder and warned, "don't mention the axe to Aganyer."

"Should I tell Matthew—I mean, Matt—about it?"

"Use your instincts," the sorcerer advised. "Just be sure he agrees to keep it a secret."

Matthew nodded. "That's crucial, Molly. Aganyer would definitely tell Fox. He loves wheeling and dealing."

"You don't think we should try to retrace your steps around here? I think that's what Matt's planning to do."

"I don't see the point, but one day won't hurt, if that's what he wants. Try to keep him happy, Valmain."

Happy? He's delirious, she grumbled to herself at dinner. Matt and Aganyer had been trading stories for hours, with the guest clearly seeing his host as a prince among men. The more Aganyer worked to impress his visitors, the more certain Molly became that he was not to be trusted, and she was relieved when she and Matt finally retired to their room, where she quickly shared her suspicions.

"What can I say, Molly? I like the guy, you don't. Maybe we're both right. Although, he's obviously very impressed with you."

"Me? All I've done since we got here is rest."

"Well, apparently, you do it very well," he teased. "Are you feeling any better?"

"Yes, much better, thanks. I'm adjusting really well this time. I'll be all ready for our exploration tomorrow."

"Then you'd better sleep now. I want to get going early."

"Tell me what you and Aganyer talked about for so long."

"You've asked me that three times," he laughed fondly. Weapons, weapons, weapons."

"Did you talk about the amulet?"

"No. What else is there to say about it? But we did talk about the axe."

"Tell me exactly what he said."

"He really wants it. Because, I guess, this guy Fox is obsessed with it, which sparks Aganyer's interest. Anyway," he shrugged, "I may try to get my hands on it."

"Why? To trade with Fox for the amulet?"

"No. I don't buy any of this intrigue stuff. I believe I was just plain robbed, probably by local thieves. But Aganyer offered me a huge commission if I can track down the axe for him. It's pretty tempting."

"A commission?" Molly frowned.

"Yeah. There are a couple of other things he's interested in, too," Matt enthused. "There's a funeral mask, made of pearl, obsidian, and jade—it sounds incredible! Some tomb robbers in Guatemala just put it on the market, and Paul wants to buy it and donate it to a museum. I've seen pictures of those mosaic masks, Molly. They're fantastic."

"You'd work for Aganyer?"

"Why not? I'd like to make some extra money, especially in case the amulet comes on the market. Right?"

"I suppose," she grumbled.

"Get some sleep, Molly. We can talk about this later."

"No, Matthew, wait. Come with me." Taking his hand, she hurried him onto the balcony and lowered her voice to a faint whisper. "I have something to tell you."

He grinned impishly. "We're really international spies?"

"Just listen. And promise you won't say anything to your buddy Aganyer about this."

"I promise. What's up?"

"We already have the copper axe. It's at Rita's ranch house, in the trunk of Jesse's car. It's a long story, but the bottom line is, once we know what we're dealing with, we can use it to trade for the amulet. Until then, we have to keep quiet about it. It could put us into danger."

"From this Fox guy? If it turns out he's the one who robbed me, *he'll* be the one in danger, not us!" Matt growled. "You really think he's got the amulet?"

"Either Fox or Aganyer."

"You're leaving out the most obvious possibility. Local, garden-variety thieves. Like Aganyer said," he added wryly, "I was stupid to wear something valuable into the jungle like that."

"Just keep the axe a secret until we're in a stronger position, please? Until we're ready to trade."

"Sure. Whatever you say. Now go in and go to sleep." He hesitated, then rested his hands on her waist and brushed his lips lightly over hers. "Sweet dreams, Molly."

"Matthew!"

"What? We're married, remember?" He seemed charmed by her confusion. "I liked the way you cuddled against me in the limo, by the way. It felt nice."

"I was *nauseous,*" she reminded him nervously. "It was hardly cuddling."

"Yeah? I liked it anyway. It made me wonder. . . ." His eyes were sparkling with suggestion. "You and me—the princess and the champion. It must have been pretty romantic."

"Matthew Redtree! Stop that!"

"You're sexy when you blush, Mrs. Redtree," he grinned. "Go on into bed now. I'll sleep out here on the balcony, for tonight, at least. Okay?" He turned away before she could answer. Not that she had an answer. But she intended to get one, and *fast!*

She rushed to the dream, summoned the baby to keep Aaric distracted, then drew her champion aside, whispering frantically, "We've got a big problem, Matthew. Our friend's getting *ideas.*"

"He's suspicious by nature," Matthew shrugged. "Don't worry about it, Valmain." His gaze was locked on the Moonshaker, entertaining a wide-eyed Kerreya in the distance with an illusion of a litter of puppies. "Look at that guy. What a show-off."

"You're not listening to me." She lowered her voice and insisted, "I think he expects me to *sleep* with him." The slow, golden burn in her champion's eyes warmed her heart and she added, almost shyly, "What should I do?"

"You get out of there now!" he ordered tersely. "I can't believe the nerve of that guy!"

"I know," she sighed.

Matthew's tone had alerted Aaric, who joined them immediately. "Is something wrong?"

"Aganyer's been hitting on Molly."

The sorcerer clenched his fist and accused, "You assured me he was harmless." Turning to Molly, he demanded, "Where was Matt when this was going on?"

She stared for a moment, unsure of whether to be amused or frustrated, then explained, "Matt's the one I'm talking about. *He's* been 'hitting on' me. Not Aganyer."

The two warriors exchanged confused glances, then Matthew reminded her gently, "You're married to him. It's okay. It's *me*."

"It's a good sign," agreed Aaric. "Encourage him. It'll foster his need to protect you. Actually, I had assumed . . ."

"What? That we've been doing *that* all along? You two are sick. He's a stranger!"

"He's your husband, Princess."

Matthew nodded his agreement. "He's me, remember? It's perfectly okay, Molly."

"He's *not* you! He's different. He says I'm 'sexy' and he compliments my legs."

Matthew shook his head, clearly perplexed. "You *are* sexy, and you do have incredible legs. What's the big deal?"

She stared, dumbfounded by the bizarre revelation. "Since when did *you* ever notice my legs?" When Aaric burst into laughter, she scowled, "Be quiet, Moonshaker. This is serious."

"A man would have to be dead not to notice how attractive you are, Princess," the sorcerer grinned. "Your champion is not dead, and neither is his zombie counterpart. Take advantage of that. Seduce him. Win his loyalty."

"Men!" she spat, turning her back on them both in complete disgust. She had expected them to be jealously protective. Especially Matthew. If nothing else, wasn't he appalled at the thought of such calculating manipulation of his counterpart?

The thought of actually making love with a stranger was intimidating, but she had to acknowledge a provocative side to the situation. For so long there had only been Matthew. And, of course, Aaric as Matthew. And now . . . Matt as Matthew? If nothing else, she was definitely in a rut.

When she awoke from the dream, the sun was streaming into the guest room through the balcony shutters. Matt's absence didn't surprise her. She rarely managed to awaken before her husband and even now, groggy from her ailment, wasn't sure she was truly ready to face the day of hiking and investigating, let alone the night of bizarre lovemaking that seemed destined to follow.

It was Paul Aganyer, alone in the garden, who greeted her when she'd finally found the nerve to venture downstairs. "Mrs. Redtree! You're finally awake. We were beginning to be concerned. How are you feeling?"

"Better, thank you. That sleep was just what I needed."

"Can I have my woman bring you some breakfast? She'll know what would be soothing for your condition."

"No, thank you. Matthew wants to get an early start. Do you know where I can find him?"

Her host gestured for her to take a seat. "He felt it would be best to leave you here while he did some looking around."

"He left without me?" Molly gasped. "Oh, no . . ."

"Don't be distressed. He'll be back in a day or two. In the meantime take advantage of my hospitality. Enjoy a walk around the grounds, or a ride on one of my horses. Or my man can drive you into town if you wish to shop."

"I *wish* to find my husband," she informed him haughtily. "Right away."

"You don't trust me?" he murmured cautiously. "Surely you don't still believe I was involved in Matthew's injuries?"

"He came here last time to see you! You were the only person within five thousand miles who even knew the amulet had any value. And now he's disappeared!" Molly stared into her host's eyes, wondering if she should reveal the fact that she was not quite as helplessly human as he might think. Of course, there was always the possibility that she was in fact totally at this man's mercy. She dared not rely upon her faulty powers, which could easily fail her completely, or surge and multiply her problems.

"You're a fascinating woman," Aganyer was marveling. "Aren't you just the slightest bit intimidated by your situation? Not that you should be, of course. You're perfectly safe. And your husband's fine, or at least he was when he left. Let me send for some herbal tea." Again he motioned for Molly to take a seat. "He left you a note. Here."

The handwriting wasn't clearly Matthew's but, as Molly slowly savored the words, she knew that he had certainly written them.

Molly, you looked so pretty and peaceful that I couldn't bring myself to disturb you. I'll only be gone a day or two. Try to rest. You'll be safe with Paul. Sincerely, Matthew Redtree. P.S. I'm sorry I couldn't say goodbye, but I did kiss you. Twice. I hope you don't mind. M.

She tried not to let Aganyer see how deeply the words had touched her. For Matthew Redtree this was the equivalent of a sonnet! Until now, she had had to content herself with a stack of postcards, tied with a silver thread, each of which bore the identical message: *Staying longer than I'd planned. Miss you. Kiss the baby and keep the doors locked.* Hardly romantic. But this . . .

"Now, Mrs. Redtree . . . may I call you Molly? Molly,

you and I must get better acquainted. Your Matthew reminds me of myself, years ago, before my unfortunate accident. How was it that you and he came to be together? You seem so different." He waited for a reply but Molly simply nodded, numb with concern, and so he continued, "He tells me you're interested in drug research. Toxicology? That must be fascinating."

"What exactly did Matthew say before he left?"

Aganyer waved his hand impatiently. "He said you were weak. That he didn't wish to disturb your sleep. That you were to rest. That I was to see that no harm came to you. That's all."

The tea arrived and Molly sipped it cautiously. Making Aganyer angry suddenly struck her as a foolish move, and so she halfheartedly resumed the conversation. "I met Matthew when I was in college. He was lecturing on mythology."

"Why does a toxicologist study mythology?"

She shrugged. "Variety, I guess. Anyway, we got married and had a daughter and that's about all there is."

"Not quite all," he noted with amusement. "He travels constantly, and you do not accompany him. Again, it makes me wonder what you have in common. Besides the child, of course."

Something in his gaze seemed almost knowing, and it was Molly's turn to be curious. "What do *you* think?"

Aganyer laughed. "If I told you, you might think I was crazy. And I assure you I'm not. So, have we reached an impasse?"

"I think we started at one. My husband wants me to rest and so, if you'll excuse me, I think I'll go to my room."

"Nonsense. You have my entire estate at your disposal. There's no need to flee from me. I promise you'll be undisturbed. Enjoy your stay, Molly Redtree. Whoever you are."

The remark caught Molly by surprise and, as she watched her host glide noiselessly away in his wheelchair, she replied softly, "Who are *you*, Paul Aganyer? What game are you and destiny playing with my life?"

"Aganyer's so strange," she confided to her champion that night in the dream. "I almost tried to use persuasion on him, so he'd send someone after Matt. In fact, I almost went after him myself, but I didn't know which way to go."

"Aganyer's bizarre, but I don't think he robbed me. And I don't think he'd hurt you. I'm sure Matt . . . I . . . will be fine. He was right to leave you behind. You need to rest, not hike all around. Try to build up your strength."

"Do you think I should summon Aaric?"

"No. He'd want to rush to Peru and I don't think that's necessary. Just wait. Does this dreaming deplete your power?"

"No. It's fine. I feel better here than out there." She cuddled gratefully against him, trying not to picture Matt, all alone, in the same hostile jungle that had almost killed him only weeks before. Stranger or not, she wanted him back. Safe. Where she could see him. Touch him. Scold him for "imagined slights" . . .

"Molly! Stop worrying. He'll be fine," Matthew was insisting. "If you're this upset, maybe you *should* summon Aaric. Ask him to come down to Peru."

"No, let's give it a few days. Jesse might just make things worse." A chilling scenario had been slowly subverting her attempt at optimism. What if Matt were to meet with foul play? Wouldn't Matthew—this dream Matthew, who loved her so dearly—wouldn't he die, too? Aaric had said this dream Matthew was the part of the old Matthew equivalent to the part of Aaric that Maya had sent into the future. That part had survived the death of Aaric's body. If she kept that part here in her dream from now on, then maybe it would survive if the worst befell its body.

"What are you thinking, Valmain?"

"I'm thinking that, until he comes back, I'm leaving you here safe in this dream. I'll feel better knowing where at least part of you is."

"Keeping me here twenty-four hours a day might weaken you."

"Having you in my dreams could never weaken me," she assured him sadly. "You make me feel strong, and alive, and loved . . ."

He cradled her close. "Don't cry, Valmain. I'm not going anywhere. We're together—just like we were always destined to be—here in the Valmain dream, and someday soon, we'll be together outside of here, too. And then"—his voice was strong and confident—"nothing will ever come between us again."

Nineteen

As Molly quickly discovered, the more familiar Paul Aganyer became with his guest, the more complicated became his games. The dining room was the main arena, with Aganyer serving loaded questions and Molly fielding them awkwardly. She wanted to take control, but he was a master. Still, his enjoyment seemed to be tempered with affection, and she began to trust that, for all his annoying, underhanded ways, he was not a threat—at least, not to her.

"Don't worry about your husband," he assured her heartily on the fourth night of her visit. "He has no valuables on his person this time, and he knows the trail well from other hikes."

"But he doesn't remember those other hikes."

"Some things he remembers, some things he forgets. A strange pattern, don't you think?"

She shook her curls, refusing to be drawn into so loaded a discussion. "Have you told Fox that Matthew and I are in Peru?"

Aganyer feigned surprise. "I've had no contact with him, I assure you. Still, he's an interesting man. You'd hate him, of course. He's quite without morals, but fascinating. Something of a magician, if you know what I mean." His silver eyes twinkled playfully and, when Molly yawned, he laughed heartily. "So? That's how we'll play it? You do not even *believe* in magic, is that correct?"

"Of course I don't."

"I, on the other hand, am a firm believer."

"Oh?"

"Look around you," he invited. "Why do you suppose I settled here? It's not my native land, as you've surely guessed."

"I give up."

"This house and its grounds are protected by an age-old spell. Magic cannot be used offensively here. No one can harm me here. Nor can they harm my guests. Do you understand?"

"Who'd want to harm you?"

"That's an interesting question. Another time, perhaps, when you've come to trust me, I'll tell you the whole story. In the meantime," he suggested slyly," put my house to the test. Try something simple. Or have you already discovered the truth of my claim?"

"I don't know what you're talking about. Try what?"

"Fine. Do nothing now. But when you retire to your room, try to . . . what? I am not versed in your 'talents.' But try something nonetheless. Try to influence or injure me. Under other circumstances I would even invite you to try to seduce me," he teased. "You will see that my house is not just a shelter from the cold and the rain. It shelters me from danger. And it shelters you, too, Molly Redtree."

"I'm not in any danger." She was suddenly desperate to change the subject. "I'd like to go shopping in Cuzco tomorrow."

"Wonderful. My driver will escort you. You'll enjoy our city. Hopefully, when Matthew returns, you'll be strong enough to go to Machu Picchu. You shouldn't leave without seeing it, you know. If I were in different circumstances, I'd take you there myself. Of course," he grinned, "if I were in different circumstances, I would do *many* things differently with you." When she blushed, he added mischievously, "The truth is, there was a time when I was absolutely obsessed with marrying a witch like yourself. At one point I thought

I'd found one, but she turned out to be simply a very sophisticated brat."

"She sounds perfect for you," Molly countered. "Where is she?"

"She divorced me after the accident."

"Oh, Paul!" She was honestly ashamed and pleaded, "Forgive my sarcasm."

"Why? Her departure was the only silver lining to that particular cloud. But you're right. I *did* deserve her. I wasn't smart like your Matthew. I went for flash instead of substance. How did he find out about you, anyway?"

"Find out what?"

"Ah, yes. Still the innocent."

"I'm tired, Paul. These games are fun, but not tonight, okay? Tomorrow," she added ruefully, "if Matthew's not back, we'll have a rematch."

"You're anxious to test my house?" he guessed. "Believe me, you'll be amazed. The spell is inviolable."

She shook her head as though completely bemused. "Whatever you say. Good night, Paul."

She could hear him laughing as she hurried toward the stairs and her first impulse was to prove him wrong by setting fire to one of his precious possessions. *Except,* she thought ruefully, *that would prove him correct. It's probably just what he wants. But how on earth does he know?*

With a new respect for her surroundings, she made her way to the guest room and rushed to the dream. After heartily embracing Matthew, she summoned Aaric and reported Aganyer's claim. Her two experts conferred briefly, then Aaric announced, "If this is true, you're safer than we'd hoped."

"You mean, such protective spells are possible?"

"I've heard of them, but they require powerful magic. This Aganyer doesn't claim to have done it himself, does he?"

"He called it an age-old spell. But my dream power works."

"Because you aren't using it offensively. You can summon us because we are willing. No one is deceived or disadvantaged. The true test would be for you to summon your host. If you're unable to bring him, we'll know his boast is true."

"And if I do manage to bring him? What would we do with him?" Molly grimaced. "We'd better save the experiments for later. Or, I could do like he suggested and try to set something on fire."

"No, save your strength. You still look pale," Matthew interrupted. "You should have started recovering from the *soroche* by now."

"I have. I am. This isn't altitude sickness. It's just that same weakness I've had for weeks."

"What do you think, Aaric?" the champion worried aloud. "Should we put all of this on hold for a while? Finding the amulet can wait, if this is endangering Molly."

"The dreaming isn't weakening her. I agree, though, no outside magic for now. And"—he was apparently still fascinated by Aganyer's boast—"it probably wouldn't work anyway, within the protected house. How far did he say the spell extends?"

"He didn't. But he stays within the outer garden walls."

"You should do the same, Princess. And you should go now and rest."

"Matthew stays here, though." She expected Aaric to protest and when he quickly agreed, her heart sank. One glance at Matthew told her that he, too, had faced the grimmest of possibilities.

"Are you leaving, Aaric?"

"I'll stay for a while. Take care of yourself, Princess."

She nodded, hugged him quickly, then threw her arms around Matthew's neck, whispering, "He'll be back. I feel it."

After she'd left, Matthew held her cape longingly. "Her cape is always here. Just like Maya's."

"Her cape *is* this dream. It's her amulet, in a way, but it's

always with her. She cannot lose it as you lost yours. And"—
he coughed—"for what it is worth, I, too, feel that Matt's
still alive. He'll be back."

"Yeah, I think so, too. You'd think I'd be the first to know,
right?" They laughed nervously, not yet comfortable with
their new roles, then Matthew absentmindedly sent his
leather bola flying through the air, wrapping it around a tree
trunk. "How's Rita doing, anyway, Aaric?"

"She's well. No discomfort at all."

"I've figured it all out, you know." The Valmain champion
retrieved his bola, then confronted the Moonshaker solidly.
"Molly's so naive when it comes to you. She doesn't suspect,
but *I* know why she's so weak. She's sharing Rita's pregnancy
somehow, isn't she? You used her egg instead of Rita's. So?"
His words became an unmistakable challenge. "Is she in any
danger?"

Aaric seemed to momentarily consider denial, then
shrugged. "It was an honest mistake. I regret the effect it's
had on the Princess. She'll be fine, though. It'll last only a
month or two." He smiled reluctantly and admitted, "I'm
glad you figured it out. If anything were to happen to me,
I'd want the child to be told, someday, that he was the Princess's son."

"What about Molly? You never intended to tell *her?*"

"It would cause her unnecessary turmoil. Do *you* intend
to tell her?"

"Again, I won't tell her until this is all wrapped up. I've
got Rita to think of, too. It's a mess." He sent the bola flying
once more through the air. "You're sure they're both safe?"

"My magic is very strong. I'll help Rita. And if the Princess gets any weaker, I'll find a way to help her, too. Of
course," he added defensively, "the altitude and worry are
also taking their toll."

"If anything happens to either of them—"

"You'll kill me?" Aaric guessed, striding alongside him
as he again retrieved his weapon. "Don't worry. It won't

come to that. I'll sustain them at any cost to myself. If only Maya had consented to use the carrying spell so long ago, I would have known what to expect."

"Maya would have killed you herself if it had started draining her power this way."

"She certainly would have tried." The Moonshaker chuckled at the thought. "She was a wildcat. We're probably fortunate she chose not to have offspring."

"What will your son be like? Yours and Molly's, I should say," Matthew added dryly.

"Obviously, he'll be amazing. Powerful. Strong."

"There's no chance he might be born without powers?"

"It's always possible, but highly unlikely. I am amazing, and the Princess is quite something in her own right. Will it bother you?" He smiled sheepishly and assured him, "It's not as though the Princess allowed me into her bed."

"These days, nothing bothers me the way it would have once," Matthew confessed. "Just back off from now on. Don't use her for any more spells or crazy schemes."

"I have no more 'crazy schemes.' Once you are repaired and my son is born, I will merely sit back and enjoy being a wealthy rancher. You could do the same, you know."

"I'll just be glad to get out of here. I feel like a caged animal." He took a breath, then exhaled deeply, forcing the tension from his chest. "For months all I could think about was getting back to this dream. Now I almost hate it."

"When I was trapped in this dream, I hated it, too," Aaric admitted quietly. "At least you'll still be yourself when you emerge—with your own body and your own past. It has been very different for me."

"It's really amazing," Matthew admitted. "You actually restored a dying man's body to health."

"It's fully recovered from the beating," the sorcerer agreed. "But there are other problems."

"Huh?"

"His body is rotting from the inside out, due to years of

bad habits. I can maintain it indefinitely, but at some point it won't be worth it. When that day comes, you'll know. They'll say my brakes failed, or I was drunk driving, but you'll know the truth." His voice softened with regret. "It'll be hard on the Princess. You'll need to be strong for her."

"Is it that bad?"

"It will be. That's why the Princess must never be told. If she knew that I, or any other of her loved ones, was in pain, she couldn't abide it. The experience in the car with her mother scarred her deeply." He seemed to notice Matthew's concern for the first time and teased, "Don't get your hopes up, Son of Lost Eagle. It won't be soon. I want to see my son's childhood. I'll be in your way for many years to come." With a rueful laugh he added, "There was one advantage in the old days, I remember."

"What was that?"

"When the day came for me to die, I could have counted on you to kill me. I could have died a death fit for a warrior. Now I suppose that would be asking too much?"

"We'll see," Matthew grinned. "I'm sure my opinion of you will continue to evolve. Who knows what's possible in the future?" His momentary amusement vanished. "When the time comes—when you can't bear the pain anymore—talk to Molly. Prepare her. Don't just leave her. It would break her heart. She loves you, man."

"You've changed," Aaric marveled. "You do not wish me gone at any price?"

"Yeah," Matthew chuckled. "Who would have believed you and I could actually coexist?"

"It's bizarre, I'll admit. Lost Eagle would be amused. And"—he studied Matthew intently—"I intend to be a worthy ally. Together, you and I are invincible, although . . ."

"Yeah?"

"You do that inefficiently, did you know?"

"Huh?"

"The way you throw the bola. There's a better technique.

My technique. I could show you. After all, as I said, we're allies."

"Better?" Matthew's pulse quickened. "You mean, you *think* your way is better?"

"I know it."

"Care to prove it?"

Aaric grinned. "The Princess will be angry if we compete. Especially if I win. She's worried about your 'fragile ego.' "

" 'Fragile' . . ." Matthew caught himself ruefully. "Trying to put me off balance? I suppose that's the secret to your famous technique? Come on, Aaric. Enough talk. Pick a target."

Aaric waved his hand, causing an illusion of a huge, fair-haired, scowling warrior to loom in the distance. "A lake wizard. Are you impressed?"

Matthew whistled. "Not bad. Can the illusion actually do us damage?"

"Of course. Otherwise, it wouldn't be a valid test."

"True. Okay, what's the contest?"

"We'll each take turns with shots as he advances. The one who can wrap his weapon around the lake warrior's neck in the fewest attempts . . ."

"Perfect. Where's your bola?" Matthew watched in fascination as the weapon materialized. "Pretty flashy. Is that solid silver?"

"Of course. Silver versus sand and leather, yet it should not matter. It's the technique that counts."

"I agree. Okay, I'm ready. Release the wizard."

"One word of warning. Don't allow yourself to lock eyes with him. A lake wizard—especially the First Wizard—can drain the energy from even a sorcerer or witch. With you it would be an instant disaster. And avoid his claws at all costs."

"Okay, let's go."

Aaric nodded toward the black-robed illusion, whose blue eyes instantly grew red with power. Within seconds both the silver and the leather bolas had flown through the air and encircled the wizard's windpipe, yet still he advanced.

"Now what?" Matthew shouted.

"Congratulations, son of my old enemy!" Aaric roared. "You won! The honor of finishing him off is yours!"

"Now that we've made him *really* mad?" Matthew demanded.

With a booming laugh Aaric disappeared and Matthew chuckled knowingly. The lake warrior illusion had remained, which meant Aaric, while invisible, had not truly left the dream, so the Valmain champion proceeded with confidence, although he heeded his new ally's advice and avoided meeting the wizard's hypnotic gaze. The obsidian dagger lay in plain sight and Matthew dove for it just as the wizard moved fury-charged fingertips toward his throat.

The claws dug deeply into his neck, inflicting a searing pain unlike any Matthew had felt. Then he plunged the dagger into the wizard's heart. The illusion shrieked, then vanished, and the champion stood alone, flush with the memory of the battle, and mindful of Aaric's lament. *A death fit for a warrior.*

The infamous Moonshaker didn't want to simply rot to death from the inside out. He wanted to leave the world in a blaze of glory. Likewise, the Valmain champion didn't want to spend eternity in a dream, with no physical self, unable to protect his dream girl or raise his daughter.

But if anything happened to the body they so cavalierly called "Matt," wouldn't that be his fate? *A death fit for a warrior . . .* It was suddenly, dangerously appealing.

Paul Aganyer invariably dressed formally for dinner and, if the verbal sparring was to continue, Molly was determined to even the match by finding something other than her simple white wool suit to wear. Unfortunately, the limousine ride into the city reawakened her dizziness, so she placed herself at the mercy of the driver, who assured her he knew of just the boutique for a one-stop shopping spree.

In hesitant Spanish she explained to the saleswomen that she wanted something elegant, inexpensive, and preferably white. When they ushered her into a dressing room and presented her with their selection, she laughed ruefully and agreed, "It's definitely white. And I guess it's elegant, in a skimpy sort of way. . . ." She held the low-cut, strapless, beaded bodice against her chest with one hand, fluffing the short, multilayered chiffon skirt with the other. "It just isn't me . . . But it's *soo* beautiful." When her attendants oohed and aahed, she bit back an embarrassed smile and, when they'd left her alone, she shrugged eagerly out of her modest skirt and blouse, slipped the gown over her head, and tugged it into place low on her full, bare bosom, then stared at her reflection in absolute awe.

It's as beautiful as my cape, she marveled. Except of course that the cape, with its air of dignity and purity, covered her regally while this dress revealed her shamelessly. Her neck seemed longer and more graceful above the bared shoulders; her breasts were seductively emphasized; and thanks to a tightly set-in silver sash, her waist seemed almost impossibly slender.

Too provocative for dinner with Paul Aganyer, she decided finally. *And Matthew would hate it. You could ransom the amulet for the price of this one, silly, fabulous dress, so take it off!*

She retreated into the safety of her own unpretentious garments and, when she again surveyed herself in the mirror, the shabby image dismayed her. *You're as bad as Matthew,* she chided herself. *When all of this is over, you'd better go shopping again.*

She didn't have the heart to search for another, less stunning dress, nor the strength for sight-seeing, so she returned, deflated, to the protected house. When the housekeeper informed her that her spouse had not yet returned, her shoulders slumped in complete defeat and she longed to escape to her room. Paul Aganyer, however, had arranged for a beautiful feast of fruits, cheeses, and breads in the courtyard and insisted upon "experiencing Cuzco through the eyes of a beautiful young woman."

She quickly regretted having allowed her ailment to interfere with what had probably been her only opportunity to understand why Matthew had been so often drawn to this area, but as Aganyer's questioning persisted, the beauty and grace of the centuries-old buildings and ruins came back into focus. Her host entertained her for almost an hour, supplying the history, detail and significance of the remarkable clash of cultures that had produced "modern" Cuzco. Then he interrupted himself, motioning toward the doorway, and the housekeeper stepped forward, handing a package to Molly. "This is for you," Aganyer explained. "My driver told me how you'd admired it. Please accept it as a token of my friendship."

When the glamorous dress spilled into her arms, she flushed, feeling confused, manipulated, and tempted, all at one time. "I'm sorry, Paul, but I can't accept this."

"Don't say 'no' just yet," he protested. "Once your husband has returned, you can decide. But I hear you are breathtaking in it. Of course," he added gallantly, "I would miss seeing you in your lovely white suit, and so you mustn't wear this for me. But consider the effect it might have on our Matthew. It might even stimulate the return of his memory."

She blushed again and retreated to her room, where she sank wearily onto the bed. Each time she closed her eyes, she saw a montage of churches, masks, capes, and dresses. She knew this feeling all too well. It was destiny, coming to call. Uninvited, of course, but coming nevertheless, when all she wanted was for it to be over.

"But it's never over," she reminded herself. "You'll always be who you are. And the baby will be a sorceress. And Matthew and Aaric . . . warriors. Whether or not the amulet is recovered, it will never really be over. Think about *that*, Molly Redtree. *Whoever* you are."

Twenty

Jesse's pulse quickened as he hurried his horse toward the ranch house. Someone had been ringing the dinner bell madly, and he was suddenly dead certain something had gone wrong with the pregnancy. Racing into the kitchen, he found Rita holding an ice pack on a shaken AJ's bruised face.

"Where's Kerreya?" he demanded.

"She slept right through this, thank heavens," Rita assured him. "But poor—"

"What happened, son?"

"I heard a noise—" the boy began, but Rita interrupted, "Someone *attacked* him, Jesse. Right in our own barn! He could have been killed." Her dark eyes were filled with distress. "I hate living out here, in the middle of nowhere."

He patted her shoulder, then turned his attention back to his son, examining his swollen eye and nose. "Tell me what happened. Who did this to you?"

"A man hit me, Dad. I can't remember right, I guess, because it seems like . . ."

"Like what?"

"Like he hit me from the other side of the barn. He was ten feet away! I promise."

"Let's not talk about it, AJ," Rita soothed him. "Be glad it all happened so quickly. Don't try to remember the details."

"Are you well enough to go hunt for your assailant, son?"

"Hunt for him?" Rita gasped. "Jesse, no!"

"I'm going after him, Rita. If AJ wishes to assist me . . ."

"Yeah! I do!"

"Don't be ridiculous," the angry mother scowled. "I called Rob. He's on his way here. Let's just leave it to him."

Jesse pulled his wife aside. "If we don't allow our son to deal with it—right away—it will always seem like a big deal."

"It *is* a big deal! He was assaulted!"

"That kind of talk doesn't do any good." Jesse turned back to the boy. "Will you be able to recognize him if we find him?"

"It was kind of dark in the barn, but I think so."

"Good. Let's go."

"Jesse!" Rita implored, and again he pulled her aside, insisting, "Our chances of actually finding the man are slim. I'm just doing this for AJ. He needs to know he dealt with the situation." He kissed her cheek reassuringly. "Think about it. Where could we even begin to look? He could be anywhere in Los Angeles!"

"Please, Mom?"

"You really want to?" She sighed, rumpling her son's hair lovingly. "I guess it's okay. But don't go for long. And if you start feeling dizzy or nauseous . . ."

"We'll come straight home," Jesse promised. "Okay, AJ, let's go." He ushered the boy toward his shiny white Cadillac. "First I want to see if anything's missing."

"Shouldn't we go to the barn for that? He was hanging around Uncle Matt's junk."

"I know what he wanted, and it's not in the barn." Opening the trunk of the car, he quickly located the axe. "Good. It's still here. I'll explain everything to you while we drive."

"Can you explain how he hit me from across the barn?"

"It's called 'infliction,' and it's a very powerful weapon in the right, or should I say, wrong hands."

"Do you know where we should start looking?"

Kate Donovan

"He's probably at the airport. My guess is, it's the same man, or men, who hit your uncle over the head in Peru."

"Wow."

"We'll find the flight for Michigan and he'll be there."

"How do you know all this, Dad?" AJ's voice was calm and trusting.

"Today is an important day for you, son. Today you will learn things that will amaze you. Today you became a warrior."

"A warrior? I got knocked out."

"So did your uncle," Jesse reminded him. "The important thing is, you were ready to fight. To protect your family. You have a brave heart and a strong body. You're ready. Of course," he added quickly, "your mother and your aunt would not agree."

"You don't want me to tell them?"

"I can't tell a warrior what to do. But when I've told you everything about myself, and about you and your ancestors, then I'll ask you to think carefully before you speak of it to anyone else. If your Uncle Matt were recovered, you could talk to him. He knows, or knew, most of what I'm about to tell you."

"Does Aunt Molly know?"

"She knows. She wouldn't want you involved, though."

"And Mom *doesn't* know, right?"

"Your mother and your brother are special," Jesse explained respectfully. "Much of their strength comes from their dedication to logic and normalcy. The truth is, even if you decide to tell them, it won't matter, because they won't believe you. And now, since we have so little time, listen and prepare yourself. We'll start with the evening at the mounds when you experimented with your uncle's amulet."

They rode together—Jesse quietly revealing secrets, AJ absorbing those secrets in wide-eyed silence—until they'd reached the airport, where they checked for flights departing for Michigan. "We're lucky, son," Jesse grinned. "He's still here. Now, look around carefully."

"What if he goes back to the ranch?"

"He won't. I'm surprised he went there even once. Stealing the axe will get him nothing. He just wanted to confirm that we had it, I suppose. The timing would have seemed perfect, with both Matt and the Princess out of town."

"Because he doesn't know about you?"

"He doesn't know about *us!*"

AJ beamed. "I'll do better this time, Dad."

"Against infliction, unprepared, you stood little chance last time. But you're right. This time will be different." He noticed that AJ was staring at a man. "Is that him?"

"Yeah. He doesn't see me. He looks sick, doesn't he?"

"Do you see?" the proud father laughed. "You injured him without even realizing it! He *can't* be Fox. Some minor errand boy. You'll handle him easily."

"Me?" The boy's eyes widened in dismay. "I'm only twelve, remember? I thought you wanted me to stay back and watch."

"When I thought we were dealing with Fox, I wanted to proceed with caution. But this is different. He's already weakened from the encounter with you. Let's have some fun." He placed his hands on his son's shoulders. "Relax. Rely on your instincts and your training. We'll escort him into that rest room where we can all talk in private."

They approached their target, who immediately took a step backward, clearly alarmed by their audacity.

"Not so fast," counseled Jesse, grabbing the wizard's arm. "My son and I would like a word with you."

"You have the wrong man." When AJ grabbed his other arm, the man frowned. "Haven't you learned your lesson yet, kid?"

"Talk to *me*," Jesse advised smoothly. "My son has a bad temper. Let's go somewhere we can talk comfortably."

The man's eyes darted from father to son, then he whined, "I didn't take anything. And I didn't hurt the kid too bad."

"Where's Fox?"

"Who?"

Jesse nodded to AJ, who obligingly tightened his grip.

"Listen, I don't know who you are . . ."

"That's obvious. *Where's Fox?*"

"He's in Detroit. Waiting to hear from me."

"And what will you tell him?"

"That you don't have the axe?"

"Wrong. We have it. We want to sell it to him. And we want to buy our amulet back. Do you understand?"

"I don't know anything about any amulet." When Jesse scowled, the man panicked. "I swear it. Fox tells me nothing!"

"Fine. Just give him a message. Tell him to come here. To Los Angeles. I'll meet with him here at the airport. Tell him not to come near my house or Redtree's. *Or* the mounds. I'll kill any one of you who does."

"Believe me, I'm not planning on coming back."

"Wouldn't you like to apologize to my son now?"

"Oh, sure. Sorry, kid."

"Do you want to hit him, AJ?"

"No, thanks, Dad."

"Fine. Go now, errand boy, before my son changes his mind."

She had desperately tried to rest, but images of her champion in danger kept floating before her eyes. She even thought she could hear his voice, whispering. So gently. Only inches from her ear. She opened her eyes and, charged with relief, impetuously jumped into Matt's arms, then drew away just as quickly. "I'm sorry!"

"Don't apologize. I'm glad to see you, too, Molly. And—" he reiterated casually, "we're *married*, remember?"

Embarrassed and relieved all in one confused moment, she gathered the blanket around her chemise-clad body and gushed, "I've been so worried! You shouldn't have gone without me."

"I thought you'd be safer here. You look a little more rested." He smiled as she moved shyly—almost primly—from the bed to a chair, the blanket still clutched about herself. "You look great, actually, Molly. Here," he held out a package to entice her back, "this is a present for *our* daughter."

"Matthew! How sweet." She tore away the white tissue wrapping eagerly. "Oh! A doll!"

"Not too imaginative, I guess."

"It's perfect. The poor thing has been forced to play 'baby' with the puppy Jesse gave her."

"Jesse gave her a puppy?" Matt muttered. "I bet she loved that."

The bitter undertone to his voice concerned Molly and she assured him firmly, "You're not in competition with Jesse."

"Are you sure? Then"—he held out another, smaller, wrapped bundle—"this is for you. For us, really."

Her hopes soared as she accepted the gift. Through the tissue she could detect a hint of silver, and, as she peeled away the layers, she became certain—and ecstatic. "The amulet! You've found it! Why didn't you put it on . . . Oh!" She caught her breath as the last layer of wrapping fell away, revealing a shining silver heart on a long, delicate chain.

"My mistake," he growled, rising stiffly, then striding toward the door. "I have to go report in with Aganyer."

"Matthew! No!" she wailed, still clutching the blanket as she raced to his side. "Please don't go. I'm sorry. This is so beautiful." Grabbing his hand, she insisted, "This is the nicest gift you've ever given me."

His eyes were cold and unforgiving. "Forget it. It was a stupid mistake. I've got to go, Molly. I'll be back later."

As she watched the door slam forcefully behind him, she berated herself for her monumental blunder. This was the kind of thing Matthew never did. The kind of thing she had always ached for him to do. A necklace! Beautiful and personal, with no connection to any legend or larger purpose. Just a gift. Because she meant something to him! Because he found her attractive!

Pressing the locket to her lips, she remembered the day by the wading pool, when he'd first admired her legs and talked about romance. And he'd left her that sweet love letter, and kissed her on the balcony, and told her she was sexy, and now this! As the full import of the silver heart hit her, she cried out in soft delight, then raced to the intercom to summon Aganyer's housekeeper.

It was as seductive an apology as had ever been fashioned from white beads and chiffon, dazzling a contrite Matt upon his return. "You look incredible," he murmured, his gaze wandering from her long, bare legs to her brazenly showcased breasts. "I'm sorry I ran out like that."

"No, Matthew, let *me* apologize." She took his hand and kissed it shyly. "Please?"

He flushed and kept her hand in his own. "I know how important that amulet is to you. To buy you *silver,* of all things, was just dumb."

"The amulet's important to me," she agreed softly, "but this locket's special, too." She fingered the silver chain, then let it drop back provocatively into her cleavage. "I adore it."

"Good. As for the amulet"—he smiled confidently— "I've decided it's time we wrap this thing up. I told Aganyer to contact Fox and to tell him to meet us in Los Angeles. We'll trade the axe for the amulet if he has it, and be done with it. No questions asked."

"Matthew! It's not that simple. He could be dangerous . . ."

"I've lost my memory, not my moves." He grinned. "Let me handle it from here on out. Now"—his gaze caressed her hopefully—"shall we go? Aganyer's car is waiting. We have reservations . . . Oh, wait. I almost forgot." Hurrying to the closet, he rummaged in his knapsack, pulling out a slightly rumpled tweed sport coat. "I hope this didn't get too wrinkled."

"Where did you find that?" Molly gasped. "I haven't seen it in years."

"It was in storage, with the weapons and all. Rita got it cleaned for me. I thought I should bring it," he smiled, shrugging into the coat, "just in case."

Just in case? Had he planned this even then? Her heart was pounding at the thought. Would he try to kiss her? To make love to her? Instead, he took her arm and led her toward the door. *Our first date,* she thought in amazement. *What would Matthew think?* The thought almost made her giggle aloud.

Her giddy mood continued in the limousine, where she chattered breathlessly about her day in Cuzco, finding every possible excuse to touch the sleeve and lapel of the jacket. She was conscious of his eyes, drawn time and again to the new locket as it swung provocatively between her breasts. Had he planned *that* too? Had he imagined . . . ?

It was not a time for analysis. Still, she couldn't help but notice that this man was falling in love with her, and she watched the progression in awe. No longer were they players in a cosmic fantasy of intrigue, betrayal, and duty. To Matthew—*this* Matthew—they might as well have been the only two people on earth.

The rest of the evening was truly a dream come true for her romance-starved heart. It wasn't just that Matt was gallant and attentive. He seemed positively mesmerized. When he actually suggested that they dance, she could no longer contain her amazement. "You're a different person! You've *never* danced with me. You said you hated dancing!"

"I have an ulterior motive," he confessed. "I want to hold you in my arms." She went to him gratefully, and he led her onto the floor, then pulled her into a seductive embrace. "Your skin's so soft . . ." He was stroking her bare back as he cajoled, "You feel so good, Molly."

"Matthew . . ."

"You're so sexy." He pulled her closer, then confided, "You're driving me crazy."

"You feel good, too," she assured him in throaty delight. "You're so strong, and warm . . ."

"You should hear your voice," he groaned. "It's got the most incredible little purr. . . ." Cupping her chin in his hand, he pleaded, "Can we go back to the mansion now?" When she nodded, he grasped her elbow with one hand, digging in his pocket with the other for a fistful of bills, which he dropped onto their table as they hurried past it. Molly heard the waiter chuckle, and blushed to realize the entire restaurant knew that Matthew Redtree had absolutely lost his mind—*over a woman!*

He escorted her back to the limousine, sliding into the seat beside her. "How do you feel? Weak?"

"No," she assured him. "I'm feeling stronger every minute."

"Are you cold?" He was draping his sport coat over her shoulders before she could protest.

"I'm not cold—Oh!" She gasped as the bodice of her dress loosened dramatically under his mischievous fingers. Then those fingers moved to her breasts, fondling eagerly, while his mouth descended to her neck. "Matthew Redtree!"

"Shh," he admonished. "You don't want the driver to notice, do you? And we *are* married. It's time we got reacquainted. I haven't done this in . . . how long?"

"You've *never* done this!" she assured him, light-headed with arousal. "Never. It's decadent! Petting? In a limousine?"

His lips had trailed down her shoulder and into the jacket.

"Quiet, Molly, you're embarrassing me. The driver, remember?"

She was laughing helplessly as Matt pushed her back onto the seat. Then he stretched over her, running his hand down low toward her stomach. "Ever since that day in your backyard, when you were wearing that bathing-suit thing, I've been fantasizing about your incredible body. And of course"—his eyebrow arched wickedly—"your pure eyes and steady heart."

"That's *steady* eyes and *pure* heart!" she scolded, her heart thumping wildly against her chest. Where was the reverence? The control? The love that transcended physical needs? It had all but disappeared, replaced by the infamous "much less lofty" love that Aaric had always favored and that she herself had apparently always craved.

His kisses and caresses—playful, yet with a sweet desperation behind them—continued as the limousine wound its way back to the Aganyer estate. Then they reached the protected house and Matt scooped her into his arms, bundling her swiftly to their room.

"I love you, baby," he crooned, falling with her onto the four-poster bed. "You're so beautiful."

"Matthew, this is heaven. I'm tingling all over! It's like your body remembers, even if your mind doesn't."

"I know. It's perfect. Our first time, even though we've been lovers for years. What a turn-on."

"Our first time . . . ," she repeated dreamily. It was true! This was so like that day, so long ago in Ireland, and yet it was also so radically different because *this man was out of control!* He was pleasing her, yes, but not at his own expense, as he had so often seemed to do in the past. Instead, he had a voracious appetite and apparently intended to devour her before the night was through.

"I've always wanted you to make love to me this way, Matthew," she enthused, arching to more completely enjoy the aroused feel of him.

"What way?"

"Like you couldn't live without it."

"Couldn't live without *it?*" He paused in his attack to chuckle. "Don't you mean, couldn't live without *you?*"

"I always knew you couldn't live without me," she sighed, confessing shyly, "I can't live without you. *Or* this."

"I intend to keep you alive," he promised with mock solemnity, then his mouth crushed down on hers, signaling an end to talk—perhaps even to thought!—and a resumption of unbridled lust.

The bodice of the gown had been pawed down to around her waist and now Matt bared his own chest, stretching over her, then groaned when her erect, appreciative nipples greeted his efforts. His tongue was thrusting hungrily into her mouth, tasting and exploring, while one hand began an even more daring adventure, traveling down, past her waist, and teasing between her thighs. She arched again, then tore mindlessly at the zipper of his jeans.

"Yeah," he groaned, shrugging awkwardly out of the pants while attempting to keep his mouth engaged with hers. Then he was in her, and the world was exploding with sensation, and they were grinding and thrusting with hedonistic abandon.

She knew he never wanted it to end, yet knew also that this time—their "first time, even though they'd been lovers for years"—they needed to climax together or perish deliciously in the attempt, and so she dug her fingernails into his buttocks and gyrated wantonly, wresting the last vestiges of dominion from him. The wild, glorious explosion that rewarded her seemed also to consume her, shattering all sense of self and delivering them both into chaotic ecstasy.

Drenched and satiated, they continued to cling to this moment, and to one another. Molly was pulsing gently as Matt's hands kneaded her buttocks adoringly, urging from her those last, luscious aftershocks that they both craved. When finally they were still, there were a million things each wanted to say, and yet their grateful, slightly sheepish gazes said it all, and they snuggled in silence until their contented exhaustion dissolved into true sleep.

That night Molly didn't even consider going to the dream. She wanted to stay in Matt's arms forever. She even found herself wondering if it would be so tragic, after all, if the amulet were never recovered. *Two Matthews.* More and more it seemed as though her old enemy, destiny, intended to force her to choose, but she slept soundly, for this one miraculous night, secure in the knowledge that she was loved.

When she awoke and Matt was there, she kissed him in gleeful amazement. "You're still in bed! You didn't get up! You've been awake for hours, haven't you?"

"Again"—his smile was devilish—"I had an ulterior motive." He was kissing her heatedly when the telephone jangled. "Damn."

Jesse, concerned over Molly's failure to report to the dream, interrogated her rapidly and, while she tried to respond soberly, Matt's insistence upon playing with the locket as he nibbled on her breasts made her replies nonsensical and brief. Finally Jesse growled, "What the hell's wrong with you, Princess? Have you been drinking?"

"We went to dinner and it was too late to phone you," she gasped.

"To 'phone'?" Jesse mocked. "Princess . . ."

"I'll explain later, Jesse. Kiss Kerreya for me—"

"And tell Rita we'll be flying home today," Matt added loudly and confidently into the receiver.

"I think I'm beginning to understand," Jesse muttered.

Her mentor's annoyed reaction reduced her to tears of laughter and she barely managed a breathless goodbye before Matt slammed the receiver back into its cradle and covered her mouth with his own, merciless in his tenderness. He amused her for hours thereafter, and she joyously welcomed a life that had suddenly, miraculously, become perfect. But could such perfection last? The answer came swiftly when Matt arose to dress, and the young witch, attempting to follow, collapsed to the floor.

"I take it your servant displeased you, Fox?" The elegant golden-haired witch sighed. "What did he do?"

Fox looked up from the dismembered corpse of his former manservant and grinned malevolently, imagining how impressed his bride must be by the sight of her new husband, the First Wizard of the Lakes, splattered with blood and victory. Gesturing for the blond beauty to approach, he assured her, "I'm glad you've arrived in time to witness this reminder of the fate of those who disappoint me."

"How did he disappoint you, darling?"

"I sent him in search of the axe. Not to retrieve it, of course. Merely to verify its location. He returned with wild tales—of hordes of sorcerers and twelve-year-old magicians who threatened his life."

"Twelve years old?" Sara scoffed. "Impossible! How could a twelve-year-old threaten a practiced wizard?"

"A cowardly wizard. A lazy one."

"A dead one!" Sara laughed harshly. "He would have been better off dying at the hands of the alleged boy magician. Where does this supposed phenomenon reside?"

"In Los Angeles. On the ranch of Matthew Redtree's sister."

"And is Matthew Redtree one of the supposed sorcerers?"

"No. His brother-in-law, Jesse Camacho, was the man named."

"Is it possible . . . ?"

"It's always possible," Fox admitted, abandoning his bantering tone. "Highly improbable, though. Camacho is reputedly a failure. And, since the deed to his property is in Molly Sheridan Redtree's name, he's also apparently a charity case." He kicked the corpse in disgust. "If this fool had done his job, we'd have our answers. Instead, we operate in the dark. And my new suit's ruined."

"Let me help you," Sara cooed, moving her fingers to the pearl buttons on his shirt. When she had bared his chest, she wriggled out of her own chic silk suit and moved against him suggestively. "Will you go to Los Angeles yourself now, Fox?"

"Eventually. For now, there are several other options. There's an old woman they call Deborah Clay. Crane learned all about her when he visited the old burial mounds."

"Is she a witch?"

"Apparently not. But the locals claim her granddaughter Angela was one."

"Was?"

"They say she was a tall, beautiful whore of a witch, who seduced a young tourist named Matthew Redtree."

"Redtree? Again?" Half to herself she added, "It would seem no woman can resist him."

"When he wore the amulet, he was powerful," Fox glared. "But now he is an injured, powerless fool. Do not lust so openly, Sara. I might decide to discipline you." When she blanched, he continued coolly, "According to Crane, the witch Angela died of a heart attack, although she was only in her twenties. The old woman moved away thereafter, although she occasionally visits a cottage she owns there."

"And you intend to find her and question her?"

"She has a nephew who keeps in contact with her. I spoke with him this morning, pretending to be interested in purchasing her run-down hovel, and he promised to convey the message to her."

"Maybe she can tell you how to operate Redtree's amulet. Then we could draw power from the mounds as well as the lakes."

Grinning, Fox pulled the silver spool from the pocket of his trousers and stroked it between her breasts. "Constance

tells me the mounds always linked such charms to blood-
lines. We can never use it. I'll try to find some other toy for
you."

"When did you talk to Constance?" Sara snapped. "That
bitch is always monopolizing your attention!"

"Her stepdaughter is the Valmain heiress," he soothed. "I
must be vigilant."

"And did you sleep with her stepdaughter also? Is there
any female left on earth with whom you have not slept?"

Fox roared with laughter, then confessed, "I intend to sam-
ple her, eventually. From what I've learned, she's already
whoring with Camacho on the side. And I'm told she's very
attractive. Thick, curly hair and cobalt blue eyes . . ."

"She's hazardous. We should kill her."

"I agree. She's a focal point for trouble and must be elimi-
nated, once we have the axe."

"You're sure they have it?"

"Camacho claims they do. But before I go to Los Angeles
to deal with him, I need to know two things."

Sara nodded. "You need to know if he's the rightful owner,
and you need to know if he is, in fact, a sorcerer, disguised
as a bum."

"This is the reason I married you," Fox murmured. "Fire
and brains. Do you think you could check this Camacho out
for me?"

Sara's eyes sparkled. "How thorough should I be?"

"I hate to disappoint you, my little whore, but I want you
to observe from a distance, not to touch. Do *not* speak to
any of them. You should be able to tell quickly from his
movements and demeanor if he's more than he seems to be."
He kicked again at the mutilated corpse, this time in unadulterated warning. "Stay out of sight, and report back by midnight. Do you understand?"

"Yes, Fox. I'll stay out of sight. And I'll make you proud
of me. Will you instruct the assembly to empower me?"

"Camacho's never seen you, so no illusion will be re-

quired. And no spells will be necessary if you follow my
orders. Service me now, then proceed to Los Angeles. When
you return, the fates of Redtree and Camacho will be decided
at last."

Twenty-one

The pilot was announcing preparations for landing in Los Angeles as Matt buckled his bride into her seat. "I still wish you had let me call a doctor for you in Cuzco, baby."

"It's not a medical problem, Matthew. I know you don't believe me yet but, I swear, I've had this before."

"Soroche."

"No. It's somehow connected to my dreaming."

"Come on, Molly. Dreams can't make you sick."

"It's not so much the dreaming, actually, as my other powers that are messed up."

"Powers? Listen, I love you, but you're nuts. I want you to see a doctor as soon as we land." He moistened his lips and added cautiously, "You're not pregnant, are you?"

"No. Or"—her eyes twinkled with memories—"at least, I wasn't as of last night." When she feigned an accusing stare, he grinned sheepishly, his arm tightening its hold on her shoulders, and she snuggled into him. "You feel so strong."

"And you feel so soft," he replied, nuzzling her amorously.

"Mmm . . ." She surrendered gratefully to the lavish attention, purring, "Matthew? If you could have anything in the world, what would you want?"

"That's easy. I want this. Forever. What would *you* want?"

"I agree with you. This is perfect. But what about making society more accountable? Saving the forests? Searching for artifacts? Seeing new places?"

"I can do those things and kiss you at the same time. Or else I'll give them up."

"Good."

"What about you? What will *you* give up?"

"What do you mean?"

"I 'mean' the amulet, of course. Can you settle for me? *This* me? Can you be satisfied with the 'us' that started in the last few weeks?"

"If only it were that simple," she sighed.

"You're worried about Kerreya? I'll win her over. I promise. I'll even get your watchdog AJ to trust me eventually."

"I have another obligation," she explained softly. "To an old friend. You'll understand someday."

"Not again," he groaned. "Rita told me to humor you, but for how long? I actually felt jealous, watching you last night while you were sleeping. Wondering where you were and what you were dreaming about. I want you to concentrate on me."

"You're always on my mind. Awake or asleep. Believe me."

"It's like there's a part of you I can't have. . . ."

"No! It's just the opposite. And I wasn't dreaming last night. I swear."

"What about this 'old friend' you owe an obligation to?"

"He's you. Can't you see? It's you—Matthew Jason Redtree—waking or sleeping. You're everything." She nestled against him as the plane bumped along the runway. "We're home, Matthew. Home and in each other's arms. That's where I want to be."

With the landing completed, Molly intended to stand, but Matt swept her into his arms before she could try. "No way. Rest. We're going straight to Rita's hospital, remember? I want a doctor's opinion on this dizziness of yours."

"I thought 'Matthew Redtree's family doesn't use hospitals.' "

"Was I really that pompous?" He grinned apologetically

and proceeded down the ramp, only to be confronted by an incredulous Jesse.

The sorcerer's eyes were blazing as he roared, *"What the hell have you done to her?"*

"She'll be okay, Jesse. Calm down. We're going to find a doctor—"

"Give her to me! Now!"

To Molly's surprise Matt immediately lowered her to the ground. Then he steadied her carefully, turned calmly to Jesse, and shoved one fist into the sorcerer's stomach while, almost immediately, punching another into his astonished face, sending him flying into a bank of chairs.

With supreme confidence Matt again hoisted a speechless Molly and proceeded through the terminal. "Don't worry, baby," he chuckled. "He'll be okay. With guys like that it's better if you just let then know exactly where you stand, right from the start."

"But, Matthew . . ." She wanted to warn him. To predict a fearsome revenge. She wanted him to know what he had done, whom he had antagonized . . . Craning her neck, she finally caught a glimpse of Jesse, rubbing his jaw with an expression of . . .

Amusement? He was almost laughing. He *was* laughing, and Molly grinned back at him with relief, then turned her beaming smile to her husband. No amulet, no weapons, no dramatic buildup. She definitely preferred his new style. "My champion," she gushed.

"Don't start with that champion stuff," he protested. "Let's get you taken care of. And then I'll find Fox and get your amulet and then"—he winked—"you can thank me properly."

The doctors at Rita's hospital were thorough, and it was hours before Molly, armed with a clean bill of health, rejoined Matt. They drove straight to their little house, where he again swept her into his arms, whisking her across the threshold and directly to the bedroom. Imagining that all coherent conversation was about to be forbidden, Molly held him at arm's length and adopted a no-nonsense tone. "As much as I'd like to melt right now, Matthew, I think we need to make some plans."

"I *have* a plan," he assured her impishly. "The doctors said there's no need to restrict your activities, and I'm feeling incredibly active." Dropping the bantering tone, he added lovingly, "You really do look stronger than you did in Peru. And even prettier, if that's possible. It seems like you look prettier every time I see you."

Molly blushed with pleasure. "You used to say that to me all the time."

"Did I? I was right." He stared intently. "Tell me about those days."

"I've told you most of it. I thought you didn't like to hear it."

"You told me about legends and dreams and Valmain and Maya. Tell me about *us*. How we fell in love. The first time. Where did we go? What did we do? What did we talk about?"

Molly stared, then stroked his cheek with her fingertips. "The first time? I think maybe, the first time, we were too busy. And then . . ."

"And then?"

"It was as though we had always been together. Always been in love. We didn't even seem to have a choice. It was wonderful, but . . ." She forced herself to think about that other Matthew. "We definitely have to talk. If we're going after the amulet soon, there are things you should know."

"I'm going after the amulet alone, while you rest. And don't worry. I'm not about to die for a trinket. I'll get it if I can. But one way or another, I'll be back. It'll be good practice for me anyway," he added pointedly, "in case I decide to take Aganyer up on his job offer."

"It really is the perfect job for you. Traveling around, searching out treasures. But for *his* collection, not yours. Wouldn't that bother you?"

"Why? I can't afford them. I don't even really have the same taste as him. But I like his style and I like his purpose. He respects his belongings. Look at all the donations he's made to museums and all. I think he's just trying to preserve a lot of these objects. To keep them from being melted down or mistreated."

"He bought your dagger just to annoy you, remember?"

"Yeah. I 'remember'," he chuckled. "I like the guy. What can I say? And he's crazy about you. He picked up on your belief in magic, I think. He goes for all that stuff, too. Anyway, look what he gave me." He reached into his knapsack and produced the obsidian dagger.

"Matthew! How wonderful! But be careful. Its blade is venomous." She touched it gingerly. "He just *gave* it to you? For free?"

"Yeah. He said he has everything money can buy, but he can't buy what I have."

"Love?"

"That was my guess, too, but he was talking about magic. He wants to know about the axe. And the amulet. He begged me to allow him to be a part of it. Strange, huh?"

"As I was saying," she countered briskly, "if *we're* going after the amulet, there are things you need to know. You have to listen and, for once, don't be so skeptical. Please?"

"Okay. What's the story, now?"

"When you get the amulet, will you promise to tie it to your right wrist?"

"Sure. That's when I become superman, right?"

"I hope so." She blushed as his meaning became more apparent and hurriedly changed the subject. "What would you say if I told you, you really don't have amnesia?"

"I'd say I'm starting to like it when you talk like a crazy

woman." He winked suggestively, refusing to be distracted from more amorous thoughts.

"It's true. You didn't really lose your memory."

"No?"

"No. It's not lost. I know where it is, so to speak."

"Let me guess. It's in the amulet?"

"No, but you're thinking along the right lines. It's in my dream. Actually, at the beginning it was still in you—in your brain or whatever—but I summoned it to my dream and then I kept it there, just to be on the safe side."

"I guess I really do love you," he grinned.

"Why do you say that?"

"Because I'm still here! Two weeks ago this definitely would have sent me running. But now I want you, crazy or not."

"Just let me finish and maybe it won't seem so weird," she laughed. "I mean, believe me, I remember how I felt about you, years ago, when you first started talking to me about dreams and legends. My reaction was exactly the same as yours. I didn't believe you until my dream started changing. If you could see the dream, you'd believe me."

"So, bring me there and reunite me with my memory."

"No. I can't. You're already there. I told you."

"You told me my memory was already there," he countered. "How am *I* there?"

"That's the complicated part."

"Ohhh!"

"Don't tease. There are two Matthew Redtrees now. The old you and the new you. Somehow, you became disassociated from your own memories. Not the intellectual ones, so much, I guess, but the emotional ones. Like the dream. And your family. And your collection. It's like your life—your experiences—never happened to you."

"But you've been in contact with the old me?"

"Right! In my dream. He's there the way Aaric was there. Remember I told you about Aaric?"

"The one who tried to fight me to get my body?"

"Yes! That's good, Matthew. You're getting it."

"Speaking of getting it, don't you think that's enough for today's lesson? Don't I get my reward now?"

"Don't be hopeless. Let me just tell you one more thing." When he ignored the serious tone and kissed her, she pulled away and began to pace. "Concentrate, Matthew. The only way we can get you back together again is to get our hands on the amulet. And we may be running out of time."

"I'll get the amulet, I promise." Blocking her path, he nuzzled her neck while accusing, "You can't expect me to live like a monk when I'm married to the sexiest woman in the world. This'll only take five minutes."

"Five minutes?" She laughed nervously. "It *always* takes a long time. That's part of what makes you such a great lover."

"Great lovers are flexible," he insisted, backing her toward the wall as he spoke. "This situation calls for the no-frills approach. Ready?"

A soft, more seductive laugh bubbled in her throat. "Try to behave yourself. You're a champion, not a cowboy, remember?"

"No problem, ma'am," he drawled as his hands traveled under her skirt, finding and removing her panties with decidedly un-Matthew-like speed. Then his mouth descended, crushing hers with a hungry, probing kiss that left her breathless. His fingers were probing, too, readying her for more and inspiring her to move her hands to the waistband of his jeans, helping him to liberate himself, then bracing herself as he hoisted her higher against the wall, penetrating her with one sure, hard thrust. He paused then, just long enough to flash her his sexiest grin, then renewed his onslaught. Soon they were kissing and writhing in frenzied unison, groaning their frantic, mutual appreciation of one another until finally, drenched in perspiration and adoration, release came and they slumped, depleted, into one another's arms.

Matt was the first to speak, his tone playful and low. "You were saying something about the amulet?"

"What?" she murmured, still slightly dazed.

"We don't have much time, Molly," he teased. "Try to concentrate on amulets and axes."

"Later," she sighed, drawing him shyly toward the bed. "For now, I want to lie in your arms and kiss you for the rest of the afternoon. Everything else can wait."

Satiated by her lover, and guilty over her afternoon of bliss in his arms, she steeled herself for a confrontation with her dream mentors. Although she trusted Aaric not to gossip unduly, she knew he must have told Matthew, by now, that "Matt" had returned safely. What *else* had he told him? Or what had they guessed, from the tumult the lovemaking must have caused in the usually quiet meadow?

When Matthew's face lit up the moment she appeared in the dream, she knew he had no idea of the sharp turn her life had taken, and overtones of true betrayal began to color her guilt.

"I was worried when you didn't show up!" he declared as he pulled her into his arms and brushed his lips across hers. "What happened? Are you okay?"

"I'm fine," she assured him nervously, feeling illogically yet completely out of place. "I'm here now."

"I was worried about you with only that mindless version of me to protect you."

Aaric laughed. "Don't worry. He's hardly mindless. As a matter of fact—"

"Aaric! Be quiet."

"What?" Matthew eyed them quizzically. "What's going on?"

"Come on, Princess. Let me tell him." Jesse turned back to Matthew and explained, with a grin, "You decked me at

the airport for showing a little too much interest in your
wife."

"You're kidding! Good for Matt." His gaze shifted to
Molly. "So? Why didn't you want him to tell me?"

"I thought you might be jealous. That's silly, I guess."

"It's ridiculous," he agreed. "If *Matt* hit Jesse, then *I* hit
Jesse. He's me."

"That's one way of looking at it," she nodded.

He studied her for a moment, then moved his hand to her
chest and fingered the new locket. "What's this?"

"Oh!" She flushed to realize it had accompanied her to
the dream. "It's a gift. Matt gave it to me."

"You mean *I* gave it to you?"

Her champion's sincere, frustrated expression intimidated
her and she suddenly felt unfaithful, not to mention guilty,
over failing to visit him sooner. "It's been confusing, Matthew. Just be patient. As soon as we get the amulet, and you
get yourself back together again, things will start making
sense."

"That may be sooner than we'd hoped," Aaric interjected.
"Matthew, you've received a telephone call from Deborah
Clay. She has heard about your affliction. She wants you to
come to the mounds—tomorrow—to meet with her."

"A telephone call? That's bizarre," Matthew murmured.
"It's not Deborah's usual style. But it's great news. You can
go out there now and confront her."

"Actually, I think the Princess and Matt should go. I don't
want to leave Rita."

"Why? What's wrong?" Molly frowned. "You've been
telling us she's doing great."

"It's just a feeling," the sorcerer shrugged. "I feel I should
be in Los Angeles."

"You said Molly shouldn't go near Deborah because she
could see how vulnerable she is," Matthew reminded him
impatiently. "Let's send Matt alone."

"No!" Molly's objection had been more resonant than intended, and she stammered slightly as she explained, "That's n-not logical. He doesn't believe this stuff and doesn't understand the danger. I *have* to go with him. To—to advise him. I'll be fine, I promise. I won't show any weakness."

Matthew's eyes had narrowed with suspicion. "You seem to have developed a pretty strong attachment to your zombie, Molly. I remember when you were too busy to go to the mounds with me. Now you suddenly *have* to go with *him?*"

"Because he needs me. And"—she bristled at his attack— "you never did. You were off on your own. In your own world."

"That's crazy," grumbled Matthew. "Everything I did, I did for you. You're *my* wife, not his."

Aaric yawned in exaggerated annoyance. "I'm going back to bed, Princess. I cannot abide this preposterous conversation."

"No! Wait! We haven't decided the details yet," Molly protested.

"Sounds to me like *you've* already decided," Matthew accused. "Marry Matt and forget about *me.*"

"Silence!" thundered Aaric. "We must reunite these Matthews if only to end this illogic. Princess, bring the other one now!"

"What? But he's here."

"This is Matthew. Now bring *Matt.* Bring what's left. Think about him—the one with whom you are so enamored—and summon him."

"Even if I could, he doesn't belong here," she countered uneasily. "He doesn't believe all this. It could shock him."

"Great," the sorcerer nodded. "Maybe the shock alone will be enough to reverse the damage."

"Can't you see, Aaric?" demanded Matthew sarcastically. "She's not sure that's what she wants anymore."

"Princess?"

"I'm trying!" she wailed. "It seems crazy, but . . . Oh!" He was there, in the meadow, so close she could have reached out and touched him, if she dared. Instead, she watched in speechless amazement as the newcomer and the Valmain champion studied one another. Each had the other's expression: a blend of curiosity and rivalry. Their bronze bodies and warrior garb were identical and compelling, and the gold-flecked eyes were like mirrors, reflecting and refracting as the scrutiny intensified. Finally, Matt turned to Molly and admitted, "You're not crazy after all. I'm glad about that much, at least." He fingered her cape in quiet amusement. "So? You really are a witch?"

She nodded proudly. "I'm a sorceress. And this is Aaric. My friend. *Our* friend. He's a sorcerer. He's also Jesse Camacho."

Matt nodded. "That makes sense, I guess. As much sense as any of this." He turned back to his counterpart. *"You're* the one who doesn't make sense. It's unbelievable."

The Valmain champion scowled. "That's an understatement. This all started with the amulet, and the sooner you and Aaric recover it, the sooner things will be back to normal."

"Normal?" Matt looked inquiringly toward Molly, touching the locket with his fingertips. "Is that the goal here? The way things used to be?"

Aaric coughed and chastised, "This is no time for philosophizing. We must concentrate—"

"No! I *want* to hear his 'philosophy,' " Matthew growled. "What do you have in mind? Do you think you can do a better job of being me than I have?"

"Matthew, please. Don't argue with . . . well, with yourself. Please."

"It's not an argument, Molly," he assured her coolly. "Just a discussion. Interesting, but ultimately irrelevant. Once we get the amulet—"

"We may never get it," Matt interrupted, just as coolly.

"I could have gotten it," Matthew taunted. "Are you saying you're not the man I was? I mean, am?"

"Aaric, make them stop! Any minute now they'll be dueling or something."

Aaric nodded. "Send yours away. At least now he'll believe you and accept your counsel. That's worth something."

Molly complied, and then, with a withering glance toward the remaining Matthew, disappeared.

The Valmain champion stared at the spot where the couple had stood. "This can't be happening," he whispered finally. "Who the hell does he think he is?"

"Before you say any more, think," Aaric advised. "He's you, after all. Stubborn and independent. Nothing he does or says should surprise you."

"He's me, all right." Matthew nodded grimly. "Gone off in a different direction."

The sorcerer's smile was sympathetic. "It should be some comfort to you that *you* ended up with the Princess. Remember? You said you would rather see her with anyone other than me. You got your wish."

Matthew seemed dazed. "You're right. Do you believe it? At this moment, I'd rather see her with *you* than with him! *And he's me!*"

They laughed ruefully at the irony of Matthew's dilemma, and Aaric observed, "You'll have to trust them. He's you, after all, and she's the Princess. That's a pretty impressive combination. They'll do the right thing, even if it kills them."

Matthew found the reference disquieting. "Will it kill him? I mean, his memories, his feelings . . ."

"I don't know," the sorcerer mused. "He was a clean slate, so to speak. Not influenced by your dream or your experiences. But once it's over, those old memories will dominate once again. Yes, Son of Lost Eagle," he admitted finally. "I think the amulet will kill him. Is that not what you want?"

Of course it's what I want, thought Matthew fiercely. *It's right. So why do I feel so guilty? Molly, why do you always have to complicate things? Why won't you let me be me?*

"This will be over soon," Aaric assured him confidently.

"I've sent for Fox and told him to meet me in Los Angeles. That's why I sent the Princess and Matt to the mounds."

"You mean, Deborah didn't really contact me?" Matthew grinned reluctantly. "Pretty clever, Aaric. Are you sure you can handle Fox on your own?"

"He will rue the day he challenged Aaric the Moon-shaker," the sorcerer promised. "I'll kill him, recover the amulet, and you'll be your obnoxious self by this time to-morrow."

"You want all the glory for yourself," Matthew accused, although not without a measure of fondness. "I can't blame you. She'll be grateful . . ."

"She'll be safe," Aaric corrected. "That is my only motive. She is the rebirth of the mounds. Protecting her, and the little one, is selfish, but for reasons more vital than glory."

"You're sure there aren't any other mounds magicians around?"

"I've visited the mounds many times. If any of my de-scendants existed, I would recognize them."

"Really?" Matthew's infamous curiosity overtook him. "How do you know if a person has magical powers? Is there some way I could have known Angela was a witch?"

"With women it's extremely difficult," Aaric admitted. "I personally could never tell, especially if she happened to be attractive. Maya's father could recognize one, but I cannot. They're all the same to me."

"They? You mean women?" Matthew laughed. "You'd better not let your 'Princess' hear you talk that way."

"I only mean that, witch or not, I regard them as equal to one another. The more beautiful one is, the less I trust myself to remain objective. I've met some particularly beautiful ones in Los Angeles lately who . . . ," he winced and added hastily, "As a man named Nicholas! I swear. As Jesse Camacho, I've been completely faithful to your sister."

Matthew groaned. "Don't mention that mess."

"You think we've been unfair to Rita?"

"Actually, I think it was Molly who was unfair to *you*. She made you stay with Rita when the real Jesse would have left."

"But I am not he. I would never abandon my sons," Aaric declared vehemently.

"I appreciate that. So. Tell me about these women you've been meeting as Nicholas. Using *my* eyes, according to Molly."

"Women trust them," Aaric chuckled. "It's quite remarkable."

Matthew shook his head. "Can you really handle any more relationships right now?"

"Relationships? These women are pleasing, but married."

"Married? All of them?"

Aaric nodded. "That I *can* recognize."

"And you still get involved with them?"

"I'm married, too, remember? It wouldn't be honorable of Nicholas to mislead unmarried women, but . . ." He shrugged and explained, "When I'm restless, or worried, seeing a woman calms me."

"So last night," Matthew grumbled, "when we were worried about Molly, you just became Nicholas and went to your bar and found a woman to calm you down?"

"A beauty," Aaric confirmed without remorse. "It was casual, yet satisfying, and I'll never see her again."

"What if you accidentally fall for one of them someday?"

"I won't," he predicted dryly. "I've decided to opt for quantity and variety. I'm through with all the rest of it."

Matthew tried to laugh, but visions of Molly and his alter ego making love were consuming his imagination. He envied Aaric his attitudes. If only all women were the same to *him*. Instead, Matthew hungered for his dream girl. He thought of the strength in her eyes and the power in her touch. Even as he craved her, he wondered if he'd lost her forever, and he stared in quiet despair toward the mounds—the resting place of his ancestors. Would he be joining them soon? Was he as obsolete as that? Would he at least be allowed the coveted death fit for a warrior?

Matt was pacing, Matthew-style, and Molly couldn't help but wonder why she'd thought the two of them so different. He was thinking through the evening's revelations, and she knew that he would present her with an ultimatum at any moment. She was ready for him, though. She knew exactly what she'd say.

"Arrogant," Matt muttered.

"What?"

"He was arrogant! Is he always that way?"

"No. I don't think he was arrogant just now, either. He was direct. So were you."

"You told me the amulet makes a person arrogant. Remember? You said Lost Eagle decided to give it up, voluntarily, so that he could be the person he really was, and not some slave to it."

"You're embellishing a little, but I remember. What's your point?"

"This champion of yours was dominated by a dream. And then by the amulet. I want to be free of all that. You say I was tied to the past. Now I want to be tied to our future. Why shackle ourselves to our ancestors again? You're happy. I'm happy."

"Happy? Yes, I guess I am. And that never mattered to the old Matthew. Our integrity, and my safety, were all that mattered."

"Integrity. There's an arrogant word. *He* decides, right?"

"There's more to it than that, Matthew."

"The old Matthew Redtree was touched by the dream and the amulet. *I* was touched by you," he declared. "The combination of dream and amulet is too overpowering. Together they'll smother what's happened between us. There won't even *be* an us." He grabbed her hands eagerly. "Do you know what I want?"

"You want me?"

"Right! But there's more. I want . . ." His eyes were glittering wildly. "I want to find the amulet. Right away. And I want you to ask me *not* to put it back on my wrist. I want to be free of all of that. Maybe if I can get the amulet back, you'll see I can be everything he was—and more—without it."

"Matthew, don't!"

"Don't say anything now, baby. Just wait. Aganyer has probably contacted Fox by now. You and I can go to the mounds to meet with this Deborah woman, and then, when we get back to Los Angeles, I'll arrange to meet with Fox. And"—his eyebrow arched sternly—"I don't want Jesse involved."

"I told you, you're not in competition with him."

"I'm not feeling jealous," he assured her. "I just want to show you we're okay on our own. You're safe with me. *Just* me. We don't need amulets or any other magic. I'm going to close that chapter in your life."

She tried again to protest, but he had resumed his pacing, making plans for their trip to the mounds. "I want the axe. Can you get it from Jesse without his knowing it? And then give me ownership? Along with yourself?"

"Matthew! I told you we *need* Jesse."

"Come on. I don't want him to deal with Fox while we're at the mounds. We'll just take it with us for safekeeping."

"Okay," she sighed. "I'll get it. On one condition. You have to promise to let Jesse help with Fox when we get back."

"No! That spoils everything."

"Take it or leave it."

"You're a hard woman," he complained, "but okay. For now, I have to agree. I can't take a chance on Jesse handling the whole thing himself! He's the type who would."

"Look who's talking," she giggled. "That's what *you* were trying to do."

"True," he grinned. "But *I'm* entitled. Get the axe tonight, and then we'll take off for the mounds. On the way you can fill me in. On everything. I'll have to know every detail. We can't be sure what's important, so we'll have to assume everything is. You'll start at the beginning. . . ."

She'd seen that look so many times. Total confidence. *Where does it come from?* she wondered. *Does he really believe so completely in himself, or is this just his way of preparing, like war paint or locker-room pep talks?* As though he'd guessed her thoughts, he winked reassuringly. "Remember our deal? I get the amulet and then you shower me with gratitude and affection. Do you need a rehearsal?"

Knowing there was no point in trying to reason with him while he was in this self-possessed state, she willingly stripped and complied.

Twenty-two

The sorceress readjusted the passenger seat of her Mustang for the tenth time, determined to remain awake. After hours of play with Matt and a joyful, albeit too short, reunion with Kerreya at Jesse's ranch, they had begun the long drive to the mounds, intent upon arriving before dusk.

In contrast to the exhausted witch, Matt was alert and inquisitive. "I need to know what I felt. What I said. What *you* felt and saw and said. I need to know every detail about Aaric. And Maya."

"Maya? She's gone."

"She's part of it. You have to describe the fight. The battles. Why did I win? Where did Aaric make his mistakes?"

"He's offered to replay it all for you with his illusion power. Kind of a mirage of the past."

Matt nodded. "Still, he can't replay what he doesn't know, right? Only the parts he saw. Or heard about in detail. So, for now, lean back and close your eyes," he directed quietly. "You were a student in my class and your exam paper intrigued me. I suspected our legends intertwined. Start from there. Describe how you felt. How I felt. Everything."

She was glad his golden eyes were now trained on the road. The irrational tears that were streaming down her cheeks might distract him from what he clearly felt to be his new imperative. Only this time, it was their love, and not some lofty concept of destiny, that he was preparing himself to defend.

She began softly, "You wanted to be sure. You had to be sure, so you tried to disprove it all. The harder you tried, the more convinced you became. The more convinced you became, the more you frightened me. No. Unnerved me, I guess. Just like I unnerved you these last few weeks with talk of spells and dreams. But my dream—my simple little sewing dream—came back and began to change. I finished my cape, put it on, and everything changed. Forever."

"Good, baby. That's what I want to hear. Go on, now. Tell me the story. But start with your earliest memories. Tell me about little Molly, growing up. Her parents. The accident. *The half sister.* Everything."

Emaciated and bitter, Deborah Clay sat in her humble cottage awaiting the prospective purchaser who had contacted her through her nephew. News of Matthew Redtree's affliction had reached her and now provided some measure of fleeting consolation to her thwarted soul. Perhaps she hadn't quite managed to avenge Angela's murder, or to gain access to magic—mounds or lakes—but she could at least know that the Redtrees were miserable. If the amulet on Matthew's wrist, along with all the powers of the dreamer, had been unable to effect a cure, then a cure was impossible, and their lives were in shambles. It was small comfort, but comfort nonetheless.

Why, she wondered, had the fates kept her dry, frail body alive? For one hundred and one years she had waited! But her waiting was over. She would sell this house and all its memories. No longer would she live in the shadows of the lifeless mounds, hungering for the magic buried so long ago therein. She could die now, knowing that the Redtrees were as helpless and unhappy as she was.

A stern knock at her door roused her from the reverie and she answered swiftly, intent upon closing this chapter—this final chapter of her worthless life—quickly. When she beheld the menacing stranger whose figure so easily filled her doorway, she was momentarily cowed. This was not a man on a simple real estate mission. He was evil, *and* he was of the lakes.

"How old *are* you?" Fox marveled, drawing back from her outstretched hand as though certain that it would turn to dust upon contact.

"I'm very old," Deborah agreed warily. "And very wise. Why have you sought me out?"

"I seek information, old woman. They say you have studied these mounds for a lifetime." The wizard's eyes flashed. "These mounds of my ancient enemies, whom we had believed to have died out!" He regained his composure and grinned. "Tell me everything you know about Matthew Redtree. And about Jesse Camacho."

"Camacho?" Deborah frowned. "The sister's husband?"

"I sent my wife to investigate him and she tells me he's a harmless family man. But he frightened my servant, and so I'd appreciate hearing *your* learned opinion."

"Jesse Camacho is a vagabond and a drunk. There is strong enmity between him and young Matthew." Deborah paused to grin. "Your servant is a coward and your wife is too kind."

"You're certain?"

"The mounds civilization has died out, except for one sorceress. Matthew's curly-haired bride."

Fox's eyes narrowed in disbelief. "Her? She *can't* be of the mounds. She's Valmain. From another culture, across the seas."

"Valmain married a mounds sorceress named Kerreya. You didn't know about that?"

"No."

"Kerreya was the sister of Maya. Surely you've heard of her?"

"Of course," he assured her, then repeated, almost joyously, "Of course! That's why Maya wanted Valmain destroyed! Jealousy, between sisters. And now . . ." He was thinking quickly as he spoke. "The stepdaughter is in the line? It's priceless."

"There's more," Deborah assured him. "The girl is a pitiful magician, who can barely cause a spark or stir the leaves, but she has one strength. She has the gift of dreaming."

"Dreaming!" Fox blanched. "Impossible! It's a lost art!"

"Even her dreams are inept, although she managed to kill my darling granddaughter by means of them," the old woman declared, then she caught herself and frowned. Why was she volunteering this information? This wizard would obviously pay well. Would he offer the power and vengeance she craved?

"Go on, old woman. Don't try my patience."

"You've asked about Matthew. He's the champion of Valmain, sworn to defend it against all threats."

"And is he also the warrior sent by Maya to destroy Valmain?"

"Maya sent Aaric the Moonshaker." She chuckled when the wizard shrank from the words. "You are right to cower, evil one. But there is no danger. Matthew killed the Moonshaker in battle in Ireland. That's how he won the dreamer's heart."

"Yes, yes," Fox murmured. "That makes sense, too. Constance says they fell in love in Ireland. . . ." His eyes narrowed. "Redtree is a warrior, but not a sorcerer? You are certain?"

"He has access to power only through an amulet that resembles a spool. If you desire further information, bring me that amulet." Her eyes sparkled at the thought. "I have heard Matthew's afflicted with a serious head injury. It should be easy to take the amulet from him. When you've accomplished that, come back to see me."

With a mischievous grin Fox produced the silver spool, dangling it before her hungry eyes. "Is this the amulet, old woman? If your information is helpful, I will gladly give it

to you." When she reached for it, he grinned. "Be patient.
Tell me first, does Matthew Redtree understand the significance of the copper axe he holds in his collection?"

"Copper axe?"

"It belonged to the lakes, but we lost possession. I'm determined to recover it. When I own it, you may have the
mounds charm, but not before."

Deborah's chest tightened with frustration. An axe? What
could it mean? And how could he ask her to wait any longer?
The amulet was here, and she was old, and the time was now.
She had to make him understand that. "Forget the axe," she
wheedled. "Trade for this instead." In desperation she
reached into the pocket of her apron and produced the one
thing of value in her worthless life.

"A spoon?" Fox hooted. "Are you senile after all?"

"Examine it closely," she urged. "It's thousands of years
old but appears newly crafted. Notice the markings."

"The same markings that decorate the amulet," he admitted. "But different . . ."

"The fourth mound is here, set apart. Do you see?"

"The fourth mound?" Fox gasped, then recovered his
equilibrium and shrugged. "Interesting. But simply a relic?"

"No. A witch used this to charm the womb of my daugh-
ter-in-law. When Angela was born, I fed her with this spoon,
and she grew powerful. And beautiful. For a time"—her eyes
glowed with pride—"she controlled Redtree."

"How?" Fox demanded.

"I'll tell you all—I'll even give you this spoon!—in exchange for the amulet. Give it to me now. A lake wizard,
even one as powerful as you, can never use a mounds amulet.
Just as the dreamer can never use the lake axe you're so
desperate to own."

"*Use* the axe?" The wizard laughed harshly. "Your ignorance is showing. The dreamer prays the axe will *never* be
used."

"Why?" As Deborah racked her tortured memory, her

pulse began to race. "I remember now! It concerns the twins. It was an axe—a copper axe!—that killed them."

"Enough of this," he growled. "Give me the spoon and I'll be gone. You've amused me and so I'll allow you to live."

"Wait." Deborah grasped his arm and proposed boldly, "I can get Redtree to come here with a snap of my fingers. When he arrives, I'll use the amulet to kill him. He's the legitimate owner of the axe. By his death he will abandon it, and then . . ." She paused, allowing the wizard to see the possibilities for himself.

He was nodding slowly. "No one will own the axe. It will be abandoned! Is this possible? Will my possession be legitimate?"

"Of course. You did not solicit his murder. You came seeking information only. It is *my* plan. To avenge my darling Angela's death. You will merely be an innocent beneficiary. Assuming, of course, I manage to get my hands on the amulet."

"I did not solicit his murder," Fox agreed softly. "I asked only for information. His death will be your doing, but *I* will recover the axe and will be remembered for all times as the greatest of First Wizards! All of the glory will be mine! Begin now, old woman, and tell me everything you know!"

The sun was beginning to set when Matt stopped the car, gently roused the Valmain Princess, and led her onto the highest mound. He had left word of their arrival with Deborah's nephew, the jeweler, who had assured him the old woman would be eager to see him. The nephew had suggested they go directly to the cottage, but Matt didn't want to meet on Deborah's turf. It was here, among these amazing burial mounds, so similar to those in Molly's dream, that they would put this matter to rest, hopefully forever. Lowering his heavily weighted knapsack to the ground, he embraced the trembling sorceress.

"It's beautiful here, Molly."

She clung to him desperately. "Let's go home, Matthew. I'm frightened."

"Would you feel safer if Jesse were here?"

"I'd feel safer if you had your amulet."

"I'll handle this without the amulet. Don't worry, baby. Even if Deborah's a witch, she's old, and if she were truly powerful, she'd have hurt you or me by now." He squinted slightly. "There! Do you see? That must be her! She got our message fast! Wow! She's older than old. She looks . . . dead. Do you see her?"

"Yes." Molly's trembling ceased. As the danger materialized, she turned to her incomplete but diligent training, and to her amazement her power seemed to swell. The mounds, she realized gratefully, were charging her as they had so often charged the Valmain champion. If only she could transfer the power to Matt, but without the amulet on his wrist, that could not be, and so she waited.

"At last we meet." Deborah beamed, patting Molly's arm. "Your champion here has told me so much about you." She turned to Matt, eyeing his knapsack eagerly. "My old friend. Has your memory returned?"

"Why did you send for us?" Matt demanded coolly.

"Send for you?" Deborah chuckled. "I intended to do that tomorrow, but I received *your* message from my nephew first."

"You telephoned me the day before yesterday," Matt growled. "That's why we're here."

"I never use telephones," she shrugged. "But I'm glad you're here." A mischievous smile played on her lips. "You're like a son to me, Matthew. How sad you don't remember our tender feelings. At least I'm meeting your witch bride at last."

Matt and Molly exchanged confused glances. Had Aaric lied about the telephone call? For what possible purpose? "Jesse was just trying to get rid of us . . . ," Molly groaned.

"So he could deal with Fox alone in Los Angeles," Matt finished quietly. "He thinks he has the axe! If he's made him any promises he can't keep—"

"Axe?" Deborah interrupted innocently. "I had assumed your visit concerned this." She exhibited her wrist proudly, allowing the silver to catch the last rays of evening.

"The amulet!" Molly choked. "Give it to us!"

"It's mine," Deborah gloated. "Remember well, Valmain. My Angela aligned it to her kin. If you try to take it, I'll kill you."

"You can't kill us both," Matt warned. "Hand it over, Deborah, and we'll let you live." He stepped close to the old woman, who reached for his arm, an affectionate light in her eyes. Then, to Molly's horror, the eyes grew cold, the mounds themselves seemed to shudder, and the body of Matthew Redtree was hurled ten feet through the air, landing motionless, and seemingly lifeless, on the ground.

Now, when it was too late, Molly recognized the extent of the danger. Angela had been nothing compared to this demonic old woman. This one knew how to use the amulet in ways that were foreign, and deadly, and definitely *not* of the mounds. Or, she had help. Either way, to panic would mean death for both herself and the man she loved, and so she forced herself to speak in a loud, clear voice. "I can't be hurt so easily, Deborah. The amulet gives you power, but the mounds fuel me directly, and so my strength is infinitely greater."

"Yet you are distracted by your champion's plight and the danger to your child."

"My child?" Molly gasped. Did Deborah dare to threaten Kerreya? "What are you saying?"

Deborah produced the silver spoon from beneath her threadbare shawl and, with one eye on the unconscious champion, stepped forward to press it into Molly's palm. "This will strengthen your child as it strengthened my Angela. Notice the markings. When the child is born—"

"Born?"

"You carry a son!" Deborah snapped. "Why do you pretend not to know this? It's clear from the weakness behind your eyes. If you wish to carry the boy to term, give me the axe. *Now!*"

"The axe?" Molly's head was spinning at the confusion of information. A baby? The axe? "How did you know about the axe?"

"Enough!" A huge voice boomed from behind her and Molly spun toward it, completely terrified. When she saw the eyes—pale green yet beginning to glow red—she cringed in helpless terror, and to her shame the show of fear made the wizard grin proudly as he announced, "Your champion is dying, Valmain. Do you wish to join him?"

"No," she whispered, averting her eyes as she spoke. "I'll give you the axe. I didn't know you were here, but please! Just take it and go." She dropped to her knees and pulled the heavy axe from the knapsack, then moved quickly away, intent upon buying herself time and repositioning the conflict far from Matt's lifeless body.

You're a mounds sorceress, she reminded herself sharply. *Concentrate! What would Maya do?* Each power seemed unusable. Persuasion? She dared not try to touch them. Confusion? It might further incapacitate Matt. Infliction? Would that serve only to infuriate them further?

Just wait for an opportunity, she decided desperately. *Keep them occupied. Keep them talking. . . .* "If you kill me, your possession won't be legitimate, Fox," she reminded him.

"It belonged to Redtree," he barked. "Now it's abandoned."

"No. It's mine. Matthew gave it to me last week."

"I see." His eyes returned to a cooler shade of green as he glanced toward Deborah. "There must be no doubt. Proceed with your plan of revenge, old one. But first . . ." He held up a hand, commanding the old woman to stop, while his gaze played slowly over Molly's shape. "Your power is flickering. As a witch, you're pitiful. But . . . ," his tone grew silky, "as a woman, you're incredibly lovely, did you know? Such soft curls . . ." He licked his lips avidly. "I've never made love to a sorceress, but I hear it's a true delicacy. And you're a princess as well! If you use your every skill to please me, perhaps I'll show mercy to you and your champion."

"She can't use her power," Deborah declared, smirking. "She's weakened by the child she carries in her womb. Can't you see it in her eyes?"

"That," the wizard growled, "is truly a shame. You will be no challenge at all then, my weak love. . . ."

"Don't be misled," Molly warned. "I'm powerful. These mounds have been waiting for centuries to reawaken, through me." When Deborah moved toward her, Molly raised the axe and cautioned them clearly, "One more step and you're dead."

"You forget the amulet." Deborah chuckled. "Why not surrender, witch? I hear consorting with a lake wizard can be quite stirring. He can do for you what my Angela did for Matthew."

Molly's gaze shifted from the old woman to the lascivious wizard, but it was a movement behind them that was demanding her attention. Matt! He had stirred, once or twice, and she had hardly dared hope, but now he was coming alive—reaching slowly for the obsidian knife strapped to his ankle—and she was determined to distract the pair of evildoers until the moment came for her champion to make his move.

Her mind raced back to Fox's words. He wanted Deborah to be the one to kill the owners of the axe. Why? So he would be technically blameless? "You want me to surrender and be killed?" she murmured slyly. "And then this axe will belong to no one?" With a burst of inspiration, she confided, "It won't be abandoned at all, Deborah. I have wonderful news for you. If I'm killed, the axe will be my dying bequest—to you. You'll be its new owner, with power beyond anything you've dreamed possible."

"Wait!" Fox's face was flushed. "What about *that,* old woman? That axe is useless to you, I assure you. If you try to own it, you'll die a hideous death. Be content with the amulet."

The old woman's eyes were shining with unadulterated lust for power. "Do you think I'm afraid of you? When I'm owner of the axe, you won't dare kill me! It will all be mine!"

"Then I'll kill you *before* you own it!" he roared, lunging with eager claws extended toward the old woman's throat. At that very moment Matt sprang to life, burying the venomous black dagger deep in the wizard's back.

"Now, Molly!" he ordered sharply, and she released the axe—the axe that *never* missed—and it connected with a sickening crunch, splitting Deborah's skull into perfect, gruesome halves. Repulsed by her own prowess, Molly fell to her knees and hid her face in her hands, unable to bear the sight of such carnage, despite the intensity of her hatred for this pair. The axe had saved them, and yet she despised it as intrinsically evil. And the dagger! Aaric had marveled at its venomous sting, and she could only imagine the agony the hated wizard must be experiencing as he lay at Matt's feet.

Deep within her, a mixture of pain and power was surging out of control, and for the first time she truly believed she was carrying her lover's second child. A male child—less than one day old. "Matthew," she moaned, rocking herself on her knees and clasping her stomach tightly. "Matthew, we need you."

When he failed to answer, she raised her pleading eyes, but the eyes that stared back were not flecked with gold. Instead, they burned, like red-hot coals. It was the First Wizard of the Lakes, towering over her, his features twisted with pain from his wounds, but driven by hatred and greed toward triumph.

And Matthew Redtree's body—bloody from the gouging and slashing of the wizard's claws—had been tossed aside, landing in a macabre heap atop Deborah's corpse. "Your champion is dead, witch," Fox seethed. *"Now give me ownership of the axe!"*

Grief and terror were conspiring, along with the blazing eyes, to immobilize her. *What good would it do to struggle now?* they seemed to taunt her. *Let him have the axe, and the amulet, and your life. Without Matthew, what does it matter?*

But destiny was there, alongside the grief, battling the terror, reminding her of Kerreya, and the new life within her, and the old sorcerer who had bequeathed his power to her, so long ago, on the condition that she would be the Valmain princess—strong and pure of heart.

Do you hear how this Fox taunts you, Valmain Princess? He killed your lover and now threatens your son! If he leaves this place, he goes to Los Angeles—for Kerreya! If ever you were a sorceress, prove it now!

With destiny's call came a burst of power and, without warning, she lunged at the wizard, dragging her fingernails across his face, stunning him with the searing pulses of pain she now inflicted by virtue of her ancient link with the mounds. "You killed my champion? You're evil! *Evil . . . evil . . .*" Again and again she tore at him, shrieking and tearing, inflicting and despising, until her strength faltered and her fingers—now useless—began to shake uncontrollably.

"Bitch!" Fox sneered, pulling her to the ground. "You scratch like a hungry woman. Shall we put you to the test?" His claws tore deeply through her blouse and into her skin, then he leaned down to taste the wounds he had inflicted on her bloody breasts. "You're mine now," he proclaimed. "When I'm done with you, there will be nothing left to bury or burn. I'll eat you alive, but first I'll teach you why lake witches obey us without question."

She was beyond struggling, yet the mounds would not

surrender, and one last jolt, unfocused and uncontrolled, empowered her pain-racked body, allowing her to wrench free of the wizard. But the magic was gone as quickly as it came, leaving her unable to stand, or even to crawl, and so she sobbed in soft despair, pulling her tattered blouse close in a futile gesture against any further assault. Then miraculously—Or was she simply hallucinating?—Matthew was on his feet again, radiating fury and vengeance. Without his knife or other weapon, his attack seemed doomed, yet he launched himself at Fox with mindless confidence and throttled him powerfully, cursing the wizard for daring to defile the Valmain princess.

Grunts of pain and profanity filled the air as Molly dragged her trembling, exhausted body toward Deborah and the axe. *The axe that never missed!* If only it would fly straight for her, just one last time. She could see it. How she hated it! How she needed it! It was almost within her grasp, but her grasp—like her life itself—was too close to death for such exertion, so her hand rested on the weapon, without the strength to lift it.

Her sobs were now bitter as she cursed the destiny that would rob her second child of life. It was only then, as darkness flooded her tortured brain, that she remembered the amulet. The remembrance came too late. Even as she reached for Deborah's wrist beneath the old woman's bloody shawl, her last shred of consciousness failed her.

". . . our baby. Please, Molly, for my son." The distraught warrior's voice was ragged and hoarse as he nestled her against his chest, stroking her curls in loving desperation. "I need you, Molly. Our daughter needs you. We love you so much . . ."

She struggled to open her eyes, succeeding only partially. "Matthew?"

"I'm right here," he whispered. "It's all over, Molly. Fox and Deborah are both dead. They can't hurt you. I promise."

"The baby . . ."

"Our baby's fine," he soothed. "He'll be just fine. Strong like his father and pure like his mother." His voice broke as he added, "I love you so much. You were so brave. So beautiful."

"It was awful," she sobbed. "I thought it was the end. But you were wonderful, just like . . ." She stopped, unable to bring herself to meet his golden gaze.

"Say it," he urged. "I need to hear this."

"I know what you want me to say, Matthew," she whispered unhappily. "That we can go on from here, start fresh together, without magic or mounds, and a part of me wants that. I'm so proud, and grateful, and I love you so much, but I can't . . ." She could feel his heart pounding against her cheek, which was damp with tears and crimson with shame. "He and I had something—we're bound to each other. Through our destiny. I need to bring him back. I have to ask you to put the amulet back on. If it means anything"—she choked on a rush of tears—"I adore you. And I know you love me. The thought that I might be giving all of that up is so unbearable, but I promise . . ."

"Tell me."

"I'll never forget you. For the first time since my childhood, I've felt completely . . . I don't even know the word."

"Happy?" he reminded her softly.

"Yes. Such a simple thing."

"I intend to see that you stay happy."

"You're everything to me now!" She lifted her eyes to his and wailed, "Everything! My baby's father, my love, my life. *But so is he!*" Her sobs deepened, until her chest felt crushed under the strain. "I . . . I never told you . . . never told you the cruelest part, darling! I never told you . . ."

"Tell me now."

"He didn't fall in love with me, but I . . . *I fell so hard!*

I burn with love for him. Can you forgive me? Can you believe that my love for you is . . . is beautiful and true, but—" She broke off, shuddering from the intensity of her despair.

"I need to hear this, Molly," he whispered. "I need to know the truth. I want to understand . . ."

"My love for you is beautiful. I'll never, never forget what you gave me these last few days. And nights. My love for you is the most beautiful thing in my life, and my love for him is *cruel! Cruel!* I'm its prisoner . . . forever . . ."

"No, Molly, no," he soothed. "Not my prisoner. Not any more. I guess I finally learned something from Aaric. And from Matt, for that matter. Things will be different now, Valmain. I swear it."

Valmain? She pulled herself free and stared in dismay. "Matthew?" An accusatory edge crept into her voice. "You're already here? No!" Her eyes, glistening with tears, focused on the amulet on his wrist, and she shrieked *"No! No!"* as her fists began to pummel his chest. "I wanted to say goodbye!"

He caught her hands in his own and pulled them to his lips. "You don't have to say goodbye to anyone, Molly. Come here." His voice was gentle and soothing. "Come here and let me hold you. It's all I want to do."

"I wanted to say goodbye," she repeated, pulling free and burying her face in her hands. "I wanted him to know . . ."

"Shh, Valmain. Listen to me," Matthew pleaded. "When Fox went for you—left me for dead—I almost believed I was finished, but he had thrown me onto Deborah, and the amulet was there. Right there under her shawl. I could feel it! Inches from my wrist. I shifted and shifted again and finally . . ." He paused for a breath, then insisted, "I didn't want to do it, but I had no choice. I had to put it on. I heard you wailing. . . ."

She forced herself to meet his gaze, so filled with pain and uncertainty. He *needed* for her to understand, and so she nodded and murmured, "You had to do it. I see that, Matthew . . ." But her tears belied her words and, as he stroked her hair, helpless to reassure her, the deep, wracking sobs returned. "Forgive me, Matthew!" she gasped. "I just wanted to say goodbye to him. He was my baby's father. I wanted him to understand. . . ."

"Don't cry, baby. I didn't go anywhere. I'm right here, with you. Try to understand."

" 'Baby' ?" She stared through her tears, stunned, not daring to hope. "Matthew?"

"Who else?" He grinned weakly. "Did you really think I'd leave you?" When she continued to stare, he fingered the silver locket at her neck. "When I put the amulet on, I remembered, but I didn't forget. I'll never forget. The last few days have been just like those first few days, don't you see? In my office, and in your little apartment in Berkeley." His lips brushed hers hopefully. "Do you see what I'm saying?"

"I-I-I thought I'd have to choose and I-I couldn't," she stammered. "It was killing me, Matthew. I needed you both."

"I know that, baby. I need you, too. And so does Kerry. Let's go home and see her, okay?" He pulled her face up to his and stared intently. "I want to start working for Paul Aganyer."

"Yes, Matthew! It's perfect for you. . . ."

"You'll get your doctorate, but you'll also practice your magic. Every day. We'll build on Jesse's land—"

"Matthew!" she gasped. "Are you sure?"

"We need him," Matthew admitted. "He can protect you while I travel, and he can teach you. If he hadn't taught us about fighting lake wizards, we'd be dead. And"—his grin was self-conscious—"he's pretty damned loyal. And the father of my sister's baby."

"Does it all make sense to you? Honestly?"

"It all makes sense." He nodded. "You can help Rita with her baby, and"—he patted her stomach fondly—"Kerry and I can help you with my son."

"Matthew . . ."
"I know." He nodded solemnly. "I love you, too, Val-main."

Epilogue

The summons was a searing, hot pain, almost knocking a very pregnant Molly to the ground.

"Damn!" Matthew, too, was reeling. "What was that?"

"It was Aaric," she whispered hoarsely. "What can it mean? He'd never jolt me like that in my condition unless it was an emergency. It must be the baby! Rita's so long overdue! Something must be wrong!"

"Let's not panic, Molly. You wait here. I'll go."

"No, Matthew! He needs *me!* Rita needs me."

"Yeah. I guess you're right." He surveyed her swollen belly grimly. "You're seven months pregnant yourself, remember? You have to take it easy. I'll get you there as fast as I can."

"I'll be careful," she assured him. "We'll be fine."

They drove in silence, each imagining the worst; each remembering Aaric's repeated assurances that nothing could possibly go wrong; each still recovering from the summons that had now belied that claim. "Are you okay, baby?"

"I feel like I have a hole in my head, but I think your son actually liked Uncle Jesse's little invitation."

"Is he kicking up a storm again?" Matthew marveled. "You're lucky Aaric targeted your head. I feel like I got shot in the gut."

"Poor Rita. What could be wrong? Aaric promised . . ."

"Just relax. Maybe he's just over-excited about fatherhood." He pulled into the emergency room parking lot and flashed her a hopeful smile as he eased her out of her seat and ushered her through the hospital doors and along to the delivery room.

One glance at Jesse's ashen face confirmed the worst. "Princess! Thank you for coming. Rita's in bad shape . . ."

Molly stared past him in horror. She had expected pandemonium and screaming, not a deadly calm body.

"They medicated her. I didn't approve but . . ." Jesse waved his hands helplessly. "Nothing I did seemed to help and she was in agony. . . ."

"You're going to have to wait outside," a nurse advised, frowning.

Jesse placed his hand directly on the woman's forehead, unwilling to spare the time or energy for subtle persuasion. "Silence," he commanded and she retreated hastily.

"Get those people out of here," Rita's obstetrician growled.

"This woman is a midwife," Aaric muttered. "My wife needs her. Princess?"

Molly nodded encouragingly as Matthew tied the amulet to Rita's wrist. "She'll be okay now, Jesse."

"Just a minute." The doctor, apparently, was not susceptible to Jesse's persuasion on this issue. "I don't want to deliver two babies at one time."

"I'm only seven months along," Molly assured him.

"If you're seven months, I'm Whistler's Mother. Go and find another delivery room. This one's occupied."

While Matthew and Aaric restrained the angry doctor, Molly powered the amulet. Slowly but steadily the color returned to Rita's cheeks and her eyelids fluttered lightly. "Molly?"

"Hi, Rita. Just relax. The baby's coming." The sorceress faltered, consumed with guilt. "I'm so sorry, Rita."

"All better," Rita assured her, groggy but suddenly stronger. When she noticed the amulet, she giggled, "Voodoo?"

"Deliver the baby now," Molly instructed, and as Rita's uterus contracted, Molly felt an echoing stab of pain. Leaning heavily on the laboring woman, she moaned, "Hurry, Rita. *The baby's coming!*"

"I know. Believe me." Rita was growing stronger by the moment and her voice was now cheerful. "Jesse! The baby's coming!"

Jesse held his wife's other hand and, to the astonishment of the obstetrician, a flawless, rapid delivery ensued. "A boy," Matthew announced, his hands trembling at the feel of the new nephew he himself had caught.

"A boy?" Rita grimaced. "Again? Jesse!"

"Sorry, Rita." Her husband chuckled proudly.

A second, searing pain shot through Molly and she sank to the floor, frightened and speechless.

"Just like I said," the doctor groaned. "Get her up here, where I can get a look at her."

"Huh?" Matthew tore his eyes away from the newborn and panicked. "Damn! Jesse, take the baby . . ."

"Princess!" Jesse ignored Matthew's plea and ran to Molly, scooping her into his arms contritely. "It's too soon, Princess."

"Aaric," she moaned. "Don't let my baby die . . ."

"No, Princess. Never. Never. I swear. I'll give my own life first if it comes to that!"

"Put . . . her . . . down!" The doctor was livid. "What's wrong with you people? Put her down and get out!"

"Let the doctor look at her, Jesse," Matthew insisted, thrusting his nephew into Rita's anxious hands. "Now!"

Molly was writhing in pain as Jesse laid her gingerly on a nearby table. Only when Matthew brought the amulet from Rita and pressed it to his wife's wrist did Aaric's magic begin to ease her distress. "Forgive me, Princess," he pleaded. "I didn't know . . ."

"It's okay now," she gasped. "The baby's okay, Aaric. I . . . where's Matthew?"

"Right here, Valmain. Relax."

"Relax?" She giggled helplessly, momentarily free from the spasm. "You try to relax when . . . Aiyee!" She pushed with every ounce of strength she could muster, then whispered, "Doctor?"

"It's a boy. Again," he muttered. "Damnedest thing I ever saw."

"Matthew . . . ?"

"He's perfect, Molly. Perfect. Look at him."

"Give him to me."

Jesse exhaled sharply, then moved back to his own family. "You okay, Rita?"

"Molly upstaged me," she complained cheerfully. "Tell me your son's name, Jesse."

"Aaric!" Molly interrupted. "Rita, look!"

Jesse looked toward his princess and, when he saw her holding her baby high in the air, laughed proudly. "Almost as handsome as ours."

"Is Molly naming her son Eric?" Rita demanded. "I thought they wanted to name him Jason, after my father. Why does she keep saying Eric?"

"Maybe she wants *us* to call *ours* Eric." Jesse chuckled. "Eric Camacho. Do you like it?"

"Eric?" Rita shrugged. "It's fine." She kissed her new son's cheek. "Hi, Eric."

The sorcerer sidled over to the curly-haired witch. "Nice move, Princess."

"Pardon?"

"Thanks to you, Rita named the kid Eric. E-r-i-c."

"I love it," Molly enthused. "This, of course, is Jason Sheridan Redtree. Of the Argonauts, of course."

"Congratulations, Matt." Jesse shook his brother-in-law's hand firmly. "You look a little pale."

"Two in one day." The Valmain champion lowered his voice and muttered, "You and I have to talk."

"Yeah. Later, okay?"

"Now." Matthew turned and waved to Molly. "Jesse and I are gonna go have a cigar. We'll be back in a minute."

"A cigar?" Molly stared. "Matthew Redtree smoking?" She eyed baby Jason with amusement. "His desire for a son must have been even stronger than I suspected."

Her champion propelled Jesse down a corridor to an empty room, then roughly slammed him against the wall. "I ought to strangle you, Camacho!"

"Go ahead." Jesse raised his hands above his head. "Kill me. I deserve it."

"You *knew* this could happen!"

"No! I swear, Matt. I thought Rita would sail through it. It scared me to death when she started crying."

"Did you know Molly would go into labor?"

"No! I never saw anything so bizarre. It was as though Rita needed the Princess's . . ."

"Contractions?"

"I hate that word." Jesse shuddered.

"Yeah. Me, too." Matthew released his hold and sat on the empty bed. "What a mess. Kerreya's birth was so beautiful."

"This was horrendous," Jesse nodded. "No more babies."

"I agree. Good-looking boys, though, huh?"

"Yeah. Congratulations, Matt. And thanks for getting the Princess here so quickly."

"You owe me one," Matthew agreed.

Jesse leaned against a white wall and considered this solemnly. "I will repay you right now. I've been meaning to offer you some friendly advice. . . ."

"Just what I need," Matthew drawled. "Let's hear it."

"Who was the 'incredibly beautiful' woman? The one you dreamed about in the hospital in Peru right after your injury?"

When Matthew hesitated, Jesse's voice took on an urgent tone. "It was Angela, wasn't it? Take my advice, Matt. When the Princess asks—and she will someday, *believe* me—tell her it was Maya."

"That's ridiculous. It was just a dream."

"A memory. The Princess won't like the idea that such memories linger in your head." Then he shrugged. "Do what you think is best. But I know more about women than you do, and I'd cut my tongue out before I'd tell a woman I was dreaming of her rival. Your life will be a living hell."

"I have enough secrets from Molly. There's the one about the baby. About the witch stepmother. The business about you killing yourself someday . . ."

"And so you intend to admit you dreamed of your former mistress?"

"I already told her." Matthew grinned triumphantly. "She interrogated me months ago."

"And . . . ?"

"And she understood. She said"—he surveyed his 'ally' coolly—"that in those days, thinking about Angela filled a need in me. Now *she* fills that need. Completely."

Jesse grimaced. "So I have observed. You're an insufferably satisfied couple. I have no more delusions in that area."

"Good. Let's get back to them now."

Rita stretched lazily and leaned across to the baby cart, placing Eric gently on his stomach. "Molly?"

"Hmm?" The witch glanced up from Jason. "Yes?"

"Do you remember when you promised to help me? That night I first told you about the pregnancy?"

"Of course!" Molly's attention now shifted fully to her sister-in-law. "I'm more available now than ever."

"Well, are you ready for your first assignment?"

"Sure. Anything."

"I want you to explain to Jesse—the new and improved *domestic* model Jesse—that I don't intend to breast-feed Eric. I've done it twice and it was very fulfilling, but . . ."

"But?"

"I'm older. I want to get back on my feet and back into the world. Jesse never used to care whether I nursed or not—I got mastitis so many times he even suggested I give it up with AJ—but I know he'll flip out now, especially if *you're* nursing Jason. So? Will you help me? You've got more influence with him than I do."

"I'll talk to him," Molly sighed, "but are you sure? You have help this time, you know."

"Molly! Don't take his side."

"Not Jesse's side. *My* side. It's so cute, the way they're so similar. I was hoping we'd do everything the same way. . . ."

"I'll buy them matching outfits," Rita suggested dryly.

"Let *me* breast-feed Eric," Molly countered.

"What?"

Molly's eyes sparkled. "I'll do the feeding. You do the . . . ?"

"Bathing?"

"Oh, no! I want to do that."

"Diapering?"

"No. Jesse and Matthew should do that." Molly grinned. "But you could take them for walks. Introduce solid foods. Teach them to ride bikes. Hundreds of things."

"What if you don't have enough milk? Matt would have the right to insist you put Jason first."

"What do mothers of real twins do?" Molly smiled, confident and completely taken with the plan. "I'll have enough! And if not, we'll supplement them both. Matthew will agree. I'm sure of it."

"I'll still have to have a fight with Jesse, but"—Rita grimaced—"having his 'princess' wet-nurse his baby will definitely cushion the blow."

The sorceress sighed with relief. The boys would be raised identically—it seemed both logical and charming. She and Jesse could have "persuaded" Rita, of course, to breast-feed the infant, but Molly was tired of manipulation and deceit.

And mastitis sounded so painful! This solution was bizarre but painless. In fact, it was perfect.

"Here they are!" Jesse grinned at his women. "The two most beautiful mothers in the world."

"Is everything okay?" Molly eyed Matthew suspiciously.

"Sure. Everything's fine. How about here?"

"Jason and Eric are perfect. The nurse says they're exactly the same height and weight! Except for the hair color and eyes, they could be twins."

Matthew arched an eyebrow toward Jesse. "Twins?"

The sorcerer seemed not to have heard. "They're sound asleep already. What a life."

"I think I'll sleep, too, Jess," Rita sighed. "You'd better go and tell the boys. They're watching Kerry, remember?"

"Yeah. I'll bring them back with me." He kissed her cheek. "I love you, Rita. Take good care of Eric."

There were tears in Molly's eyes as she watched him depart. "Wasn't that beautiful, Matthew?"

"Yeah. What a guy," Matthew growled. "Now, what about you? Should I go with him and get Kerreya?"

"Take me home, Matthew. I want us all to be together in our new little ranch house."

Matthew nodded. "I'll get your things. Rita? Want to come, too?"

"No way. Molly, you're crazy. They'll wait on us hand and foot here."

"I'll wait on both of you, hand and foot, at home," Matthew promised. "But you can stay if you need to, Sis. We'll understand."

"Come with us, Rita," Molly cajoled. "Please? We won't have to lift a finger. These babies are more like twins than cousins. They shouldn't be separated. Please?"

Rita shrugged. "Do I have a choice? Jesse'll die of jealousy if Matt's son comes home before his. I can already imagine the years of competition we have in store for us."

"Yeah." Matthew grinned, lifting his son in his arms and

smiling proudly. "I'm counting on you, Jason." The brown-haired baby hiccuped dutifully and, less than two yards away, the raven-haired infant gurgled in return. It had begun.